We Maxwells been right here at Falconhurst since before the war of 1776.

We put down our roots in this good black dirt of Falconhurst Plantation. We drinks our vigor from the richness of the old Tombigbee. . . . A man don't break off from deep roots like that.

Our roots here at Falconhurst, not a root that breaks off easy. Masta Ham go off to the Texies—restless like young boys git—been gone eight long years. A long time. A long sad time.

But he comin' back home. He comin' home, Lucretia Borgia, where he roots are, where he belong. . . .

About the Author

Ashley Carter traces his Deep South ancestry back at least nine generations to Noble Worthington Hardee (1693–1743), who settled on the James River in Virginia. His great-great-uncle, Lt. Gen. Wm. J. Hardee CSA (1815–1873), was one of Lee's generals. His great-grandfather, Maj. Charles Seton Henry Hardee (1830–1927), was treasurer of the City of Savannah, Georgia, for forty years.

Fawcett Books in the
Falconhurst Series:

FALCONHURST FANCY 13685-X $1.95

MISTRESS OF FALCONHURST 13575-6 $1.95

MANDINGO 23271-9 $1.95

FLIGHT TO FALCONHURST 13726-0 $1.95

THE MUSTEE 13808-9 $1.95

DRUM 22920-3 $1.95

MASTER OF FALCONHURST 23189-5 $1.95

HEIR TO FALCONHURST 13758-9 $1.95

Fawcett Gold Medal Books
by Ashley Carter:

MASTER OF BLACKOAKS 13585-3 $1.95

PANAMA 14025-3 $2.25

SECRET OF BLACKOAKS 13960-3 $1.95

SWORD OF THE GOLDEN STUD 13842-9 $1.95

TAPROOTS OF FALCONHURST 14090-3 $2.25

TAPROOTS
OF
FALCONHURST

Ashley Carter

FAWCETT GOLD MEDAL • NEW YORK

TAPROOTS OF FALCONHURST

Published by Fawcett Gold Medal Books, a unit of CBS Publications, the Consumer Publishing Division of CBS Inc.

ISBN 0-449-14090-3

Printed in the United States of America

10 9 8 7 6 5 4 3 2 1

For William T. Brannon

Author's Note

The eight Falconhurst novels are based on themes, settings, character, atmosphere and situations created by Kyle Onstott in his novel *Mandingo* (1957).

The next seven Falconhurst novels were written by Onstott and Lance Horner. Two of these books—*Drum* and *Master of Falconhurst*—carried the by-line of Kyle Onstott. The by-line Kyle Onstott and Lance Horner appeared on *Falconhurst Fancy*. The last four —*The Mustee, Heir to Falconhurst, Flight to Falconhurst* and *Mistress of Falconhurst* (1973)—carried Mr. Horner's by-line.

In the sense that Mr. Horner extended and expanded ideas orginally created by Mr. Onstott in *Mandingo,* these books were collaborations, though most of the writing was done by Mr. Horner.

In this present novel, the writing is entirely mine. However, in the same way Mr. Horner extended and expanded ideas created by Mr. Onstott, I am continuing and developing the work, ideas and situations carried forward by Mr. Horner. In this sense, this book is a collaboration, and Mr. Horner a full partner in its development. Without Mr. Onstott's creations and Mr. Horner's extension of them, there would be no basis for the present novel before you.

Ashley Carter

Prologue

FALCONHURST 1840

I

Lucretia Borgia awakened abruptly, frightened and fevered in the murky gloom of this somber night. She held her breath, afraid she had screamed aloud in her sleep. She lay taut for a long time, listening in the silence that enshrouded the old house. No one stirred. She exhaled heavily. Her howl of terror must have been a lingering shard from her fragmented dream. Nightmare. A nightmare—that's what it was, all right. The old vapors moiling up from the depths of memory; too painful to remain denied.

"Oh Gawd," she whispered. "Wishin' I could fo'git. Gawd knows I wish I could fo'git."

Her eyes burned. She couldn't forget. That horror and pain, and none of it hurting like the degradation, the public humiliation and the naked indignity. The whip wales were healed, her lashed back and buttocks no longer bled; it was in her heart that the bleeding persisted, that the shame festered, the outrage flared to haunt her melancholy dreams.

"I'se cold. I'se so cold," she said.

She scrubbed her hands along her bare, icy arms. The cold drizzle still blew in her window on erratic gusts that whipped and ballooned her sodden feedsack curtains. For the moment she was too numbed with panic and chill even to get up and close the window. The rain had started before she finished her late-evening chores. Charging in on a rising wind, it had settled into a steady, unbroken barrage of thunder, sleet and hail. She'd stood in the lighted kitchen doorway and watched the shattering cloud-to-ground lightning crackling through the quarters and across the pine hammocks. The yard was a black swollen pond, littered with floating islands of debris and cow dung. Her rain barrels reverberated with the thundering freshets through the downspouts. The last candles winked out in the shanties beyond the work barns, and the Alabama night surrendered to the storm. She felt as if she were alone, like a single star winking in the cosmos, but it was a good feeling. This was her home. They needed her here.

Lucretia Borgia. Falconhurst Plantation would collapse into decay and dilapidation without her. Only Lucretia Borgia stood between this place and blight. It would crumble into sere and yellow leaf without her. She felt alone, but not lonely.

She'd climbed up to her attic room, and she'd gone to bed pleased by the soothing dissonance of the downpour. She slept better in the rain. The house was still warm and comfortable, secure against the onslaught of the elements. She lowered her magnificent bulk into her cot, the bed ropes squealing. She repeated her nightly prayer for Masta Ham's safety out across the Texies, and was lulled quickly into exhausted sleep. It had been another long day, another hellish long day, with old Masta Warren growing daily more pettish and vexatious, afflicted by crippling rheumatism and suffering the mollygrubs over the loss of his son.

She did not ever escape her master, even in her nightmares. He was there to castigate and scourge and expose her to public ridicule.

She shuddered. The dream never changed, nor did its sick terror lessen with repetition. She saw the same crowd of silent blacks, summoned by the clanging plantation bell, that sound still ringing inside her skull. The blacks stood in a sullen semicircle, the slaves who had to respect her authority, who had to obey her

12

orders, who looked up to her, almost as if she were as white as the Maxwells themselves. *Yes'm, Miz Lucretia Borgia, ma'am. No'm, Miz Lucretia Borgia, ma'am.* They were all there to witness her flogging. All watched her patched black-and-gray calico dress ripped away. She stood naked before them. Naked. Disgraced. Stripped of her vast pride.

Within the semicircle of slaves, young Hammond stood with his father. Master Warren Maxwell's seamed face was the countenance of a stranger. He gazed at her, cruel, detached, unyielding, without pity. Master Ham looked ill, but determined. She had defied them, disobeyed them; they had decreed her punishment: she would take twenty lashes—if she lived.

She shivered with shame, standing naked before them. Not even when Master Warren bought her at auction had she been compelled to stand naked like this for so many to see. She felt this malevolent moment would never end. All the blacks would talk about her disdainfully now, laugh at her, ridicule her behind her back. The domineering Lucretia Borgia, debased to a fat nigger wench; naked, belittled, branded.

She tried to stand straight and unbending, head erect in her red turban, as long as she could. Her eyes, olive-black and liquid, held fixed on some middle distance, something none of the rest of them could ever see, her own inner agony. Her mouth, with its perfect set of gleaming white teeth, remained taut, her chin thrust forward, uncompromising. A quadroon, Lucretia Borgia was big-girthed, statuesque and colossal. She wasn't fat. Though her breasts were over-full, they quivered, high-standing, amber-nippled. Her sculptured legs, her rounded belly, her whole body gleamed with the warm flesh tones of Gaboon mahogany. Until this moment of mortification, she'd been a laughing, majestic woman, cognizant of her size, aware of her beauty, alert to her power. She'd been surrogate to old Master Warren in his life-and-

13

death dominion over four hundred slaves. She carried herself like a queen.

Her authority at Falconhurst Plantation was absolute. There was no appeal. No slave's word had coinage against Lucretia Borgia's. Lucretia Borgia, descendant of a Sudanese tribe, with a mixture of Jaloff, was set apart. When one glimpsed her striding about the farm in her calico dress with its mother-of-pearl buttons, her bright-red turban bound rakishly around her head, her single gold earring glittering, one respected her position. She was not merely big, she was impressive in every way.

Naked, she was reduced to nothingness, debased, discredited and defiled. She barely felt ropes being tied around her ankles and wrists. Her inner agony overwhelmed her.

"Heist her up, boys." Warren Maxwell shouted the order almost as if it were some sort of sport. She would hear those words into eternity. She would carry them echoing inside her to the hottest hole beyond hell.

Suddenly those ropes yanked at her ankles. She was thrown forward and her legs winched upward above her head. She was held suspended in the air, her fingers clutching for but not quite reaching the plank flooring. Ropes creaked as they were wound about the stanchions. Blood rushed to her head. She choked back sobs. How ridiculous she must look, strung up like a slaughtered sow. Her spectacular breasts bobbled loosely, making her look even more comic and defiled. When the whip struck, she swung in an arc over the floor. The lash stung and burned across her buttocks. The leathers sliced her flesh. Blood seeped and then spurted from the ripped seams. Each stroke seared her and cut her. She chewed at her mouth until her torn lips dripped blood. And then she wailed. Her mindless screams drowned even the sound of Maxwell's counting off the strokes.

She plunged downward into the vilest world of pain

14

and torment. She was less than human, lower than a beaten animal. Her mind blazed, a red haze. Blood pounded at her temples. Blood smeared and squelched under the bloodied whip on her back.

It was impossible, yet it was old Warren Maxwell's contorted red face she saw as she hung there. Upside down. Disembodied. He had not laughed at all. Yet in her nightmares she heard his crazy laughter rattling inside her mind. Laughter. Wild and savage, maniacal laughter. His eyes, huge and empty and red rimmed, glittered with madness. They flew in like bats homing in on her bloody nakedness. Fixed. Staring. Gazing not in lust but in derision, insult, contempt.

She could endure the dream no longer. She wakened, sweated, cold, crying out. "Oh, Masta! Oh Gawd, Masta, no!" She threw her great arm across her face to ward off his flying eyes, his insensate laughter, to keep them from colliding with her, incinerating her.

She breathed raggedly. Hard to believe she had not screamed aloud. Yet, Mem slept, snoring in the cot beside hers. Damn him. She hated him, if only because he could sleep and she could not. He had been whipped, often and pitilessly, and yet he slept. What she had lost in her single flaying, he had never possessed.

Her eyes filled with tears and she closed her eyes tightly, squeezing the mists away. The pain and the damage had not been permanent, but the humiliation and outrage burned as furiously now as they ever had more than twenty years ago.

Instinctively, reading that timepiece of her mind, Lucretia Borgia knew it was at least two hours before dawn. The darkest hours of the night yawned before her. She could not go on lying on her cot. She couldn't stay in this bare, chilled room. She had learned over the years one response to sorrow, rage, fear, disappointment, anguish old or new—she worked. The harder she worked, the less she thought, the less she remembered.

She tossed off her flannel gown and slipped her

15

calico dress over her head. In the dark she wound the red turban about her crisp black hair—a certain heritage from the ancient Sudan. She pushed her feet into her loose slippers and let herself out of the small unplastered crib. She padded down the narrow, tunnel-dark stairwell to the unlighted kitchen. She didn't need a candle to light her way. She knew every inch of this house.

The kitchen was cold, a large square room with lye-scrubbed pine flooring. Still haunted by the unforgivable affront to her dignity, the scorn and debasement, she struck fire to a sulfur match and lit a lamp wick. She stood a moment before she replaced the polished shade, watching the pale, limber flame guttering in the night draft. She stacked shavings and sap-oozing kindling and soon had a blaze roaring in the great field-stone fireplace.

The room grew gradually warmer, but she remained chilled. She removed the cheesecloth from the loaves of yeast-risen dough and set the bread pans in the brick oven to bake. She built a fire in the huge old iron wood-burning stove, set a gallon pot of water on to boil while she ground fresh coffee beans. Cats of various breeds, tints and temperaments mewed at the door. She let them in and set down a dish of yesterday's milk on the floor for them.

"You ra'nchy devil cats, you has it easy, don't you?" she said to them. "Out cattin' round all night. Come in here first light you see, get warm milk an' a place to sleep under the stove. Oh, you live high . . . don't give milk, don't lay eggs, skins ain't even no 'count fo' nuthin' . . . you jus' eat and pester and spit at people that tries to pet you . . . you look at me when I'm talkin' to you, you no good cats."

She placed floured chicken breasts and drumsticks and wings in a large black iron skillet to fry, prepared a large pot of grits to boil. She busied herself with scores of tasks ordinarily left to her underlings. She

16

was glad to occupy her mind and her hands. But no matter how busy she kept herself, her melancholia remained, her sense of depression deepened.

"Nobody on this here place care how much work I do round here. Nobody. They let me do it all—every last lick—if I would. . . . Sometimes I reckon it'd be done heap faster and one hell of a lot better if'n I did do it all myself. But nobody care. Nobody evah once say thankee, Miz Lucretia Borgia. Nobody say, you-all tired, sister Lucretia Borgia? You jus' set down, Miz Lucretia Borgia, and I gone fix you a nice hot toddy. . . .

"All them white people think about is makin' work for me. Now that no-good brother of Miz Blanche's here again. . . . Come and stay like he own the place and he sister dead these eight years—an' him nuthin' but a cousin. He don't make nuthin' but work and trouble. So cross-eyed he thinks them spots in front of his eyes is freckles."

She permitted herself a faint smile that quickly died in a vinegary twist of her lovely full mouth.

They came all the time to Falconhurst Plantation, from every road—the relatives, slave buyers, itinerant slave traders, plantation owners and hangers-on like Miz Blanche's brother, Charlie Woodford. To Lucretia Borgia's mind, the strangest guest of all had been the perverted Roche, until the arrival of cross-eyed Charlie and his male companion they called Brass Door. Lord God almighty, such goings-on in that bedroom up there. Skinny Charlie Woodford taking big brawny Brass Door in his arms as if the Nordic giant were a wench, using him in his bed.

"Ole Masta Warren, he don't care who set his feet under his table, don't make me no trouble in my mind," she said aloud. "Seems to me, though, a man ought to pester a woman, not another man. . . ." She shuddered, repelled by her imaginings. "An' it goin' on, likely, right up in that bed right now . . . whips an' chains an' cross-eyed Charlie."

These white men! Such gods before the world, such geldings in private. These arrogant, swaggering white lords! What were they really, under all that hypocritical posturing? Were they virile men to pleasure a woman, plant seed in her as God must have had in mind? Or did they stride about cursing, lashing out with riding crops, yelling orders—and secretly hiding in a closet with another male? As long as nobody suspected the truth. No wonder white women cared so little for pleasuring with such hypocritical changelings. Skinny-shouldered, soft-assed, keg-bellied, flat-chested, scrawny-legged, hairy milksops. Who could want such a frog when she looked at the wide-shouldered, strong-legged beauty of a black man?

Her mouth twisted. No wonder those white men preferred each other rather than attempt to satisfy a healthy woman with their skimpy little tools. No wonder they feared, reviled and debased the black man. No wonder they called it an unforgivable crime for a black man to touch a white woman. Only death would remove the stain if a white woman knew a black stud's virility, caressed his thick muscles or submitted to his robust manhood. No wonder white men treated blacks like animals, castrating them, hanging them. They must deny or destroy the black man's manhood, or admit their own inadequacy.

This morning she hated them all, all white men, equally and without exception.

She tilted her head. "They done whupped me once. Hung me naked by my feet. Made a low, howlin' animal out'n me. Once . . . jus' once in this heah life. That I vow. No mo'. Nevah no mo'. . . ."

She straightened and went purposefully to the large cutlery drawer in the high-standing walnut chest. She selected the sharpest knife, stood gazing at its gleaming blade. Then she walked with it to the grindstone. She sat before the wheel and worked the treadle with her foot until sparks flew from the fine-honed blade. She heard movement behind her. Without turning, she said, "What you doin' up this early, Mem?"

"Come down to ast you the self-same question, woman. You cattin' round with that big Jingo Jim nigger, ain't you?"

She turned, gazing at the shrunken, round-shouldered black man in contempt. "Sure. Don't you see him? He right here, 'tween my legs."

Mem hesitated, winced. He knew his valuable days were behind him, the time when he'd been strong-thewed, yellow-fleshed and potent. He was almost forty plantings old and Miz Lucretia Borgia and the other wenches he had covered over the years had drained him badly. He said, "You ain't foolin' me none. You not in your bed. . . . Sneakin' out to meet Jingo Jim, warn't you?"

"Yes! I told you! Yes. Went out in the rain. So randy jus' couldn't wait. Laid down in the mud under that ole chinaberry tree—"

"They plenty dry places—"

"They all in yo' head. . . . You got no call comin' round accusin' me of nuthin' . . . with Jingo Jim or nobody."

"You my woman." He spoke without much hope, little conviction.

Her laugh seared him. "You sick in yo' head. I ole Masta Warren Maxwell's wench. I belongs to him. I his slave. That's the way it is. That's the law. But I don't belong to nobody else. Specially I don't belong to no dried-up, triflin' limber-cock like you."

He seemed to shrivel as he stood there. He looked as if he might cry. "You know I crazy 'bout you, Lucretia Borgia."

"I know you crazy. Weak-juiced. Triflin'. Lazy. Stupid."

"I seen the way you always lookin' at that Jingo Jim, smilin', and lettin' your eyes crawl over him like flies."

She shrugged. "That Jingo Jim he somethin' to look at."

Now his ebony eyes did fill with tears. "Please, Lucretia Borgia. Don't chase out to that nigger. Not him. I a better man than him when I was twenty. I forty now. He treat me like dirt. He take you—he laff in my face."

"Everybody laughs in yo' face, you had sense enough to see." She shrugged her shoulders again. "I didn't make this world. I didn't make things the way they is —but I takes 'em the way they is. That what you better do. You gittin' to be a scrawny ole rooster. You better face it."

"Please, Lucretia Borgia, I begs you."

"Ain't no good you beggin'. You ain't gettin' your big muscles back. You ain't gittin' back yo' thick juices. You gittin' old. You gittin' limber. You jus' make me sicker'n evah." She stopped spinning the grindstone and stared engrossed at the glittering blade.

"Why you got the knife?" he said.

She laughed sourly. "Gwine cut a little ole hole in you, Memnon, let some of the p'isen sawdust run out."

"What for you needs a knife that sharp?"

" 'Cause this heah my knife." She stared at it for a long beat. " 'Cause it mean nobody evah whup me again."

He caught his breath. "You gwine knife the ole masta?"

Her voice was flat. "Knife not fo' the masta. Not for nobody but me."

His eyes stretched wide and round. "You? What you mean—for you?"

"For *me*, nigger. 'Fore evah I lets *nobody* whup me—'fore I evah lets nobody make me live like a animal ag'in, I die. Quick and clean. I die like the lady I is. I die like I live—pridey—Miz Lucretia Borgia."

II

The barbarous night thunderstorm eased south and east on the wind, leaving the farmlands washed clean and fresh-smelling. The sun winked from puddles and rivulets which coursed through deep-cut wagon tracks in the red clay. Clouds glowed pristinely, puffy and gleaming white, soft bolsters against the laundered tapestry of the skies. Morning heat dispelled the last traces of nightchill, and faint mists smoked up from grassy fields, glittering ponds and marshy low ground. Lucretia Borgia found no time to enjoy the startlingly new azure, green and bright-yellow morning. There was a plantation to run; and by default there was only Lucretia Borgia to run it.

She heard commotion upstairs as the house came awake in the false dawn, servants and white masters alike. From old habit she straightened her fancy red turban and patted at her dress. By nature she was a warm, uncomplicated, curious and friendly soul. As the house grew louder, some of her natural exuberance returned. She hated and despised many of the cruelties and injustices of life, but she found boundless joy in living itself.

"Git out from underfoot, you Memnon," she ordered the black butler. "You see to them fires in the dining room an' the parlor this instant, or Masta give you a dose of the snake. He don't, I will."

"Got plenty of time," Mem protested, but he obeyed her, shuffling toward the darkened front of the house. He wanted to make her swear allegiance to him. He yearned to hear her deny any interest in Jingo Jim, but he didn't push her. He'd only exacerbate matters by defying her direct orders.

She heard Masta Maxwell and Cousin Charlie and another voice she reasoned to be that of the strange blond slave Brass Door. She heard their faltering steps on the stairs and Masta Warren Maxwell yelling for Mem to fetch a lamp to light the way for his guests. Hearing these familiar sounds, caught up in the swelling buzz of early-morning activity, she warmed, her spirits lifted. She did not forget her inner agony, but her desire to run things drove everything else from her mind. She had the hoecakes and fried eggs and ham sizzling hot, the coffee boiling, the fried chicken cooling just enough to make it crackling crispy the way Masta Warren hankered it.

She shouted up the rear stairwell to hasten the kitchen help and the table servers, the scullery maids and the cleaners. "Masta gwine be ready fo' he bre'fust. Stir yo' lazy stumps, you triflin' niggers."

When she turned, Cousin Charlie Woodford stood grinning fatuously at her from beside the huge stove. She supposed his gaze was focused on her; he was so crooked-eyed it was hard to tell what he was looking at. She was thankful she wasn't superstitious as some of them Bantu niggers, or seeing those angled eyes, she'd run screaming for the woods. She bit back a derisive smile, thinking, *whips, chains and cross-eyed Charlie*. Her voice, however, would have melted butter. "How's yo' health this mawnin', Masta Cousin Charlie? What can I do fo' you?"

"Needs a quick cup of black coffee to wake up, I do," he said.

She nodded. Probably Charlie had had another rugged night. Whips and chains and cross-eyed Charlie.

She poured a goblet of steaming brown coffee. The aroma pervaded the room. Cousin Charlie sat down at the long pinewood table and sipped tentatively at the scalding liquid. "How'd you like to be rich, Lucretia Borgia?"

"What I need money for, Masta Cousin Charlie? Can't spend it at Falconhurst. Seldom gits anywhere else. Masta, he give me all I need."

"You was rich enough, you could buy your freedom. Be a freed woman of color. Go live free in New Orleans."

"Lived once in New Orleans. Wasn't too partial to it, Masta."

His voice rasped. "Well, hell, you must want *something*. You had money you could buy your freedom, go north to live."

She shrugged her shoulders, watching him uninterestedly. "I seen white folks from the no'th. From the south. They ain't all that different."

He leaned forward, glanced around oddly with his bleached blue eyes askew. He lowered his voice to a confidential pitch, as if fearful of being overheard. "You tell me where ole Cousin Warren keeps just one of his money pots buried, I'll halve it with you. Enough gold eagles for both us to live high the rest of our lives."

She showed her teeth in a bland smile. "If'n I knew that, Masta Charlie, I could dig up a pot and keep it *all*."

"You smart-talkin' nigger. You'd never git away with it."

She tried to meet his eyes. "How come you think you would?"

He smiled, showing yellowing teeth. "I wouldn't *try* to git away with it. I'd jus' take it. Once I was gone, Cousin Warren might someday find out I took it. But what could he do, all stove up with rheumatism like he is?"

"Naw suh, Masta Charlie. I cain't help you none."

23

"It might be years 'fore he even found out a pot was missing."

She shook her head negatively.

"Dammit. Why not? You know damn well you know exactly where ever' one of his pots of gold eagles is buried. Cousin Warren, he trust you."

"Maybe he trust me 'cause he know I ain't gwine tell nobody."

He sweated, mopping at his face with a soiled white handkerchief. "Dammit, Lucretia Borgia. I *need* that money. I'm in debt. Bad in debt. Gambling. These New Orleans gamblers could kill me. I know Cousin Warren would *want* me to have that money an' he understood."

"Yassuh. Why don't you talk to him 'bout it?"

"I did." He spread his hands helplessly. "He was real kindly. But he got *one* idea in his head. He means to keep that money—every penny—hid till Cousin Hammond come home from the Texies. . . . Hell, Lucretia Borgia, you know Cousin Ham ain't nevah comin' back heah . . . and I need that money now."

She lifted her massive shoulders and let them sag. "Wish I could help you, Masta." Her tone was fawning. There was no harm in smiling falsely at this critter. She had no interest or faith in his promised bribe. She knew Cousin Charlie too well. Once that pot was in his scrawny hands, he'd cancel all vows.

"Damn you, Lucretia Borgia, you uppity nigger. You'll regret this."

"Yassuh. Prob'ly I will, Masta."

"You damn well will. You gone die a slave on this backwoods farm. Never have nuthin'. No diamond rings. No red silk petticoats. Nuthin'." He finished off his coffee and stood up. "Don't you say nuthin' to Cousin Warren 'bout what I say to you. Won't do no good. I'll jus' say you lie. He take my word ever' time over a biggety nigger's. He my own cousin. You jus' keep yore tater trap shut. You tell him nuthin'."

24

"No, suh. I don't say nuthin'." She smiled, deciding to let this polecat steam a little in his own broth. "I don't nevah say nuthin' to Masta Warren—less'n he ast me."

Mem came in from the dining room to fetch Master Warren the first of his morning toddies. Charlie glared at Lucretia Borgia on the bias and strode from the kitchen. The room was suddenly alive with kitchen helpers, grinning, giggling and relieved that Lucretia Borgia had done the work of ten of them already this morning. They felt no gratitude, only relief.

Her voice raked them, stirring them like ants. She vented on them the hostility Cousin Charlie had roused in her. They hurried under the lash of her scorn. They set the breakfast in the dining room, filling silver goblets with fresh cold spring water so the metal sweated enticingly. They placed platters of hoecakes and ham and chicken along with bowls of grits upon the table, and they filled cups with coffee. And then it was Lucretia Borgia's prerogative to walk up to the front parlor and announce breakfast.

When she returned to the kitchen, hoping for a moment to gulp down her own breakfast, Dide was there. The black midwife wore a scarf over her corn-row plaited hair and an oil slicker about her shoulders. Lucretia Borgia offered her coffee, but Dide shook her head and waved her hand impatiently. "Can you come down to Dixie's cabin, Miz Lucretia Borgia?" Dide said.

The room went silent. Black eyes fixed on Miz Lucretia Borgia and Dide, even when Lucretia Borgia ordered them to get about their work. Everyone knew Dixie was gut-busting swollen in her pregnancy. They also knew Dixie had lost three suckers to miscarriage. Master Warren was waiting for her to deliver this git before he sold her off. He could have fetched a nice profit for her knocked up, but he never knowingly sold inferior animals. He wanted to be certain his dams could foal in season. Falconhurst Plantation had a prideful reputation to uphold.

Lucretia Borgia snatched a knitted shawl from a wall peg and followed Dide out the rear screen door, letting it slam behind them. Mud oozed ankle-deep as they plodded across the yard, and they hurried to escape it.

Jingo Jim strolled out of the barn, proud as a stallion, as they passed. Jingo Jim was nearly twenty plantings old and was by far the prize stud at Falconhurst. He was dark-skinned, a Ugandan black. His face was round, his nostrils wide and his lips thick. But not since the Mandingo Mede's murder had there been such a breathtaking physical specimen on the plantation. Muscles rippled on his bared chest and bulged chunky across his wide shoulders. He stood tall on stalwart legs straight and thick as cypress boles.

Lucretia Borgia, even hastening as she was toward a crisis, felt a confused and not unpleasant mixture of emotions when she glimpsed the arrogant Jingo Jim. She felt a flushed feverish heat at her thighs. She couldn't deny that. He stirred her up, all right. But she felt more than a physical response to his rugged virility. There was also a sense of fierce pride in recognizing that Jingo Jim was the fanciest of Falconhurst's high-quality stock. Pride of the herd. She herself had traded for Jingo Jim more than five years back. Master Warren had said nothing at the time. He'd asked only if she'd gotten boot in the trade. He figured himself bested in any transaction in which he didn't collect cash as well as flesh in trading. He said nothing about the chances of the muddy, skinny boy growing into a real saleworthy buck. But over the years, Master Warren had watched Jingo Jim with growing admiration and had long since forgotten who'd bought him. But Lucretia Borgia had not forgotten.

All this flashed through Lucretia Borgia's mind while she and Dide walked toward where Jingo Jim stood bare-chested, in Osnaburg britches chopped off raggedly at the knees. He grinned self-confidently. Though he would never approach the weight, beauty or sale value of the Mandingo Mede, Jingo Jim possessed a cocky, endearing self-confidence totally unknown to the dead Mede. Mede had been a mild-mannered, gentle, quiet man—he had lived almost as quietly and bravely as he had died.

"Well, lookaheah," Jingo Jim said to the clouds. "Where you fine gals headin'? Bet you think you died and gone to heaven, runnin' cross me like this."

"Be careful where you step, Dide," Lucretia Borgia said. "It pilin' up knee-deep round here."

Jingo Jim laughed. "I been meanin' to come up to the big house to talk to you, Miz Lucretia Borgia."

"You want to feel the whip, you come messin' round the big house, boy." Lucretia Borgia kept walking.

"Jus' gone ask you to meet me somewhere we kin be alone."

"Why I want to be 'lone with a young boy like you?"

"Got a powerful hankerin' to show you what you bin missin' all yo' life."

"Go on back to work, boy. I got red bandanas older'n you."

"No red bandana ever keep you warm as ole Jingo Jim," he called after her.

Dixie was wailing as they came along the lane to her whitewashed cabin. They could hear her anguished sobs, split by mindless screams which in turn died away in a whining, pleading gasping for relief from intolerable pain. She wanted to die. She didn't want the baby. Dixie kept promising God if He just took this git from her body, she'd never get herself in such a predicament again as long as she lived.

Though there were already three other women in Dixie's cabin when she and Dide got there, Lucretia Borgia felt it meet and right that they should have sent for her. Whatever went wrong at Falconhurst, she had to know about it sooner or later. She nodded curtly and spoke briefly to the magnificently proportioned Mandingo girl, Big Pearl, and with less warmth to Big Pearl's mother, Lucy.

Lucretia didn't bother wasting a smile in Big Lucy's direction. There was little love lost between Big Lucy and Lucretia Borgia. Before Lucretia Borgia came to Falconhurst, Lucy had been the white folks' pet. There were a hundred reasons—all of them valid—why Lucretia Borgia had replaced Big Lucy as proxy-margravine of Falconhurst Plantation. Only Big Lucy recognized none except the incurable itch between Lucretia Borgia's thighs. Their hatred flared intensely. It had cooled only slightly in a quarter of a century.

Valerie, the older woman, boiled water at an iron stove and whispered soothing words in Dixie's direction whenever the sweated girl was silent for as long as a moment. Dide pushed a pillow under Dixie's hips and pulled her legs apart for an examination of the parturient canal. The fetus was partially exposed, the top of its head showing. "Been like that—ain't moved a blessed inch in more'n an hour," Dide whispered.

Dixie went off into a paroxysm of screaming.

"Hit's dead," Lucretia Borgia whispered. "Likely cord got wound round its neck. Strangled."

Dide nodded. "What we gone do?"

Lucretia Borgia tugged for a moment at the exposed cranium. Dixie's screams rattled the walls. Lucretia Borgia shook her head and straightened up. "Got to send for Doc Redfield," she said.

"Why?" Dide straightened. "What that dirty-handed ole vet know that we'uns don't 'bout birthin' suckers?"

"Nuthin'. But this heah is Masta Warren's wench. We got to git that sucker or she gwine die. We gits blamed if she die. Masta Warren, he don't take kindly to losin' wenches in childbirthin'."

Dixie howled hysterically. Lucretia Borgia smoothed the girl's sweated forehead gently. Dixie screamed.

"Don't wanta die. Don't wanta die. Oh Gawd, help me. Help me, Gawd."

"Gawd is helpin' you all He can," Lucretia Borgia said. "I here. Dide here. Dide and me, we ain't gwine let you die, honey."

"Me neither," Big Lucy said.

"We got to cut her to git that sucker," Lucretia said. "That means Doc Redfield. He can sew her up. . . . He can take the blame if anything does happen to her. We done all we could that way. Masta Warren he say we ain't done all we should, less'n we git Doc Redfield."

Dide nodded. "What we do for her till he gits here?"

"My Gawd." Lucretia Borgia stared at the unceilinged roofing. "You don't know what to do? Many suckers as you delivered, Dide?"

"I ain't delivered dead ones."

"You keeps her comfortable as you can. I send down a mason jar of Masta's corn whiskey and some long sweetenin'. You give it to her—hot—till the pain lets up—and don't you ole women drink it up neither. Hit's for Dixie." She smoothed the girl's contorted face with her fingers. "We gone do fo' you, Dixie. All we can. You hang on an' you howl much as you like."

"Hurry . . . I splittin' open! I in pain, terrible pain, Miz Lucretia Borgia. I dyin' in pain."

"I know you hurt, honey. I knows. I gwine hurry." She turned and went to the door. "Y'all takes care of her, now."

She closed the door and left the shanty, moving swiftly with the grace of a ballet dancer despite her size. She raced her bounding shadow along the lane, shouting for Jingo Jim. He came grinning from the barn. "You makes up yo' mind you want somethin', you sho' come a-runnin'."

"Got no time fo' yo' smart talk, boy. You hitch a light buggy to the fastest horse we got and you git it up

29

to the house fast as you can." She was already striding past the barn.

"Sho'. Have that horse up there 'fore you gits there good. . . . But tell me somethin' that's real important, Lucretia Borgia. When I gone git you nekkid on a bed?"

"When I gits time fo' you, that's when," she said over her shoulder. "An' that sho' ain't now . . . maybe you get yo' full growth by the time I ready fo' you."

He yelled after her, "I gits a full growth ever' time I looks at you, Lucretia Borgia."

She called for Mem as she entered the kitchen. He stood, shoulders sagged round, at the kitchen window. His face was bleak, his mouth pulled down. She saw he'd been watching her talking to Jingo Jim at the barn. He looked ready to cry. She shook her head impatiently. A buck was getting old when he cried over a woman he could no way hope to keep satisfied. She sent a girl running to Dixie's shanty with corn whiskey and sweetening. Then she lashed out at Mem. "Get ready. You got to go fetch Doc Redfield."

He did cry now, openly. "Cain't. Cain't go."

"Why not?" She was ready to hit him.

"Hit way over Widder Johnson's place. On Six Mile Road—"

"I know where he lives. So do you. And you waste time, I crack your triflin' skull."

He shook his head, crying. "Don't know the way fo' sho'. Forgits, I do. Besides, I go, them paddy-rollers gits me—call me a runaway slave—cuts off my balls. Anyway, I git lost . . . I cain't do it."

Fists clenched, Lucretia Borgia stared at Mem. He had never been much; he was just a husk of what he had once been. She looked around, scanning the faces in the room. "You, Clarissa," she said to a sixteen-year-old quadroon wench. "You bin to Widder Johnson's place, ain't you?"

30

"Yes'm. An' I got no wish to go ag'in. I scairt of that old Doc Redfield."

"Hell, he can't hurt you. Now you git a wrap." She heard the wagon pulled in at the rear door. She wished all the slaves moved as fast as Jingo Jim. "Mem will drive you. You show him the way."

"Cain't," Mem wept. "I scairt when I gits off the place."

"I scairt, too," Clarissa sobbed.

"Goddammit," Lucretia Borgia said. "When I give a order on this place, I want you niggers to jump. You got nuthin' to be scairt of but me. You, Mem. You, Clarissa. You want to go fetch Doc Redfield on the run, or you want me to whip your bare asses with a birch cane? You make up yore minds whilst I git you a road pass."

Old Maxwell Warren dawdled over his coffee and cigar at the breakfast table. Cousin Charlie sat across from him behind a blue screen of smoke. Brass Door ate at a small table beside the far window, alone. He was a mustee. This meant by legal definition he had a trace of Negro blood. He was too elegant for Cousin Charlie to allow him to eat with the house niggers in the kitchen, but not white enough to share a table with his white betters.

"Hit's that wench Dixie, Masta Warren, suh," Lucretia said. "She's lost her git. It died. But it died right in her hole, you excuse me, suh. Looks like it strangled on its cord. We got to send fast for Doc Redfield. Dixie got to be cut down there to git the dead sucker or we gone lose Dixie too. . . . Needs a road pass for Mem and Clarissa, I do."

"Goddam that Dixie wench," Maxwell said. He chewed angrily at his cigar. "Got to git shed of her. She no good on this earth for bearing suckers. Won't have her on the place. Want nuthin' but perfect stock in my herds here at Falconhurst."

31

"She gone die if we don't get Doc Redfield fast, Masta."

Maxwell shook his head. He sat and stared at his gnarled hands. His joints ached, his knuckles and fingers were swollen out of shape. "No way I can write nuthin' this mawnin'. If'n I could write, I'd git off a letter to my boy out in the Texies. . . . No. Jus' let 'em chance it. Them slave patrollers prob'ly in where it's warm."

"Can't risk it, Masta, please. Dixie shorely gwine die we don't hurry."

"I'll write the pass for you," Brass Door said. "If Master Maxwell don't mind I sign his name."

"Don't mind nuthin' at all, long's we save that wench Dixie." Old Warren Maxwell shook his head. He waved his arm, granting all necessary permissions to carry out Lucretia Borgia's plan. He winced and scrubbed his painful hands together. "Got to keep that Dixie wench alive long enough to sell her. Got to git shed of her, we do. Mayhap she be good for choppin' sugar cane. She sho' ain't worth a shit as a breeder."

III

When Lucretia Borgia came out of the kitchen door, she saw Jingo Jim loitering under the chinaberry tree near the open well. She ascertained that Mem and Clarissa had left the farm in the buggy, then she walked toward the quarters and Dixie's shanty.

"What you doin' hangin' round this house, boy?" She squinted at Jingo Jim in the high-slanting sun.

He fell into step beside her and grinned confidently. "Waitin' for you."

"You ever been whupped?"

"Who'd want to whup me? Nobody wants to scar up nuthin' as pretty as me."

"You keep hangin' round the big house when you supposed to be workin', you find out."

"I knowed you'd be goin' back to Miss Dixie's house. . . . Can't be no harm in me walkin' with you."

She didn't smile but she was pleased. She found pleasure in the world for the first time this morning. God, it must be wonderful to be as young as Jingo Jim and so certain of one's self and one's world. She'd purentee forgotten how it was to be so innocent. She winced. There was a bate of pain and a lot of hard learning ahead of him. Too bad, too. He was like a high-stepping colt, spirited and unbroken. Well, that wouldn't last, either. She'd learned one truth about her world: Nothing lasted in it. Not beauty. Not kindness.

Not the joyous unbridled mettle and strength of a Jingo Jim. Her voice was not unkind. "Depends on what you got in mind."

"Got you in mind."

"You stopped to think I old enough to be yo' mammy?"

"Ain't the way I think of you at all."

"You just a baby."

"You give me a chance. I show you who's a baby. You know Miss Dixie—what's droppin' her sucker this mornin'? I knocked her up. She's howling now but you should have heard her carryin' on and beggin' for more when I planted it in her."

She glanced at him but did not bother telling him his natural son was dead. The Falconhurst blacks were casual in their mating—this was the design of the old master of the stud farm. Any paternal feelings were firmly discouraged. There were no black "families" at Falconhurst. A sucker was taken from its mother when it was weaned. None ever knew its own father. Masta Maxwell wanted it this way. He wouldn't have it any other way. He raised black flesh to sell; he didn't want them growing attached to each other. Usually, by the time they were twenty-two or twenty-three, they were gone off to some slave auction. "You jus' too young for me," was all she said.

"You what I want. I got the craving for you. Something fierce." His voice lightened, urgent. "You know what a man need . . . nobody have to tell you what to do. . . . You a fine woman. Lawdy, all I got to do to git my pecker standin' is to lie in bed and think about you."

She did smile now. "I think kindly about you sometime, too. You a mighty comely buck, all right."

He put his head back, laughing. "Ain't I, though? . . . But I ain't nuthin' an' I don't git you nekkid in a bed."

"I got no time. I tole you."

34

"Please, Lucretia Borgia. I got you in my mind. Like a sickness. Can't think on them other wenches. It you I want."

"Got to git on up to Dixie. Got things to do."

"Jus' a little while. Please . . . I got the miseries."

She hesitated. She glanced toward the big house where Masta Warren and Cousin Charlie had repaired to the front porch. Masta Warren sat with his bare feet planted against the belly of a naked nine-year-old black boy. He was "dreenin'" out the miseries of his rheumatiz into the body of the slave child, a remedy he'd faithfully followed for nine or ten eternal years. He got only slight and infrequent relief but it was the best prescription he knew, though he searched constantly for miracle cures or quick palliation.

She turned, looking along the row of cabins to where Dixie lay agonized. If Dide plied Dixie with enough corn whiskey and sweetening, the girl would likely survive until the vet arrived. If Dixie began to fail, or the pain became intolerable even to her numbed senses, they would have to go ahead and cut her, remove the dead fetus and let Doc Redfield sew her up.

She exhaled heavily. "I might jus' drop by the hay barn on my way up to Dixie's," Lucretia Borgia said, almost as if talking to herself.

She saw Jingo Jim respond instanter. The sudden and enormous bulge at his fly quickened her own juices. She turned and walked away from him.

He was waiting for her when she stepped into the dark, musty-smelling hay barn. She let the door slap shut behind her. She was bat-blind for the moment after the sunlight. Before her eyes adjusted to the cavernous gloom, Jingo Jim caught her breasts in his hands, kneading them roughly as he must have done in a hundred orgiastic dreams.

She let him kiss her mouth and her throat. His hands were busy, one loosening the mother-of-pearl buttons decorating her bodice and slipping inside to fondle her bared breasts, the other working in the padded eminence of her fevered femininity. "Oh, lawsy," he whispered, delighted. "You sho' is even more gyascutus than I reckoned. . . . Come on, Lucretia, let's lay down in the hay."

"Can't. Ain't got time." She kissed him hungrily. "Besides, I git all messed up—hay all over me. Might as well wear a sign telling ole Lucy and Valerie where I been, what I been doing."

He panted, frustrated. "If you ain't gone lay down with me, why'd you come?"

She laughed and stroked his bulging crotch. She pulled away from him, rolled up her dress above her hips and tucked it in about her waist. He gazed enraptured at her gleaming mahogany beauty. His hand pushed between her naked thighs, finding her wet, heated, receptive. She loosened his fly. "I jus' take him out," she said. "Been wonderin' what he like."

"He like a cannon, gwine blow your head off, that's what he like." He worked his fingers faster.

She murmured, pleased. "Ohh. He is nice." She turned around in his arms. Then she bent over, facing away from him, and braced herself against the baled hay.

"Standin' up?" he sounded frustrated.

"I tole you I got no time. You want what you can git, boy, or you want to waste time complainin'?"

He said no more. He grasped her pelvis bones in both hands and drew her roughly to him as she guided his rigid staff home. She gasped with pleasure as he mounted her. "Oh . . . you wondrous . . . do it . . . do it. . . ."

He moaned, sobbing for breath, as he assaulted her. Even with her legs planted apart, he had to rise on his toes to drive himself totally into her. He gasped in lungsful of air and wailed in delight. "You a big boy," she panted. "You is truly growed. . . . Gawd knows

36

—what you be—when you gits—to be—a man. . . ."
Her voice trailed off in a keening cry of ecstasy.

Suddenly, he was bucking his hips so frantically she
had to bite her lip and dig her fingers into the bales of
hay to keep from being driven to her knees—or run
across the barnyard like a bitch in heat. She felt her
own desires rising to match his. It was good. It was
good. . . .

He thrust himself to her with a fearful final lunge,
clung to her for uncounted seconds and then staggered,
his knees buckling. He sank to the ground, dragging
her with him. She sprawled atop him, laughing. "You
kill me dead," he whispered, grinning. "Gawd, what
a way to die."

She pulled free, kissing him. "I got to go. I got work
to do."

He caught her hand and clung to her. "When I
gone see you ag'in?"

"When I can. I tell you when. . . . You a fine boy,
Jingo. You make gals outrageous happy when you
grow up."

He laughed, knowing she was teasing. He had
brought her all the way past a climax and left her
gasping for breath. Her hands grasping him with a
greedy tenderness told him better than any words how
delighted she was in him.

He waited until she straightened her dress and turban, brushed off her skirt and stepped through the
door and let it swing shut behind her. Then he
crawled on his hands and knees into a pile of loose hay
and plunged instantly into sated, exhausted sleep. . . .

Outside the barn door, Lucretia Borgia hesitated.
She leaned for a moment against its rough facing to
catch her breath. She wanted nothing more in that
instant than to sleep. Maybe relieve her kidneys and
then sleep. Oh, that Jingo was a caution—a heavy-

hung caution! She was tired out, wrung limp as a dish-rag. The backs of her legs trembled like a calf's spindly limbs.

There was no time to rest. She checked the road through the oaks, tupelos, pines and elms, looking for some sign of Mem's buggy. There was none. She sighed, walking up the lane toward Dixie's shack. If Doc Redfield didn't come soon, she and Dide would have to go ahead and cut Dixie. Mayhap she'd bring the knife she'd sharpened like a razor in her fury before dawn. Couldn't let the girl die. That was like throwing away Masta Maxwell's money—at least that's what he would charge, raging.

She heard Dixie's mindless laughing as she came up the steps. At least the girl wasn't dead. Drunk. But not dead. Not yet. She stepped into the quiet room. The women sat around helpless. Dixie laughed when she saw Lucretia Borgia. "Thank you, Miz Lucretia Borgia. That sweetening sho' is plumb soothin' . . . little devil's head a-hangin' out down there, an' I don't even care."

Dixie's pretty mouth twisted in a sudden spasm of pain, but she did not wail. Instead she cried out merrily, "Better pour me some more sweetening, Miz Dide. Think the last glass is plumb wearin' off."

Lucretia Borgia soothed her forehead. "You gwine be all right, baby."

"I all right now." Dixie went off into gales of laughter.

Someone was shouting Miz Lucretia Borgia's name from the lane. She went out on the porch. A small boy had come running from the big house. She recognized him as Marcus Aurelius, the nine-year-old who served as old Maxwell's latest "dreenin' pan." The boy's voice shook. "Masta say he yellin' fo' his toddies—and no-body to fetch 'em, please ma'am, Miz Lucretia Borgia."

Lucretia Borgia shook her head, her smile wry. Things must be in bad shape if Masta Warren would spare Marcus long enough to send him on an errand. Her gaze dragged the trace beyond the Falconhurst property line. There was no sign of the buggy or Doc Redfield. Damn his trashy white hide. Damn Mem. Wait till she got her hands on that Clarissa gal. "All right," she said. "You tell yore masta I be there." She searched the road again, looking for Mem's buggy. The trace was empty. The boy turned and ran ahead of her toward the big house. Lucretia Borgia walked tiredly in the sun. She saw Cousin Charlie prowling the yard, kicking at grass clumps.

IV

Mem's buggy slogged through the obscuring mists of the damp forest. Water splayed out from under the hooves of the horse and sprayed around the iron rims of the wheels. In places the ruts were hidden in black puddles. The sun blazed down pitilessly through soiled clouds. The rain had destroyed the roadbed in spots and slowed the horse. Mem fought to keep the animal on the ill-marked trace, cursing him when he balked or faltered.

"You best hurry," Clarissa said.

"I scairt to race this horse."

"Why? Ain't you man enough to handle him?"

"I man enough. Don't have to be a young stud like that Jingo to handle horses or women. But we go racin' long Six Mile Road, paddy-rollers take us for runaways sure."

"We got a road pass."

"Yeah. We know it. But do we know them trashy slave patrollers can read writin'?" He shivered visibly.

"Well, we got to go faster. Dixie maybe dyin'."

Mem slapped the whip over the rump of the horse, but with the other hand he held a tight restraining grip on the reins. He'd heard too many stories about what paddy-rollers did to slaves when they caught them on the road.

When Mem pulled the wagon into the drive before the Widder Johnson's farmhouse on Six Mile Road,

Clarissa left him sitting in the cart and ran around the old house, hounds sniffing at her legs. Drawing a deep breath, she knocked timidly but insistently at the rear door. After a long time, Doc Redfield opened the door. He was a scrawny man who had married money and cultivated a beer belly. His hands were arthritic, twisted and liver-spotted, with a funereal line of black at the tips of his nails. Prosperity had improved the color of his cheeks. His wife insisted he shave daily and trim his V-shaped beard and sparse red whiskers. He looked almost respectable in twill trousers and flowered waistcoat. He squinted and stared at her. He glanced over his shoulder and then said, "You one of them Falconhurst wenches, ain't you?"

"Yassuh. Masta sent me to—"

"Come on in then."

"Don't need to come in." Clarissa retreated a step.

"Can't do nuthin' for you an' you standin' on the stoop. Either you come on in or you git on off the place." He went on holding the screen door ajar for her, his eyes fixed on the fullness at her dress front.

Trembling, she nodded. "Yassuh." She came into the kitchen. She waited politely for him to inquire the reason for her visit. She'd been taught to talk when spoken to. But the vet did not speak to her at once. Instead he closed and locked the door which led from the kitchen to the inner house. Then he rolled up his sleeves above his elbows and soaped and scrubbed his black-nailed hands at a basin on the drainboard.

When he turned around, he seemed surprised to see her standing there. "Well, lay down, girl."

"What?"

"How can I 'xamine you, you don't take off that dress and lay down?"

"I don't need no 'xamination, Doctor. I tryin' to tell you."

"You don't have to be timid with me, wench. I a doctor. Well, a black and horse doctor. I a vet. But I seen hundreds of gals like you buck nekkid. I can tell

42

in a hurry what ails you. Now git that dress off and lie down on the table."

Frightened, she nodded and slipped the dress over her head. She stood as if chilled, trying to cover the lush planes and escarpments of her tawny body with her hands. He swallowed abruptly and adjusted his spectacles, which appeared suddenly steamed. His voice remained businesslike. "Go on now. Lay down on the table and put—your legs—apart. Wide apart now."

Blushing, the blood suffusing her face and throat, Clarissa hoisted herself up on a chair and lay down upon the table. She lay staring at the ceiling, her arms over her breasts until Doc Redfield pulled them down and placed them firmly at her side. "Old Warren gittin' set to sell you off, eh, gal?"

"Oh no, suh. He not figurin' to sell me—"

"You gits knocked up, I bet he sells you." Doc Redfield laughed. "Old Warren mighty sly, sick as he is with the rheumatiz and all. He don't sell a wench less'n her belly swolled up with a sucker in it—gets double price then. . . . Yassuh, smart ole coot."

"I'm not pregnant. Not sick. Masta sent me—"

"Masta sent you. Sent you to me. Right? Then shut up and let me get on with it."

He thrust his fingers into her tender parts, probing extensively. She closed her eyes and bit down on her underlip. After a long time, he said, "Well, you right. You shore ain't knocked up. What's wrong? Masta think you got the clap? He shore don't want that spread in his herd."

"I ain't got what you said. We clean. We all clean wenches at Falconhurst."

"That's God's fact. But it don't take but one case in baggage pretty as you to foul up a whole herd. Got to be sure."

Her head jerked up. "I ain't never had no such thing."

"All right. We see. You got it, we got some of Mrs.

Redfield's herb medicine clear it up. Stings bad, but effective. Powerful effective." He continued to probe and press and stroke inside her thighs. Once he said, "Can you tighten them muscles on my finger? Do it." Agonized, she tightened the muscles of her vulva. He nodded. "Do it again . . . again. . . . You real fine gal, all right. You evah been to see me before?"

"Yes. . . . I came once—with a sore throat, and you made me undress."

He smiled, nodding. "Knowed I'd examined you before. Ain't one to forgit a perfect animal. Ain't forgot how you looked—all tawny. Maxwell likes wenches black, but I prefer the light tan—like you."

Her voice sharpened. "Masta nevah sent me fo' no examination. . . . We got trouble over at Falconhurst. He say fo' you to come. Soon as it convenient."

She tried to get up from the table, reaching for her dress hung over the back of a kitchen chair. He pushed her back down brusquely and with such authority she was afraid to oppose him. "It ain't convenient just yet," he said.

"You let me alone."

"I lets you alone when I gits through heah. I know my job."

"I ain't ast fo' this."

"You threatenin' me, gal? What you gone do? Tell Maxwell on me? He only laugh at you. He pleased to have me finger any of his slaves, when I want. You want to tell the sheriff maybe? Go ahead. Word of a high yeller gal—against mine. Who you reckon to tell, gal?"

"I'll—tell God."

He laughed. "You do that. An' you best do it in secret. Else you'll feel a whip on your back, peddlin' tales about me. I a respectable married man." He worked his fingers faster in her pudendum.

She cried out. "Masta say you to come to Falconhurst in a hurry—"

"When it convenient. That's what he say. It be convenient soon's I through here. Now lay still."

"Please. Don't do that. I don't want you to."

"Reckon you ain't got much to say about it, gal." Doc Redfield laughed and closed his free hand over one golden breast. "I been a nigger doctor, handling black wenches, a long time, gal, and I've learned that a lot of wenches start out hatin' it when a white man fangles 'em, but most of 'em wind up not able to get a bate of it."

"Not me—I ain't like that."

"You ain't yet. Now lay still and take it an' we be through heah in a minute."

Coming around the side of the old clapboard house, Lucretia Borgia cursed Doc Redfield volubly, if under her breath. She outlined a comprehensive program of pain for the trifling Memnon and that flighty Clarissa. It would be a long time before they didn't follow her orders to the letter. She heard a sound which brought her up sharply. Puzzled and troubled, she stood and looked around, scowling. The sound was like the mortal whine of a sick hound, the stifled, agonized weeping of an ill woman.

"Oh my Gawd," Lucretia Borgia said. "What's the matter, Masta Warren?"

For a moment she hadn't even realized that the form hunkered over in the old rocking chair was the aging master of Falconhurst. He crouched, doubled over, his arms across his face. Sobs wracked his entire body. She had seen Warren Maxwell in strength and weakness, rage and anguish, in sickness and robust health. But she had never heard him weep aloud like this. She had seldom encountered such a sound of heartbroken agony in all her life—and she'd seen her share of mortal woe.

He sagged forward, his shoulders quivering. He sat alone, as if totally abandoned, his heavy blanket discarded on the floor beside his chair. His bare feet were liver-colored with jagged, malformed nails.

"Masta! What's the matter? Talk to me, Masta. What happened? What they done to you?" Her first thought was that Cousin Charlie had harmed him trying to find out where his money pots were buried.

Lucretia Borgia ran up the plank steps to the wide porch and fell on her knees beside Maxwell's chair. She put her arms about his shoulders as tenderly as though he were a child. She whispered to him, smoothed the graying red hair that was more a dirty orange now. He had not shaved; his scraggly red-gray beard was wiry on his leathered cheeks. She blamed Mem. She'd skin the lazy nigger this time for sure . . . if he ever got back with that no-account doctor. Maxwell's shirt smelled sour too, and she realized she'd have to attend him more closely. The older he got, the more careless he became about his appearance. He'd wear the same shirt and pants until they rotted off him if she let him. "It's all right, Masta. It's all right. Lucretia Borgia here. Lucretia is here, Masta."

At this display of compassion, Maxwell wept afresh, louder. At last, he got himself slightly under control and sat straighter in his chair. He put his head back, crying brokenly. She couldn't help thinking how decrepit and worn-out he looked. He sniffed, hawked deeply and spat thickly into the yard. He rubbed his swollen-knuckled fingers in his bleached blue eyes, drying them.

"Goddam you, Lucretia Borgia." He gripped her wrist so fiercely she winced. He quickly loosed his grip; the pangs of pain flared maddeningly in his joints when he made a fist of his liver-spotted hands. "Where you been? I been callin' you an' callin' you. An' that no-good Mem. Nevah could rely on that nigger, even when he was young. But you, Lucretia Borgia. I could die right here and wouldn't nobody on this place give the first damn. Nobody."

"I'd care, Masta." She soothed him gently. "You

know I'd care. Why it'd break my heart something bad happened to my masta."

"Somethin' bad is happenin' to me, Lucretia Borgia. Terrible bad."

"What is it, Masta? Tell me what."

"Everything, goddammit. Goddammit, everything. I send that boy Mark lookin' fo' you—and he sneaks off to play. Who's to dreen the rheumatiz from my pore hurtin' feet? Ain't had a toddy all this goddam mornin'. Know I has to have my hot toddy 'gainst the weather and the pain. Where's that Mem? I want a toddy."

"I gits you a nice hot toddy, Masta. And I canes that Marcus Aurelius till his bare ass bleed. He won't nevah sneak off no more." She moved to rise from beside him, but he caught her, almost in panic.

"Don't go," he said.

"No, Masta." She turned her head and shouted. "Millie! You black Millie! Get yo' ass out here."

Millie came as near as the screen door. She stood inside it, trembling, waiting. Lucretia Borgia spoke over her shoulder. "You fix Masta a nice hot toddy this second, Millie. An' you keep that water b'ilin' hot and sweetening poured, ready. You hear me?"

Millie sniffled. "I cain't, Miz Lucretia Borgia. I ain't nevah made no hot toddy. That's Mem's work. . . . I don't know how."

"You don't know how to screw, either, but that don't no way keep you from heistin' yo' skirts at every black boy on this farm. You don't know how to make a toddy—then by damn it's time you learned. Don't talk back to me, gal. Git." She made as if to pursue the scullery maid. Millie cried out and fled.

Lucretia Borgia returned her full attention to the master of Falconhurst. He sat sniffling. He massaged his knees and scrubbed absently at one gnarled hand with the other. He was seldom liberated from the sharp bite of pain in his joints.

"Goddammit," he said. "I just ain't got the strength no more to go on like this, Lucretia Borgia."

"You got to go on."

"Fo' what? Who care if I live or die?"

"I care, Masta."

"You jest a nigger. You ain't white, or flesh-and-blood kin. You a good wench. But you black. It ain't the same as needin' a human to care for you."

"They's Masta Ham. He loves you."

"Goddammit. How can you say he loves me? If he loved me, would he be clean out across the Texies, the way he is? He ain't comin' back home. I feel it in my bones—when I can feel anything but that paralyzin' pain, that's what else I feel. Sorrow that my son ain't nevah comin' home to Falconhurst ag'in."

"You jus' been listen' to that no-good Cousin Charlie."

"Now I can't have you low-ratin' a white man, Lucretia Borgia. Folks forever chidin' me how I lets you talk uppity and forgit yo' place, disremember you ain't nuthin' but a kitchen slut. That's what you is, and no matter yo' airs, you nuthin' but a black kitchen slut."

"Don't be able to abide that critter."

Maxwell leveled an accusing finger at her. "Don't matter a damn bit who you like and who you don't like—an' he a white man. An' I was well enough, I'd touch you up with a whip, round the edges some. That put you in yo' place."

"No," she said. "Nevah nobody take a whip to me ag'in, Masta. . . . You done it once—"

"Goddammit, I can whop when I want. Who I want. I master here. Don't be argufyin' with me. You talk about what you can't abide. I can't no way abide no argufyin' nigger. I has you whipped. Can't no way tolerate a back-talkin' black wench."

"I Lucretia Borgia, Masta. An' I loves you. An' I reckon I dies fo' you, if I hasta. . . . But I ain't nevah being whipped no mo'—by nobody."

His face flushed to the roots of his fading red hair. Though he still clung to her forlornly, his voice raged. "By God, we see. You wait till my boy Ham come home from the Texies. Whop you then. He whop you when I say."

She shrugged, matching his cruelty. "Maybe he don't come home."

He burst into sudden unexpected helpless tears. He caught her in his arms and pulled her against him with all his strength, sobbing. "Oh, he got to come home, Lucretia Borgia. He got to. Sometime I feel like I can't jus' live inside my own skin no mo', my boy don't come home to me." He wept, strangled, and clung to her.

"It's all right," she whispered. "It's all right."

He straightened, sniffling. "I needs him, Lucretia Borgia. Here on the place. I swan I don't know how in hell we managed as well as we did all these years without Masta Ham. . . . I give you some credit, Lucretia Borgia. You done what you could. You jus' a nigger, but you done what you could. An' I appreciate it. . . . Got no wish to whop you—jus' can't have a nigger actin' biggety and talkin' like she human. Can't you see that, Lucretia Borgia? I know you got some human blood. And I know it made you uncommon clever—for a nigger—but I needs my son. . . . Got no reason to live no more 'thout my son."

"Masta Ham comin' home. . . . One of these days, we look up and we see him a-comin'—a-laughin' and a-callin' to us up that lane from the road."

He almost smiled, nodding. "Be a great day when he come home from the Texies. This place be somethin' fine then. Been meanin' all these years to build a great new manor house—like the Hammonds' Anglebranch Plantation mansion down there near Selma. I do it when Ham come home. A place finer even than the Hammonds'. . . . Them Hammonds real quality people. Masta Ham's mother—she a Hammond. Old

Theophilus Hammond's own daughter. We named Masta Ham for ole Theophilus Hammond.

"Yes suh, when Masta Ham come home, we gone build a fine mansion. Yonder in them pines. Meant to build a mansion for Mrs. Maxwell when I brung her up here from Anglebranch Plantation. But I just stayed so busy—kept puttin' it off, like a man will. Busy raisin' and sellin' niggers. An' this sickness come on her. Miz Maxwell poorly. Just kept puttin' it off. . . .

"I purely wanted a fitten place for her to live. We talked about it. Planned. Some folks think this ole nine-room clapboard is a purty good place. But it not fancy. Fancy in it day, but not much no more. My pappy built it—mighty showy in his time."

Millie brought Maxwell's hot toddy. He tasted it, his mouth twisting sourly. "Goddam. Fix me another, Millie-gal. Mo' sweetenin'—an' hotter. . . . This ain't no good at all. Taste like pig piss . . . but you'll learn." He forgot the black girl, who retreated, closing the front door so quietly behind her that they scarcely heard her leave. When Lucretia Borgia moved to get up from her knees, old Maxwell clutched her with surprising restraining force.

His mind followed the memories he'd roused by speaking of his wife and her family, and the plans for a new house. "My boy belong here. That's why I *know* he is coming home. No matter what that no-account Charlie Woodford say, no matter what nobody says. Our roots, they go deep here at Falconhurst. Hit like a taproot that grow so deep it can't never be pulled loose. My grandpappy built a log house right in this clearing. And he raised niggers to sell. We Maxwells been right here at Falconhurst since before the war of 1776. We put down our roots in this good black dirt of Falconhurst Plantation. We drinks our vigor from the richness of the old Tombigbee. . . . A man don't break off from deep roots like that. Our roots here at

Falconhurst, not a root that breaks off easy. Masta Ham go off to the Texies—restless like young boys git—been gone eight long years. A long time. A long sad time. But he comin' back home. He comin' home, Lucretia Borgia, where he roots are, where he belong. That much I know."

"Sho' he is, Masta. Sho' he is." She saw the buggy race into the yard carrying Mem, Clarissa and the white vet. But when she tried to get up, old Maxwell restrained her with his frantic grip viselike on her arms. The buggy rolled past the house and into the quarters. At least Mem had enough sense to keep Doc Redfield from getting a chance to drink and talk with the master.

"What was I sayin', Lucretia Borgia?"

"Doc Redfield's here, Masta. He gwine to cut Dixie's dead baby loose—"

"Yeah. Yeah. I seen 'em. . . . I was sayin', I know my boy is comin' home most any day now. The longin' for Falconhurst gone bring him home. He don't break away from his taproot that goes so deep in this earth. No, suh. An' he knows I need him here, gettin' on like I am, an' stove up with rheumatism. Oh, you done what you could. But no way you can block a coffle and march it to New Orleans or out to Natchez. We sellin' nigger flesh—to them as comes to buy it. Reckon you made us some money, doin' best you could. Can't take nuthin' away from you. But sellin' niggers here at Falconhurst ain't like auctioning a hundred or so at a time on a New Orleans vendue table. . . . To make big money we needs to put whole herds up fo' auction at New Orleans—leastways out at Natchez. That's where you gits your price for the fancy flesh we raise. That's one reason why we needs Masta Ham so terrible."

"Yassuh. Be a great day when he come home."

"I miss him so terrible, Lucretia Borgia. Bein' a black animal an' all, you can't know what it is to miss yo' chile so terrible. Oh, I recall how you moan and carried on when we sold off yo' twin boys. But I not talkin' 'bout nigger carryin'-on. I talkin' 'bout human misery."

He wiped at his eyes with the back of his hand. "I swear to you, Lucretia Borgia, sometime I think all I want is jus' to have Ham here to set and rock and drink a toddy with me. I get so lonely for him, I swan I feel like I can't stand it. You even understand what I talking about?"

"I understand, Masta. But he is comin' home. I know it."

"How you reckon he stay away so long? Knowin' I needs him? Knowin' this place needin' him? . . . Why, he loved Falconhurst, loved raising and trading niggers . . . come natural to him." He breathed raggedly. "I gittin' old, thinkin' 'bout preparin' myself to go to my Maker. But I can't go in peace till I see Masta Ham again. . . . I sick-hearted, fifty, gettin' old . . . not wantin' to die 'thout I hold my boy close ag'in."

Mem came running breathlessly around the corner of the house. "Doc Redfield say Miss Dixie screamin' somethin' fierce an' you best come, Lucretia . . . Miss Dixie, she in some howlin' pain."

Lucretia Borgia nodded. Reluctantly, Maxwell released his deathgrip on her. She sent Mem to run things in the house and walked tiredly out toward the quarters. But she'd barely stepped into Dixie's shanty when Mem came running for her. She had to come back to the house. Clarissa was crying in her room and wouldn't come out. Nobody knew what to fix for dinner and Masta Warren had thrown a scalding hot toddy in Millie's face.

V

Doc Redfield sweated, working devotedly, and only dimly resembling the horny old satyr Lucretia Borgia had come to know and despise. It was hot in the shanty and he perspired heavily, his shirt growing discolored at the armpits, rivulets dripping along his face and glittering in his scraggly beard. Finally, he sewed the girl's raggedly torn paravaginal and periproctial tissues. Dixie writhed, wailing with the pain of puerperal convulsions and high fever. The veterinarian spoke to her brusquely, telling her often to shut her goddam mouth, but he was incredibly gentle, and he prepared a potion of a powder from a small jar he took from his medical kit. He poured the mixture into Dixie's mouth. He held her nose pinched closed with thumb and forefinger and clamped his palm over her lips until she swallowed. Within minutes, Dixie quieted, grew silent and sank into a stunned sleep.

"That jus' a purentee, bonfide miracle," Lucretia Borgia said.

The doctor was not too modest to accept her praise warmly. "It's a laudanum derivative. A dose will knock a man flat-ass on his tail in under a minute. Pain gets where a patient can't bear it, this helps him to sleep it off and give nature time to make repairs. . . . I always say, nature could cure one hell of a lot of ills an' doctors and patients just be smart enough to let her alone and give her a chance."

He hesitated a moment and then held out the bottle, giving it to Lucretia Borgia. "You put this stuff away, Lucretia Borgia. Sometime people hurt monstrous. This here won't cure, but it knock 'em out like a pole axe—put 'em out of pain, sometime long as overnight. Depend on the constitution of the patient. They don't have to suffer so much whilst you send for me."

Lucretia Borgia thanked him kindly and dropped the bottle into her apron pocket. Later, in the pantry off her kitchen, she put it away carefully, though unmarked. She trusted her remarkable memory in all matters of preserved and bottled goods, since she couldn't read. As desperately as old Warren Maxwell needed her assistance in running Falconhurst, he refused to allow her to learn to read and write or even to sign her own name. His excuse was that teaching Negroes to read or write was not only a waste of time, it was against the law. This statute was one of the few he did not violate with that impunity peculiar to the white ruling class of the South.

Doc Redfield joined Maxwell on the front porch. Lucretia Borgia saw that little Mark had been found and now lay prostrate and naked at his master's feet, crying and sniffling after his corporal punishment.

Maxwell cursed the child as hopeless. "Recollect when Alph—he were one of Lucretia Borgia's twin boys—laid quiet under my feet for hours at a time."

Redfield laughed. "I recalls you kept Alph grogged out of his gourd on hot toddies most of the time. Kid just laid there and grinned—and belched."

"I'd be as kindly to Marcus. But he got no stomach fo' corn whiskey. He vomit it right up."

Redfield smiled in sympathy. "This boy is no fit companion for you to have around."

"I say amen to that. But till I find me another one,

he have to do. Or less'n I come on another cure. Been usin' this one more'n ten years now. Kinda losin' it strength. Don't dreen the rheum out'n me the way it usta."

"I been givin' it some thought," Redfield said. " 'Course you know, I ain't no medical practitioner—not for white folks."

"Hell. Few regular sawbones with fancy diplomas half as smart as you." Maxwell nodded emphatically, reinforcing his praise.

Redfield nodded, accepting the accolade with seeming immodesty. "Be that as it may, I am a veterinarian, not a purentee M.D. But somethin' else I is—especially since I married Widder Johnson. I is a Bible reader."

"The Bible? What's that got to do with my rheumatiz?"

"Well, that's it. That's where I found this cure that jus' might work for you. The widder reads from the Bible every blessed night before she go to sleep—or anything else. And every morning she reads it after breakfast, come hell or high water. Lots of begets and fool talk and gossip about people been dead six thousand years, but some hellish interestin' stuff, too."

"If you gone talk about faith to me, save your breath. I believes in Jehovah God much as the next man. More, maybe. But I believes a man's a fool to try to live on faith. God gives you a brain. He gives you hands to work with—though He did let mine git in one hell of a condition. But what He give you to work with—that's your faith. Faith in your own strength. Your own smartness. That's what God expects you to believe in. He got too much to do to fool around answerin' jackass prayers."

"Ain't talkin' about faith. Ain't talkin' about prayers. I'm talkin' about what I *read*. Widder Johnson skipped the first part of the first part of the first book of kings.

Got me curious. So I sneaked back and read it myself. That Bible! It's a dirty book, you know where to look."

Maxwell scrubbed his painful knuckles impatiently. "What's that got to do with my rheumatiz?"

"Maybe nuthin'. Maybe everything. The king—David—got up in years. Gat, the Bible says. The king grew old and stricken with years and they covered him with clothes and he gat no heat. Figure he was pretty much like you, Warren. A active man suddenly struck with rheumatiz—cold all the time."

"Gawd knows that's me."

"So the medics and the vets and the other wise sages of the time, they came to David and tole him they was just one way to gat the kind of heat that was going to loosen his stiff joints and git his blood stirrin' ag'in."

Maxwell leaned forward, his gnarled hands trembling. Unconsciously he scrubbed at the chloasma spotting the backs of his hands. He grew so excited he expelled gas abruptly, loudly and repeatedly. "What did he do?"

"They tole him the kind of heat he needed would come only from a young virgin. That the only place he goin' gat heat, they tole him."

"A young virgin!" Maxwell broke wind again. "What's a young virgin got to do with rheumatiz?"

"She heated, that's what. Inner heat. She young and soft and hot-blooded, inside and out. . . . So they brought the king a young virgin—and the king he laid with her and, brother, he gat heat."

Maxwell stared at his old friend, incredulous. "That in the Bible?"

"I swear on the widder's warts." Doc Redfield finished off his hot toddy and held his glass where his host had to notice its emptiness. "It worth a try. I ought to git on home and be with the widder. But I could stay over to be sure that Dixie gal stay alive—and see how your experiment come out. You gets

Lucretia Borgia to wash you up a young virgin, put her in yo' bed every night. Sooner or later, you bound to gat heat." He sat rocking and laughing.

Maxwell hesitated. "Do she has to be a virgin?"

"Bible say. Virgin. Lay with a virgin. Gat heat. King was old and stricken with years. Laid with a young virgin. Gat heat. Shore hell worth tryin'."

Maxwell shouted for Mem, ordered their glasses refilled with toddy. The two old friends talked until dusk. After supper, with Doc Redfield in advisory capacity, as Bible student and medical man, Maxwell outlined to Lucretia Borgia the doctor's prescription. "A hot one," he said. "She got to be a virgin—but I'se delayed so long now she's got to be a hot one."

"That not so easy." Lucretia Borgia glared at Doc Redfield. "With yo' friends takin' every black cherry they find—hard to keep a wench a virgin."

"What the hell you argufyin' about now?" Maxwell demanded.

Redfield laughed. "Think Lucretia Borgia upset with me. . . . I kinda used your Clarissa gal for a little relief over at my place. Had her layin' on the table. Just eased it in, that's all. Got relief. Anyhow that Clarissa ain't no virgin. Hell, she's at least sixteen plantings old."

"She scairt of you," Lucretia Borgia said. "You make her scairt of all men."

"Hell," Maxwell shook his head, snorting. "She scairt, that one fear she sure hell outgrow. Now you stop talkin' when you ain't talked to—an' git me a virgin fo' my bed wench tonight."

"You know how many years it been since you needed a bed wench?" Lucretia Borgia asked.

"Goddam you. You know how many years it been since you had your bare ass whopped? Ain't ast you. Ain't ast you nuthin'. *Tole you.* Git me a virgin fo' my bed wench."

"You gwine be sleepin' with a six-year-old. Likely git your bed wet."

"That's 'nuff of yo' backtalk, goddammit. You ain't sure they hymen secure, you bring 'em up and let Doc Redfield check—"

"That sounds entirely reasonable." Doc Redfield nodded.

Lucretia turned and strode from the room.

Warren Maxwell fidgeted, restless, the remainder of the evening. His mind wandered and he was unable to follow the thread of the conversation. His hot toddies lost their efficacy as well as their taste. He was relieved and somewhat excited when Doc Redfield stretched, yawned and announced it was his bedtime —well past the widder's Bible-reading hour over on Six Mile Road. Warren felt only faint stirring in his loins, almost like the memory of fire and fervor. But his mind spun as he groped with rekindled hope toward that potent remedy which would bring him succor and surcease. What better prescription for the relief of human misery than one right out of the Bible itself? His heart thundered erratically in his rib cage and he sweated mildly going up the steps, leaning as much of his weight as possible on Mem, who struggled to hold a candle aloft and to keep his footing on the steep stairwell.

"Can't you no way hurry yo' lazy ass?" Warren demanded.

When Maxwell hobbled into his bedroom, his virgin —chosen, bathed and instructed by Lucretia Borgia— lay curled under the thick pile of covers on his bed. Mem helped his master undress and slipped a flannel gown over his head, his dark face expressionless. Neither of them mentioned the bulge in Masta Warren's bed.

Ready for bed, Warren jerked his head and Mem got on his hands and knees and pulled the porcelain thunder chamber from beneath the bed. Holding the huge pot with both hands, Maxwell relieved himself. Mem replaced the slop jar and backed from the room. Holding his breath, Maxwell turned back the covers and got in beside his virginal concubine.

"Gal? What yo' name?"

"Missy, Masta. I'se Eleanor's Missy."

"Don't recollect you. Let me look at you."

The covers were hesitantly turned back and the girl smiled tentatively at him. She was unabashedly naked and looked to be around nine or ten plantings old. Warren was unprepared for the beauty and delicacy of the child. You could always count on Lucretia Borgia to select only the best, no matter her personal feelings. Missy looked virginal. The innocent appearance of wide-eyed childhood, the youthful bloom of chastity and April freshness glowed in her dark creamy cheeks. Her eyes were disturbingly candid and unblinking. She was frightened, but resigned. Those olive-black eyes stared at him from under sooty lashes with uncompromising honesty. She was such a young child. Yet, she might be his last best hope for a peaceful sunset of life. . . .

Under the directness of her gaze, Maxwell found himself faintly discomfited. He said, "You sure yo a virgin, Missy?"

"Yassuh. I a virgin."

"You know what a virgin is?"

"Ain't nevah been nuthin' inside me, Masta. I a virgin, all right."

He touched her arms and rosy-pointed nipples. "You sho' heated, all right."

"Yassuh. These covers mighty hot."

He continued to stroke, caress and fondle her. He found her pliable, willing and pliant. The stirring deep in his loins rose slightly, like mercury in a thermometer. "What did Miz Lucretia Borgia tell you?"

"She say I not to fart . . . I do whatever you tell me . . . an' I not to cry even if I hurt."

He winced slightly. "Is that all she tole you?"

She responded to his caresses by slipping closer to him. Her eyes closed sleepily and a smile pulled tremulously at her lips. "She say I gwine make you feel better, 'cause I gwine help you gat heat."

"That's right." He drew her closer and caressed her small, rounded hips. "I mighty cold—you gwine have to help me get lots of heat. Can you do that?"

"I do anything you want, Masta. Miz Lucretia tole me to say that. She tole me some of the things I suppose to do. . . . I do all of 'em if you wish."

"Don't know what she tole you. But I reckon I wish whatever it is—the whole business. I want you close. Close as you can git."

She moved closer, closing her tiny hand on his flaccid manhood. He said, "You evah seen one of them, Missy?"

"Nevah saw one like that, Masta." Smiling up at him, she stroked him down there, at first gently, and then with fiery vigor. Astonished, he found himself responding. She pressed herself against his body, and her heat *was* radiant, like high fever. His arms went about her. Her lips, moist, pink and flower-soft, touched his mouth, at first as innocently as a baby's, and then with surprising undulation. Jesus, he thought. Nine years old. A virgin. Hell, this is instinctive with them. He reached down and guided himself against her. Holding her breath, pressing her parted mouth over his, she eased herself upon him, thrusting suddenly and violently. She cried out, sharply, but when he looked down, those doe eyes were smiling up at him, reassuring him. She worked her little hips like vibrating pistons.

Maxwell breathed through his mouth. He said, "Don't sweat, gal. You smell like a nigger if'n you sweat."

"I is a nigger, Masta."

"Yeah. But you don't have to stink like one."

60

She moved faster. Her voice rose. "You makin' me sweat, Masta."

He didn't care. He was sweating, too. For this brief moment he was conscious of no pain in any joint of his body. He seemed floating lightly, wafted toward some irrecoverable past. He tightened his arms, working her harder upon him. "Nevah mind, Missy," he said. "Sweat if you got to. Jus' shut up an' fuck."

VI

The king gat heat.

Old Warren Maxwell, stricken with years though he might be, and chilled to the bone marrow as he certainly spent most of his days and nights, was suddenly exultant. Perhaps his relief was all in his mind, but its force was potent and restorative. True, he was not yet ready to relinquish Mark's bare belly for "dreenin'" his feet and legs, but in a burst of unwonted good spirits, he promised the child that he might soon be freed from his obligations to receive into his body the poisons from his master's and be allowed to play in the yard with the other small boys.

"Goddam miracle," Maxwell said. He tottered about the house on his tender feet, talking about his miracle to cleaning girls, houseboys, portraits on the wall, or his own reflection in a wavy mirror. "A purentee goddam miracle . . . and right out'n the Bible, too!"

Missy became Lucretia Borgia's newest burden. The pretty child was installed in the big house as the master's pet. A pallet was ordered for her and placed in old Maxwell's bedroom. But Maxwell decided he didn't want Missy sleeping on the floor like a common nigger. The carpenter shop was ordered to produce a trundle bed. A thick soft mattress was stuffed and sewn to specifications and goosedown pillows were supplied. Only the freshest sheets and most delicate coverlets were permitted to be used on Missy's new bed.

Missy soon learned there were no visible limits to her power over the other slaves at Falconhurst Plantation. She was Master Maxwell's cosset—petted, fondled and made much of. As a sop to Lucretia Borgia's position as mistress of the house, Maxwell at first permitted her to assign to Missy the lightest possible household tasks to occupy her during the day. Missy soon tired of these dull domestic duties. It was nigger work, no matter how one looked at it. She neglected these tasks or forced Millie or other underlings to perform them for her under threat of reporting their infractions to the master. The servants complained to Lucretia Borgia, but Miz Lucretia found herself impotent against the youthful tyrant. If Missy were crossed by anyone she had only to whimper prettily in old Maxwell's presence and the matter became a life-and-death proposition. And everyone else might retract, compromise, back down, but Missy never would. She remained imperiously in the right, and wounded, until the wrong was redressed to her satisfaction. To Lucretia Borgia at least, Missy soon became an intolerable brat. The childish innocence hardened into the corrupt, appraising, satiny texture of the harlot.

The jealousy which burgeoned between Missy and Marcus Aurelius was so intense that the atmosphere inside the old house fairly crackled, and only the white master remained unaware of it. Mark at first saw Missy's presence in the master's bedroom as his own means of deliverance. But until she pushed him out of favor, Mark had not realized the life of ease, privilege and comfort he was about to forfeit. Escape to play meant also returning to live among field Negroes, to eat and work and sleep—and finally to be sold with them. He learned quickly to hate Missy.

Sometimes, Miz Lucretia Borgia felt the burdens were too onerous to be borne. Despite the fact that life had taught her incredible patience and forbearance, she felt her blood boiling. If only she could write! She would compose a missive which would follow Masta Hammond across the Texies and lay before him the sorry state of affairs at his beloved Falconhurst, the peril to its continued existence if he did not soon end his long self-imposed exile.

"But I *cain't* write," she muttered. "I can only work and work and let new troubles pile up on my shoulders. . . . Wonder my hair ain't the color of cotton. . . . Sometimes I think I just walk away from heah." Because she was exhausted and discouraged, she smiled, tiredly letting her mind consider what she would take if she decided to leave Falconhurst and go north to live in freedom. It never occurred to her as a serious possibility that the slave patrollers might capture and return her. Not her. She was Miz Lucretia Borgia. She held her head high and folks knew she was somebody, even out on the highways. Hadn't she walked all the way home to Falconhurst from New Orleans? And no paddy-roller dared question her. What would she take? Maybe a pot of Master Warren's gold eagles Cousin Charlie was obsessed with finding. A pot of gold eagles and maybe Jingo Jim. She almost laughed aloud in her fatigued reverie. Wouldn't that be a fitten life for Miz Lucretia Borgia—the finest existence possible this side of the Jordan? All them gold eagles and Jingo Jim! She smacked her lips, dreaming it. . . . But there was suddenly the abrupt chill, the dark other side of the bright coin. She'd been away from Falconhurst. What had she dreamed all the time she was away? She'd dreamed of home, of Falconhurst.

Her eyes filled with tears. She'd wanted nothing more in life than to come back. It had gotten worse, never better, the need for Falconhurst, until she'd been no longer able to resist the lure of this ugly old stud farm. Wouldn't that same longing draw Masta Hammond home from the Texies? She could only pray it would—and soon. . . .

She heard old Maxwell shouting her name. She walked out to stand beside the deacon's bench on the front porch where the master sat with his new pet and the nude boy at his feet. Missy lolled against the old man's shirt front, her tiny hands caressing him, her disenchanted eyes playing over the exposed genitals of the boy on the floor. Lucretia Borgia shook her head over the picture they presented. She followed the direction in which the master pointed his trembling finger. "Someone a-comin', Lucretia Borgia! Hit's a man alone in a carriage, ain't it? Praise God, it might be my boy Ham a-comin' home."

Lucretia Borgia's heart lurched at this possibility. She squinted, staring across the yard toward the property line along the trace. After a moment, she shook her head. "Tain't Masta Ham." Her voice betrayed her own deep and bitter disappointment.

"You sure? You gettin' old. You might be gittin' blind."

"Hit's some stranger. Tain't my Masta Ham," she said.

Missy sat up straight. Even the boy on the floor lifted his head, shaded his eyes with one hand and watched the man in the buggy approach along the driveway.

"He's got a slave running along behind the wagon," Lucretia Borgia reported. Then she saw the black youth was chained to the rear of the buggy, with a heavy metal collar locked about his neck. He had to keep running or he would fall and be dragged or choked to death.

The three people on the shaded porch remained unmoving until the cart pulled directly in front of the wide plank steps and drew to a halt. The driver took his time. First, he gazed up at them. When no one spoke either to welcome or repulse him, he shoved the whip socket into its holder, looped the lines around the stock and got down gingerly from the wagon boot. He looked as if he'd been riding for a long time and his muscles were cramped and sore. Behind the wagon, the black boy sank to his knees, his mouth parted, eyes wide, staring in a mindless exhaustion, his head back. He quivered with fatigue, but the chain was so short that he had to hold his head tilted awkwardly to keep from being choked by the metal collar.

The white man came around the front of the buggy in a loping stride. He was tall, with a protuberant belly. He wore a black slouch hat, its brim hanging as shapeless as a lily pad. His face was wind-and-sun-burned a fiery red, his eyes bleached blue. His front teeth on the right side of his tobacco-stained mouth were missing. When he spoke he whistled through the cavity. His trousers, worn and unpatched, hung loosely on a single gallus that traversed a filthy, nearly buttonless shirt. Everything about him said "poverty," despite the fact he had a slave in tow.

He took out a brightly colored bandana, wiped his face, forehead and the sweat band of his slouch hat. His straggly hair was a mustard yellow. The back of his neck was baked a ceramic red with crosshatchings of seams, lines and wrinkles. Lucretia Borgia believed that from behind, every white farmer in Alabama looked alike—sun-blistered, wrinkled red necks.

She seldom sustained pride in Masta Warren, and she felt even less proud as he piled up the years without the saving grace of dignity. But, looking at the visitor, she was glad she belonged to Maxwell. Despite his faded red hair, the beet-colored skin of his leathery face, the tight, squinted blue eyes, sun-bleached and pain-scarred, he was stations above his guest. Maxwell's long trunk was wide-shouldered, thick-chested. He would have been impressively tall except that, like his son, Warren had short legs. Just the same, he stacked up favorably in comparison with the new-comer.

"Howdy," old Maxwell said. "What brings you way out here to Falconhurst, suh?"

The man stopped at the head of the steps. He also stopped smiling. "See you don't recollect me a-tall, eh?"

" 'Fraid not," Maxwell shook his head. "Should we?"

The visitor appeared affronted that he'd been forgotten so easily. "Bought this here slave from you." He jerked his head toward the youth slouched on his knees in the blazing sunlight. "Just last year."

"Don't seem I'd forgit—your teeth givin' you that look an' all," Maxwell conceded.

"Name's Eldon Close." The visitor did not offer his hand, nor did Maxwell. The man was a dirt farmer and Maxwell owned this plantation and five hundred slaves. "An' though I did most of my dickerin' to buy with your black wench there, you an' I did meet—over a hot toddy, as I recall."

"Should recollect." Maxwell evinced not a trace of interest. "Would you care to set a spell? Have a hot toddy? An' mayhap a gourd of water for your slave? The boy looks ready to collapse."

Close shrugged. "Nevah mind him. He git jus' what he deserve."

"Mayhap. He your slave. But, personal, I'd never treat a nigger thataway. Not faultin' you, mind. A man kin treat his animals anyway he like, and that's his business. But that boy look kinda wild—look ready to fall in his traces. If he do fall, he dead, choked or broken neck."

"He know that." Eldon Close shrugged again. "He good daid as he is alive. If he daid, I shed of him. But daid or alive, I through with him. That's why I here."

Lucretia Borgia stared at the slave crouched awkwardly upon his knees on the ground. The black was thin, emaciated, but he had wide shoulders, good bone

68

structure. He should have weighed nearly two hundred muscular pounds. Instead he was skin and bones. "Why, Masta," she said. "That's Vulcan. That's our own Vulcan."

"Vulcan?" Maxwell leaned forward in his chair. "My good lord. That really you, Vulcan?"

The boy on the ground merely put his head further back, gasping for breath through his parted lips.

"None of my business, Mr.—uh, Close? None of my business," Maxwell said, "but you leave that boy out there like that you gone lose him—stroke, choked to death—but for sure, he dies on you."

"Makes no difference to me," Close said. "Like I tole you, I shed of him. I brung him back to you."

Lucretia Borgia sent Mark running to fetch Jingo Jim. Glad to escape his hard place on the flooring, the boy raced across the yard toward the work barns.

Angered at being deprived of his "dreenin' animal" and by Lucretia Borgia's butting in, Maxwell glared at her, but said nothing. She had made the correct decision. Instead of speaking to Lucretia Borgia at all, Maxwell turned his sour scorn upon the dirt farmer. "What you mean you bringin' Vulcan back to Falconhurst?"

"Jus' what I said. Inferior merchandise. Oh, I heered of yore fine reputation fo' quality slaves. That's why I come heah in the first place. Why, I paid more'n I could really afford for that boy. . . . I can tell you, suh, this place was better run when your son was in charge."

"Can only amen you on that, brother," Maxwell said. "But no matter where my son is, I take it as a personal affront that you come here down-ratin' the quality of my stock. Our stock all quality animals. Clean-limbed. Sound."

"All I know is, this boy is worthless. Lazy. He doesn't refuse to work—he falls asleep with his hoe in the air. When you like me and got only six slaves to work your place, all of them animals got to work, all the time. Hell, with the hundreds you got, one's lazy, it don't matter. It matters on my farm. I put up with him, long as I could."

Maxwell's face was set, livid, the blood throbbing in the exposed blue vein in his temple. He was enraged that a white-trash dirt farmer would return a Falconhurst slave as unsatisfactory, blemished. He said, controlling himself with great effort, "Bring the boy up here on the porch. Let me look at him."

"He been runnin' a fair piece. He stink with nigger musk."

"I use to nigger musk. Wanta to see what you done to him."

"Ain't done nuthin' to him. He no good. He worthless."

"I'll just thank you to let me judge that."

Reluctantly, Eldon Close went down the steps into the yard. He loosed the chain from the wagon bed. Wrapping a length of the metal links about his wrist, he led Vulcan up the steps. When the slave stood before him, Maxwell swore. "My God, Close, what you done to this boy? He was a fine specimen when I sold him to you. Now he whip-marked, got sores, pustules . . . Jesus Christ, man."

"Vulcan is Belshazzar Two's boy, Masta," Lucretia Borgia said. "Out'n Didie. He a fine boy—or he was."

"He looked all right when I bought him. I grant you that," Eldon Close said. "Till I got him home. He cried to come back here till I whupped that out'n him. Then he got sickly. Throwin' up. Broke out in them boils. Lost weight. No good for nuthin'. That's when I made up my mind to bring him back here."

"Hell, Vulcan he sick. Has you had him to the vet?" Maxwell demanded.

Close shook his head stubbornly. "Vet's right costive. Ain't got money to take my own family to no doctor."

"You willin' to let a strong slave boy die to save a

few dollars the vet gone cost you, you got no right to have a slave. This boy prob'ly got hookworm. Sure hell got pellagra. Likely picked 'em up at your place. Ain't been treated. He got all the signs. He run down. Scaly with sores. Eyes look dull. He got no energy. No wonder! Probably carryin' a gutful of hookworms."

"Well, whatever he is, I say he was like that when I bought him here from this thievin' black wench."

Maxwell started to speak, caught himself. His voice was low-pitched but taut. "We don't have no thievin' niggers here. We don't sell no inferior merchandise. This boy is from Khoisan stock—his forebearers spoke what they called the 'click' tongue. He a bushman. He what he is. We tole you all that. Wasn't nothing physical wrong with him when you got him." Maxwell ceased speaking when Jingo Jim came to the edge of the porch and stood in the slight rim of shade staring up at them.

"Now there's the kind of specimen I want," Eldon Close said.

"Reckon you do. You got two thousand dollars you can walk away with him. You paid—what? Four, five hundred for Vulcan. You got what you paid for. A good field hand. But you've ruint him—and now you comin' here low-ratin' my stock." Before Close could speak, Maxwell cut him off by speaking to his slave. "Jingo, take this here boy to the hay barn—not to the cell or anywhere he'll be round the rest of my herd. Get that metal collar off his neck—"

"You best chain him, or he run away," Close advised. "Finally got so I had to chain him up every night. . . . He lost now, he your loss. Not mine."

Maxwell ignored the dirt farmer. He continued giving orders to Jingo Jim. "Give him a cold drenchin', and all the cold well water he want to drink. But no solid food. Tonight when Doc Redfield come, we give Vulcan a strong dose of herbs. Bet he shit a bucket of hookworms by dawn. We send for Doc Redfield right away." He smiled down at Vulcan. "It gone be all right, boy. We take care of you proper."

He waited, but the slave boy did not speak. He seemed drawn into a taut ball of pain and hatred.

Vulcan appeared hardly aware of his old master. His eyes were frantic, glassy and as empty as a rabid animal's. Maxwell waved his arm in dismissal and Jingo Jim led the boy across the yard toward the barns. There was a brief silence on the porch, broken only when Mem showed up with fresh toddies for the master and his guest. Maxwell seemed reluctant to enter into further conversation with the farmer, and Lucretia Borgia didn't trust herself to speak at all. Vulcan had been healthy, bright-eyed and vigorous when this white man took the boy away from Falconhurst.

Eldon Close sat in a rocker, moving it in a rapid rhythm. "What sort of adjustment you figure to make —on a sick nigger an' all?"

Maxwell smiled tautly. "Don't no way anticipate to make *any* adjustment, suh. You took a hardy buck and you starved and mistreated him. He was well and healthy when you got him."

"I fed him good as I could. Good nigger food."

"Hell. Don't tell me that. You think I spent my entire life raisin' blacks and don't know when one been ruint by neglect, starvation and purentee cruelty?"

Close sat forward. "Reckon you think to talk to me that away because I'm a pore farmer. If I was a fancy-suited gentleman in a fine carriage, you'd be lickin' my ass."

"You bastid—"

"Don't think, suh, that I can't spread the word about the kind of no-account animals you sell here at Falconhurst, same as some rich dude."

Maxwell's fist closed over his canehead. "Wish to God my son was here. I'd die happy—after seein' him kick your ass from heah to Benson."

Close waved his arm, untroubled. "No call for us to

rage at each other. I feels I been cheated. We got some-way to reach some common ground where we can settle this matter."

"There ain't no common ground for us, suh. I feeds my niggers good. You starves yourn, or feed 'em slop. You can't no way work a nigger no more'n you can a human white man—or a horse, for hell's sake—'thout decent feedin'. You feed him well, keep him healthy, he be well right now."

"I admit he didn't eat from my table. I grant he didn't—no more'n your field hands eat frum yore table. But he ate sound."

"Ham fat and corn pone, I wager."

"Gave him best I had. Best I could afford."

"Afford? You got to afford what keeps 'em well. Nigger can't work on an empty belly, or on food got no iron in it. Hell, you took one of my good field-grade niggers—and you ruint him, that's what you did." Maxwell spat. "Wasn't for this rheumatiz, I'd throw you off this place myself. Comin' here tryin' to git somethin' for nuthin' 'cause you know my boy's away—"

"You wrong, suh." Close shook his head. "Admits I do feel you ought to trade me a sound nigger for that unsound one."

Maxwell cursed impatiently. "Tell you what, Close —that your name? When Doc Redfield gits here, he say that boy *ain't* been ruint in the past year—at your place—I lets you pick the best field-grade nigger on the place and he yours for five dollars."

"Five dollars?" Close shook his head, protesting.

Maxwell's mouth twisted in contempt. "A man ain't got five dollars shouldn't own slaves in the first place." He shrugged. "It don't matter. I know in advance what the vet will say."

Eldon Close stared at Maxwell, at his bare, purple feet, his twisted fingers. "You a great one to be talkin' about how healthy your niggers are. Look at you.

Walkin' around with rheumatiz—no wonder this place no good since your boy run off."

"My boy never run off. He took a hankerin' years ago to go off to see the Texies. He had a unhappy marriage—his wife died—and so he went to the Texies. Don't deny we miss him. But Lucretia Borgia and me —we runs this place just as my son would run it if he was here. Nuthin' but quality blacks fo' sale."

"You could run this place a heap better—an' not depend on no nigger wench—if'n you got cured up from your ailin'."

"Doin' all I can."

"Is you? You soakin' in hot hog blood and entrails?"

"What?" Maxwell sat forward. "I nevah heard of that one." His cold hauteur toward his guest relaxed noticeably.

"Old receipt." Eldon Close shrugged and sat taller in his chair, assuming more importance in his own eyes. "Never dreen but dribs and drabs out'n yo'self with that nigger boy—an' you run a chance of ruinin' the boy, crippling him so he won't be no good for sale. I seed that hog blood and entrails work. My own dear pappy. Had rheumatiz worse'n you. Stove up total, he was. He slew a hog. Got it ready and got hisself cured —fast."

"How'd he do it?"

Eldon Close sat back, enjoying his sense of elevated position. "Well, paw took the fresh innards—you got to take 'em whilst they fresh, an' still got the curative powers. Somethin' 'bout the way them hog organs jus' kindly *pulls* the p'isen and ache out'n you. But they got to be fresh, so's they still got the pull. Liver, kidney, heart and intesines—and all the drained blood. Put it in a wash pot over a low fire—one that keeps the blood tepid—at a simmer, like. Pappy kept his hands and feet in that mixture. Strength and heat an' pull of the hog innards purely cured him. He got up from his chair—that very day!—and danced a jig."

Maxwell gazed at Eldon Close as if the farmer were sent from God. He put back his head and yelled for Mem. When the servant limped out to the porch, Maxwell ordered a hog slain and prepared.

"Where you 'spectin' to put a stinkin' mess like that?" Lucretia Borgia demanded. "You ain't messin' up this house with all that stink and mess."

"Goddam you, Lucretia Borgia, shut your mouth."

"Tetch her up with the whip," Eldon Close advised. "No nigger'd ever talk to me like that and live to tell it."

Lucretia Borgia simply stared at the farmer, her mouth twisted, her black eyes glittering with contempt. But Maxwell was too engrossed in preparing the latest cure for his rheumatism. He ignored Lucretia Borgia, and after a moment, Eldon Close dropped his gaze under hers. In silence they watched three slaves prepare a slaughtered hog. The drained blood, entrails and organs were tossed into a black wash pot.

"Jus' douse your hands right in," Eldon Close told Maxwell. "Leave 'em long as you can. Longer, more effective. Then yore feet. Day or two you'll notice a difference—one of these days you'll be walkin' round this place like new."

"Don't know how I'll ever thank you, friend," Maxwell said.

"I know how you can thank me, you got a mind to." Eldon Close bent closer. "Four hunnert—odd slaves —you'd never miss a sound one—in trade fo' that no-count Vulcan."

Maxwell laughed and ordered fresh toddies for himself and his guest. "No problem," he said. "We have no problem workin' somethin' out."

He sent a slave riding a mule with word for Doc Redfield to return to Falconhurst posthaste. Then he turned his total attention to the tepid blood and hog entrails in the wash pot. His hands trembled as he lowered them into the gently simmering liquid.

Lucretia Borgia watched for a moment, nauseated. She was convinced that Eldon Close's remedy was as dishonest as the dirt farmer himself. She had no use for white trash. She turned to enter the house. She stopped cold when she heard a scream from the direction of the barns.

Instinctively, she turned and ran down the steps. A small boy sobbed, running toward her. "Oh, laws, Miz Lucretia," the boy wept. "Hit's Jingo. That Vulcan done jabbed a pitchfork in Jingo's belly and run. . . ."

VII

Lucretia Borgia ran. Inside her mind she screamed Jingo Jim's name; she wept, sobbing out her agony and sense of horror. Around her, the familiar world of Falconhurst Plantation looked alien. The same faces of the slaves were fixed on her, and they saw her strength, her silence, her self-reliance. She moved faster, her aching muscles holding her face immobile, impassive. This was the only way they would ever see her, in command, totally in charge, of this farm, of them, of herself. *Please, Gawd, let him be all right. In the name of holy Mary, let him be all right.*

She found Jingo Jim slumped against the bales of hay where—on another day—they had found bliss together, standing up. She felt heated blood suffuse her cheeks. She spoke sharply to the slaves knotted helplessly around the fallen Jingo. Her hands tightened into helpless fists. Blood oozed in half a dozen wounds along what would be the youngster's belt line. He held his hands tightly against his belly. The deep-red liquid spilled between his fingers. *Oh Gawd,* Lucretia Borgia thought, *he gwine die, and he jus' a chile yet.*

"Can't let him die," she said aloud.

"I with you on that—all the way," Jingo Jim managed to say with a grin that twisted into a grimace.

"An' you . . . jus' you keep your sassy mouth shut.

You save yo' strength." She glanced around at the other male slaves. "Let's git him to his cabin."

"Yes'm, Miz Lucretia Borgia." They all agreed, but none moved. At last, huge Polon bent down to take Jingo up in his arms as if he were a child.

Lucretia Borgia's voice crackled. "Not like that, Pole. You makes him bleed to death, you carry him like that. . . . Get some canvas and two poles. We got to have us a stretcher, and fast."

Once told what to do, the slaves reacted swiftly. Soon, with Lucretia Borgia walking beside Jingo Jim on the improvised stretcher, the small procession moved out of the barn toward the slave quarters. Lucretia spoke softly to Jingo, brushed the flies away from his face and bloodied hands and warned the bearers to walk swiftly, but carefully. Slaves came out of their shacks to stand on stoops, steps or in the sunlight to watch them pass. They saw little violence at Falconhurst. They stood in silence, troubled by the sight of Jingo Jim sprawled in pain on the canvas litter.

As they moved through the dazzling sunlight, Lucretia Borgia heard old Maxwell yelling for her from the big house. She hesitated, torn between letting the master yell his lungs out or leaving Jingo Jim's life in the hands of willing but stupid field hands. As always with Lucretia Borgia, prudence won over compassion. She warned the stretcher bearers to lay Jingo Jim down easily on his bed and she promised she'd return as soon as possible.

"Surely hope so," Jingo Jim said between clenched teeth.

She strode across the yard, her slipper heels slapping at the soles of her feet. She found her aging master bent over the simmering pot of hog blood and entrails, his hands immersed above his wrists, his feet pushed to the bottom of the smelly vessel. The fire was so hot Maxwell was forced to lift his feet in a weird little dance step.

"Mr. Close is worried about his nigger, Lucretia Borgia," Maxwell said, staring upward at her.

"Worried about his nigger?" Lucretia Borgia's turban bobbled as she shook her head. "It our nigger what got whopped with a hay fork—them tines right into his belly. That Vulcan he never learned that kind of evil here at Falconhurst. Niggers here trust other niggers—trust even white folks. Vulcan he wild. He don't trust nobody no more."

"Never mind, Lucretia Borgia," Maxwell said. "Mr. Close's nigger has run away."

"Then Mr. Close best jump in his cart and head out to find him," Lucretia Borgia said. Her voice shook. "I got more to do than worry 'bout his sick nigger. We got us a prize stallion that might be bleedin' to death."

"Sick nigger ain't my nigger no more, black wench," Eldon Close said. "Vulcan he yo' nigger now. But I agrees with Brother Warren here—we ought to git him back an' they goin' to be a fair trade."

Lucretia Borgia stared at the two white men with contempt enough to shrivel their leathery hides had they not been totally insensitive to her estimation of them. At last, she spread her hands helplessly, surrendering to white supremacy.

"Yassuh," she said. "I send a couple boys to tell Mr. Gassaway that we got us a runaway. Also let the paddy-rollers know. . . . Though, 'fore Gawd, sick as pore Vulcan is, I don't see how he can git very far."

Lucretia Borgia turned on her heel. As she walked away, Maxwell called after her, voice blistering. "An' us got to have fresh toddies, you Lucretia Borgia."

Lucretia Borgia stopped walking, shoulders set. She stood absolutely immobile for a long beat, then she yelled for Mem and relayed the master's orders. In less than three minutes she'd dispatched slave boys on mules to notify the nearest farms and plantations, as well as the slave patrol, that Falconhurst had a runaway. From long experience, Lucretia Borgia knew most of the farmers and the gentlemen of leisure from the plantations would enter enthusiastically into a manhunt. They would bring their hound dogs, their slaves, horses and guns. Only a fire provided as much excitement for them as a manhunt offered.

She shrugged her shoulders, putting them all out of her mind. When she stepped into Jingo Jim's shack she found the four field hands who'd brought Jim from the hay barn. They stood silently about, not willing to leave him unattended, but unable to think what they should do for him. They simply waited, arms at their sides staring at the man writhing on the bed. Jingo Jim lay grimacing, the whites of his eyes showing, his strong white teeth sunk into his lower lip. He looked gray, as if the blood were drained down from his face. Lucretia Borgia's heart lurched. They were going to lose him. He was losing too much blood. There was no way to save him. She swung her arm, dismissing the four men. "You all through in here now. Git out."

"That's right." Jingo Jim spoke between clenched teeth, forcing a horrible smile. "We'uns don't need you no more. Git out—and close that door a-hind you."

"You keep quiet," Lucretia Borgia told him. She glanced at the other boys, who smiled at Jingo, wishing him well. "And you, Pole. You go stand down there to the gate at the trace. Instant Doc Redfield gets here, you lead his cart past the big house and bring him up here. Don't you no way let him stop to drink and talk with them white men up to the big house."

"And close the door a-hind you," Jingo Jim said broadly.

Lucretia Borgia laughed despite herself. She said, "You bad boy, Jingo Jim. Heah you is a-dyin' and still ain't but one thing on yo' mind."

He reached for her with bloody, sticky hands, but pain almost overwhelmed him and he lay back, gasping for breath. "That Vulcan," he whispered in awe. "Reckon he got me better'n I thought."

Lucretia Borgia said, "Don't talk. We find that Vulcan, I peel the skin off'n him myself—in strips."

She tore a ragged sheet, made pads for the bleeding tine wounds in Jingo's flat, muscular belly. "Little lower and he'd have broke the hearts of a heap of women," Jingo said.

She set the pads in place and bound them with a sheet. Jingo's head rolled from side to side. "Is the pain bad?" she asked.

"No. Fo' pain hit's real good." He grinned up at her. "You gwine make my last few minutes on earth happy, Lucretia Borgia?"

"What you talkin' about?"

"Talkin' 'bout you climbin' nekkid in this bed and sending me across the Jordan with all my sails a-flyin'—"

"You crazy. You near nuff dead without me killin' you."

"You want me to die with a hard-on?"

She laughed. "It's the way you lived, ain't it? . . . Now I want you to shut yo' mouth an' rest."

He rolled his head back and forth on the pillow a moment. Then, "You lets me die a-pokin' up hard like this, they nevah gone git that coffin lid nailed down."

Lucretia Borgia gazed at him tenderly. She soothed his brow with her hand. She got a basin of fresh water and washed his face and chest. He suggested she might massage him a little lower—and a lot faster. She shook her head. "Ain't but one way to keep you quiet, is there?"

He smiled wanly. "That's right. Shuck that dress and lay down."

She stood up. "You lie quiet. I be back quick as ever I can."

"No." He cried out. "Don't leave me like this, Lucretia Borgia. You leave me like this, I gone die for sure—or I rapes the first wench pokes her head in that door."

She laughed at him. "You too strong to die, you too weak to rape. You'll keep."

She sent two black men to sit with Jingo Jim and to keep him quiet. She hurried from the quarters and across the yard toward the big house. The sun slanted through the trees, throwing a netting of shadows about her as she hurried.

As she approached the house she heard Missy screaming and found her near the kitchen, pressed quivering against a wall. When she spoke Missy's name and the girl continued to wail, Lucretia Borgia struck her sharply across the face. She felt a twinge of guilt, admitting she'd been looking for an opportunity like this. It worked. Stunned, Missy stared up at her and then fell silent, sniffling. "Now. Tell me. What's the matter with you?" Lucretia Borgia said, still kneeling beside the girl.

"Hit's Masta. He want me to massage his feet—in that—that blood and mess! That ol' fat man tole him it help to have the blood and stuff massaged right in. Masta want me to put my hands in that—mess." Missy wailed again.

Pleased that the matter was no more serious than a minor altercation between the old master and his small concubine, Lucretia Borgia entered the kitchen. She crossed it silently, refusing to become embroiled in the questions and complaints which barraged her. In the pantry she found the laudanum. "I give Jingo 'nuff to shut him up till the vet git here," she said aloud. "Mayhap we can save him if'n we can keep him quiet."

She met Doc Redfield in the barnyard as she left the kitchen. The vet drove his single-seat buggy with his medical kit beside him. Pole ran alongside the wagon. Pole panted, grinning when he saw Lucretia Borgia.

"I brung him right past the front porch." His voice vibrated with pride.

Doc Redfield halted his horse while Pole helped Lucretia Borgia up beside him on the buggy boot. She explained what had happened as they rode between the slave shacks to Jingo's cabin.

Doc sent the slaves out of Jingo's single-room cabin. He set Lucretia Borgia to boiling water while he examined the tine wounds in Jingo's belly. A taut silence stretched out inside the cabin, broken only by Jingo's involuntary whelps of pain when Doc pressed at the tine holes across the youth's stomach.

Lucretia Borgia stood at the vet's shoulder, watching. Doc spoke to her, twisting his head. "Don't it bother you none, staring at a buck's privates this way, Lucretia Borgia?"

"Why should it? I proud of him. I bought this boy. Five years ago. He was skinny, underfed. Look at him now."

"Shore ain't skinny no more—an' I've treated stallions no heavier hung than he is."

"So . . . I proud," Lucretia Borgia said.

"I proud, too," Jingo whispered. "Sho' hates to die—deprive so many deservin' ladies a look at my . . . privates. . . . "

"Privates," Lucretia Borgia scoffed. "They 'bout as private as an outhouse."

"I better sew him up." Doc Redfield reached for his bag. "Keep him from bleedin' any more external. . . . If he ripped inside—artery or somethin'—he'll bleed internal; nuthin' we can do. . . . If nuthin' vital inside is punctured, he'll recover in time."

Doc prepared a mixture which Lucretia Borgia recognized as the laudanum derivative in her own apron pocket. In less than five minutes, Jingo Jim lay unconscious. With the smallest of the large needles he carried on a card in his kit, the vet repaired the tine punctures, leaving small gray mounds tightly sewn.

"Done all I could," he said. He winced with the acknowledgment of his own inadequacy. "All I could. Know how you hate to lose him. Fine specimen. Seen few better stallions in all these years here at Falconhurst. Know you hate to lose him."

"You don't know how bad I hate to lose him," Lucretia Borgia said. "Ain't they nothing more I can do?"

He shook his head. "Keep him quiet. That's about it." He washed the youth's belly with hot water and stood up, shrugging. "Nuthin' now but wait and see. You want to git somebody to sit with him?"

"I stay," she said.

He gave her an odd look, but nodded.

She sat the rest of the long afternoon beside Jingo's bed. She washed his face and chest with fresh cool cloths, she soothed his forehead and the tight cap of black hair with her gentle hands. She brushed away the flies with a palmetto fan. He slept so long and so soundly she became afraid he might be dead. But his heartbeat was regular; he breathed, if only shallowly.

Just before dusk she heard a commotion in the lane outside Jingo's cabin. She got up, padded to the door and let herself out. She saw Polon running from the barns and she called to him.

"Pole. What is it? What all happened?"

He stood at the edge of the high stoop and gazed up at her. "It's Vulcan, Miss Lucretia Borgia."

"Them white men found Vulcan?"

Pole nodded, his face set and bloodless. "Yes'm. Them white men run Vulcan down. . . . He were right down yonder at the end of our field—a place where he used to go to hide when he was a boy. They say he was a-layin' there vomitin' . . . didn't put up no fight a-tall, they say. Them white gen'mum and the paddy-rollers took Vulcan out to the hardroad and hung him to a tree. . . . After that, they shot him full of buckshot. Left his body hangin' there—alongside the

84

road—as a 'zample to other niggers, Master Lewis Gassaway say."

Lucretia Borgia felt her eyes sting with tears. Poor Vulcan. Seemed to her the man who ought to be hanging as an example was the fat-bellied Eldon Close who had driven Vulcan out of his mind, starved and beaten and mistreated him. Vulcan hung dead at the end of a dangling rope, and Jingo Jim lay dying with pitchfork wounds, while fat Eldon Close laughed and drank hot toddies up on the porch of the big house. Lucretia Borgia didn't know who was in charge of the daily existence of this cosmos, but it seemed to her whoever it was was hellish busy or fearfully incompetent. Sighing heavily, she turned and went back into Jingo's cabin.

VIII

A post-hanging party was in noisy progress as Lucretia Borgia walked across the yard in the late afternoon to the big house. She recognized most of the guests—Lewis Gassaway and his sons, the Colton boys, the Athertons, the majority of the landed gentry and all of the area farmers. They were drinking Warren Maxwell's corn whiskey and recounting the lynching in every graphic detail for Maxwell's, and their own, edification and enjoyment. Eldon Close kept reminding everyone who came within earshot that the dead Negro was no longer his property—he'd returned Vulcan to Falconhurst. No one listened. No one cared.

"Onliest regret I harbors anent this heah hangin'," Maxwell said, and most voices lowered, his guests attending him politely. "Hangin' a nigger's a waste—less'n it done right."

"Oh, it done right!" Floyd Colton shouted. "I guaran-damn-tee yuh, it done right."

"We strung him up until he was dead," Lewis Gassaway said in his quiet, firm way.

"Then we filled his carcass with buckshot to make sure he daid," Floyd Colton yelled. "When that nigger gits where he goin', they gone spend most eternity pickin' buckshot out'n his black hide."

"Amen, brother, it purentee done right—that hanging," somebody said.

"Like I say," Maxwell persisted. "Less'n it done in a way that serves as a lesson an' warning to other niggers, a hangin' is a waste of a perfectly good nigger. Nigger's worth money—alive. You kill one, ought to be some profit in it somewhere."

"Warren's right about that," Doc Redfield agreed.

"You hang a nigger, you don't do it for no pleasure," Maxwell said. "Now, 'course I admits with you-all, blacks ain't human. But they is beasts that talk. They ain't human but they is God's critters. We destroy one of God's critters, we can't replace him—"

"Hell, Mr. Maxwell, I can replace niggers fast as I can knock up a black wench," Floyd said, laughing. He pounded the man nearest him on the back, almost overcome with laughter.

Maxwell smiled tolerantly, lifting his gnarled hand to silence the laughter. "Just the same. To do it right, you hang a nigger where as many other blacks has been called to witness it as possible. . . . You let them know what he done to deserve hanging—same as they'd git for the same crime. You got to show them blacks what a hangin' is, what it does to a critter. You can *tell* a black till you're blue in the face. But them blacks they like airy other animal. They fo'gits fast. But when they *see* a buck hanging—they purentee remembers that. His head broken off to one side, hanging crazy-like, his eyes poppin' out'n his head and his tongue pokin' out thick and swelled up and ready to burst. They remembers that fo' a while—and then a hangin' ain't wasted. Then they's some reason for it beside just punishin' a animal for doin' what he don't know better than do in the first place."

The other white men quieted for a few moments, deeply impressed with the sage logic of the elder Maxwell. After all, you expected a man who'd devoted his life to breeding and selling blacks to know the most effective way to deal with them in every situation.

"Maybe we acted hasty," Lewis Gassaway agreed.

"But I know what my own thoughts were—what most of the rest of these gentlemen felt—when we come on this murderin' black. We saw we'd caught a runaway— a nigger that had tried to kill his guard and run. . . . We didn't want that kind of thinkin' spreadin' to our niggers—"

"Amen," several men said in chorus.

"No way," said others, already feeling justified in whatever action they had taken.

"—so we acted in a way that seemed best at the time," Gassaway continued.

Filled with a vast sense of emptiness and despair, Lucretia Borgia entered the kitchen. She agreed with Mem they'd likely have twenty hungry white men for supper. She supervised the preparation of fried chicken, baked yams, white gravy, grits and field beans. She set kitchen boys to squeezing lemons into a huge crock of cold water and she pretended she didn't glimpse Memnon urinating in the lemonade when he set the earthenware vessel in the underground chamber to cool.

She ordered her favorite rocking chair sent over from her kitchen to Jingo Jim's cabin. She satisfied herself that Millie and the octoroon Ellen could handle the serving of the repast. Taking her shawl from its peg near the kitchen door, she pushed open the screen door to leave.

Mem caught her arm. He looked desolated. "You going back over to that Jingo?"

"Jingo likely dyin', Memnon. He ain't gwine do nuthin' to me that you need worry 'bout."

"I don't trust that nigger till I see pennies laid on his eyes," Mem said.

"Let me shut this screen door," Lucretia Borgia said impatiently. "We lettin' in flies."

Missy came mincing across the kitchen. "Miz Lucretia Borgia, the masta he wants to see you in the parlor. This instant."

"You tell him I be there directly," Lucretia Borgia

said. She turned and looked on Mem tenderly, pityingly. "You don't fret, Mem. You go up to bed tonight an' wait fo' me. . . . I don't git there, you start without me." She laughed and patted his face. She walked past him, going toward the front of the house. She left Mem slumped against the doorjamb.

She found Masta Warren and the dirt farmer Eldon Close alone for the moment in the parlor of the old house. The other men shouted, drank and laughed on the front porch. It was growing dark, but inside the room was bright, warm and pleasant with candles lit and a fire roaring on the hearth. A large-bellied lamp on the centertable glowed yellowly. The parlor was certainly not elegant in any way, but it was comfortable and looked livable and lived-in. Home-loomed rag carpets spiced the scrubbed floors with islands of dusty color. The furniture had been bought or constructed in the plantation carpentry shop, as necessity dictated. There was no sense of decor, design or coordinating. The master's aged Empire mahogany rocker, swatched with pillows and quilts, dominated the carpeted space before the huge fieldstone fireplace.

Two houseboys helped Masta Warren ease himself into his big Empire chair. His calves, feet, wrists, and ankles were still discolored from the hog-blood bath. He moved no less painfully, but declared himself encouraged and totally satisfied with his first medication.

Maxwell gazed up at Lucretia Borgia, his beetled brows warning her not to oppose him. He said in a bright and cheerful tone, "Mr. Close here say he wants his nigger boy in trade."

"What's he got to trade?" Lucretia Borgia demanded.

The farmer glared at Lucretia Borgia, but spoke, pleadingly, to the master of Falconhurst. "Your word. That's what I got. I got your word, Brother Warren. Afore that Vulcan runned—'fore them people hung him—you agreed to a trade. It was good as closed right then."

Maxwell nodded, agreeing. "That's right. Morally, if not legal, I got a bindin' agreement with Mr. Close—"

"Right." Close continued to stare coldly and balefully toward Lucretia Borgia. What enraged her was that Maxwell would normally never have consented to this highway robbery on the basis of the poor hulk of Vulcan returned after a year of cruelty, mistreatment and neglect. He was entranced by Close's stinking prescription for curing his rheumatism. The dirt farmer could probably have walked off with a dozen slaves if he'd had the intelligence to realize it. For likely the first and last time, Close had old Maxwell exactly where he would want him—deeply indebted and anxious to display his gratitude.

Maxwell was nodding with enthusiasm. "So I want you, first thing tomorrow, to line up some field-grade nigger boys and let Mr. Close make his choice—"

"So he can ruin another nigger?" Lucretia Borgia protested.

"What Mr. Close do with his animals ain't our concern, Lucretia Borgia, and it sure to hell ain't none of your'n." Maxwell's voice shook with self-righteous indignation. "You show him the niggers. You lets him make his choice—and the nigger is his'n—fo' ten dollars boot."

"Ten dollars boot?" Now Close protested. "That hardly seem fair."

"It fair," Lucretia Borgia said.

"Whether it fair or not," Maxwell said, "it the way I do business, Mr. Close. Much as I'm beholden to you, I don't close no trade without somethin' to boot. That jus' the way it is. Always been. Always be."

Reluctantly, Close nodded his head in agreement and the two men shook hands. Lucretia Borgia hid her disgust. She shrugged and nodded. "Whatever you say, Masta."

"That's what I say." Maxwell's voice raked her.

"When Masta Ham git home from the Texies, I gwine see you flogged, you black slut—"

"I do hopes you invite me over to view the ceremony," Eldon Close said, nodding and grinning.

"—an' Mr. Close goin' spend the night as our guest. You tell Mem to fresh up a bed and wash Mr. Close a nice bedwench to warm his sheets."

Lucretia Borgia nodded, telling herself that if and when Masta Ham returned from the Texies, this man's spending the night was something else that would never happen again at Falconhurst.

The two men watched Lucretia Borgia stalk in majestic dissent from the room. The clap of her slippers against her heels was like small gunfire. She coldly passed down the orders given to her by the master and escaped the house as if running from a place of pestilence. . . .

Jingo Jim slept exactly as she had left him when she walked into the silent cabin. "He still alive?" she said, panic moiling in her belly.

"Reckon. He breathing," Zeus Four said.

"Ain't moved a muscle," Pole told her, worried. "Lay like he daid. But like Zeus Four say, he breathin'."

"Barely."

Lucretia Borgia thanked them and waved them from the cabin. She found several large tallow candles and placed them beside the broken-dish candle base on the bare pine table near Jingo's bed. She looked forward without relish to a long night watch.

As the cabin door closed behind Pole and Zeus Four, Jingo opened first one eye and then the other. He grinned weakly. "They gone yet?"

Lucretia Borgia shook her head, laughing despite herself. "Jingo, you a devil, that what you is."

"I hopes you can fo'give me, Miz Lucretia Borgia, ma'am," he said in mock servility.

"How you feels, boy?"

"Terrible. I dyin'."

"Oh, Jingo. No. What can I do?"

"Get nekkid and git in this bed. This heah hard-on is killin' me."

"Now you jus' hush that kind of talk," Lucretia Borgia said. "You may not have sense enough to know you are on the point of dyin', but I do."

"I know I dyin' . . . I even know what I dyin' of . . . I dyin' of need . . . for you. You some gyascutus gal, Lucretia Borgia. I want you—nekkid—on my deathbed . . . then I dies happy."

"You want horns but you gone die butt-headed," she said. "What you think I gits nekkid in your bed? Long's I got my dress on, I can 'splain anything. But who gone believe me when I nekkid in your bed—and you dead from excitement?"

"What's best, Lucretia Borgia?" he inquired in a plaintive, innocent tone. "To die fum excitement—or fum neglect?"

She laughed and shook her head. "I don't know an' we ain't gone find out. . . . Now you hush. Save yo' strength. You go to sleep. I gone sit right here by you. All night. Anything you need, you jus' tells me."

"I needs *you*."

"Anything 'ceptin' that."

"Then I don't need nuthin'. You can go on back up to the big house. I jus' gone die—in terrible pain."

"Where you hurt?"

"You know where I hurt."

"Where else?"

"Nowhere else. . . . Least you can do is lie down beside me on my deathbed. Can't hurt nuthin'. You keeps yo' dress on, nuthin' happens. But I got you close, where I needs you. I die—I die peaceful."

She rocked and thought this over. The buldge in his blanket showed he was not lying, he was not at peace. He might lie quieter if she lay beside him. She heard the undiminished sounds from the manor house. The white men extended their party into the night hours. Be a passel of drunks trying to find their way home in the dark. She hoped most of them stumbled and broke their goddam white necks.

"Cain't lie with you," she decided. "You jus' get mo' excited."

"Cain't git no more excited than I is, Lucretia Borgia. What you think I want most all these years? To git you all by yo'self in my cabin. Had to git a pitchfork in my belly to git you here. An' now here you sit, a rockin' and a shakin' your head."

"It you I thinking about."

"It you I thinking about, too. Ever since I first laid eyes on you—when they brung me here to Falconhurst in that coffle—I knew I wanted a big, full-growed, full-bloomin' lady like you. With tits like you. With hips like you. With a beautiful pretty like you—all throbbin' and hot like you. . . . Knew I wouldn't never be satisfied with nuthin' less. . . . You what I want. What I want since I was a boy with my voice changin' and my first hard-on."

"I what you want, all right. I what you want 'cause I the onliest female in earshot," she said, but she was flattered.

"All right. Jus' go git any other two wenches. Put 'em there—nekkid—beside you and see which one I gits up and reaches for."

"You ain't no way gittin' up at all."

"Ain't stayin' here, less you lay down with me."

"You cain't git up. You bad hurt. You ain't gittin' up."

"I is, less'n you lies down here beside me. I gits up on my feet, likely I bleeds inside somethin' fierce— might jus' finish me off."

"All right." She waved her arm in surrender. "Let me blow out the candle."

"Don't blow out no candle. Wants to look at you, I

do. Don't see no gyascutus beauty like you every night in the world."

She set her mouth stubbornly. "Ain't gone leave no candle lit. You want me to lie beside you—jus' lay quiet beside you—we do it, but we do it in the dark."

He spread his hands. "All right. I hate to be in the dark so I can't see them big titties with they nipples all hard for me. . . . "

"You gone sleep."

"Yeah. Yeah. I gone sleep. . . . Blow out the candle."

Her mind aswarm with misgivings, Lucretia Borgia blew out the candle. She heard a rustle of movement at the cabin window and hesitated a moment in the darkness. She could hear retreating steps on the ground outside and she thought with pity of poor Mem. But then if he came peeping around in windows, he found what he was looking for. He was so miserable, so torn with jealousy of the youthful Jingo Jim. She was sorry but she didn't belong to Mem. She belonged to nobody.

Somewhere in the night darkness a melancholy baritone sang to the night mists. She listened to the sadness that was as old as slavery, as old as the night itself. Her eyes filled with tears she could not explain and she exhaled heavily, lying down beside Jingo.

She found that Jingo had kicked off the covers and lay naked on his back. His manhood reared erect as a mast in the darkness. "You gone kill yo'self, boy," she warned.

He laughed, pulling her hand over on his rigidity. "We have us a double death. I pesters you to death, an' I dies a-tryin'."

She laughed at him but did not pull her hand away. Gently she caressed his quivering staff and his gonads. She heard his deep breathing, his breath hot against her neck. "If only you'd git nekkid, too," he whispered. "Nekkid like me."

"Ain't," she said. "I expects you to die any minute,

carryin' on like this. Suppose you do die—how I explain why I was layin' nekkid in your bed with you? How I gone live with myself, knowin' what I doin', knowin' I kilt you when you should be lyin' quiet? Lord knows, I can't live down being caught nekkid in your deathbed."

He lay quiet. He moved his hand along the heated inner surface of her legs, carrying her skirt before him. His fingers closed on the mound of her femininity. He played with her for a long time. She felt herself growing weak with need, her whole body fevered. When at last he told her he had to have her, or burst inside, she could not protest. All she could say was, "God help us both."

"God helps *me* right now, He gone have the best time of His life," Jingo whispered.

Lucretia Borgia bent her legs at her knees and held herself open to receive Jingo Jim. In the misty darkness she could see his twisted, agonized face, but she could also tell that no amount of pain—internal and intense—was going to deter Jingo Jim now. He wanted her. He had to have her.

She cringed at his sharp, agonized intake of breath. Even now, she wanted to stop him, but she could not. Perhaps he was mortally wounded inside, an artery nicked by those vicious pitchfork tines. There was no doubting this was the way he chose to die. There was no doubting he wanted her more than he wanted life. . . . She drew him to her, cradling him upon her magnificent body, at first tenderly.

She was lifted up, transported from this bed in a slave cabin. It was as if she sailed free in the deep vaulted night, light as vapor, disembodied, spinning in ecstasy, removed from all reality except the sweet agony of his possessing her with every ounce of his strength.

She held him close for a long time after they had reached a final climax together. He did not speak. She pulled away in panic, lighted a candle. He looked gray, lifeless. "Jingo," she whispered, frantic. "You all right?"

He winced and fell away from her.

Deeply troubled, Lucretia Borgia stared down at him. She remembered the bottle of laudanum in her apron pocket. "When the pain gits monstrous," Doc Redfield had told her. She got up, prepared the mixture as she had seen the vet do. But when she returned to Jingo Jim's bed, the flickering candle showed her he was sprawled unconscious across the mattress.

Terrified, Lucretia Borgia knelt over him. "Oh Gawd," she whispered. "I done kilt him. Jesus Gawd, I kilt him."

Jingo opened one eye. "You ain't kilt me," he said sleepily. "Leastways not kilt total. It'll be fifteen, twenty minutes—'fore I got strength enough to pester you ag'in, that's all."

He closed his eyes and sank into an instant and blissful stupor. She stayed in her rocking chair a long time, watching him sleep. Overwhelmed with relief, she blew out the candle, kissed him lightly on his bared belly where the stitches made small rough ridges in his heated skin, and then let herself out of the cabin.

In the kitchen at the big house, she entered the pantry and replaced the small jar of laudanum carefully. She'd learned frugality over the years running Falconhurst Plantation as Masta Ham would have wanted it run were he here. Waste not, want not. And if this compound of laudanum was only half as potent a tranquilizer as Doc Redfield claimed, it would come in handy as an antidote to the pain of existence in this place. There was a lot of pain among the Negroes of the stud farm; there was pain in being black in this white world. . . .

These days dragged past slowly at Falconhurst. Old Warren seemed ashamed that he'd sunk so low as to cry aloud his loneliness for his son—and worse that

97

he'd been caught in his unmanly weeping by Lucretia Borgia. Lucretia carefully never mentioned that day when he'd been so depressed and heartsick. She sensed instinctively that it was a shameful subject with the master of Falconhurst, and she avoided it. She fixed him his special toddies when he sat alone. He would express his gratitude by nodding his head. Sometimes she would stand beside his overstuffed chair before the fireplace and they would talk about Hammond, but they never spoke of old Masta Warren's tears for his son.

They watched the trace beyond the property line for some sign that Masta Ham was coming home, but the hot days and nights remained empty, as did the road, and he did not come. . . .

Warren Maxwell felt he was destined to the tedium of watching the fire and waiting for Hammond to return from the Texies. Sometimes he got up on his purpled and painful feet and limped gingerly to the window that overlooked the lane and the road beyond. Often, he'd stand, biting his mouth against the pain, and watch that empty road. At times Lucretia Borgia came and stood silent vigil beside him. They didn't speak, but their concern was the same, for Hammond's safety and his welfare in that strange and distant land far across the Texies. . . .

I

ACROSS THE TEXIES

IX

Moonlight filtered through the chaparral bearding the dry creek bed, touching man and animal. The slaughtered heifer dangled by the hooves from the shaky tripod the man had hastily constructed of cottonwood poles and hemp. The man moved in closer to the suspended beef. His long knife glittered in his fist. With a practiced slash of his arm, he slit the throat of the beast. Hot red blood spewed in a torrent, smelling nauseatingly sweet in the stillness.

The man stepped back, watching the blood spilling from the slaughtered cow. He wiped his hands and the blood-covered knife. His satin tan face, gaunt though youthful, was set in rigid lines. He was not quite twenty years old, a Mexican national, his black eyes harried but as chilled as the steel of his knife. He was a handsome boy, with sharply defined features beneath his flat-brimmed sombrero with its bright band and small feather. Everything about him except the fierce pride in his delicate face spoke of deprivation, poverty and gnawing hunger. There was about his very movements a sense of frustration and bottled violence, as if he had been pushed until he could be pushed no more. His boots, which he had stolen, were run-over. They fit badly and hurt his feet so that every step he took was painful. But he moved with the grace of a puma, with the mindless instinct of a hungry animal with the scent of fresh blood.

He worked swiftly but confidently, carving the carcass and placing the cuts of beef, as well as the tongue, heart, liver and eyes, upon a canvas roll near the mesquite bush where his sharp-ribbed horse waited, ground-tied.

A rustling sound from the shadowed darkness paralyzed the youth for a long beat. He stood unmoving, for that instant unable to move. When he could react, he turned, knife held ready, low in his taut fist. A disembodied voice said, "Drop it or die, greaser."

The Mexican boy stood gray-faced as three men converged on him from the whiskered mouth of the arroyo. The boy dropped his knife. It winked, silvered in the moonlight.

The man in the lead swung down easily from his saddle. Walking stiffly, as if he'd been a long time on his horse, he came to the boy, took up the knife. A lean, tall man with sharp features, dead-flat gray eyes and a soup-strainer mustache, he inspected the knife, wiping it on his chaps. "Goddam," he said. "No matter how hungry they kids are, these greasers always carry the best knife they can steal, Mr. Maxwell."

Hammond Maxwell awkwardly swung down from his saddle, his right leg extended stiffly. He dropped his reins and stalked forward, limping. He was about thirty-two years old, of medium height, with long stocky trunk and short, thick legs. His hair and brows were a sandy blond, but his skin was so leathered by exposure that wrinkles were baked in around his eyes and mouth and he seemed older, weathered. His jacket —of fringed antelope leather with a thick wool collar—looked well tailored, though dusty and briar-scratched.

He peered into the youth's face until the boy dropped his gaze under Ham's. Hammond's blue eyes were tired, disenchanted, with a chill remoteness that made him appear aloof and unapproachable, even when he laughed. Something about him—perhaps the expensive whipcord trousers, hand-tooled boots and light gray planter's hat, wide-brimmed and flat-crowned marked him as a man of affluence and authority. An air of faint arrogance about him suggested he'd been born into a feudal hegemony and accepted despotic power as a divine right, as he had assumed wealth, youth, good food, freedom and deference as his due. The way he held himself declared he'd been bestowed all advantages and embraced them as casually as he viewed sunrise, sunset—all God-given, part of a divine plan. He was a Maxwell and a Hammond, of Alabama, and this in itself set him apart from ordinary mortals of any hue, political persuasion or social background.

The boy wouldn't meet Hammond's gaze but he set himself as if he would protect the slaughtered carcass with the armor of his own frail body.

Hammond's foreman inspected the suspended animal. "It's our beef all right, Mr. Ham. Dumb greasers. Brand oughta be the first hunk they cut out—always the last. Grab the meat and run, huh, greaser?"

"All right, Paley," Hammond said. "We knowed it was our beef." He gazed at the slender youth in the silvered light. "You wasn't smart as you thought you was, boy. Line rider saw you cuttin' that heifer out before sundown. Reckon you figured yourself all alone in this part of the Texies, huh? You and my stolen beef."

"I'm hungry," the boy said in halting English. "Maria goin' to have our baby. Maria need meat. Red meat. I ask you for work, Señor Maxwell, I beg, but you would give me none."

"That give you the right to squat on my land?" Hammond bent forward over the youth, the very size of his body threatening. "That adobe hut you greasers slapped together out'n mud an' cow dung is on my land."

"*You* say it is your land, Señor. We say it is a Spanish grant. We say—"

"We don't give a shit what you say, greaser." Paley tapped his shoulder with the flat of the blade. "You admit that there beef is Mr. Maxwell's?"

The boy shrugged, but his voice sounded weak, lost. "It has his brand. But everything up here has his brand. He come—from where? He buy. Or he take. He ride onto a piece of land and he say this is my land. And it is his land. He put his brand on everything. Even the Mexican girl he will not marry, but who bears his sons, his brand is on her—"

"Watch your tongue, boy." Paley struck harder with the knife blade.

The boy spread his hands. He felt as if he were talking to the cactus, the armadillos, the night runners, himself. It did not matter what he said. They did not listen. "When Maria, her parents and me, come north across the Rio to make our home, we have a milk cow, two beef calves I raised from birthin'—and an aged bull. . . . They gone . . . all gone among all the cattle wearing Señor Maxwell's great brand. Your cattle trample my garden, dirty my spring water—"

"That there spring is *my* waterin' hole, greaser." Hammond shook his head, unable to comprehend the stupidity of these people. "An' you buildin' an adobe hut in the willows beside that spring don't no way make one inch of it yourn."

The man behind Maxwell shifted impatiently in his saddle. "Stop foolin' with him, boss. He admits it's your beef. The brand is yourn. We seen him steal it. He's a rustlin' greaser-squatter—and rustlers hang in the Texies."

"Relax, Lambdin," Hammond said over his shoulder. "My ole pappy back in Alabama always said, don't be in a hurry to be hung, and don't be in a rush to hang nobody." He raised his arm in a restraining gesture.

"Now, I'm a fair man. He says he lost his cows in my herds—"

"Shit, he's lyin'. You know that."

"Still," Hammond said. "We hang this greaser—then we get a greaser family to git shed of. . . . I got a better plan."

"You can't let him go, boss," Lambdin said. "Word spreads. They'll steal us off the range."

"Cale's right, Mr. Ham," Paley said. "Out here, the only rustler you can trust is one hangin' by his neck."

The boy remained standing, but it was as if through some supreme exercise of fading will. His face had gone pallid in the moonlight. "Maria—pregnant . . . she hungry, Señor . . . don't you see?"

"I see jus' one thing, boy. You broke the law. Range law says you got to be punished. I a respecter of the law, boy. Firm respecter. Always been. Always be. Now that damn heifer more or less means nuthin' . . . we finish butcherin' it—an' we take it to your adobe. Your folks can eat it while they pack to clear out. . . . But you broke range law, and you gone pay. You squatted on my land. You stayed when we warned you off."

"I had my family—no place to go, *patrone*. My garden. My chickens. Without these things how could we live?"

"I could of burnt you out. But I kept hopin' you'd show some sense." He swung his arm. "Instead you made it worse—on both of us."

Cale Lambdin laughed, cold and mirthless. He slipped his pistol from its holster at his hip. "Hell, boss," he said, "I'll settle it for you—nice and quick."

As the gun came up, the Mexican boy gasped, retreating a step. Hammond turned swiftly and smoothly, considering his stiff, misshapen knee. Hammond's whip cracked in the somber quiet. Lambdin's gun toppled from his numbed hand and thudded to the hard-packed ground.

"Tried to tell you. We ain't killin' him, Cale," Hammond said in a cold tone. He picked up his employee's gun, held it negligently. After a moment he returned it to Lambdin, butt first. "I figure to use this here boy in a way that do us some good. We kill him, he just a carcass to bury. We make a 'zample of him—maybe we spare ourselves more rustlin' trouble with other nesters later on."

"An example?" Paley stared at Hammond in the vague dark. "Seems to me—a greaser hangin' from a cottonwood is the best example you goin' to find."

"I do it my way," Hammond said coldly.

Brazos Crossing sprawled prostrate in the early-morning sunlight. A random sowing of adobe and slab-sided shacks where trails crossed, the town was built around a large well in the plaza before an imposing Catholic church. The stone-walled public well offered the only safe watering place for fifteen miles in either direction. The church drew the spiritually thirsty. For travelers there was a saloon–general store. Sooner or later everyone in the territory came to the well, or the church or the saloon.

Since an hour before dawn the great cast-iron bell in the church steeple had been ringing at five-minute intervals. It seemed the breathless atmosphere still held the sound of the tolling bells when their clamor started again. People gathered outside the wide church steps, waiting in the plaza, puzzled and silent. They sought what shade they could beneath two scabrous, dust-choked cottonwood trees. Every strata of life was represented—Texicans, Mexicans, Indians, pilgrims from the north and east, white gringos who bought or staked out the arable land for their own.

The cowed Mexican youth was led from a locked crib inside the monastery. His wrists were thonged at his back. He had spent most of the night on the stone floor. He was chilled to the bone in the blaze of sunlight, terrorized, without hope. The priest had prayed with him, but even this dedicated man seemed to mumble indistinctly as if his mind were elsewhere. The boy didn't blame the priest. What could they do? He was guilty. Even had he been innocent, they would have been helpless against the will of the Señor Maxwell. He slumped against the four-foot stone wall of the well. He glimpsed his pregnant wife and her mother in the silent crowd, but he lowered his eyes, staring at the ground, and could not look at her.

The priest, a stout young man, his face pied with old and advanced acne, reluctantly and hesitantly translated into Spanish what Hammond had to say to the gathered crowd. The priest wished no part in this. It would not enhance his image with the bishop, but the rancher was very wealthy, arrogant and adamant. What could he do? What could he hope to say that such a man would hear?

"This man is a rustler," Hammond told the assembled people. "Under range law, I could have hung him where I caught him slaughtering my branded beef. . . . I did not want to do that. He has a family. If he were hung, that family becomes a public burden. On all of us. Another burden.

"And there is another reason why I chose this kind of punishment. I have seen it work—most effective— back where I came from. I think it can work here. If I hung this rustler, we'd have one more dead criminal, but others would hardly be aware this boy had lived or died.

"That's why I've called all of you here. All of you. Texicans. Mexicans. Injuns. White folks. What you see happening here today to this cattle thief is what will happen to every rustler we catch on our range. I vow that to you. Public flogging. . . . We're goin' to give this thief twenty lashes with a bullwhip. If he lives, he carries the scars and the memory of this pain to his grave. When it's over, he'll tell you—if'n he can tell

107

you anything—how unbearable that pain gets . . . he will think well before he trespasses on our land again.

"I warn you all. Were he to steal from me again, I would chop off his hands. I want you people—all of you—to *see* what will happen if you steal from me. There ain't much law in the Texies. But by God, there will be law in this part of it."

Paley and Cale Lambdin half-carried the trembling youth. A rope secured him, arms stretched tall above his head, to the pulley-support stanchions over the well. At a signal from Hammond, the boy's cotton blouse was ripped off. The boy's wife screamed and tried to run to him. Her grim-faced relatives and neighbors restrained her.

Paley stood, legs apart, his own shirt removed, the sun glinting on the corded muscles and faint padding of blond hairs on his shoulders and chest. He was aware of the striking figure he presented. He hefted the bullwhip in his hands, letting it slip across his palms in a serpentine way. At a sign from Hammond, Paley brought his arm up. The whip crackled like a rifle in the taut silence. The second lash brought blood.

The priest clasped Hammond's arm. His pocked face twisted, pleading. "Please, Señor Maxwell. In the name of *Madre de Dios*. No more."

"He gits whupped," Ham said in a flat tone. "Or he hangs. It don't make no nevah mind to me."

The priest nodded, subsided. The black-frocked man sank to his knees, a portly figure on the steps, his head turned away from the flogging, crouching as if trying to melt into his own shadow.

Ham felt queasy. The air seemed heavy with dust, oversweet cow manure and sweat. The whip cracked loudly. The boy's screams rose to a hysterical pitch and then abruptly ceased. He slumped against the ropes. Blood spouted from the torn gashes across his back. The whip dripped blood and flicked huge globules when it cracked. At last, long before Cale reached twenty in his measured counting, Ham lifted his arm to stop them. No sense whipping the boy further. Either the youth had fainted or he was dead. Ham did not go near him to check. Paley washed the blood off the bullwhip with water from the well and then cracked it a few times to dry it. Then he stood in the intense sunlight, coiling the thick leather about his arm. Ham saw many women eyeing Paley hungrily. No matter how civilized people became, the ruthless shedding of blood always proved a most powerful aphrodisiac.

Most of the Mexicans and Indians crowded in about the boy slumped against the stone well.

Ham gave them only a brief glance. With Paley and Lambdin beside him, he limped across the plaza toward the leather-slicked hitch rail where their horses dozed, idly slapping flies with their tails.

A tall thin man paused in the center of the hard-packed street. His accent suggested the Virginia tidewater. "You must be from the Deep South, Mr. Maxwell."

Ham paused. "I'm from Alabama, yes suh."

"Figured you'd dealt with niggers. Whoppin' always makes a real lastin' impression on blacks. Wonder 'bout greasers, though. Different hide. Different temperament. You rob a Latin of his pride, you kill him." He jerked his head toward the group knotted about the well. "Likely, that boy died under the whip."

"Well, now they know what to expect." Hammond did not glance toward the well. His stomach roiled, and sweat ran down from his hat brim. He swallowed back bile and kept his face expressionless.

The man grinned to show it was none of his affair, that he intended no affront. He shook his head. "Funny. No matter how long you live out here in the Texies, you're still livin' in Alabama, or Virginia, ain't you?"

Hammond shrugged. "A man's roots go deep," he said.

X

Sometime within the first hour of the ride home, Hammond and his two lieutenants entered into unfenced range owned, controlled by, or assumed to belong to the Maxwell ranch. The trees hung desolately in summer heat, leaves sere, and the winding dirt road was rock-hard. They passed no other travelers and expected to meet none. The land, Hammond thought, giving it only a casual glance, was ugly, barren and brown. It was really desert land, but desert land on which grass grew, grass rich enough to sustain great expanding herds of cattle. He had never found the beauty he'd dreamed of, back in Alabama, when he thought in longing of the open ranges of the Texies. In fact, it was generous to call the clumps of weeds *grass*. Grass grew green in the Alabama summers. In the Texies, the summers were hot and the wind blew; in winter it was chilled and the wind blew. This day was dry, the air pungent and acrid in the nostrils. A man's breath burned in his throat. They crossed the river and found a faint trickle of muddy water dribbling yellowly through its narrow bed. It looked as if it had been raining in the distant foothills—they lay in the haze with a heavy cloud cover that would dissipate long before it reached these dry plains. If there were ever any rain out here it was always in some remote region. One saw far lightning, cloud-to-ground, but one heard no thunderclaps, felt no drops of cooling water.

Hammond slumped in his saddle. His right stirrup was extended to accommodate his "game" leg. His knee bent only slightly and then with excruciating pain. He was dog-tired. He could smell his own sweat in his clothes, the sweat of the horses, and the unpleasant odor of the other two men. They'd been two days in the saddle. Ham looked forward to a bath in a tub of tepid water, Lydia's scrubbing his back, a toddy like his father always had, and then into bed early. He yawned, almost helplessly.

He wanted to hurry, but there were still miles of hot open country, and he couldn't push the other two men, their horses, or himself. They'd all been pushed to the limit now. There was the smell of exhaustion about them, almost as strong as the ammoniac odor rising from the sweated horses. When Lambdin broke out a quart of whiskey from his saddle bag, Hammond salivated slightly. Even hot raw whiskey was wet.

Lambdin drank first. He took a long pull from the mouth of the bottle, wiped his mouth on his sleeve and then offered the uncorked bottle. "Want a drink?"

Paley hesitated. Hammond said, "Thanks."

He drank, with Paley watching him thirstily. "Jesus," Hammond said. "This stuff is terrible." He handed the bottle to Paley, wincing.

"You got to hold your breath," Lambdin said. "After a while, it tastes fine."

"Hell, I don't want to get drunk," Ham said. "I just want to cut the dust."

"Lot of dust," Lambdin said.

"I don't want to get drunk," Ham said again.

"Me neither," Paley said. He took a second drink, gasped, belched, and leaned over in his saddle, returning the bottle to Lambdin.

"I do," Lambdin said. "I'd like to ride in to the

112

place drunk, fall in my bunk stewed and then sleep it off."

"Jesus," Ham said. "Don't you want a bath first?"

"What for? Liquor can wash out anything water can wash off," Cale said.

"What in hell does that mean?" Paley asked.

"Have a couple more swigs," Cale said, grinning. "Then you'll either know what I'm talking about or you won't give a shit."

"Already I don't give a shit . . . but I'll take another pull. Against the dust. Against snakebite. Against slavery."

"What you got against slavery?" Hammond said. He jerked his head around and stared at Paley fiercely.

Paley waved his arm. "Who the hell cares? I was just drinking—against something. Against anything. Hell, make it against cold weather. Forget slavery. Hell, I'm not even against snakebite, if it leads to drinking."

"You know what drinking leads to?" Cale asked.

"What?"

"I don't know. I thought maybe you did." Cale shook his head. "If I was in town, I'd know what drinkin' would lead to. A Mexican whore. But way out here there's nuthin' but the boss's woman—and my fist."

"Shut up that talk," Ham said. "Don't you talk about Lydia like that. I don't care what you do to your fist. I ever catch you with my—wife—I'll kill you."

Cale grinned at him. "Is she your *wife,* boss?"

"If you want to stay healthy, Cale, you'll shut your teeth about—her," Ham said.

"Hell, boss. It ain't like she was a—white lady. She is a greaser. And no matter what you say—she ain't your wife."

"That's enough, goddammit."

"Hell, boss, I don't mean anything. I was just having fun. If I had a woman, you could say anything you

113

wanted to about her—and I'd laugh along with you—long as it wasn't true."

"Shut it up, Cale," Paley said. "Have a drink."

"A woman is just a woman, that's all," Cale insisted.

"Well, that's where we're different, you and me," Ham told him. "Where I come from a gentleman treats women with respect."

Cale and Paley exchanged glances. Neither of them said anything. Paley drew the back of his hand across his mouth and Cale took another long pull at the bottle. The road was steep for a couple of miles and the horses slowed in the blazing sun, plodding upon their shadows.

The land lay unchanging. Cale and Paley lagged slightly behind Ham, sharing the bottle. Hammond didn't want any more to drink. The sun drew the liquor through his pores, adding to the stink of his own body. He heard Cale and Paley talking about white women and Mexican women. Cale said that after a man hit the hay with a Mexican girl, he never wanted a Texican or American girl again. Ham sweated, thinking Cale was right. He preferred a tawny Mexican or a mustee wench every time. Except for his brief marriage to Blanche he'd never bedded himself with a white woman, or wanted to. He'd had a black bed wench since he was thirteen.

He smiled tiredly, remembering. A bed wench had been his father's idea. It was good for him, father had said, better than using his fist and feeling guilty. A colored bed wench was fine, but it was not the same with a white woman. Since birth, he'd been taught that all white women were sacred—just below the mother of Jesus, who'd had an immaculate conception. Carnal relations with a white woman was forcing something ugly upon them that they were too genteel and respectable to want. A man married, and if he wanted children, he and his wife bedded together; pleasure had nothing to do with it. Somewhere, he had lost all desire to touch

114

a white woman—actually he found the stark whiteness of their naked flesh almost revolting. His marriage to Blanche had been one of the most evil times of his life, and he could not endure to recall it even now.

"Reckon I agree with what you say, Cale, about Mexican women," Ham said. "Not interested in marryin' up with one—not even my Lydia. But I can tell you, I never have liked the idea of white women for pestering. They too pink and soft for me—it's like lookin' at the belly of a dead fish a-layin' there."

"Was you ever married to a—white lady?" Paley said. "Maybe you'd feel different then."

"Wouldn't feel no different," Ham said. "A black wench takes natural to pleasurin' a man, and like Cale said, Mexican women are as hot as tamales—"

"An' they taste better," Cale said.

Again, Hammond retreated, withdrew, his face going cold. "I don't go in for unnatural stuff, neither. No, nor that perverted talk, neither. Ain't what God meant between a man and a woman."

Cale put his head back, laughing. "What the hell you think God did mean, boss? God meant you to do anything you can do—any way that makes you and your lady happy. That's all God meant. God put it here —and He put you here—you don't enjoy it, hell, don't blame God."

"Look who's talking for God now," Paley said.

Hammond consciously closed his mind to the two cowmen. As far as he was concerned, Cale Lambdin was low-minded white trash that would have to be watched out at the ranch and never left alone on the place with Lydia. Lydia never had looked at any other man in the past six years, but she was a greaser, and hell, everybody knew how hot those women were. He'd run Cale off the place if he even looked at Lydia. Goddammit, he'd lay her bones bare with the whip if he caught her. He sweated, sick. Thinking about the whip brought back the Mexican boy and the public flogging in the plaza at Brazos Crossing. He turned slightly in the saddle. "Did the greaser die?" he asked.

"No." Paley's voice thinned with disgust.

"He was alive when we left town," Lambdin said. "They took him into the church." He shook his head and laughed. "That priest with the pocked face. He was like an old woman out there."

"I thought sure hell he'd burst into tears," Paley said.

"I was expectin' him to vomit up his holy guts," Lambdin said. "I'd of give you odds."

"A woman in a black frock, that priest," Paley said.

"Ready to cry. Did you see that? A grown man. Don't that beat hell? A grown man cryin'. That's something I ain't never seen. Made me sick to my stomach."

"Like a woman." Paley nodded. "Soft hands. Maybe that's why he became a priest."

"Hell," Cale said. "I heard them priests ride them nuns all the time. Reg'lar."

"Shit. Most priests don't care about women. Nuns or no other kind. They'd rather ride each other."

"You're shittin' me."

"So help me God. I heard that. An' the way that priest swung his wrists around—limp-like. I knew a flirty girl back in Georgia usta use her hands like that. Didn't seem manly in her, neither."

Though Ham was convinced he'd done the right thing in publicly flogging the nester, he regretted people like that Mexican boy. Nameless nester. He'd never had to deal with the very poor back in Alabama. He saw them occasionally but seldom came in contact with them. Seemed to him the world was easier back where divisions between classes of people were sharp and definite. Master. Slave. You knew where you stood in that world. You knew what your rights were and also your responsibilities and obligations. Out here, a greaser family, or pilgrims from the east, squatted on your land. They were like thieves. They robbed you of your land. Soon they were actual thieves, stealing beef, horses, blankets, food, anything that wasn't nailed down. They lived free on your land. But they owed you nothing; you owed them nothing. They stole from you to underline their independence. And when you punished a theft, a priest sank to his knees, ready to weep. Not for the crime, for Christ's sake—for the criminal.

He shifted in the saddle, hotter, sweatier, stickier than ever. What was to become of a man's property and his property rights if this kind of thinking continued and was carried out to its illogical limits? A man could sweat and work all his life to ensure his family's security, build his property—and then lose it overnight to violence and vandals. And the priest would weep for the thief. Jesus.

He wished for home—for Falconhurst. It was the first time in eight years he felt overcome with homesickness. A man does not determine to throw over one life for another quickly. Not the old for the new, or again the new for the old. It begins with an empty-bellied sense of insufficiency, something lacking in one life that existed certainly and reassuringly in another. Hammond looked back to Alabama after eight years away, first inside his mind.

Thinking of home—of the oaks and elms and pines of Alabama, the cold deep clear sweet of the old Tombigbee—he felt a sickness in the pit of his stomach. Nothing he'd accomplished out here had the good and exhilarating taste of success anymore. He sweated, frustrated and miserable, for the first time truly longing for home. He had for years kept it all out of his mind, but suddenly he was facing the truth. He belonged at Falconhurst. The taproot went deep in that Alabama earth. No matter how wealthy he became, or respected, or feared, or envied, or admired out here in the Texies, that taproot sank vertically downward. That taproot sustained him, despite any smaller lateral roots in what-

117

ever acropetal succession. He could reach out, but he could never break free. He had never left home. Just as that stranger had said in Brazos Crossing this morning, he'd never really left the Deep South. He had tried to bring it with him.

His skin felt tight, as if he could not go on living inside it. He suddenly realized he had not brought his home with him. He had simply tried to go on clinging to it even when it was no good, even when he knew it was lost to him.

"Something scratchin' at your craw, boss?" Paley asked.

Hammond shrugged. "Thinkin' about home," he said. He shook his head. "Must be overtired, I reckon."

The horses plodded in the sun. With a conscious effort of will, Hammond shook off the sense of homesickness. He was just tired, that was all. Hell, he owned this world. He gazed out across the flat brown plains, thinking, *I own all this.* He tried consciously to renew that old sense of achievement which had buoyed him these past six years. The first two years away from Falconhurst, he'd wandered lost in Texas, miserable, driven. He'd raised himself some hell, until raising hell itself lost its appeal. He'd looked around for the career that was going to make him rich—richer even than he'd been back at Falconhurst. There was no traffic in black slaves out here or he'd have become the kingpin slaver. Cattle multiplied like sand fleas, lived on the country like rabbits. Land was cheap, plentiful. In six years he'd become one of the most successful men in Texas—as he'd have found success, affluence, anywhere he went, in whatever direction he turned his energies and strengths and will, as well as his innate acceptance of his own superiority among men.

He demanded position and power as his birthright. He was a Maxwell, a Hammond. He knew who he was.

He was proud of his achievement out here. His land spread forever, his, as far as he could see in any direction, and beyond. Flat and gleaming under the hot sky, from the dusty green willows and cottonwoods marking the course of a dry river bed to the stark foothills, hazy in the distance. For a long time this wide-flung land had stirred him faster than hot whiskey. The sunrise was overwhelming, the sky burning into infinity, the plains were wild and free, the ranges an immense region to tame and to own. The days were long and slow and relentlessly hot. This was savage land where not even the water was sweet, often tangy with an unpleasant oily aftertaste. The wind fought him and the sun wilted him and he stayed forever thirsty for clear, clean, sweet water. He'd made up his mind six years ago. He could run or he could bend this land to *his* will, make it pay him as the Hammonds and the Maxwells had beaten gold out of the black dirt of Alabama. He saw the gray plains, touched almost mockingly with willow green where one unbroken horizon line stretched out forever to merge with another. And it was his.

In six years his cattle rimmed the hills and sought meager shade in arroyos. His men beat cattle out of the chaparral thickets and out of rocky plateaus. He could sell off three thousand head today and round up countless more tomorrow—all wearing his brand. Back home in Alabama realizing a profit in slaves was a matter of eighteen or twenty years. Here you turned bulls and heifers into the grasslands and they began to multiply.

Suddenly, Cale Lambdin sank his spurs into the flanks of his exhausted horse. The animal lunged forward and Cale went racing into the ranchyard. "Damn fool will kill that horse," Paley said.

"He's beginning to turn it to clabber with me," Hammond said.

"Hell, he's just likkered up. Glad to be home. Tired. He don't mean nuthin'."

Watching three small children run out of the ranch

house, Hammond said nothing. But he wasn't sure Cale didn't mean anything riding in yelling. Lydia stood just outside the front door, her apron caught in her hand. Cale knew she'd be there, and it was Cale he wanted her to look at first. Damn white trash. He'd run him off the place.

The children ran screaming to meet Hammond. He swung down painfully from the saddle and tossed the reins to Paley, who led his mount to the corral. The children clutched at Hammond's legs, but he ignored them. One of them cried to be picked up, but he ignored that, too. He tossed them each a small poke of candy from the general store at Brazos Crossing and then he forgot them.

Lydia ran out from the shadowed stoop. She put out her arms as she ran and her lovely face was contorted with a smile of welcome and tears of relief. She flung herself against him with such force that he staggered and almost fell. As he recovered his balance, Lydia was kissing his face and throat and ears, laughing and pulling his head down to hers.

Angrily, he jerked away from her. He caught her arm, twisting it until she calmed down and stood silently at his side. Her dark face was bleak. He said, "Goddammit, Lydia. How many times I got to tell you? I don't no way appreciate displays like this in front of people. Goddammit, you're a grown woman and you got to act like it. And I purentee mean that thing."

XI

Soon after eight o'clock that night most lamps, lanterns and candles had been tamped out on the Maxwell ranch, even in the bunkhouse. A soft, impenetrable dark like that of a silent and bottomless pit settled in over the range, horizon to horizon. Even the distant blaze of stars did nothing to temper the obscuring darkness, rather intensified and reinforced its shadowy labyrinths and gloomy corridors.

Ham lay on the bed and watched Lydia undress. He felt a rush of warmth toward her, though he tried to remain angry. Anger was his most effective fulcrum for balancing their positions as master and—woman. This was what she was, no more, no less, though he admitted to a feeling of affection for her. But of course this could not be, her being a greaser and all and not purentee white. What he felt was not love. It couldn't be, could it? There was so much difference between them. She was dark-skinned. Not a nigger, admittedly, but a Mexican. Certainly she wasn't a white American like he was. He'd had little experience with love—he loved his father and he loved Falconhurst, but he had never been in love with a woman. Certainly not with Cousin Blanche, though he had married her, and dammit, had tried to make their marriage work. Still, he couldn't love Lydia, could he? He was a Maxwell, and his mother had been a Hammond. This in itself made him superior, different from Lydia, as his white skin set him apart and above her. He doubted he would ever love a white woman, and he couldn't let himself love a racial inferior like Lydia. That wouldn't help either one of them.

Watching her, feeling himself growing excited by her olive beauty, he was confused and troubled inside. Had he ever really *loved* any human being except his father? He knew he had not, and lying there, he recalled the aging man with a twist of agony. His eyes burned. You could almost say he had loved Lucretia Borgia—as much as any man could love a black woman who had been a surrogate mother to him. But that was different, too. Lucretia Borgia was black, but not like other niggers. She was almost human.

He watched Lydia remove her clothing in the lamplight. This made her different from white women. A white lady would hide in the closet to undress. At least, he'd always heard they did. But Lydia was as natural and unaffected as her children. She undressed right in front of him, though he had asked her a couple times not to do it; he didn't like a brazen woman.

His sweated anger dissolved under the loin-shocking charge of her tawny beauty exposed to him. She was a breathtaking goddess of a girl in her thin blouse and skirt of printed cotton. Out of them, she was stunning. There was beauty even in the high-arched perfection of her bare feet. Her Latin beauty, heightened by an ethereal, ancient sadness haunting her gentle black eyes, had captivated him the first time he saw her. In six years he had overcome that sense of wonder; he'd grown accustomed to her. She was his mistress, domestic, lackey, washerwoman; she bore him dark-skinned children toward whom he felt nothing more than the delight one might take in a litter of playful puppies. Despite all this, her loveliness could still make him ache across his nose, make him ill in the pit of his belly. He felt *something* for her. Something more than he'd ever felt for anyone else.

The lamplight lunged after her when she moved, drowning in the golden smoothness of her flesh. She loosened the slack bun of hair at the nape of her neck and it spilled almost to her waist. She wore her black hair parted severely in the center and brushed straight back. But when she grew heated during the day, soft tendrils, glittering with perspiration, curled about her face and neck like small promises, faint whispers of secret excitements. There was something of Aztec Indian in the squared lines of her delicate jaw, the slender column of her throat. Her inviting, sensual smile, brilliant and warm against the depths of old and unnamed sorrow swirling in her ebony eyes, gave her an aura of mystery, an allure that lingered hauntingly in your mind when you were away from her.

She reached out to take up her shapeless cotton gown from the back of a chair. Her body, despite three cruel labors and difficult deliveries in three years, was a bronze vision—round-breasted, flat-bellied, rounded hips, sculpted thighs, calves and ankles. He denied there could any longer be any air of mystery about her. She was honest and uncomplicated and devoted. And yet sometimes he wondered, could he ever entirely own her, body and soul? And no matter what happened to them, would he ever be able to wipe her completely from his mind?

Lydia sat for a moment on the side of the bed. He wanted to reach for her, but he did not move, though he felt himself growing rigid, engorged with blood. "The children missed you," she said.

He shrugged. "I was away because I had to be."

"I missed you."

"Told you. Had business," was all he said.

"I know." He watched her slender shoulders rise

as she drew in a deep breath and held it. "You hung the young boy from sweet springs . . . Ramon."

"Ramon? That his name?"

"His wife, Maria, is pregnant. He came here and asked you for work."

"How do you know all this?"

"I heard him ask you."

"I mean—about the trouble—at sweet springs?"

"A rider. For Kinlaw. Passed through on his way to town. He told me you were taking Ramon to Brazos Crossing to hang him."

"I'm tired," Ham said. "I haven't slept. An hour this afternoon. A couple hours before dawn. I'm dead tired. Blow out the lamp. Lie down. Whether you want to sleep or not, I do. I got to sleep—if it ain't too hot."

She went on sitting on the bed, facing away from him. He turned toward her but still did not reach out. "Do you want me to take off my gown?"

"What for?"

"To make love to you—if you want me."

"No. I'm tired. It's too hot."

"Are you punishing me?"

"For what?"

"Because I ran out to meet you—and made you angry—in front of Paley?"

"Blow out the lamp. Lie down."

She did not move. "Did you—kill the boy?"

"He stole a heifer. Slaughtered it. Right on my land."

"Do we have so few cows he cannot have one for his hungry family—for his pregnant wife?"

"You'd have me feed every greaser this side of the Rio, wouldn't you?"

"We have so much. Ramon—his family—they have so little. That's all."

"I work for what I got. Let them work."

"It is not always that easy."

"It wasn't easy for me. Nobody says it's easy. Nobody

says it's got to be easy. But there is law. We don't have law, we have nothing."

She shrugged those shoulders. "Laws say—a man and a woman—living together. Unwed. Have children together. Unwed. They break God's law. They live in sin."

"You knew I wouldn't marry you."

"No. I hoped. I prayed. I did all I knew."

"God almighty, Lydia. I'm too tired. Don't start that. You are my woman. You are—mine. I take care of you. I give you what you ask. But I can't marry you."

"You won't have me because you have no respect for me—no more than you have for Ramon and Maria."

"What in hell does that mean?"

"It means I cook for you, I wash for you, I bear your children, but I am not even a servant. I am less than that. Because a servant has respect. One must respect a good servant."

"Who says I don't respect you?"

"I do. You don't respect me—and so no one who comes here—or works here for you—has respect for me."

"They better. By God, they better."

She turned and stared at him, her ebony eyes brimmed with tears. "Those men out there. In that bunkhouse. Men that come here. They've all heard about me. They call me your—squaw. Your greaser woman."

"They sure hell better respect you. Or I'll run 'em off."

"Respect, Hammond? Respect? What you mean by respect? That they don't try to get under my skirt?"

"Yes, dammit. Yes. I call that respect. They better respect you. Or I'll sure run 'em off—if I don't kill 'em first."

She shook her head and wiped at a tear with her knuckle. "Is that because you care—about me? Or because you are—the boss? *El hombre muy grande. El patrone. El caballero.* The boss man with—the woman. They cannot touch *her*."

"That's right. They cannot."

She sobbed suddenly, helplessly.

"Aw hell, Lydia. Don't take on. You are mine. *Mine.* I take care of you. An' I take care of your suckers—"

"Those—suckers—Señor, damn you, are your suckers out of my womb."

"All right. I feed 'em well, don't I? No other half-breed kids live nearly as well, I can tell you. They'll always have what they want. Just like you will. I'll see to that."

"I will never have what I want. Not from you. Nor will our children."

"Jesus, Lydia. I'm tired. What do you want from me?"

"Is it too much—after six years—to ask you to marry me, before a priest, so I can live in peace, with myself, and with God?"

"Yes. Well, dammit, yes it is. You're a gr—a Mexican, Lydia—and I'm—well, a white man. From Alabama. It wouldn't work."

She spread her hands. "It works all right—like this. For you."

"Yes. And for you. . . . Try to understand me, Lydia. I don't want no white woman. No gringo woman. None. I want *you.* Ain't that enough?"

"Is it?"

"Well, hell yes. You—got your religion. I got mine. The Baptist Church is for Christians. It don't make no place for mixed marriages. I got my family name to think about."

"The wonderful Maxwells. And the Hammonds. Of Alabama. I've heard how *muy grande* they are."

"Well, they are good people. An' I'm sure yours are—good *Mexican* people."

"You think these Hammonds and Maxwells of Alabama—she would not think so high of me, eh?"

126

"They'd prob'ly like you, Lydia—an' they got to meet you. But that's it. It ain't *what* you are, Lydia. You're a wonderful girl. You work hard. You're good in bed—when you behave yourself and do it the way like God meant. . . . But it's *who* you are. I mean, I am a Maxwell. My mother was a Hammond—that does make me different."

She laughed in scorn. "You want I should rattle off names, Señor? You think I have no *grande* names in my past . . . only my babies—our *suckers*—have no name."

"Now you stop talkin' like that. You just make yourself sick."

"I talk as I wish. What can you do? Beat me? Run me off the place? Hang me, as you did Ramon? Sooner or later, these things will come to pass anyhow. Just be honest. For once, *por un momento,* look at the truth."

"Now, goddammit, Lydia. Anybody will tell you I am honest. Fair. Truthful."

"Oh, I am sure you believe you are all these things. You are so careful *what* you think."

"Lydia. I give you all I can. That's all I can do."

She shrugged and nodded. "I'll blow out the lamp now. . . . Do you want me to take off my gown, after all?"

"You might as well. I sure as hell can't sleep now."

She stood up and slipped the gown over her head. He felt himself go achingly rigid, his whole crotch in pain. With the light still on, she knelt beside the bed and said a prayer to the "little mother of Jesus," and asked a special prayer for Ramon.

She was silent for a moment and he lay watching her, aching with need. Suddenly she sprang forward like a lynx, thrust the cover away and began kissing his navel, his pubic hairs, his glans.

"Goddammit, Lydia." He pulled himself up and struck her backhandedly across the head. She cried out and toppled to the floor. He let her stay there for some moments. He raged inwardly. She had some perverted, Latin ideas about sex that were in terrible conflict with his ideas of what was appropriate in a bed. He'd had to slap her face before to keep her from loving him—down there—with her mouth. How revolting! In any good Christian home a woman laid flat on her back—white lady or bed wench—and a man mounted her. All the rest was perverted, a fearful sin in God's sight, and he wouldn't tolerate it.

At last she pulled herself up from the floor. She held a hand against the livid imprint of his knuckles on her face. She lay down with her back to him. Heaving a heavy sigh, he lay down on his back and stared at the ceiling. At last he said in a flat cold voice, "Blow out the lamp."

"Go to hell," she said.

"I won't have you doing that perverted stuff, Lydia. I've told you often enough."

She did not answer. He lay there, empty-bellied. His hands trembled. He wanted to reach for her. He could not force himself to do it. He closed his eyes. He sweated. He heard her ragged breathing. Distantly, one of the children coughed in its sleep. He heard the heavy knocking at the front door twice before he realized what it was.

He got up, slipped awkwardly into his pants without Lydia to help him. He did not ask her assistance and she did not move. He buttoned his fly, got his gun and took up the lamp as the knock was repeated.

The lamplight bounced yellowly across the sparsely furnished living room ahead of him. Its glow touched at the huge fieldstone fireplace, at handwoven rag rugs, bright with Aztec reds, at pine tables sand-smoothed and pillow-piled wooden chairs, a dilapidated leather-covered couch. It was a comfortable room where children played. It was a scrupulously clean room, scrubbed.

Holding the gun negligently at his side, Ham opened the thick wooden door. A shaft of saffron from the lamp illumined a long rectangle which showed a young boy and beyond him, a lathered horse quivering in its traces and a young girl slumped on the boot of the wagon.

Ham hefted the lamp slightly, checking the youth for a concealed weapon. He found nothing. The boy held his hands lax at his sides. Ham heard Lydia behind him padding across the parlor in her bare feet. "Who is it?" she asked.

Ham shrugged. "Who are you?" he said to the boy outside the door. "What do you want?

The youth answered, his voice edged with fatigue. Ham was not aware of what the stranger said. Pushing the lamp forward, he stared at the boy in the tightly buttoned black coat, Osnaburg britches and heavy run-over boots. But he was not seeing any of these external details. He was seeing himself—gazing incredulously at himself precisely as he most certainly had looked fifteen years ago—the blond hair, the gray eyes, showing exhaustion but a faint arrogance, the sandy brows, the thick-chested, wide-shouldered long trunk, the stocky legs. It was like peering into a time-lapse mirror, seeing oneself as you once were, and would never be again.

XII

"You people are plumb off the big trails," Ham said. "What you doin' out here?"

The boy flinched. "We're on our way to Waco."

"Waco? You're a hell of a jump from the trace to Waco." Ham continued to peer unwaveringly at the boy.

The youth hesitated, glanced over his shoulder. "Reckon we got lost." He tried tiredly to smile. "Lot of room in Texas to get lost. Yes. We got lost."

"You been lost a long time to get down this far." Hammond's chilled voice remained flat and uncompromising. Lydia touched his arm.

"Hammond, please," she said. "The boy is exhausted. You can see this."

"I am pretty well beat, ma'am." The blond boy smiled. "But me, I'm all right. I would most humbly appreciate food—hoecake, clabber, anything—for my wife . . . and water for my horse."

"Of course," Lydia said before Ham could speak. "Tell your wife to come in."

"They all right," Ham said. "Right where they is."

The boy's head jerked up. For a moment his tired gray eyes clashed against those of the older man, and they held. The boy bit his lip, forced himself to smile. He nodded, accepting Ham's dictum. "We all right out here, ma'am."

Lydia gazed up at Ham for a moment as if she had never seen him before, would not understand him if she spent the rest of her life with him. She stepped past Ham and went out into the vague shaft of light illumining the overhang. Ham followed, the lamp flickering in the sudden gusts of nightwind. "Help your wife down from the wagon," Lydia said to the boy. "What is your name?"

"Name's Frazee." The boy glanced oddly at Ham and then added, "First name is Tige, ma'am. Tige Frazee." He reached up and swung the dainty girl down from the wagon seat. He set her carefully on the stone flooring of the stoop. "This is my wife. Mrs. Tige Frazee. Her name is Nell, ma'am."

Lydia caught her breath. It was difficult to be certain about the girl's age. But she couldn't have been more than fifteen. Her pregnant condition was plain to see. She was far along in her pregnancy. Lydia, who had suffered agonized labor and perilous deliveries winced in sympathy for the girl's battering ride in the open wagon over broken country.

Nell tried to smile, but she appeared on the verge of collapse. Her face was pallid, her eyes dilated and swirling with exhaustion. Despite all this, she was incredibly pretty, with delicately shaped features, soft violet eyes and a gentle full-lipped mouth. Lydia saw at once that the girl had never done a day's housework— those dainty hands and long slender fingers had never scrubbed a floor, wielded a broom or been immersed in hot lye soap dishwater. This in no way prejudiced Lydia against her. She felt the pity well up inside her, and her eyes burned with compassionate tears. There was no law which said that everyone who wandered blindly into hell had to be prepared for the ride.

Lydia's first impulse was to take the girl in her arms and lead her into the battered parlor sofa. Ordinarily, Lydia acted on her impulses, and she would have now except that Ham had been so adamant in refusing to invite these poor young derelicts into his house. She glanced toward Ham again, sure that the wretchedly tired girl's condition had now softened his attitude toward Tige and his child wife. She believed that Ham was not cruel—often thoughtless, a compound of his blind prejudices—but he was a kindly man. She could not have lived with him even for these past six years were he less than kind. She found his face chilled, his manner unrelenting. Her shoulders sagging, Lydia said to the girl, "You should be in bed."

"We got no place for strangers," she heard Ham say. "No place at all except the bunkhouse. That ain't no place for a pregnant white lady."

"Of course it is not," Lydia said. "I will fix for her."

"We got no place," Ham repeated, his voice hardening. He stared straight into the face of the young boy. "I'm sorry. We got no place."

The boy did not retreat. He even managed to smile and nod. "I understand, sir. . . . If we could have a little food—and water for my horse—we'll move on."

"Yes," Ham said. "We'll get you some food while you water your horse."

"Sorry we can't pay you," the boy said.

"We've plenty," Lydia said. Her voice matched Ham's now, flint-hard and set against him, almost as if she dared him to oppose her. She placed her arm gently about the girl's shoulders. "Come with me into the kitchen while Tige cares for his horse. It will be all right. It will all be all right."

At Lydia's display of kindness, the girl burst into sudden tears. Lydia gazed for a moment at Ham's rigid face. Then she took the lamp from his hand and led the girl across the open breezeway, which was called a "dog-trot," and into the kitchen area of the house.

Ham went on standing under the overhang in the darkness. He said, "The waterin' trough's straight yonder, near the barn."

"Thank you, sir," the boy said. "I appreciate it—

whatever you're willing to do. It ain't been easy on Nell—crossin' the Texies."

"No. I reckon not," Ham said. "And followin' backtrails ain't made it a lot easier on her, I'd say."

Ham lit a lantern and hung it to one of the pinewood-pole supports of the overhang. The light did not reach the place where the boy had led the horse. Ham could not see him, but he went on standing there. The wind rose around him, gusting through the dog-trot and rushing in chill blasts against his bare chest on the stoop.

He glanced along the overhang, which ran across the wide front of the Texas house. The kitchen area, where Lydia had lighted three more lamps, built a fire in one of the fireplaces and was now stirring up the ashes in the wood-burning stove, was across the dog-trot from the living area, the parlor and the bedrooms. The house was shallow, the depth of two rooms, but it had a long, rambling look—like a hundred other Texas houses across these plains. The walls were adobe but, unlike most of his neighbors, Ham had hauled in planking for wooden flooring.

He felt a sense of pride, thinking that while his place followed the standard design, this was a rich man's ranchhouse. Each bedroom had its own fireplace; a larger fieldstone fireplace dominated the parlor. The kitchen and dining area across the breezeway—left open to invite prevailing winds—were heated by fireplaces and boasted an iron wood-burning stove which had been shipped from Dallas.

In the silence he could hear the horse snuffling up water at the trough. From the kitchen he could hear Lydia speaking softly, reassuringly, even finding something to laugh about. He felt the cold knot of anger against her congeal like a taut fist in his solar plexus.

The boy returned, leading the exhausted horse across the barren yard. He glanced at Ham, who did not speak, then he swung up on the wagon seat and sat waiting.

Ham would have left him there, but the screen door

at the dog-trot whined open and Lydia called, "Don't sit out there. Come on in. I've got hot coffee and eggs and ham. You'll feel better after you eat."

The youth glanced at Ham, his face taut. When Ham said nothing, Tige leaped down from the wagon and crossed the dog-trot. Lydia said, "Come on in, Ham. You can eat with us."

Ham entered the dining area, but shook his head. "Reckon I'm not hungry," he said.

Lydia laughed at him. "Maybe you'll feel better after you eat something. I've—never seen you act like this. . . . Well, not very often."

Nell was slumped at the table, drinking coffee from a large tin cup. Tige went to the chair beside hers, where Lydia had set out plate, knife, fork and spoon. He stood a moment, hesitant, until Lydia laughed at him again. "Sit down. Eat. You are among friends— really you are. Aren't they, Ham?"

"Sit down," Ham said to the boy. "Eat."

"Thank you." The boy sat. For a brief beat, the boy and girl bowed their heads and said a brief, inaudible prayer and crossed themselves.

Lydia spoke happily. "You are Catholics?"

"Nell is," Tige said. "I try to do what pleases her."

"Looks like you tried too hard," Lydia said, laughing. For a moment, the exhausted Tige didn't understand. Then he laughed.

"She was trying to please me," he said.

Nell tried to smile. "We love each other. Very much."

"Why, I am sure you do," Lydia said. She turned toward where Ham had slumped into a rocker half across the room. "Can you believe it, Hammond? They've come all the way from Louisiana."

"Yes. I can believe that," Ham said without warmth.

"We are truly sorry—to cause you trouble like this, so late at night and all," Tige said. "Maybe you can tell us how far to the next town?"

"Fifteen miles," Ham said. Both the boy and his

wife seemed to sag inwardly at the distance, but Lydia shook her head.

"Fifteen miles. And then what is there? A general store—and a mission. Why, with that tired horse it is four hours, at least, to Brazos Crossing."

Ham shrugged. "But—like you said—they've come all the way from Louisiana. Fifteen miles can't seem like much."

"Oh, no," the boy agreed.

"Well, they didn't come all the way from Louisiana in one night." Lydia said. "We can fix beds for them in the children's room. We can put the two little ones on the couch in the parlor."

"No," Tige said. "That would be asking too much."

"Nonsense. Poor Nell. Look at her. She is ready to drop. You eat your supper. I'll fix the bed."

"No," Ham said.

All three of them turned and stared at him. Only Tige seemed unastonished at the sharp cold tone. Ham said, "They can't stay in the house. I said it. We got no place for them."

Lydia's voice matched his. Her dark eyes glittered like puma's eyes in the lamplight. "They can't go on tonight."

"There's a bed in the tack room. Out at the barn. They can stay there—tonight. Or they can go on."

Lydia peered at Ham for a long beat. Then suddenly her olive face lighted with a smile. "Yes. You will be fine out there. While you eat, I'll get sheets and spreads."

"Please don't go to any more trouble, Mrs. Maxwell," Nell said.

"Oh, I am not Mrs. Maxwell," Lydia said. She stared directly at Ham. "I am his housekeeper. I take care of his house—and his children. Also, I bear them."

Ham's face flushed red. He said nothing and went on sitting immovable in the rocking chair. Tige and Nell ate in silence. Ham felt his congealed rage against Lydia distending in his belly. It was enough to make him sick. Damn her. She'd been a spitfire since the day he met her, but she had no business in this world trying to disparage and embarrass him in front of these people—especially in front of these people.

Lydia sat at the table with her guests. She drank coffee and nibbled at the bread she'd heated for their supper. She chatted casually, urging Tige and Nell to have more food, more coffee. She did not glance toward Ham again. Tension crackled between them in the room.

When they had eaten, Lydia and Nell carried folded sheets, blankets and pillows, Ham carried a lantern and Tige led the horse out to the tack room at the barn.

Cale Lambdin came out of the bunkhouse. His hair was tousled, and he wore only his boots and britches. His bared chest glowed in the lamplight, his muscles thick and corded. Ham said, "Get some clothes on." Cale stared at Ham's own bared body.

"What's wrong?" Cale said. He bowed toward Lydia and Nell. "Ladies. Forgive my undress. I was afraid something was wrong, Miz Lydia."

"Nothing's wrong," Ham said. "Go on back to bed."

Cale gazed directly at Lydia. "Good night all—Miz Lydia."

Ham felt his inner rages and frustrations mounting. They fired up a second lantern, and by its light, Lydia swept out the tack room and Nell helped her prepare the aged mattress on the rope supports of the iron frame. "It'll just be fine," Nell kept saying, to Lydia, to herself, to the tack room. She shivered suddenly, chilled in her own private hell.

Ham watched Tige rub his horse down. The boy knew animals, obviously loved them. He was careful with his horse, thoughtful, taking his time. At last Ham said, voice flat but not grudgingly, "There's hay there.

Some corn and oats. You might want to make the animal a mixture. You can stable him there—keep him away from my animals."

Tige thanked him and smiled, but Ham merely shrugged. When they returned to the tack room, it was clean, lighted, the bed made with thick blankets turned back. "Gets real cold before dawn," Lydia said. "Soon as ever you see a light up at the house, come on up to the house. Old Estelle and I will have breakfast ready."

Nell went close to Lydia. She tried to contort her tired face into a smile. "I want to thank you—for all your kindness." She burst into helpless tears and Lydia drew her into her arms.

"You're just tired," Lydia said. "You're just tired. It's going to be all right. In the morning, things will look better. You'll see."

Ham gazed at the boy. Tige had taken a step toward where Lydia stood holding Nell in her arms, and then he stopped. He glanced toward Ham; their gazes brushed, touched, held. Ham's face remained chilled.

Ham and Lydia walked slowly across the bare yard toward the ranchhouse. Ham carried the lantern at his side. The glow lunged ahead of them and Lydia watched it silently. Behind them, horses stirred and whinnied in the corral. The wind rose and sand whipped against them. Lydia pushed her hair back from her face. Stars prickled the highest heavens. They could hear Nell's muffled weeping and Tige's whispering to her, concerned but helpless.

"You got to stop taking in every tramp that comes to the door," Ham said. He held open the screen and Lydia preceded him into the parlor.

"Why? They were not Mexicans."

"No. They weren't Mexicans."

"In fact, they were *norteamericanos*. From the South. Your own home. And yet you would not even allow them to sleep one night in your house."

"House ain't no place for a nigger to sleep, no more'n it is for a dog."

She turned, staring at him, her face bleak.

Ham nodded. "That boy's a nigger."

"Why, he's whiter than you are—looks much as you might have when you were only a boy. . . . Only I guess being a *muy grande* Maxwell y Hammond, you were never tired and scared."

"Never had the reason to be scairt like he does. That boy is a nigger, all right. A nigger and a runner. And he's the worst kind because the black bastard has taken a young white girl as his wife."

She drew a deep breath, held it. "Well, at least he married her," Lydia said.

XIII

The next morning Tige awakened early. There was a pungent, acrid freshness in the air that invigorated him and lifted his spirits. They were far from the swamps and mildew of Louisiana, the sight and smell of slavery. Maybe that was freedom he could smell in the chill new morning.

When he saw lamplight glowing in the kitchen window at the ranchhouse, he roused Nell gently, shaking her shoulder lightly and kissing the nape of her sleep-heated neck. She opened her eyes and looked around, troubled, but trying to smile "No. Don't kiss me," she said. "My mouth's so dry." He laughed and tried to kiss her forcibly, but she buried her face into the pillow. He said they ought to get up. All the day promised was to be long—and they might as well get started.

Nell was still shaky, disoriented, frightened and so tired she yawned helplessly as she washed her face in the bucket of well water Tige brought her. Once she was dressed in fresh underthings and a cotton print dress she'd called a "morning house frock" back in Louisiana, she felt a little better. She was young; she had hope, and despite everything, she had Tige. She refused to think back to Louisiana. She was afraid to remember, afraid to believe in this present or to trust their reluctant host who looked at them so coldly and yet let them sleep in his tack room. And she was most frightened of all to look ahead. What was to become of them? Where would they go?

She clutched Tige's hand tightly without speaking and clung to him fiercely. He brushed her cheek with a light kiss, but he didn't try to reassure her, afraid to trust his own voice. Nell was young, in many ways still a little girl, but in others she was wise far beyond her years; often she interpreted Tige's true meanings not from what he said at all, but from the tone of his voice. There was much she understood intuitively. This had to explain her wisdom, because she'd been overprotected and almost wholly inexperienced on the backwater Louisiana plantation where she'd grown up.

"Are you hungry?" he asked.

She nodded, holding tightly to his hand. They walked across the yard together in the extraordinary brilliance of the orange, cerise and scarlet sunrise that splashed the sky and tinted the earth from horizon to horizon. They found the cowhands already at work. The men they met bobbed their heads or touched their battered work hats in polite greetings. "What's your name, fella?" one cowhand asked Tige. When Tige told him, the young man asked, "Goin' to be round long, Tige?" Tige shook his head and said he reckoned they'd move on today. The young cowpuncher smiled. "You do what you got to do, Tige, but I wouldn't git that little lady too far from a midwife." Nell smiled, blushing, and pressed close to Tige's side. Tige waved toward the boy. "We'll be all right," Tige said. "We'll be fine."

Lydia greeted them warmly when they entered the ranchhouse kitchen hesitantly. Her heart sinking, Nell saw that Lydia's eyes looked tired—as if she'd spent a sleepless night. She hoped that she and Tige had not caused trouble between these people—the woman whom she loved and the man she feared.

Lydia smiled and drew Nell into her arms as if the girl were her younger sister. She held Nell tightly a moment to reassure her. Then she lightly touched Tige's

142

cheek and invited them to sit down to a table of steaming food. Lydia introduced them to Estelle, a stout aging Mexican woman sprouting a faint gray mustache on her upper lip. "Eat," Estelle said, nodding toward the table. "Eat." She waved them toward the chairs. Her English obviously was limited, but her smile was warm and generous.

Ham Maxwell limped into the kitchen while Tige and Nell were eating. The small children looked up from their plates, smiling and screaming his name, but Ham ignored them. Lydia poured coffee into an earthenware mug before the large chair at the head of the table, but Ham sat in the rocker. "Ain't hungry yet," he said.

Tige finished his meal hurriedly and said he'd better check on his horse. He thanked Estelle and Lydia for the excellent breakfast. He gave Nell a quick kiss on the cheek and went out the door. When Tige was gone from the room and his place setting had been removed by Estelle, Ham sat down at the table.

When Nell finished her meal, she wanted to help Estelle and Lydia, but Lydia would not let her. "You're a guest," she said. "We don't get too many guests, eh, Hammond?"

Eating, Hammond shrugged his shoulders. He bent over his plate, sopping a biscuit in gravy. While Ham was still eating, Tige returned from the barn. He stood, stiff and awkward, just inside the kitchen door. "Our horse looks rested. He ate good too, thanks to you, Mr. Maxwell. . . . I reckon Nell and me better get started—unless you got work you want done, for our food and bed and all."

"You don't owe us anything," Lydia said. "We were glad to help you. Weren't we, Hammond?" Lydia stopped speaking when she turned and found Ham pushed back in his big chair, his right leg extended before him. She was shocked when Ham said, "We got

143

work around here—things the cowhands don't relish doin', but that's got to be done."

"I'm not afraid of work," Tige said.

Ham glanced up, peering from under his sandy brows at the boy. "No. I reckon you're not. Come from good stock, I reckon. And it's likely work you're used to—cleanin' out stables, stalls, pitching hay, cutting firewood, milking the cows in the pens. Them white boys hate milkin'."

At the words "white boys" Nell's head jerked up and Tige flinched slightly. But his voice remained flat. "I'll do whatever you think I ought to—to pay what I owe you."

"It ain't that you owe me nuthin'," Ham said. "It's like Miz Lydia told you—you and your wife, last night, you-all our guests. Don't owe me nuthin'. But you might want to make a few dollars—if you stay on for a few days."

Tige glanced at Nell. She nodded almost imperceptibly. Tige hesitated a long beat, then said, "That's tolable kind of you, Mr. Maxwell—suh."

Tige spent the entire morning out in an open wagon with saws and axes cutting firewood. He returned a little past one. The rear of the wagon was stacked high with dry pine, oak, gum and elm cut in stovewood lengths. The wagon rattled up to the rear of the kitchen where the logs and firewood was stacked.

Ham limped out into the dog-trot. He stood in the shade with the children hanging onto his booted legs and watched Tige unload and stack the firewood. The boy's fair skin was sun-blistered and his shirt was sweated through. Ham said, "You done a good job, boy. I've had two of my cowpokes go out in the hammocks and come back with less many times." He smiled. "Most times."

"Thank you, Mr. Maxwell—suh."

144

Ham shook one of the children from his leg. "You look familiar, Tige. I evah seed you before, boy?"

Tige went on working. He didn't look up. "No, suh. I don't think so. I'd recollect."

"Nevah been in Alabama?"

The slight hesitation, then the shrug. "No, suh. Nevah have had that pleasure—suh."

Ham lit a cigar. "You say your name is Tige?"

"Yes, suh. Real name is Adam. But friends call me Tige."

"Nobody ever called you Tiger?"

The boy returned with a stack of firewood from the wagon before he answered. He shook his head. "Uh . . . no, suh."

"Not even when you were—a little boy?"

"No, suh . . . not that I remember, suh."

Ham drew deeply on the cigar and exhaled a long spume of gray smoke. He watched the boy work and spoke, in an idle tone, as if recalling something unrelated from his past.

"Knew a mustee child once. You know what a mustee is—part white, part Nigra?"

"Don't know much about that, suh."

"They look almost white. Some of them do look white. You didn't know, you might take a mustee for white. But a mustee ain't white. That's the law. They got one drop of Nigra blood, they is Nigras and that's what they is, no matter how they try to change it. You can sell a mustee Nigra just as you could sell the blackest *bozal* off the boat from Africa."

"Never heard anything about all this—where I come from," Tige said.

"Where you say you hail from?"

"My folks was pore—dirt farmers. From up Kentucky way."

"That you—practically a Yankee."

Tige grinned faintly and shrugged. "Almost, I reckon."

"You sure hell got one runny-grits accent—for a Yankee, boy."

Tige spread his hands. "You catch a Louisiana accent quick, I reckon. My pa was—overseer—on a plantation in Louisiana."

"That where you met Miss Nell, I reckon."

"Yes, sir. We decided to come out to the Republic of Texas. We heard stories about people gettin' rich out here."

"What was the name of the plantation where your pa was overseer? Where you met Miss Nell?"

Tige chewed at his underlip a moment and then he shrugged. "It was at Hiddenbrook Plantation, suh."

"Hiddenbrook . . . Hiddenbrook . . . I know that plantation. Met the owner a few times at slave auctions in New Orleans. Did some business with him over the years. Name of Randolph. Foye Randolph."

Tige nodded. "Yes, sir. That's the name. Mr. Foye Randolph. He was—he is Nell's stepfather."

"Stepfather, eh? What'd he think about you two up and runnin' off to the Republic of the Texies like this?"

Tige smiled. "He didn't like it very much. I won't pretend he did."

"No. I reckon he didn't." His face remained implacable. "You might as well go in the kitchen and git something to eat. You done a good day's work. . . . How much you reckon I owe you?"

"I leave that to you, suh."

"Well, I figure if you was one of my white cowhands, you earned about a dollar this morning."

"That'll be a big help to me, suh."

"Yes. Well, suppose I just hang on to it for you . . . till you and your lady are ready to move on. Then we'll figure room and board and any other deducts, see what I owe you then."

"Yes," Tige said. "I see." Their gazes met and held.

Ham leaned against the wall. He watched Tige take up three small bouquets of wild flowers, stems wrapped in a soaked crokersack, from the wagon boot. Tige carried the flowers into the kitchen. Ham stayed where he was, hearing Estelle, Lydia and Nell exclaiming over the wild primroses, daisies, asters, bluebonnet, redbud, plum and catclaw blossoms. Ham shook his head. You'd of thought the boy brought them diamonds at least. . . .

In the next few days, Tige continued to work, and nothing more was said about pay. One night, in their tack-room bed, Nell asked Tige if Ham was planning to pay him. "You work so hard. Work those other men hate to do."

"Yes. They like having me here. They hate milking cows worst of all. The older ones won't do it, no way. They'd quit and haul stakes first."

"You're doing a lot of their work."

"I don't mind. You're resting. You're gettin' milk to drink. Clabber. Good food. Miz Lydia sure likes having you around."

"She lets me take care of the children all day."

"An' we ain't runnin' scared—"

"Still, he ought to pay you."

"We need the money, all right."

"I'll ask Lydia. In the morning."

"No. Don't do that."

"Why not?"

"Might make him mad. Easy for me to make him mad. No sense doing that."

"Why doesn't he like you?

Tige sighed heavily. "Don't worry about it. When we're ready to leave—likely he'll settle up with us then."

"I don't trust that man. He treats you—so cold. Like you're not even human. . . . Yet he keeps us on here. . . . Sometimes, I get scared. I feel like if we tried to leave, he wouldn't let us go."

Tige drew her into his arms. She was trembling as

147

if cold. "Maybe he just wants to help us—because we're all from the South, even if he does think he's—better than I am."

"I've known planters—and plantation owners—just like him."

"So have I." His laugh was rueful.

"I didn't like them. . . . Sometimes, this Mr. Maxwell—he reminds me of Foye Randolph." She shuddered, pressing closer.

"He ain't Foye Randolph, Nell."

"He could be so kind—sometimes he looks like you—"

"Yes—"

"Like you might look in ten years—or fifteen. Except he looks mean and tricky—and you're pretty. And honest."

"I am pretty, all right."

She tried to smile. "That's why I married you." Her eyes clouded and she sobered, her voice chilled. "That's why I want us to get away from here—before something bad does happen. Away from here . . . away from him. . . . Maybe we ought to go now, Tige. Tonight."

"No." He stared up into the darkness. "I won't let *him* make me run. I'll go—when I want. When we want to."

"I want to go now."

"Tomorrow then. If you want to go, we'll talk to him—about pay. . . . Meantime you go to sleep. We can't mistrust him. I want to trust him . . . we got to trust somebody."

The next day was a long one which Tige spent pitching hay in the barn. He saw Nell playing with the Maxwell children in the yard. She looked healthy again, rested, the terror gone out of her eyes. For the moment he was content. It was suppertime before he got to speak to Ham at all. He came into the dining area while Ham and the children were eating. Tige did

148

not move to join Ham at the table. Lately, Lydia
had been preparing her meal to eat with Estelle, Tige
and Nell, after Ham and the children were fed. At
those times, Ham sat across the room and watched
them, his face chilled, and he never joined in their
laughter. Lydia found much to laugh about—the sound
lovely and musical, even in this lonely place.

Tige stood near the door, a battered hat Ham had
given him gripped in his fists. He said, "Nell and I
been thinking, Mr. Ham. We been here long enough.
We don't want to wear out our welcome. You-all been
most kind. . . . We thought we might move on—in the
morning."

"Oh, no," Lydia said. She turned from the stove,
her face sweated.

"Where you think on to go?" Ham said, chewing.
He looked up, his face expressionless.

Tige shrugged. "Where we can find work for me—
a place for Nell."

Ham's laugh was cold and not meant to be shared.
"Ain't we found work enough for you around here?"

"You've been most kind. It's just that we know we
got to move on sooner or later." Tige glanced toward
Nell. "We thought—if you reckoned to owe me a few
dollars over our room and board, we'd have a little
stake."

"Don't reckon I owe you much yet," Ham said.
"Not enough to git you very far."

Nell caught her breath audibly, and Lydia turned
again from the stove, her face taut. Tige's shoulders
sagged, but his voice remained level. "All right, sir.
Whatever you think is fair. Nell and me, we're real
beholden to you—and pay or no pay we reckon to
move on."

Lydia said, "You've worked hard, Tige. You've
earned some money—but that's not important,
Tige. . . . It will be dangerous on the trail—in open

wild country—for Nell. In her condition. She'll be due soon."

"We got to move on sometime," Tige said.

Lydia enclosed Nell in her arm. "But not now. Wait. Until Nell has had her baby. . . . I promise you, Estelle is the best midwife north of the Rio Grande. And I know."

"Yes," Ham said in a flat tone. "I don't think you ought to try to leave yet. Stay on awhile. . . . You ought to be safe here."

They said no more. Nell shivered, in the heat of the kitchen, in the security of Lydia's light embrace. Tige said, "I got some milking to do." He left the room, deeply troubled. He could not say why, but he was dead certain Nell's intuition was right again. They should move on. They should leave this place. Now.

Ham came out of the kitchen door about an hour later. The sunset was purpling the dry plains, deepening arroyos, shading the trees in several tints. Tige stood near the milch cow pens. The boy leaned heavily, sagging against the gatepost.

Ham limped out across the yard toward where Tige stood, squinting, staring eastward, to the horizon and beyond. The mustee was gazing along his back trail. Ham said, "Something on your mind?"

Tige spun around, startled. He had not heard Ham's approach. He shook his head. "No. Nothing."

"Just watching the sunset? Or is somebody out there chasing you?"

Tige sighed. "Why you ask anything like that?"

"Wasn't asking, exactly. That's your concern. Don't pry. Just meant . . . nobody in his right mind would chase a man from Louisiana clear this far. Not this far across the Texies."

"No. I guess not."

"Not even a runaway nigger," Ham said, watching the boy's face. "Even a nigger—an' he made it acrost the Sabine River into the Republic—he'd likely be safe."

"I reckon."

"No nigger worth such a long chase."

"No."

Ham spat. "Still. They is crimes that keeps the law on the man's trail . . . eh?"

"I don't know . . . I don't know anything about that, Mr. Maxwell. I got worries enough—thinkin' about Nell and me—and our baby. . . . I don't know nuthin' about no crimes, or runaway niggers—nuthin' like that. Nuthin'."

XIV

Despite the tensions, Tige was able to find some laughter in the uncertainty of life at Maxwell Ranch. He was naturally a cheerful, optimistic and buoyant person, able to overcome melancholy. In fact, he'd decided if he were less resilient he wouldn't have made it this far. You had to believe in tomorrow when there turned out to be nothing in today. He liked people; he liked the people at the ranch. Lydia was a pleasure to be near; she found fun in the simplest things. You'd think she'd never smile, never find a reason for smiling in her oppressive existence as Ham Maxwell's "blanket squaw." Yet the musical sound of her laughter brightened the ugliest day at the ranch, kept her children secure. Nell was happier—if not content, at least well-fed. Her complexion was lovelier than it had ever been. She loved Lydia, loved being near her. Tige visited with the younger hired hands at the bunkhouse. They accepted him warmly, invited him into their five-card poker games. He never joined them because he couldn't bring himself to admit aloud that he'd never learned poker. He watched; he laughed when they did, but he didn't comprehend. His ignorance of poker reminded him of Estelle's eternal skirmish with *inglés*. The fat Mexican woman was warmth itself. She wanted to please—she would do anything to make the members of Lydia's family happy. But the rudiments of the

English language were beyond her; she was never going to *comprender*. Often she smiled and said, *"Bueno,"* when she had no inkling of what had been said to her. Her empty, hopeful smile betrayed her.

She had his deepest sympathy and understanding. What did he know? Nell had taught him to read a few words, to sign his own name. Law in Louisiana forbade teaching a black to read or write. But they had broken more serious statutes. It didn't seem important that they shattered this one, too.

Tige loved to talk with Estelle, to watch her unwavering smile, the way she nodded and understood nothing. The way the glassy emptiness of her ebony eyes gave her away.

He sat with Estelle sometimes, exchanging an English word for a Spanish one. Estelle wanted to learn obscenities because she had the powerful suspicion that the unprincipled young cowhands smiled at her and said unspeakable things to her in English. She would like to be sure. She would break *unas cabezas* if what she suspected proved to be true.

They would work for a while, but Estelle grew restive. She was an old dog, she told him in Spanish. Too old by far to learn anything as tricky as *el inglés*. Why did they not in English put the subject where he belonged? In Spanish it was clear one spoke of *el caballo* because one put the horse up front in the sentence where it belonged.

Lydia translated all this, and they laughed, and Estelle gave them blank stares, incredulous that she had said so much.

Despite his fears, the life at the ranch was not all miserable or filled with tensions. There were—with Lydia and her children, with the young fellows and their horseplay in the bunkhouse, with the smiling Estelle, and most important of all, close to Nell—moments of delight and love, and laughter, and they hoarded all these treasures, each in his own way. It could not last. It would not. But from Lydia they learned perhaps the most important lesson of all. One let tomorrow take care of its woes; one found what happiness one could in this present moment.

Ham stood waiting in the bright sunlight of the barnyard when Tige came from the kitchen door. Ham bobbed his head in a curt greeting but didn't meet Tige's eyes. Ham said, "Glad you decided to stay on— for a while."

Tige spread his hands. He couldn't tell this man he was afraid to stay on, afraid to try to leave, afraid of *him,* could he? He managed to smile. "I don't know what to do. I am worried about Nell. Out on the trail and all. Miz Lydia's right—Nell could have our baby most any day now."

"Have you thought what it's going to be like, traveling with a new baby and all?"

Tige shook his head and attempted another faint smile. He felt uncomfortable with Ham, drawn taut in the belly. "Nuthin's ever real easy, is it?"

Ham did not bother to answer the boy's smiling. He said curtly that there were fallen trees down on the south range, dried logs that would make good firewood if cut in lengths and hauled in. He offered to send along one of the younger men with Tige, but Tige refused the offer. He could handle it alone.

Still deeply troubled, Tige touched the slouched brim of the old work hat they'd given him and walked past Ham toward the barn. He hitched a dray horse to an open wagon, loaded axes and gear, telling himself he should be hitching his own horse, his own wagon, preparing to clear out. He and Nell had to move on— and yet, with the baby due momentarily, how could they?

Ham was just finishing a leisurely breakfast of fried ham and eggs about an hour later when the sound of hooves of horses and the rattle and squeal of carriage wheels reached in from the yard. The children ran screaming out to the overhang, jumping up and down with excitement. Dogs barked loudly. Ham wiped his mouth with a napkin and went out to greet the arrivals. Two men sat in a black buggy, smartly painted but dust-caked. The single-seater carriage had large thin wheels for speed, and oilcloth roofing and supports to which curtains could be attached in foul weather, for comfort. A glass shield was turned down over the splashboard.

When Ham sent the children protesting into the kitchen and silenced the dogs, one of the men dismounted stiffly while the other remained seated, watching Ham with a tentative smile. The first thing Ham noticed about the men was that both wore guns holstered to their belts.

The man who swung stiff-muscled down to the hard-packed earth was extremely tall, towering over Ham, and his height was exaggerated by a formal beaver high hat. He seemed somewhere in his forties, his sandy mustache salted with gray, his wide shoulders slightly stooped, lines baked about his eyes and mouth. The other man was stout, rotund, sweated and miserable in the heat. One saw he stayed in the buggy for no reason other than that he seldom moved anywhere until he had to. He was a few years younger that the tall man; he wore a slouch hat and a whipcord suit, and his potbelly lapped over his belt. Another common denominator about the two was a predatory look—a watchfulness of the restless eyes, perhaps more vulture than hawk. . . .

The tall man introduced himself. "Name's Milford Thigpen, sir. Friends call me Mil. Hope you will. Hope you will. And yonder in the buggy, hugging any shade he can find, is my partner Zack Bugas."

"Pleased." Bugas bobbed his round head and let his eyes travel, watchful.

Ham introduced himself and asked them into the

parlor. "Out of the heat. Texies hot is like no other."

"That's the truth." Bugas mopped his face with a soiled handkerchief and with deliberate caution alighted from the buggy. He steadied himself, one pudgy hand on an iron wheel rim. He breathed heavily, breathless from the exertion.

"Reckon you're wonderin' what Mr. Bugas and I are doin' so far off the main trail?" Thigpen said.

Ham shrugged. "Folks do wander over this way. Usually when they do, though, they're lost. Bad lost."

"We're not lost, sir," Thigpen said as if somehow his honor had been impugned.

Ham held the door open for them. They entered the comparative cool of the parlor. Estelle brought in glasses, a pitcher of lemonade freshly made with cold well water and an unopened bottle of corn whiskey. She retreated. Ham waved his hand toward the refreshments. Thigpen bowed and poured himself half a tumbler of whiskey, splashed in some lemonade. The stout Bugas drank his whiskey straight, wincing and wiping sweat from his furnace-fiery face. Ham could see the livid red pustules of prickly heat lining Bugas's collar. The fat man sat heavily on the old divan. Ham sank into his own comfortable easy chair. Thigpen, less at ease, placed his tall smokestack hat on a table and sat, as if at military attention, on a straight chair.

"Mr. Bugas and I are detectives," Thigpen said.

Ham nodded. "Figured you might be."

"Not with any regular law-enforcement agency," Bugas said. "Though both Mil and I did serve with the New York City police for a spell."

"We got us what amounts to a profitable line," Thigpen volunteered. "We hunts down people—fugitives—men mostly who have run for one reason or another and somebody wants 'em brought back. That's what we do—for a profit."

"For a bounty?" Ham suggested. "Met several bounty hunters here in the Republic. Reckon it is profitable, returning fugitives from the United States."

"Yes, sir. It's a lucrative business. Mr. Bugas and I have our offices in downtown Natchez. Though we spend a lot of time on the road. Been an alarmin' increase in nigger runaways these past few years. Don't know why it is. . . . These young blacks—they's restive, you know."

"It's all that goddam abolitionist propaganda that's got 'em all stirred up," Ham said. "Used to have no trouble at all like that with our slaves." He shook his head. "My pappy and me, we never had a runner. We treated our niggers good, but they knowed we was master."

"I see you know where you're at when it comes to niggers," Bugas said.

Ham mixed some whiskey and lemonade. "You could say that."

"Things happen nowadays you never dreamed of a few years ago back in the States," Bugas said. "Nigger uprisings. Nigger murders. Runners that will kill if anyone tries to stop 'em."

"I can see payin' fellows like you for running down a prime buck that the slave patrollers can't find—"

"Slave patrollers!" Bugas laughed. "Pardon me, sir. But slave patrollers is political jobs. Anytime you got a government worker, you got a political worker, and he ain't worth a shit, usual. Slave patrollers catch slaves just about when some slave turns himself in to them. An' too they's been some bad trouble with rednecks on slave patrol. Rabble that just plumb hates a nigger because of his skin. Nigger haters. They mutilate when they catch a runner. Sometime they returns a wench—or a prime buck—and they ain't fittin' for use no more for nuthin'."

"We run a quality service. Satisfaction guaranteed," Thigpen said. "Or it don't cost our clients one thin penny. You got to be reputable to have a warranty like that."

158

"I can see that. But—fellows like you. Right costly. Chasing a buck into the Republic like this. Must be some prize animal you're after."

"No, sir. Hit's a killer we're looking for," Bugas said.

"We're working kindly semiofficial this time," Thigpen said. "Oh, we ain't connected with the law. But the law has put a price on this killer's head—five thousand gold dollars. Dead or alive. . . . Now, we can afford even to pay out a little here and there for real helpful information and still make our expenses."

Ham nodded. "And you think your killer came this way?"

Thigpen spread his long-fingered, scarred hands. "We think so. We're sure only what trails he *didn't* follow. We don't yet know where he *is*. What we know for sure is where he *ain't* been seen."

"That's what brought us down here," Bugas said. "It was a heinous crime, Mr. Maxwell. This nigger— he's a mustee—sandy-colored hair and kind of gray eyes with spots of brown in 'em. His papers say his dam was an octoroon and his pa a purentee white man. . . . Well, what happened was, he was sold to Hiddenbrook Plantation. That's a showplace, sir. Not too far north of New Orleans. Some fine old homes, great old families down there. An' none finer than Hiddenbrook. Used to be called the Murdoch place, too. Maybe you heard of it when you was back in the States?"

"Yes." Ham waited.

"Well, Neville Murdoch—that was Murdoch's name —got the yellow jack. Died. His wife, Miz Myrtle, married a young man named Foye Randolph. From a fine old family. Mr. Foye Randolph ran the plantation—maybe even more profitably than Mr. Murdoch had. They had money. Lovely home. Looked like they had everything."

"I've met Mr. Foye Randolph," Ham said.

"Have you now?" Thigpen shook his head as if he

could never cease to marvel at the smallness of this old world. "Then you'll be doubly grieved I'm sure to learn that Mr. Foye Randolph was foully slain—upstairs in a bedroom of his own mansion—by one of his slaves."

"The mustee nigger?" Ham prompted.

"That's correct, sir. Roused the entire white population of the area into a frenzy."

"I can reckon it would," Ham said. "A man ain't safe in his own house no more?"

"Exactly, sir. That's what we all got to ask ourselves these days," the tall thin man said. "This mustee not only killed Mr. Foye Randolph, a most respected plantation owner, he stole a horse and wagon. And, by God, you won't believe this, but he taken Mr. Foye Randolph's stepdaughter—a young white lady of fifteen years, mind you—and he run."

"How long ago this happen?" Ham inquired.

"Some months now. Maybe six months ago. We think the mustee—they called him Tige, and he was most trusted at Hiddenbrook—took the girl first to New Orleans. They stayed there until the money ran out—"

"You mean this white girl went with this nigger willing, of her own accord?" Ham asked.

"I hate to make such an allegation about a white lady, sir. But they ain't a shred of evidence turned up that she fought the black at all. Went willing, all right. They is talk she was even three months pregnant—when she ran away with him."

"One of them white sluts," Ham said.

"She come from the finest stock. Both Mr. Murdoch and Miz Myrtle. Highly respected. Churchgoin'. God-fearin'. But, yes, sir, it do look like she may be, like you say, a no-good slut."

"They got to be all kinds, I reckon, much as we hate to believe it." Ham stirred uncomfortably, remembering Blanche and her unnatural desire for the Mandingo.

160

Thigpen raised his hand in a calming gesture, as if trying to put a better light on the subject. "We don't know. Maybe she was deathly scared of this mustee. Afraid for her very life. She seen him kill Mr. Foye Randolph. She might be livin' in terror this minute. Or maybe she did go of her own free will with the mustee. . . . But we ain't after the mustee for runnin'—or miscegenation—nuthin' like that, bad as them crimes are. We want him for murder."

Bugas cleared his throat. "We—might be willing to pay you—up to a thousand dollars—in Texas paper—for accurate information. This is information that led us to apprehend the mustee—and git him back to the United States where he'd be convicted."

"We'd see him all right, if he passed on this trail," Ham said.

Thigpen placed a hand-lettered card on the table beside the Bible. "This here is a list of the places where Bugas and me can be reached. . . . Now, we wouldn't recommend you tryin' to stop the mustee, or hold him. No, sir. He's got to be considered dangerous. You just git word to us. . . . We arranged to receive letters and notes in the towns listed there. Whatever you do, don't try to jump him."

"Ain't ever lived the nigger I feared," Ham said. "They like airy other animal. Dogs or horses. You gits bad ones—just like you gits horses that fights the traces, or bites or kicks, or dogs that'll suddenly turn on you. . . . But if'n you know how to handle an animal—a dog, a horse or a black—they handles easy. It's when you ever once let an animal think you're scairt of him—Lord help you then. I never once done that. Never will."

"You do sound most knowledgeable about slaves and slave handling, sir," Bugas said.

"Like I say. My pappy and me raised slaves. Top-quality. Fancies. Falconhurst Plantation. Near Benson, Alabama, on the Tombigbee River."

"Well, sir, an' here you are way out here in the Texies," Bugas said.

"Been out here eight years, nigh on," Ham said.

Thigpen looked at him oddly. "An' ain't been home since?"

"Think on it a lot. Get homesick, sometimes. But never been back. You men know Falconhurst Plantation?"

"Laws yes. Ev'body south of Mason-Dixon know the Falconhurst Plantation. On the Tombigbee. Raises quality slaves."

"That's right. You passed that way recent?"

"Did, few months past. . . . Your folks still at Falconhurst?"

"Yes. My pappy."

"Old Mr. Warren Maxwell. We spent the night with him onc't."

"Yes. He's my pappy." Ham leaned forward, eager for news from home.

"Old Warren Maxwell," Thigpen said. "Not another man in the States knew nigger flesh better. Old Warren could look at a black and say not only was the animal worth buyin', worth feedin', but also the old fellow could tell you what part of Africa the black had come from—or what tribe his people had belonged to over there."

"How is he?" Ham asked.

The two men glanced at each other. "You ain't heard?" Bugas said.

Ham stood up awkwardly on his game leg. He stared down at the two bounty hunters. Whatever he may have had in mind about Tige was pushed out of his consciousness by the tone of voice and expression in the face of the sweated fat man. "How is he?" Ham repeated.

"Well, we hates to be the one to bear ill tidings, Mr. Maxwell. But your pa. Well, he's dead, Mr. Maxwell. . . . I can't say how sorry I am to bring this news to you."

Ham went on staring at them. "How did he die?"

Bugas spread his hands. "Don't rightly know, Mr. Maxwell. Hearsay, it is. . . . Believe his heart just failed."

"That's the way I heard it, all right," Thigpen agreed. "His heart—heart failure."

Ham strode back and forth in the room, limping like a wounded animal. He did not look at the bounty hunters again. He said in a savage, broken voice, "Is that all you know?"

"That's all, Mr. Maxwell. I'm sorry."

Ham swung his arm in a brushing gesture, as if to remove them from the room. The two men stood up. When they saw that the grief-stricken man was no longer aware of them, or of anything outside himself, they went out the front door. They waited several minutes on the shaded stoop. Then they got in the buggy and rode out of the yard. Lydia, troubled, ran from the kitchen into the parlor. She found Ham slumped in his big chair rocking back and forth. He was sobbing, inconsolably.

XV

Tige first glimpsed the black buggy far along the trail ahead. At the sight of the steadily approaching vehicle his heart sank and beat erratically. He did not recognize the smartly appointed buggy; he had never seen the two men riding in it. But he was gripped by a sudden panic.

In spite of the paralyzing sensation of apprehension, Tige gripped the worn leather lines and moved his horse steadily forward in the sun-stunned morning. He forced himself to reason away the dread that immobilized him. It didn't make sense to run. He could not run. Those men were still some distance away, but as he'd seen them in the open chaparral-and-mesquite plains, so they'd spied him. Running was an admission of fear. If those men were on his trail—and he didn't for an instant doubt this—his running now would only send them in hot pursuit. He had a head start; he'd learned the back trails and hidden arroyos in this range country. But his horse was slow, his wagon piled high with what he'd seen as his final delivery of cordwood on the Maxwell ranch. Those men had a fast horse, a light, steel-rim-wheeled buggy built for speed. He couldn't hope to outrun them. He couldn't hope to hide. He had to stay on the trail.

He sweated, the wild fibrillation of his heart refusing to stabilize. How quickly they approached even at that steady, unforced pace! He saw them clearly now—a stout man, a tall high-hatted driver. Gray dust bolls smoked upward behind the buggy. The vehicle rattled, bouncing over chugholes in the trail, the fat man grabbing at his bowler with one hand and the roof support posts with the other.

Tige looked about irresolutely. He was unarmed except for an axe. Damn! Why hadn't he and Nell got away from Maxwell's while they could? They should have kept moving. Running was their only hope and now they'd lost it.

Why had he let Ham Maxwell buffalo him into staying on day after day when he could almost smell the peril in the air? Nell feared Maxwell, and Tige admitted that something about the former slave breeder turned his own spine to clabber. But, now that it was too late, he admitted something he had kept from the forefront of his mind until this moment when it was loosed by panic: When he had seen Ham Maxwell standing in that lighted doorway that first night he and Nell came to the ranch, he had felt his first surge of hope since the day he'd killed Foye Randolph.

Hope? Why had he felt hope at the sight of the white man who'd once been his master? Why hope? Because he remembered his childhood—those hot easy days of security at Falconhurst? Partly that. He'd recognized "Masta Ham" at once. But more—it had not been lost on him when Ham's eyes widened in recognition—and more than recognition.

Tige swallowed back bile. As a child—they'd called him Tiger at Falconhurst—he'd been taken from his mother as soon as he was weaned. He never knew her. She'd been sold off in those earliest years of his life for which there was no recall. But he'd known—and idolized—Masta Ham. He'd tagged in his master's shadow from his earliest memory. White slave buyers, the vet, visitors—they all teased Masta Ham when Tiger was around. "That un's your spit-and-image," they'd say. "Know who sired that un, all right." Master Ham would grin and old Warren Maxwell would explain that Ham had indeed sired Tiger—out of an octoroon bed wench—when Ham was no more than fifteen. None of the white men cared that the child overheard them. He knew Masta Ham was his father. This had no real meaning on a black stud farm where families were strictly prohibited, but the knowledge set Tiger apart in his own mind. It gave him some special claim on his white master. This added to that other deeper warmth which he felt and in no way understood. When the blacks teased him about being "one of the masta's own suckers," he only grinned. There was a feeling of assurance, a sense of security, in knowing he was the white master's own son—his firstborn, if he'd known. . . . Well, he hadn't known. The young Ham left Falconhurst abruptly after the Mandingo Mede was slain. Years passed. Tiger grew, and forgot. . . . He was sold to a passing coffle and after an interminable time of marching, ankles shackled, of fear and loneliness, he had come to Hiddenbrook Plantation. . . . It was not until he stared into Masta Ham's face in that lighted doorway that he'd remembered. It had all rushed back in a torrent—he was his master's drop, his son; he was set apart.

He remembered now the way he'd stood there shaking inside, wanting to laugh and cry at the same time. His master—his father! This knowledge once had given him a sense of security and, despite all reason, he found himself hopeful again and deeply moved at the sight of his father. In these recent days he'd learned to fear Hammond Maxwell, because the rancher would destroy him without thinking twice about it—he certainly betrayed no paternal interest. Still, that blood was there! One thing none of them could change! He, Tige, was Hammond Maxwell's flesh and blood, his son! He felt a depth of emotion he was afraid to define or examine closely, but surely Masta

Ham had to feel something toward him? Despite everything that happened, he'd kept telling himself they were safe here at Maxwell ranch—he and Nell. They had come home—to his own father.

But, trouble bore down on him now and he knew one thing now for certain. He could not turn now for help to Ham Maxwell.

His hand trembling, Tige took up a small axe and laid it on the seat beside him. They weren't going to capture him without a fight! In his mind, he figured the only move open to him—he could handle that axe the way some men threw hunting knifes. One of those white bastards was going to die, his face split open. As to the rest of it—he could not think beyond that moment. Instead, he kept thinking of Nell, pitying her, wondering what would happen to her and their baby without him.

Dammit, he had to survive—and if he were going to stay alive, elude these men, he had to think. Time ran out. He'd lived out this moment of confrontation in a hundred chill nightmares. Sooner or later, the law would run him down. He had killed a white man. Nobody would ask why. Nobody would give a damn why. All that mattered was that he was a nigger and he'd killed a rich white plantation owner.

It occurred to him that if he surrendered quietly they might return him alive to Louisiana. As long as he was alive there was hope. He was young and strong and determined to live—every extra hour gave him new chances. No, goddammit, he wouldn't let them take him easily. It was going to cost him, but they were going to pay dearly too. He could never go back into that black world of slavery again. Never! He could not. As he could not imagine life without Nell, so he could not endure the thought of living in bondage again.

All these thoughts sped through his mind as he approached the on-coming buggy. His heart battering, blood pulsing in his temples, he forced himself to sit quietly, the slouched brim of his work hat shading the iron-brown sunburn of his face and, he hoped, concealing the agony of terror in his gray eyes. He would not be taken back, damn them, not when he and Nell had run so far, were at last so near freedom.

Forcing himself to remain slumped on the seat, he pulled one wheel off the hard-packed trail to permit the buggy to pass comfortably—even when he knew it would not. It did not. The tall man pulled on the lines. His horse halted, quivering in the broiling heat.

"Hey, boy, you," Thigpen called. "I want to talk to you."

Almost as astonished as his auditors, Tige heard himself reply to the tall man in an unassailable imitation of Estelle's blank answers to incomprehensible *inglés,* "*Sí, señores. Buenas tardes, señores. Sí.*" He kept the horse moving slowly forward.

"Hold it, you son of a bitch," Thigpen yelled. "I want to talk to you."

"Greaser bastard," Tige heard the fat man say. "He *no comprende.*"

"*¡Te paras!*" Thigpen yelled. "Damn you, don't that mean 'halt' in your lingo?"

Tige pulled up on the lines, troubled that they might speak Spanish. He was slightly beyond the buggy. The two men had to turn awkwardly on the carriage seat to look down at him in the wagon. He continued to peer up at them blankly, smiling broadly and emptily from beneath the slouch brim of his hat.

"Let the Mex go," the fat man said. "What's he know—a dumb grinning greaser?"

"Might of seen something. You *comprende inglés,* boy?"

"*No habla inglés, señores.*" Tige shook his head, giving them his brightest, blankest smile

"You—live—round—here?" Thigpen made signs

169

with his hands and spoke loudly as if addressing the deaf.

"Sí, señores. Muy grande luz del día. Sí. Gracias." He bobbed his head, smiling. *"Muy gracias."*

"Go on, you stupid bastard," Thigpen yelled at him. "Go on, get out of here."

Tige went on sitting slumped in the wagon. His smile remained unaltered. His heart continued to pound raggedly. *"Perdone me, señores. No comprende. Si?"*

"Oh, fuck you!" Thigpen yelled, his face red and sweated. He slapped the reins and his horse lurched forward. The fat man grabbed for support. Tige went on smiling and nodding. *"Hasta luego, señores, asnos, hijos de putas."*

Ham remained inconsolable. Lydia tried to talk with him but he only waved her away impatiently. There was nothing he wanted to hear from her. His sorrows and loss could not be shared with a Mexican woman.

Lydia watched him prowl the room, limping, his stiff knee, his contorted face, his taut body giving him the look of a wounded animal ready to lash out at anything or anyone that approached him. "Won't it help to talk about it?" she asked.

He gave her a look of raw agony. "No. Let me alone."

"I am hurt to see you suffer like this."

"Then get out. Get out. Let me alone."

She reached toward him, let her hand fall. "What did they say?"

"Who?" his voice rasped.

"Those men, Hammond. What did they say to you?"

He swung his arm. "Nothing. They are looking for a mustee killer. . . . And—my father is dead."

She caught her breath. "Oh, Ham . . . I am so sorry."

"Are you?" He paced, sweated, looking ready to

burst with pressures of inner hurt and rage. He stared at her, his pale eyes agonized, but he said nothing more. The room seemed too small to contain him in his grief, but then, so did the world. He continued to prowl from one wall to another, one window to another. He tried to drink and could not. He tried to sit down in his chair, but when Lydia came near, compassionate, he struggled up awkwardly and paced to avoid her.

"Why won't you let me share?" she said.

"Share? Share what? My guilt? Because I went away and left him in his old age, when he needed me? Share what? What do you know of sorrow—of the death of a person close to you? . . . People like you don't have—feelings like that. Let me alone."

Whatever Lydia might have said was lost when Estelle came reluctantly into the dim parlor. Outside the windows, the yard, the land beyond and the bleached sky itself were intensely white, the whiteness almost blinding, and that very intensity of whiteness deepened the shadowy dark of the room.

Estelle spoke in halting but rapid Spanish.

Lydia stared at the stout woman, incredulous. "Ramon?" she said.

At the name of the Mexican boy he'd publicly flogged, Ham glanced up. But he could not care. Whatever it was Ramon wanted, it was not important enough to eat through the impregnable shell of Ham's grief.

Estelle nodded and spoke rapidly again. Lydia came across the room and laid her soft hand gently upon Ham's arm. "Ramon's wife, Maria," she said. "She is in labor. In terrible pain. They wish Estelle should come at once. But they plead too that I come. . . . I can't leave you in your grief—"

"I'm all right." Ham shook her hand away and straightened. "Go on. Go on. I want you to go."

Lydia stood for some moments, peering into Ham's face. But when he turned and stalked awkwardly from her, staring into the cold fireplace, she let her shoulders sag. "I'll return," she said. "As soon as I can."

He appeared not even to hear her, and she turned and left the room with Estelle. Ham heard Lydia speaking with authority and confidence, ordering a carriage brought, a cowhand to drive. He heard her speaking quietly with the children and then talking with Estelle as they prepared food, milk, medicine and instruments to take to the sweet springs nester hut. Through a window, Ham saw the boy Ramon waiting, slack-shouldered in the sun beside a half-starved horse.

The carriage was brought, rattling on the hard-packed ground, to the front stoop. Lydia—a light mantilla over her head—and fat Estelle, panting and grunting good-naturedly in the heat, were helped into the vehicle. Goods and baskets were stacked into the carriage tonneau. The young ranch worker slapped the reins, the carriage rolled across the yard toward the trace, Ramon lagging in their wake. The children ran laughing and calling with the yard dogs, as far as the gate. They stood waving after their mother.

The parlor door opened behind Ham and Nell stepped inside. Ham turned from the window and glanced at her without warmth. He said nothing.

Her voice was low, uncertain. "Miss Lydia. Asked me to stay with you. She is very worried. . . . Is there anything I can do?"

He shook his head negatively. "No." He did not bother to look at her.

She mixed a drink for him. She brought the glass to him. She said, "I used to fix drinks for my father—before he died."

Ham stared at the mixture for a long beat, finally took the tumbler from her. "You don't need to stay in here," he said.

"I want to say, I'm sorry—about your father."

"Yes . . . all right."

"I know you loved him very much."

He shrugged. She drew a deep breath. At last, she said, "I know you are deeply grieved . . . but—those men—what did they want?"

"Why?" He looked up and held her gaze without a trace of compassion in his sun-weathered face.

She bit her lip. "Were they looking . . . for Tige and me?"

He continued to gaze coldly at her. "I don't know," he said. "Were they? They were looking for a mustee nigger who killed a white plantation owner and run — from Louisiana—with a white wench."

She was silent for a long time. Flies batted ineffectually against the screen. The children played, yelling with laughter, distantly in the yard. The old Seth Thomas clock could be heard wheezing and striking away the seconds. She waited for Ham to say more, but he did not. He offered no comfort, no hope of comfort. He did not suggest what those men had said to him—and more important, what *he* had said to *them*.

After a long empty silence, Nell said, "Is there anything I can—get for you?"

"I told you. No."

"I think you should know—Tige is good. One of the few really good people I've ever known—like Lydia."

"I don't want to talk about it."

"Whatever those men told you—"

"I don't want to talk about it."

Nell heard the children cry out, the dogs barking excitedly. She walked dispiritedly to the screen door. Her heart sank. She watched Tige drive into the yard, the wagon piled high with firewood. She spoke over her shoulder. "Tige's back. If you're sure you'll be all right, I'll go—see him."

"I'm all right," he said through clenched teeth.

She let the screen door close quietly behind her. She winced against the blinding brilliance of the sun reflected in the bare yellow sand of the yard. The children grabbed at her skirts. She walked with them across the shadowed dog-trot and they waited in the narrow shaft of shade while Tige drove around the house and brought the loaded wagon close to the kitchen.

Tige smiled—tautly, she thought, but supposed it was her own troubled imagination—and swung down from the wagon boot. He unloaded the firewood. She'd just moved to walk out to him when he looked up and motioned her to him with a sharp gesture of his head.

Feeling hysteria building inside her, Nell sent the children to play on the shaded front stoop and went close to the old wagon where Tige worked. She leaned against the rear wheel, gripping its rim, her knuckles white. "Two men," she whispered. "Came this morning."

Tige nodded without looking up. "I know," he said under his breath. He glanced beyond her. "We've got to get out of here. Today."

XVI

Walking unhurriedly, trying to appear as guileless as possible, Nell crossed the sun-struck yard toward the tack room at the barn. Their meager belongings were there; it would take her only a matter of minutes to gather them together. "Get everything we've got," Tige had told her as he continued working. "Get ready to leave—fast—as soon as I can hitch our horse."

Nell was thinking a hundred disparate things as she crossed the blazing yard. Her mind was aswarm with thoughts, fears, anxieties, memories and flashes of despair without form enough to be a thought. She was glad to leave this place. Yet she was afraid to run. She hated leaving without saying goodbye to Lydia. And what would happen to them out on the trail? Neither she nor Tige knew anything about delivering babies. The child in her belly was kicking frantically.

"Be still, damn you," she said. "I liked it better when I thought we'd find you in a cabbage leaf."

She turned and looked back from the shade of the tack-room entry. Her heart sank. Tige was no longer in the yard. The wagon stood empty, the horse sagging, head drooping in the heat. She searched, for the moment frantic. She could not find him. She leaned against the doorjamb, staring toward the ranchhouse. . . .

Ham looked up when he heard a knock on the parlor door. He caught his breath in the middle of a stifled sob and drew his sleeve across his face to erase any signs of his tears. He recognized Tige through the screen, the sun blindingly white behind him. Ham limped across the room. He said, "What you want at my front door, boy?"

Tige caught his breath, ready to rage back in a matching tone. Instead, he clenched his fists at his sides and spoke softly. "I want to talk to you—sir. Want to thank you. . . . You been passing kind to Nell and me."

Ham stepped out into the narrow ledge of shade afforded by the roof overhang. "Sounds like you figurin' on leaving?"

"Yes. Nell and me, we're going. Now. Today."

"Oh." Ham's eyes held Tige's relentlessly. His voice remained level. "How far you think you'll get?"

Tige shrugged. "I don't know."

"I can tell you. You won't get far."

Tige's voice held the same resolute tone that rang in Ham's. "Still—we got to try."

"Had a couple men here this morning. . . . They was looking for a murderer."

Tige drew a deep breath, waited.

Ham seemed almost taunting him. "Them men—like you—they come out here clear across the Texies, all the way from Louisiana."

Tige remained silent. Ham's mouth pulled slightly and he added with chilled malice, "Yes. All the way from Hiddenbrook Plantation."

The words verified Tige's worst fears, confirmed what he'd suspected when he met the two men on the trail. He had been certain; there was no longer any doubt; no longer any hope. An icy wave of helplessness washed down through him. His spine seemed too limber to support him. He was weak and empty inside, waiting for the accusation which had to follow—murder, murderer.

But Ham only watched him intently, his pale eyes insensitively hard, almost glittering with chill. Tige spread his hands. "I reckon they told you . . . about me?"

"They told me about Nell Randolph's father—murdered in his bedroom—"

"Nell's stepfather . . . in *her* bedroom."

Ham shrugged, seeming hardly to have heard him, and unmoved by anything he might say. "Still, a white man."

"A bastardly—"

"A white man. Murdered by a *nigger*."

"Won't you listen to my side of it?"

"Don't need to. Already heard your side of it—all you'd be allowed to tell in a court of law back in the States. You killed a white man. And you run—"

"Listen to me! Please. There's more to it than that—"

"Not for me. You might make some accusations against a white man. A dead white man that can't answer you back. But I wouldn't listen to you even if the white man had lived. . . . Niggers don't kill white men. Niggers don't attack white men. Niggers don't make accusations against white men. No court in the States will take a black's word against a white man. You know that. A nigger can't testify against a white man. A nigger can't accuse a white man in a courtroom. . . . An' you kill a white man, ain't nuthin' more to be said *for* you, or against you."

Tige's face paled, but his eyes grew as hard as Ham's. He would not chip away at the granite of this man's prejudices with no sharper tools than the simple truth. The hell with him! He had believed Ham was a good man inside because that's what he had wanted to believe. But Ham Maxwell wasn't a good man inside; inside as out, he was only a white man. He said, "What are you going to do?"

"That's up to me to decide, I figure."

Tige's voice lashed out, frustrated. "It's my life. It's Nell's life. Doesn't that mean anything to you?"

Ham merely shook his head.

Tige straightened. "You think to turn me over—to them men?"

"Them men?" Ham shook his head. "No. They bounty hunters."

"Bounty hunters?"

"They after a five-thousand-dollar re-ward."

"A lot of money." Tige peered into Ham's face, trying to read something in it, but finding it flat, implacable. "A man might help them—for money like that."

"You'll find men that will. Not me. No. I tole you. They bounty hunters. They scum. They lower'n paddy-rollers. Lower'n skunks. Lower'n snake bellies. Got no time for bounty hunters. . . . Besides, this white nigger they're lookin' for is wanted dead or alive."

Tige swallowed hard; the sense of despair swelled inside him. He stared at a ladybug crater in the sand between his boots. He said nothing.

"Dead or alive. That means first thing them bounty hunters do is kill this nigger. . . . Easiest way to cart him east across the Texies is dead. His body gits to stinkin' but that's better'n takin' a chance on a live mustee. Mustee's smart. They so smart sometimes they dangerous. Little too much white blood in a black animal can make him plumb treacherous."

"What would you care?" Even now, Tige watched his father hopefully, yet not daring to hope.

"I care. Slaves been my life." His voice cracked slightly. "My pappy's life before me. . . . Don't neither of us hold with killin' a nigger senseless. A waste." Remembering the way he'd slaughtered Mede, stewed the meat from the Mandingo's bones, Ham shuddered faintly.

As if yanked roughly back from some unrelated reverie, Ham winced and shook his head. His voice rasped. "Anytime you kill a nigger, you rob yourself—of a profit. . . . You kill a nigger only when there ain't no other way to deal with him . . . or you kill a black as a 'zample to other slaves. . . . Killin' a nigger out here in the Texics don't profit nobody."

Tige said, "Then you're not going to try to stop me?"

"Stop you?"

"From leaving. . . . I hope you won't try to stop me, sir."

At the chilled, yet reluctant threat implied in the boy's tone, Ham jerked his head up. A nigger had dared to threaten him. Until this moment, no black had ever done that and lived. He saw that the boy's hands were clenched at his sides—the mustee meant what he said. Tige was half a head taller than he—fourteen or so years younger. Whether or not he was stronger was a point Ham didn't even consider. It had never occurred to him to fear a Negro, and he did not now. But for the moment at least, he controlled the rage that boiled up in him at this nigger insolence.

"No. I won't stop you," Ham said. "An' you want to take a pregnant white girl—"

"She's my wife—"

"—an' try to fight off two professional bounty hunters that would rather take you dead than alive—"

"We can't stay here anymore."

"Can't you?"

Tige spread his hands. "Please—don't try to stop me. I know what you think. . . . You can kill me if you have to to stop me—but that's what you'll have to do. I'm not afraid of you . . . I'm not afraid to fight. We're not in Alabama now. I'm no blacker than you are."

Ham's mouth twisted as if he'd tasted something nasty and indigestible. "Smart talking. . . . Come a long way from bein' a slave, ain't you?"

"I'm a man. Out here—I'm free. . . . I'm as good as you are."

"Are you?"

"I won't be a slave again. Ever."

"Fact is, you *are* a slave. You born a slave. You gone die a slave. . . . But you figure that's back in the States—and you're a big free *white* man out here in the Texies."

"That's why I hope you won't try to stop me—sir."

"An' what about them bounty hunters?"

Tige met his gaze levelly. "I'm not afraid of them. I know them now. . . . I'll kill them—if I have to. It won't bother me to kill them . . . but I don't want to kill you."

Ham's mouth pulled down. "That's real considerate of you."

Tige hesitated. Then he exhaled heavily. "Goodbye," he said. And then he added, hopefully, "Will you— shake hands?"

It was as if lightning erupted from the sun-stunned sky. "Shake hands? With a stinkin' nigger?" Ham struck suddenly, driving his left fist deep under Tige's belt.

Tige staggered. He felt nauseating sickness gorge up from his groin and burn in his throat. He buckled forward, gripping his crotch with both arms. As he bent over, Ham brought his two fists, locked together like a club, down across the back of Tige's neck.

Tige plunged forward at Ham's feet. He struggled, trying to get up, but his body refused to obey commands from his brain. Dimly he heard the three children screaming in terror. Over their wailing, Ham's voice rode in rage, telling them to get to hell in the kitchen and shut their goddam mouths.

Tige reached out and caught the rough overhang support pole. Gripping it with all his strength, he tried to pull himself up.

Ham let the boy get almost to his knees, then he kicked him in the face, his boot smashing into Tige's flesh. Tige sagged to the ground and lay still.

Tige came up slowly from the heated depths of unconsciousness, rising through a thick stratum of total pain. He became aware that he was moving, of rattling noises, the plod of hooves of horses. He opened his eyes, stunned, and found he was lying in the bed of the firewood wagon. He tried to pull himself up. At that instant, the wagon left the bright sunlight and entered the thick darkness of the feed barn.

The wagon rattled to a stop. Ham looped the lines around the whipstock and swung down over the wheel. He limped to the rear of the wagon. He caught Tige by the ankles and dragged him from the wagon bed.

Tige toppled helplessly and struck the ground heavily, the breath blasted from him.

He lay still, unable to move, for what seemed an interminable time. Pain flared through him. For an instant it was as if his heart had stopped. He sprawled on the hay-matted dirt floor of the barn. He gasped helplessly, like a fish out of water, trying to get his breath.

When he opened his eyes, he found Ham standing over him, face cold and eyes dead.

"Why are you doing this?" Tige begged. Crouched on the dirt, the boy reached out toward the rancher.

"No sense you askin' no goddam questions. You gittin' no answers. I ain't beholden to no stinkin' nigger. You do what I tell you an' you stay alive longer."

Staring up at the white man's rigid face, Tige knew better than to speak again. Why ask for mercy where he knew there was none? His head reeled. Between shaky awareness and unconsciousness, he kept praying that Nell would not come in this barn. He did not want her to see him like this—beaten, helpless, groveling on the floor like a black slave . . . like what he was, as far as Ham Maxwell was concerned.

Ham bent down and caught Tige by the shirt collar. He dragged him across the rough, hard-packed flooring. Weakly, only barely conscious, Tige stared back at the path his body raked through the hay and litter.

He gazed at that wavering wake and thought it was like a short trail depicting his own brief life—dragged though the dirt to this place to die in this free Republic of the Texies. It was as if everything he'd done, every road he'd followed, every action he carried out or left undone, all had led to this place—a lost, Godless place without pity.

Dazed, Tige lay and watched as Ham snapped a rusted iron shackle about his ankle. Tige struggled weakly and Ham cursed him. "Lay still, goddammit."

Dimly, Tige saw a second man enter the vaguely lighted barn. He recognized Paley, Maxwell's foreman. Paley's voice betrayed his surprise and shock. "What you doin' to the boy, Mr. Ham?"

"I chained him here so he don't run away."

"Good God. Like a animal."

"You don't like it, Paley?"

"He seemed a good kid, boss. Hard worker. That's all."

"Then you let me handle it."

"But—why would he run away? Ain't his wife here?"

"He ain't got no wife. A black buck can't have no wife."

Alone, Tige jerked at the chain, raging inwardly. His eyes burning with helpless tears, he pressed his back against the barn wall. The rough splintery wood chewed into his skin. He did not feel the pain. In his mind he could see only one image—Ham Maxwell. This was the man he'd loved despite everything that should have taught him better. This was the man he'd looked at that first night and felt his first surge of hope. This was the man he'd prayed would help him and Nell. The cruel son of a bitch who was his father.

XVII

There is a silence more alarming than any violent fulminations. For what seemed an interminable, tense vacuum, the Maxwell ranch sprawled suspended in such a zone of refracted stillness. The children waited, forgotten, in the silent kitchen. The children crouched on the floor in a benumbing kind of terror without any inkling of what inspired their fears. At the bunkhouse, the cowhands who rode herd or checked fences close enough to come in for a noon meal ate in an unexplained atmosphere of tension. Paley said something about the new kid's being shackled "like a goddam dog" in the barn. He could explain no further because he didn't know any more.

The hands talked in subdued tones as they ate. They were puzzled, troubled. They liked Tige. He worked hard, laughed easily and got along well. They were worried about Tige's pregnant wife. She was just a kid. Had Paley seen her? He had not. They knew Maxwell's temper, they didn't push the matter. They finished eating, sopping biscuits in the remains of their gravy, pushed tin plates away on the rough table, stood up, stretched, returned silently to their chores.

Hammond walked away from where he had shackled Tige. He paused in the barn doorway, the stunning sunshine reflected off the fulvescent sand behind him,

183

and looked back at the mustee boy writhing and fighting against his shackles in the gloom of the barn.

Outside, the sun tilted immobile at the apex of a dazzlingly white sky. Hammond limped across the hot dry sand toward the ranchhouse. The plains lay still around him from horizon to horizon. A buzzard lazed in looping circles above the broken land. As Ham came near the dog-trot he remembered impatiently that Lydia was gone. He walked into the parlor, intensely alone. Damn her, wasting her time on those nesters. He poured himself half a tumbler of raw corn whiskey and then did not drink it. He felt sweated, uncomfortable. He wanted Lydia to remove his boots. He almost yelled for her before he remembered she was at the sweet springs squatter's hut. He sprawled in his big chair, but it was heated and not comfortable. He laid his head back and stared out the window at heat waves rising in the white sunlight. He felt sadness gorge up in him when he thought of his father. His father—dead! His eyes filled with tears, but he wiped them away with the back of his hand, thinking in rage of that mustee out there talking like a white man; this offended him almost as much as the nigger's murdering the master of Hiddenbrook. His mind would not hold on one thought for any length of time, even the heart-rending agony of death. He vacillated between sorrow and rage, between grief and hatred, and then a spreading cancerous growth of guilt.

Ham heard them coming across the yard from the barn, dogs yapping, two men talking, but he did not move. He remained sprawled in the big chair, his stiff leg stretched out straight before him.

"Boss! Mr. Ham! Goddammit, where are you?" He heard Paley's yelling as he approached the stoop. Ham went on sitting, unmoving.

He heard the screen door yanked open so violently it was almost ripped from its hinges. He pushed himself up to his feet and turned, his pallid face gray and rigid.

Cale Lambdin held the door open. Paley, carrying Nell prostrate and deadweight in his arms, turned and sidled into the room. "Where'll I put her?"

When Ham didn't answer at once, Paley's voice, accustomed to fighting high winds in the broken range, raged at him. "This kid's in bad trouble, goddammit. Her water's broke. . . . She's goin' to have her goddam baby in my arms, you don't show me where to put her."

"Why didn't you put her in the tack room?" Ham said.

"Fuck you, you heartless son of a bitch," Paley said.

With Cale Lambdin at his heels, Paley brushed past Maxwell and crabbed his way along the narrow hallway into the alien territory of the boss's chambers. He paused before the first open door, which he recognized instinctively as a guest bedroom. Lydia's touch—her impeccable taste, bright spread, high ornately laced pillows, the Spanish paintings decorating the paneled walls, plus the unused look of the immaculate room— assured him this was the place he sought. He jerked his head toward Cale. Lambdin, as if reading the foreman's mind, turned back the spread and blankets. He stepped back. Paley laid the girl down gently on the spotless sheets. Then Paley straightened, yelling savagely, "Boss, stir your stumps. Get in here."

As if pulled forcibly—and reluctantly—back to the reality of this hot Texas ranch and the primiparous wench writhing on that bed, Ham stalked into the guestroom. Paley spoke over his shoulder, "We got to get her ready, Boss."

"What are you talking about?"

Paley straightened. "This girl. This little girl. Shouldn't be deliverin'—but by God she is . . . an' she needs help. . . . I've helped foal colts and bring calves . . . I know nuthin' about this."

"Me neither. I can't help." Cale retreated toward the door.

Paley jerked his head around. "The hell you can't. You get Cook over here from the buckhouse. Tell him to git water hot—"

"Then you take a buggy, ride to the nester hut at sweet springs," Ham said. "Tell Lydia to get back here fast. And bring Estelle. Tell her I said the hell with them squatter bastards, I want her here."

Cale nodded and retreated, relieved to be allowed to escape. They heard the parlor door slam behind him.

On the bed, Nell writhed, twisted her sweated head back and forth on the pillows. "Lydia . . . Mama . . . Lydia . . . I hurt . . . so bad . . . oh God, I hurt."

"Lydia ain't here, girl." Ham's voice was surprisingly gentle. Birthing of babies had been a major part of his existence since his earliest memory. They didn't always arrive at the most convenient hours, or come out smoothly and head first, nor in a standard size, but he had been in at almost every type of emergency or easy delivery. "We sent Cale for her. You hang on. . . ."

Her head rolled back and forth, her lips pulled white and taut across her teeth. "It's started . . . oh God . . . my baby . . . it's coming."

Ham swore under his breath. He glanced at Paley, who stood, arms akimbo, helpless, gray-faced, wincing every time the girl cried out. "Better get them clothes off her, Paley."

"Don't know much about that, neither."

"For hell's sake. Pretend she's a Laredo whore—an' you're in a hurry." When Paley hesitated, Ham's voice hardened. "You seen naked women before, ain't you?"

"None this young. I wait till they ripe . . . and *none* in this fix—"

"Well, tear them clothes off, get 'em off. I'll have to find my sharpest knife."

Nell screamed. Paley had touched at the buttons on her cotton dress. He retreated. "Hadn't we better get her husband in here?"

"That mustee stays where he is," Ham said. "He's done his part."

"Tige!" Nell wailed. "I want Tige."

Ham bent over the writhing girl. "Now listen to me. We got all the trouble we need, right here. Tige would just be in the way. . . . I thought he could help, I'd carry him in here. I know better. Paley and me . . . we goin' do for you what we can. . . . I delivered dozens of pickaninny drops back home. White ladies . . . nigger wenches . . . ain't all that different . . . down there. We don't have no trouble, we make it. You got to help."

The girl's bloodless face was like papyrus. Her eyes were huge and round. Her hands were stretched, fingers widely splayed, at her sides. "What—you—want—me—to do?"

"Lie still. Let Paley git yore clothes off."

She tried to nod her head, but cried out involuntarily. "I burn . . . oh God, I burn." She wept. She did not move. Presently she tried to focus her gaze on Paley. "It's all right. I'll try to help."

"You're a good girl." Paley's rough hands fumbled at her tiny buttons. "A good . . . pretty . . . girl. You goin' be fine . . . jus' fine." He could not loosen the small buttons.

"Tear the goddam dress off," Ham told him.

"Tear the goddam dress off," Nell said, in a spasm of pain.

Paley ripped the fabric as easily as if it had been cotton lint. He threw the dress behind him. Her petticoat was easier. He slipped the straps down over her bared shoulders, pulled the damp garment along her legs. Her wide-legged drawers were soaking wet. Pushing Paley aside, Ham ripped the fabric with his

187

knife. Paley gasped, retreating a step, involuntarily. "Jesus. I can see its head."

"All right." Ham nodded. "That means it's coming out the right way. . . . It ain't goin' to be easy, girl—I ain't gonna lie to you about that—but it'll be a hell of a lot easier long as the drop does his part."

"He's a—good baby—" Nell said between clenched teeth. "He'll—do—whatever you tell him—"

"Now you listen to me," Ham said. "I want you to take a deep breath . . . a real deep breath . . . and push down in yore belly like you was bad constipated— or you been eatin' green persimmons and got a belly ache . . . bear down, girl."

"I hurt . . . oh God, I hurt," Nell whispered. But she drew a deep breath, sucking air into her parted lips. She held it, grunted with the effort of downward pressure.

"You feel him move, you help him," Ham told her. "You feel him stop, you rest. . . . Another deep breath now. Push. Hard."

"Yes," Nell whispered.

"Now . . . let out yore breath, girl. . . . Relax a minute. . . . It's a comin' . . . I got ahold of it. . . . Now—another breath . . . bear down . . . hard . . . harder, girl, harder. . . ."

Tears welled in Paley's eyes. "Jesus," he said. "I got to have a drink."

Ham's head came up. He spoke over his shoulder. "Bring us all one."

"Bring us all one," Nell called, laughter spinning off upward into agony. . . .

Cale drove the buggy across country as swiftly as the horse could cover the rough, hard ground. The sun had slipped a little, a fiery globule as alone as he was, in a sky that stretched thin and clear, still—an empty void with the life broiled out of it by its own savage red eye. The plains wavered in the heat, vast and tan,

188

with ridged arroyos and gray slopes. Far westward, the spiked foothills promised verdure and graze, but this was a green lie, a deceit no cattleman ever bought, a spell cast by blue veils of distant haze.

He kept the horse trotting, concentrating on the jagged path ahead. He kept thinking about that girl, the way he and Paley had found her, crouched over her shackled husband, screaming, in hysterics and already in labor induced by her terror. Cale wiped sweat from his face with the back of his arm. Gave a man the shakes, almost discouraged him from sexing, seeing a woman in labor.

He rode in close to the adobe hut, a single room and thatched roof, built in a copse of willows near a small artesian spring. He saw Tyler lounging in the ranch carriage, a few scrawny chickens clucking in the shade, clothes dripping from a rope line.

The Mexican boy looked up from where he sagged on a broken chair near the adobe entrance. When he recognized Cale, he winced and lowered his gaze. Ramon didn't look like the arrogant greaser they'd caught with the slaughtered heifer. He didn't look like much—he looked whipped. Maybe Maxwell was right. A hanging left only a dead man. A whip left a broken-spirited one who was a walking example to other thieves. Be a long time before Ramon rustled another heifer.

Cale halted the buggy near the open doorway and called, "Miz Lydia! You in there, Miz Lydia?"

Lydia stepped out of the doorway. Her face was pink with fatigue, damp with perspiration, glowing with a Latin beauty that raged through Cale like a virus. He stared at her, spellbound. She said, "What is it, Cale?"

"It's the girl, Miz Lydia. Tige's wife. Nell. We had a spell of trouble. . . . For some reason, Mr. Ham chained Tige in the barn. Well, the girl seen him chained up and had hysterics—and—well, she went into labor, Miz Lydia."

"Yes. All right." She turned to reenter the hut.

Cale called after her. "Mr. Ham said to tell you he wanted you home. Now. Estelle, too."

She paused and looked at him calmly across her shoulder. Under her steady black eyes, Cale fell silent. He said, tentatively, "I'll run you back home, you want me to."

"You wait," she said. "I'll see."

He nodded and gazed after her, hungry.

She was gone what seemed an uncomfortably long time to Cale. He heard Maria's screams from within the hut. Every time the girl cried out, Ramon started up from the broken chair, then subsided. The Mexican boy looked ill, ready to vomit. Cale didn't blame him. Pleasuring a woman was worth whatever it cost you. But this part of it was enough to turn a man's stomach, or give him religion. Sometimes, three sheets to the wind, he'd briefly considered marriage. Thank God, you always sobered up. This sort of thing convinced him he was right. A woman's place was in a cathouse.

When Lydia came out of the adobe hut, she wore a mantilla over her dark hair. "We'll have to leave Estelle and Tyler here," she said. "Maria's having a—difficult time. The baby is turned."

"Yes, ma'am." Cale didn't know what she meant, only that the idea somehow turned his stomach. He leaped from the buggy and ran around it. He boosted Lydia easily up into the seat. A charge flashed through him from his fingertips when he touched her. His heart beat faster and he went around the rear of the vehicle, empty-bellied, his breath suddenly tight in his throat. He was going to be alone with her—in that wild, open country. Just her and him. He shivered suddenly.

He turned the buggy, waved in response to Tyler's farewell, and kept his face averted for fear Lydia might read something in his eyes. He slapped the reins across the rump of the horse and kept it moving at

190

that steady pace for more than a mile. He was no longer conscious of the heat, the bounce of the taut-springed buggy on the hard-packed ground, the land around them. He gripped the lines tightly, afraid she'd see his hands shaking.

He could *smell* Lydia beside him, a heady, mind-boggling scent. It was the first time she'd actually been alone with him like this, but not the first time he'd imagined it, alone in his bunk, or hunkered out on the range behind a boulder, his aching staff gripped fiercely in his fist.

"How is she?" Lydia said.

"What?" Cale's head jerked up.

"Nell. How is she?"

He shrugged. "Oh . . . she was—all right. When I left. Mr. Ham had her lying down in the guest room."

"That's good."

"Yes'm. I think she'll make it real good." Jesus. Even her voice was musical, with just enough accent to give it spice and charm that enthralled him.

"We'd better go faster—"

"Got to watch for chugholes—"

"We've got to hurry, Cale." She spoke impatiently. Hell, you'd of thought she was Maxwell's wife instead of his woman.

"Yes'm. But we don't want to push the horse in this heat—"

"Push him." Her voice crackled.

"Well, look," he said. "Maybe I give you the wrong impression—about how big a rush there was and all, Miz Lydia."

"Oh?" Strange, a woman could invest so much chill in one small word.

"I mean—they ain't that big of a rush. The girl's in bed—"

"You said she was in labor—"

"Well, I think so."

"I want to go faster, Cale."

He let the horse slow, half-turned on the seat, aware only of his own pounding pulses, the aching rigidity at his crotch, her Spanish loveliness that had haunted him through a hundred wet dreams and bucking orgasms. "We ain't never been alone like this, Miz Lydia—"

"Do you want me to drive?"

"No . . . I want you to listen to me. I'm in agony. I seen you—in that house—every day. Every night. I watch you in those windows. I see you walking in the yard, that head held up like the pertest thoroughbred that ever paced. I see them—them breasts standing up full. . . . A man goes crazy inside, Miz Lydia. It wouldn't matter was I in a town big as Dallas—it'd still be you drivin' me out of my gourd. . . . Ain't many spicy-hot Mexican beauties like you—on neither side of the border. . . . I'm crazy for you—you gotta know I am."

"I warn you, Cale. Stop this. Now. If you touch me, Hammond will make you regret it—as long as you live, however long that is."

"I don't care—a man figures the cost. He's willing to pay it. . . . All right. I want you. Like nobody never wanted no other woman. . . . I seen stallions go insane—and they don't want it like I want you."

"Hammond will kill you—"

"But that's it, Lydia. He don't have to . . . he don't have to know. . . . It ain't like you're his wife. . . . He gits it—he got no more right to it than I have. He gets it—more beauty than I ever seen . . . so beautiful it makes me hurt. He gits it. . . ."

"I *will* tell him . . . and he *will* kill you."

"Wait," he pleaded. "You might not want to tell him. Feel it. Touch it. My God, look at it! Standin'—you could hang a bucket of mud on it—"

"Why don't you?" She tried to laugh at him.

"You'll like it, Lydia. It's something hard—bigger, harder'n you're ever goin' to git with him. . . . I know you like it . . . I know at night when *he's* ridin' it. . . . Hell, he's rode you—once with me ain't goin' hurt. . . . I know you're a Mexican wench. I know how hot you women are. . . . I can give you what you need. Just wait—let me—hold you . . . you won't *want* to tell him."

The horse had halted. Panting, his face flushed, Cale dropped the lines and buggy whip. He reached down, jerked open his fly and exposed himself to her. "Look, baby. *Look* at it. Touch it . . . you'll go crazy for it . . . crazy as I am for you."

Almost sobbing for breath through his parched throat, Cale caught her hand and pressed it upon his rigidity, forcing her to hold it, stroke it. He gasped, trembling violently.

Lydia sagged forward against him. Encouraged, mindless, he pulled her to him, clutching at her breasts as he had in a hundred orgasmic dreams.

When Lydia straightened, she had the whip in her hand. Before he could release her and throw his arm up to protect himself or grab at the whip, she struck him across the face, the coarse-braided whip butt slicing his cheek like the honed blade of a knife. Blood spurted. He growled and lunged upward to beat her down to submission. It was as if this was what she anticipated. As he came up off the seat, she drove both hands into his chest, shoving him with all her strength.

Cale lost his balance. He wavered and caught wildly at the roof support. Her whip broke his grasp. He toppled out over the wheel.

Lydia lashed the horse's rump. The buggy lunged forward crazily, racing away before Cale could scramble to his knees.

Cale sprang up, standing, his fly open, in the mesquite clumps. He sobbed, raging and cursing. "I'll get you for this, you greaser bitch!" he yelled after her, crying helplessly. "I'll get you. Goddam you, if it's the last thing I ever do, I'll get you for this."

He stood, slack-shouldered, still painfully rigid, and watched the buggy speed away in the heat waves. . . .

Paley stood aside watching impotently as Ham delivered Nell's baby. Two or three times it looked as if the teenaged girl might faint, but Ham's voice kept pulling her back, a dull monotone that was at once gentle, yet mocking, reassuring, challenging, soothing and prodding. "Push . . . bear down . . . he's coming right to me now . . . relax . . . breathe . . . push . . . grunt, damn it, grunt. . . ."

Paley wanted to be anywhere else rather than here, but he did not move. He wanted to escape this breathless room, pull his riveted gaze from Ham's working between the girl's widespread thighs. He could not move. He ached and winced with the girl with every agonized cry; he swallowed back bile. He remained near the wall but not touching it. A bottle of whiskey stood on the table beside him. He did not touch that, either. He remained immobile, benumbed.

As Ham worked, his mind raced back across the Texies, east to distant Falconhurst. He recalled unwanted births. He remembered Blanche's black infant, knocked in the head by Blanche's own mother. He remembered what the vet had done with monster births, unwanted cripples, black drops from white wombs—they cut the umbilical cord short and let the infant bleed to death. They accidentally suffocated it. They didn't help it catch its first life-giving breath. They let it strangle. . . .

Sweated, he stared at this fifteen-year-old girl sprawled before him. She was nothing but a child. Daughter of a quality family, the Murdochs of Hiddenbrook Plantation. Wouldn't he be doing her a favor in the long run if he *accidentally* let the infant strangle, or bleed to death from a cord he cut but didn't tie off? She was mated to a black buck. This was a crime before God, before the state, before every Godfearing

194

human being. In the States, it wasn't even a legal marriage; no miscegenation was legal. But worse than that, she was coupled with a murdering mustee who had to pay for his crime . . . if the infant died, she could start anew, free of the nigger and his git. Hurt would be short-term, a kid as young as she was. She'd get over it, she'd forget.

"There," he said. "We got it." Sweating, he jerked his head toward Paley, motioning him to cut the cord. Hand shaking visibly, Paley used the razor-sharp knife to make the cut. Ham drew string about the stub, winding it tightly, tying it off.

A spasm of reaction pain struck Nell, almost stunning her. She lay back, gasping for breath and only barely conscious.

Dimly, she saw Ham heft her baby by the heels and slap its buttocks sharply. The infant gasped, cried out, breathed, lived. . . .

Nell sagged back against the pillow, overcome with exhaustion. Ham yelled for the cook and washed the infant while the cook removed the sheets from Nell's bed and replaced them and covered her. With a basin of tepid water, Paley gently bathed the girl's ashen face, pushed her hair back from her forehead with the washcloth. She tried to pull her face into a smile to thank him. She could not.

Ham wrapped the baby loosely in a blanket. He stood for a long beat gazing down at it, his face chilled. Then he placed the infant on the pillow beside Nell. His expression did not alter. His old aloof and curt manner returned. He said, "Well, there he is. Your little black bastard."

He turned and limped toward the door. Paley followed, raging inwardly. He wanted to kill the monstrous bastard, but he managed to keep his voice low and level. "Just when I decide maybe you ain't a heartless son of a bitch, after all. Why'd you have to hurt her?

Ain't she hurt enough? Ain't you done enough to her? Why'd you have to say that?"

Ham kept walking. "It's the truth."

"That baby ain't black."

"No. He looks white." Ham shrugged and kept walking. "But he ain't, he's a nigger."

XVIII

Disquiet settled over the Maxwell ranch. The raucous laughter that rattled bunkhouse walls flickered out. Fights flared over card games, and knives glittered threateningly. There were some grins, but there was savage bite in them. They taunted Cale Lambdin in a dozen ways. Tyler told how he and Estelle, returning from sweet springs, had come across the plains and found Cale stumbling along, mumbling to himself like a wanderer lost in a desert. Tyler said they'd asked Cale about Miss Lydia, but Cale only growled and refused to discuss it. They had gotten separated, he said, and that's all he would say. No amount of taunting would force him to explain the cut across his cheek. The men tormented Cale, but slyly. There was an unspoken pact to keep his secret—whatever it was—from Hammond Maxwell, and not for Cale's protection alone.

Cale remained sour-faced. When his partner Paley inquired about his trouble, Cale cursed him. "Just let me be. Goddam it, just let me be."

Cale went silently about his chores, tense, awaiting some challenge from Maxwell. Cale lived in sweated tension. He was going to be fired, or he was going to have to fight Maxwell. He didn't relish either alternative. He considered pulling stakes and drifting, but he delayed, afraid that if he left Maxwell would run him down. It was like Maxwell to play a cat-and-mouse game, and then pounce on him when he no longer worked for the ranch. He remembered the way the Mexican boy had screamed under the whip like a woman.

The uneasiness had settled in the day Nell's baby was born. Lydia returned from sweet springs to find Nell sleeping, exhausted, and the cook feeding the children pancakes and cane syrup in the ranchhouse kitchen. By now they had forgotten their terror at seeing their father assault Tige in the yard. Lydia tried to tell Ham how proud she was of what he had done for Nell. He merely stared at her or, since she couldn't make him meet her gaze, through her.

"Why not? I done as much for nigger wenches. I'd have done it for a bitch a-whelpin'."

She stared at him. "Has Tige seen the baby?"

"Tige's chained in the barn. He stays there until I decide what to do with him."

"You've got to let him see his son."

"I don't *have* to let him do anything. We never let the bucks at Falconhurst see their whelps. He ain't no whit different. Hell, he's one of them. He talks uppity, acts white, but he's a Falconhurst nigger." His laugh was cold. "A fancy. A Falconhurst mustee, but still a black slave."

"He's your son," she said.

He looked up. " 'Cause he favors me?" He shrugged. "I covered the bedwench that dropped him, that's all. He ain't no way my son."

She drew a deep breath, clenched her trembling fingers. "And his mother?"

"What about her?"

"What was she to you?"

"I tole you. Nuthin'. Hardly recall her. A bed wench. A octoroon, I think."

She shook her head, unable to believe what she heard. "You *fathered* Tige—but he's not your son?"

198

He shrugged. "Not far as I'm concerned. Nor far as the law is concerned. He's got nigger blood. He's a black animal. That's law. I didn't make the law, but I know it's right. He's got nigger blood. No matter how much, how little, he black. "Ain't *nuthin'* to me. No more than airy other farm animal."

"You never felt—*anything* for him?"

"Figured he'd grow to be a fancy. Bring a good price at vendue."

She stared at him, face taut, black eyes bleak. It was as if, after sleeping in Ham's bed for six years, she had never really seen this stranger before. He might walk out in the morning and she would never see him again. Isn't that what he'd really meant, even if he hadn't bothered to give it a thought? She shook her head. She didn't say anything. There was nothing left to say. He had said it all. . . .

Just before sundown, Lydia wrapped the baby in a blanket and took it up. Her children clamored to go with her. She forbade them to leave the kitchen. Smiling, she kissed each of them, and allowed them to brush the infant's cheek with their lips. Then she motioned her head to Estelle, who followed her, carrying a tray of food covered with a cotton dishcloth. Together they crossed the yard toward the barn.

Lydia glimpsed Cale leaving the barn. She bit her lip, kept walking. She had to meet with him eventually; she ignored him now.

"Evenin', Estelle. Miz Lydia," Cale said. They gave him a brief nod.

Cale stopped walking and stood, legs braced apart, head up. He peered at Lydia defiantly. Lydia looked through him and past him; as far as she was concerned he was less than dirt, he was not even there. Cale felt a rush of relief. She had not told Ham Maxwell about what had happened on the way home from sweet springs. But he felt no trace of gratitude. Instead he was angered anew. Rage moiled in his belly. He hated her almost as fiercely as he desired her. He was obsessed with the need to show her how good he'd be shoved up inside her, the need to humble her, to break her spirit as Maxwell's bullwhip had destroyed the greaser Ramon. He'd get her down and she'd wail and scream and beg him for it. By God, she would!

Estelle walked silently beside Lydia. She had delivered Ramon's son after long hours of struggle at the sweet springs adobe hut. The infant was scrawny, mewling, already gnawing at its own fingers. "Starved. Right inside its own mother's womb," Estelle told Lydia.

They found Tige crouched against the wall. His hands bled, the flesh torn from his unrelenting fighting at the cleat driven into the wall stud. He stared up at them, eyes as empty and savage as a caged animal's. Lydia knelt beside him. "Here's your son," she said.

Tige laughed in savage rage. "Don't let him see me like this."

She smiled wanly. "Look at him, dear one. He's beautiful. So beautiful."

"*¡Mira!*" Estelle urged Tige. "*Que grande un muchacho, querido. ¡Mira! ¡Mira!*"

Tige gazed up at them, helpless tears blurring his vision. He reached out, took the baby in his arms. "How is she—how is Nell?"

"She is well," Lydia said. "Hammond delivered your baby."

Tige stared up at her, incredulous. Lydia nodded. The baby grasped Tige's thumb. "My baby," he whispered. He grinned, rage and pride contorting his handsome mouth. "My own son . . . " He lifted his head, jerked it savagely toward the ranchhouse. "How can he not even care?"

Lydia could not get Tige out of her mind. No matter what she did, she saw his agonized, enraged face, his

200

bleeding hands. She saw him sprawled on the ground in chains.

Lydia waited until after she'd bathed and put the children in their beds, helped Estelle clear away the kitchen. Then she came into the parlor, where Ham slumped in his big chair, stiff leg extended, his gaze fixed on the dead ashes piled on the cold hearth.

"What are you going to do with that boy out in the barn?" she said.

"I reckon that's my decision. Don't no way need to concern you."

"It does concern me. . . . I want you at least to put him in the tackroom."

"Why?"

"He'll at least have a bed to sleep in—a chamber pot."

Ham shrugged, scowling, his sensibilities offended. "He's all right where he is."

"He can't sleep on the ground."

"Why not? Nigger don't need to sleep in no bed." Hammond's mouth twisted in disgust at this irrational idea. "He can jus' curl up like a dog on the ground. Don't really even need a blanket. He keep warm, same as a dog does."

"Do you believe that, Hammond?"

His voice chilled. "I don't want to talk about it, Lydia. What I believe is because of what I been taught, because of what I am, because of who I am. I know who I am. I know what is right." He shrugged. "Throw him a blanket an' you want to. You'll only spoil him. He's a Falconhurst nigger and he ain't used to bein' pampered. Less'n maybe they treated him like a pet at Hiddenbrook—made him uppity, ruint him. . . . Ground plenty good enough for him. He uppity . . . but by God, he's still a nigger."

"Ham, he's your own flesh and blood."

"Cain't be. I'm a human. He's nuthin' but a nigger, even if'n he's got more'n a passel of human blood in him. A mule's got horse blood, but that sure hell don't make him a horse. Don't make a damn bit of difference how much human blood a nigger's got—or *whose* blood it is—he still black. By God. By law. He can be white as me. Whiter. But law say if he got one drop of nigger blood, he a nigger, purentee. Sell black nigras, sell white nigras, but you don't treat nigras like humans—an' you don't call no nigra your son."

"You can't keep him chained up like that."

"Who the hell tells me I can't? There's just one thing I *can't* do. One thing I *won't* do. I *can't* and I *won't* let no murderin' mustee nigger run free."

XIX

The cleat broke free in Tige's hand. The long, grooved metal screw was smeared and sticky with his blood. He was unaware of the blood, the deep cuts in his palms and across his fingers, or even the flaring burn of pain in his hand. He had broken the chain free from the wall stud! He felt strong, stronger than a god—hell, stronger than Ham Maxwell, and that was the urgent strength to possess in the next critical hours.

He crouched for a long time listening for any suspicious sound. There was none. The ranch lay quiet with stunned after-midnight silence. He peered around him at the cavernous vault of the barn. He heard the skittering of field rats in the hay and along the loft plankings. This had been the music played for him and Nell every night in that tack room. At first the whispering sounds had terrorized Nell. Even when she was assured the noise was only rats, she shuddered in fear and revulsion. Suppose one of the filthy little creatures ran across their bed? Or touched her arm? Brushed against her in the darkness? She'd scream, she'd warned him, trying to laugh, scream and never stop screaming. He'd held her close, soothing her, quieting her. He'd hated Hammond Maxwell as much for putting Nell in the barn as for his cold and calm refusal to pay him for his work on this ranch.

Tige scrubbed at his wrists. He had every reason

for hating Maxwell. He vowed, kneeling there, that if Hammond tried to stop him and Nell from leaving tonight, he would kill him. That thought gave him a charged thrill of exultance that etched through the bone-weariness of his mind and body. He grinned savagely, wondering if he'd be like Nell, who was afraid if she screamed, she'd never stop screaming. If he started killing Ham Maxwell, could he ever be stopped?

Tige remained there on his knees a moment longer. With the back of his bloodied hand he wiped away the beads of perspiration that dripped down into his eyes and ran saltily into his mouth. Only by killing Ham Maxwell could he cleanse the agony in his soul. He had loved him—his father—but now he hated him a hundred times more violently because once he had loved him. He gazed through the dark toward the ranchhouse with hatred, and his lips twisted with contempt at the thought of the treacherous white man who'd sired, abandoned and forgotten him. That man would oppose him, and he would kill him, and his spirits would lift and he would feel like a man again— with the courage and power and bravery a man ought to have. The kind of guts a man had to have if he were to protect and provide for his wife and son in this lawless land.

He exhaled as if he had been holding his breath for an interminable time. A sense of urgency spurred him to action, and yet he forced himself to think ahead for each step. Haste wouldn't buy him much if he bungled one move of his carefully planned escape. He had lain chained thinking how he would break free, and how he would stay free. Free. That was the word that mattered.

He pushed himself up and winced, pain flashing through him. His legs felt stiff and weak. The iron shackles tore his ankles, weighted him down. He felt as if he could barely lift his feet despite the strange elation of being free which raced through his mind, hurrying him. Get out of here! Get Nell and your son and get away from this place! Once he and Nell escaped Ham Maxwell, they'd run deeper into the Texies, where words which shaped and informed Hammond Maxwell's slave-breeder existence were unknown or meaningless—slave, mestizo, mulatto, Negro. His father a white man, his unknown mother an octoroon slave. Out here in the Texies, who the hell cared? He was a free man out here. Nothing less.

Holding the shackle chain taut to keep it from clanking when he moved, Tige crawled across the hardpan flooring of the barn to the work bench. This roughly made table was a deep shadow hulking in deeper shadow. He could not risk a light, but that didn't matter the exact position of the serrated rasp he needed was fixed in his mind, glowing like a holy grail in some stygian abyss.

His hand touched the cross-grained table planking and fumbled blindly along it. His fingers closed on the flat file. His heart lurched. He was one move nearer freedom. He knelt beside the dark table and sawed steadily at the chain link which secured the two metal plates of his leg shackle.

A huge ball of fire took form and blazed behind his eyes as he worked, a swelling pustule of fatigue that was going to burst and smash him to smithereens. That strange dancing flame warned him he was too tired to go on kneeling there, his bleeding hands could no longer drag that rasp back and forth across the heated, impervious link of steel.

He wanted to plunge forward into exhausted sleep, to extinguish that orange fireball erupting in his skull, but he was driven forward by a stronger and uncontrollable force he could no longer master—he had to be free, he had to break this chain. His toes ached, his breath burned in his throat, his legs were too shaky to support him, and only the fiery orb had reality. He kept stroking the rasp over the chain link. The violent red and green and purple flames flickered and roared inside his mind, threatening to overwhelm him. Suddenly, the chain link snapped.

Tige sagged against the thick leg and hung there a long moment before he realized he had broken the shackle lock. With that realization some of the pressure inside him ebbed. The fiery orb subsided.

He set the rasp on the ground with exaggerated care. He wanted to laugh aloud, he wanted to sob out his exultance, but for the moment he remained unmoving, missing the exquisite torture of the rasp, his bleeding hands, the chain, the shackle. "Slowly," he whispered to himself, repeating the warning that he had to remember and heed that command. No matter how urgently he wanted to run, he had to be smart enough to move cautiously, catlike in the dark shadows.

Holding his breath, he slipped the broken chain link through the thick eye, parted the metal shackles and set them aside, along with the chain. He was free; he wasn't an animal anymore; he was a man—and he was free.

He massaged his stiff, swollen ankle with his bloody hands. The liquid—his own oozing blood—refreshed his sore, torn flesh. Gradually, he felt life and circulation returning to his foot.

He stood up and walked awkwardly—his legs lifting high and extending forward oddly, as if he stalked through a rough surf—across the barn to where his old wagon was shoved into a deeply shadowed corner. Taking up the shafts, he bent over, straining and tugging, and plodded out to the deepest indentation of shadow just within the barn entrance. The gear, harness, collar and iron hames, was stacked in the bed of the wagon where he'd left them the day he and Nell arrived here.

He washed the blood from his hands and legs at a wooden bucket. He didn't want to unsettle his horse. He went stealthily across the shadowed barn, opened the stall bars and led his horse out. Thank God—and Ham Maxwell—the animal was rested, well watered, well fed. "You're in a hell of a lot better shape than I am," Tige told the big dray beast. A thousand pounds of tendons and muscle and sinews . . . they could hope for at least ten or twelve miles a day without too many rest stops. Tige stroked the animal's sleek neck.

He set the harness, the iron bit, the tugs and collar, then backed the horse between the shafts, securing the rigging leathers and metal rings to the shafts. He buckled the girth and straightened the back strap from collar to crupper. He attached the tow straps through loops in the breeching and secured them to the singletree.

Moving as silently as possible, he played the reins back over the splashboard and laid them in the boot of the wagon. Holding his breath, he caught the cheek-strap and led the horse and wagon from the barn.

He paused just outside the barn. Moonlight filtered a blue haze over the yard, the house, the bunkhouse. Dogs sniffed at his legs but were too accustomed to him to bark. After a moment they slunk back into the deep shadows and curled in their own body-warmed sand.

He carried no weapon. This was as much a part of his planning as was the way he scrupulously refrained from taking even a bag of mixed oats and corn for his horse. Ham owed him that much, but according to Ham's reasoning Tige was a slave and no matter how much work he performed, Ham would never owe him anything. To hell with him; he wasn't going to take anything. No one would be able to accuse him of theft; they couldn't run him down for stealing. If possible, he'd get Nell and the baby and leave without violence. He dreamed of throttling Ham Maxwell. But that was a dream. All he wanted was to take his family and go free.

He sweated. If only those damned metal and leather riggings didn't ring with every step the horse took. Too, the wagon creaked and rattled with each turn of the iron-rimmed wheels.

He glanced toward the bunkhouse, checking it carefully. He discerned no movement. With eight or ten men over there, you could never be sure one of them wasn't up for some reason in the night. He could be stopped accidentally as certainly as through design.

He exhaled heavily and tugged on the checkpiece, moving the horse across the silent yard.

He sensed a dangerous presence, heard a soft whisper of movement behind him, already too late to heel around and protect himself. In the darkness, he'd been outmaneuvered. When the mouth of the gun was jabbed into the small of his back, Tige simply sagged against the shafts and the horse stopped at once.

"Sorry, boy." It was Paley's voice. "I'd a-stopped you before you went to all the trouble to hitch up, but I fell asleep."

Tige's voice was flat, unastonished. "You were guarding me?"

"Hell, kid, you shoulda knowed somebody was. You know Ham Maxwell. He's ready for any dirty trick you could ever think up."

"Hell, why not? He probably invented them."

Lydia and Nell came into the parlor, where Ham stood at an east window, staring out at the gaudy afternoon dusk. Nell walked slowly. Lydia had told her she should not be out of bed, but Ham made Nell's decision for her. She made up her mind to get out of bed if it killed her—and at first she thought it might.

It happened when Ham overheard Lydia protesting Nell's getting out of bed so soon after the delivery of her baby. Ham said that black wenches at Falconhurst were up the second day after a delivery and back at their chores on the third.

"We don't spoil our niggers at Falconhurst." Lydia

mocked Ham's words, her voice quavering with sarcasm.

Ham was so convinced of the correctness of his position that he missed her heavy-handed irony. "That's right," he agreed. "You too all-fired soft-hearted where Nigras is concerned, you do spile 'em. . . . And Nell—she's a young girl. She oughta recover fast."

Hammond limped from the room. Nell gazed after him, her face chilled, eyes cold. Despite Lydia's insistence that she remain in bed, Nell was determined to get up, dress, wait on herself. As a compromise, Lydia bound the girl's abdomen with wide swaths cut from bed sheets. Nell walked oddly, stood ramrod straight and breathed only shallowly.

Now, he did not turn from the window, seemed totally unaware of their presence. Lydia said, "Ham. Nell and I. We want to talk to you."

He went on gazing across the far flat fields into the blue haze of the east. Nell said, "I'll be forever grateful for what you did for me, Mr. Ham—delivering my baby."

Ham shrugged, scarcely aware of her. "You were kind," she insisted. "Gentle. I can't forget that. I just want to say, I won't ever forget that kindness no matter what happens."

Lydia's gentle voice rode over the girl's. "I too have seen you in those moments when you had kindness, were gentle . . . I don't want to forget those times, either, Ham."

Ham turned his head slightly, glanced at Lydia as though he'd never seen her before.

"Tige is a good boy, Mr. Ham—" Nell said.

"A murderer—"

"You know better. . . . He's your son, even if you don't claim him, even if his mother was an octoroon," Nell said.

"An octoroon bed wench." Ham's voice was cold.

"You're right. . . . Tige did kill my stepfather.

. . . But Foye Randolph was a vicious man. Tige killed him to save me."

Ham made a sharp cutting gesture. "I don't want to hear no such talk."

"Why not?" Lydia's voice lashed at him. "Are you so afraid of the truth?"

"It ain't fittin' . . . an' won't do no good. Ain't no circumstances that make it right a nigger kills a white man . . . an' I won't hear no more.

"Please, Mr. Ham," Nell said. "You saw me suffering—and you were compassionate. You had pity. You helped me. I am suffering now. Be kind. Let us go! Tige and I can be free out here in Texas. No one knows us. No one knows anything about us."

"I know," Ham said. "God knows."

"What are you going to do?" Lydia said, gazing unblinkingly at him. "Keep that boy out there chained in that barn until he dies—of blood poisoning or gangrene?"

Ham drew a deep breath, exhaled slowly. He straightened, unaccustomedly putting his weight on his stiff leg. They saw his fists knotted at his sides. They expected him to lash out, raging, or to stalk from the room.

Instead, he talked quietly—almost as if half to himself—of Falconhurst. "I got to see the place where my pa is buried," Ham said.

Lydia straightened. She drew in her breath and held it, not even aware she'd stopped respirating naturally.

"When my pa died, I should of been there to see he was buried in the right place—like my mother was. When my mother died, Pa put up a beautiful headstone at her grave. With her birthdate and the day she died . . . and her surname . . . she was a Hammond."

Neither Lydia nor Nell spoke. They stared at Ham, incredulous. He seemed hardly aware of them, or aware of where he was. In his mind he may have been at a window in the old house at Falconhurst, staring out toward the family burial plot on a knoll in a pine copse.

"You could see the little cemetery from the house," Ham said. "Just our family buried there. My grandpa. Grandmother. An uncle that never married. . . . It was our own family plot, you see. . . ."

Watching him, Nell shivered involuntarily. Lydia went on gazing at him as if bemused.

". . . Sometimes . . . sometimes . . . when the sun was bright . . . it would glitter on that marble of Ma's headstone. . . . It gave you a good feeling to see it . . . as if Ma was there and everything was all right. . . . Pa ought to have a nice marble marker. . . . I know Lucretia Borgia saw to his funeral, and people coming and a proper burial and all . . . but a headstone . . . his grave needs a headstone, don't it?"

He waited a long beat. Neither of them said anything. He seemed not to have expected them to reply. Perhaps he would not have heard them if they had.

"Way I see it, them marker stones ought to match up as much as possible. . . . I worry for fear maybe Lucretia Borgia didn't have Pa buried beside Ma. On her right. His body ought to be on her right, you see, and their headstones ought to be as much alike as they can be . . . and maybe when the sun shines on 'em right—early in the mornings . . . that's the way it's got to be. I got to see to it. I know it's got to be done right or I cain't rest. Cain't no way rest less'n I know. . . ."

They went on peering at him, deeply troubled. Nell scrubbed her hands along her bare arms as if this room were as cold as the tombs Ham saw in his mind.

Lydia shook her head. She touched Nell's arm. She motioned with her head that they should leave. They walked silently out of the parlor, going along the stoop, across the dog-trot and into the kitchen. In the big

211

dining area, Lydia looked around as if caged, her eyes like chipped china.

She gestured helplessly. "No sense trying to talk to him," she said: "He's—not even here. Maybe he's never been here, really. He came out west—his body did— but he never left Falconhurst."

They worked desultorily in the kitchen, each lost in her own thoughts, prey to her own fears. Nell worked even when standing up was torture. She felt as if her womb were slipping down through her vagina. She couldn't stop because she couldn't endure thinking about Tige chained and bleeding in the barn while she stood helplessly here.

The kitchen door whined open and slammed shut. Ham entered the room. He walked to the dining table and stood gazing at them, his rigid face pallid. "You-all been houndin' at me as to what I aim to do—about this ranch, about that nigger chained out there in the barn. . . . Well, I ready to tell you. I've made up my mind. Quick as I can, I'm headin' back east to Alabama. . . . I'm going home to Falconhurst."

Lydia gasped softly but she did not speak. Raw hurt spilled across the dark bitter liquid of her eyes. She went on working.

Nell whispered, "And Tige? What about Tige?"

"I'm takin' the mustee with me. I'll turn him over to the law when I git him back to the States."

XX

Unable to sleep, Nell tossed and twisted on her rumpled bed. Her back ached, her legs felt numb. The house grew silent, as did the ranchyard, the distant bunkhouse where the last lantern was doused, the corrals where horses milled and snuffled in the darkness, and the silence spread to the open ranges where a coyote bayed, an owl hooted, a lost dogie bawled, intensifying the stillness. But the quiet was oppressive and she could not sleep.

She pressed the back of her hand over her mouth. She could not believe what was happening to her and, forcing herself to believe, she was unable to accept it. The whole world was crazy, with all the meaning and human decency and hope gone out of it. Tige chained in that filthy barn like an animal. Doubts assailed and overwhelmed her. She couldn't pray, because there were no gods left to pray to, no one who would listen, no one to give a damn. She felt like a mesquite sprig, a grain of range sand, lifeless and sterile, and unnoted in this immense universe. Not the farthest star, winking alone in the unrelieved cosmos blackness, was as lonely, as abandoned as she. Perhaps, as far as the gods were concerned, she was dead . . . she and Tige. They had committed murder, taken a human life—an evil, lecherous and lustful life, but they had slain another being. Perhaps the gods had brought them this far—this close to freedom—as some monstrous joke, to torment them. To know what hell is, you first must see what heaven might have been.

Young as she was, when Nell abandoned prayer and the gods who'd always coddled and favored her and now totally abandoned her, she looked around frantically for help on earth. Somebody. Something. She reminded herself that Ham had been good and gentle when she most needed his aid. He had saved her life. He had saved her baby. If only she could make him listen to her now.

But he would not listen. He was more remote and withdrawn than ever. The least opposition or imposition set him into a rage. Violence seemed tamped down inside him, just beneath the surface.

Nell tried to stifle her sobs in the mausoleumlike darkness of the somber house. Her crying wracked her, and not even the deep feather pillow could muffle her weeping. She was inconsolable, and unable to think how she could help Tige. Yet she could not believe he was going to be returned to the States without her. She could not let herself acknowledge this and go on breathing. She loved him and she needed him and she could not give him up.

She had loved him for so long—and so deeply! Since they first brought him in shackles to Hiddenbrook, she'd loved him. Something—a look, a shared sense of delight, that mysterious intangible magnetism which sets *one* person apart for us from all others. These emotions and her devotion deepened over the years, leading directly to murder. . . .

She saw him in the fields working—and her heart lurched. She dreamed of him in the night—and she yearned for him, a little girl who would never love but one man. Her mother—unable to credit or even suspect that a wellborn southern white girl could ever regard a Negro—even a white-skinned one—as anything more than a pet—brought Tige into the manor house at Hiddenbrook as a footman. Nell herself brought him into her bed, night after breathless night. They lay together in the jasmine-scented dark and planned a life together, far from the rigid race oppression of the States, in the new free land far across the Texies. Listening, sweated, aroused, driven, was the one man to whom their love was totally obscene, totally sexually stimulating, stirring in him lustful appetites that could not be sated outside her bed. Foye Randolph became obsessed with desire for her. She shuddered, remembering in agonized, horrifying detail the way Tige—terribly overmatched—had killed for her. And he had run with her—back into shackles—into hell. . . .

Nell heard a sound somewhere in the living area of the ranchhouse. She stopped crying, held her breath, listening. Something moved, something scraped, and then there was deeper silence. Her heart lurched. Tige had gotten free again! He was breaking into the house; he had come for her and their baby. They were going to get away together, after all.

Brushing at her tears with the backs of her fingers, Nell sat up in bed. Her breathing was labored and seemed to echo inside her own ears, deafening her to the faint rustle of sound. She had to hear! She leaned forward, straining, waiting for a movement in the still parlor.

Holding her breath, she swung her legs over the side of the bed. She wore a filmy lace gown, the only nice one she owned, the only one she'd hastily packed when she and Tige ran from Hiddenbrook.

She heard the movement again. She was convinced the muted sounds came from the parlor. Trembling, she slipped off the bed, her feet touching the chilled floor. She prayed the rope mattress supports would not creak.

She tiptoed across the room, bumped a chair. She winced and bit back her outcry.

Taking the doorknob in both hands, Nell turned

it infinitely slowly, not breathing. She cracked the door open, then sagged a moment against it. Lamplight beamed along the hallway from the large parlor. Someone was up there, merely muffling their noises, probably not even consciously trying to be quiet.

She opened the door and stepped into the hallway. She saw Hammond Maxwell. Puzzled, she paused, watching him. He had a chair pulled close to the fireplace. There was no fire in it; the hearth was cold. Then she saw Ham had removed several bricks from the support wall. He was crouched forward, intent, totally preoccupied. She could not tell what he was doing.

She went along the hall thinking only that she wanted to talk to him—she had to talk to him! She would be unlikely to find him at a quieter, less hurried time. He had to listen to her.

As the sound of her bare feet on the flooring ate through his concentration, Ham jerked his head up. He stared at her, startled, scowling. Almost he looked as if she'd caught him in commission of a crime. He said, chilled, "What do you want?"

For the moment stupefied at the sight of the incredible stacks of gold he was transferring from wall receptacle to a sturdy iron box placed between his boots, Nell could only shake her head. She had never seen so much money.

His warning voice carried a threat of reprisal. "You keep your mouth shut about this."

Nell spread her hands. "I don't want your money."

"Could buy you and your nigger boy a lot of freedom." Then he softened slightly, his tone kindly and concerned. "You ought to have some clothes on."

She smiled, forcibly reminding him of his kindness and gentleness toward her. "I guess it wouldn't matter anymore if I walked around naked before you—"

"No." He shook his head. "But you'll get chilled walkin' around in the night."

216

"You've seen me—as naked as I'll ever be," she said. "You worried about me then. You worry about me catching chill. . . . I *know* that inside you do care about—me and Tige."

He astonished her by gazing up at her with an almost gentle smile. "Yes. I do care about you. You're a very pretty, very young little white girl—from the very best sort of family—in deep trouble."

"It doesn't matter who I *was*—where I came from, Mr. Ham. It's what I *am*."

He nodded. "Yes . . . I started out hating you . . . for betraying your family, your upbringing. I despised you. But you are a sweet child. I can't deny that. You get to know you, you come to love you. You have made all of us love you in spite of everything."

She stared at him. Was she dreaming this? Were these quiet words coming from the Hammond Maxwell who chained a human being in his barn? Then she realized.

Yes. As one white person responding to another— as one of the superior class to another—he could love her, care for her, worry about her. It was when she crossed the line and admitted she loved a boy with black blood in his veins that Hammond Maxwell became her implacable foe.

She crossed that line now, purposely. "I love Tige," she said. "No matter how much you deny him, he is your son, and I love him."

"You're all mixed up in your head." His voice was cold now.

"But it's my life, my life that's destroyed—without Tige."

"That's where you're wrong," he said in that low, reasonable tone of logic. "I'm doin' you a favor, girl. You—and your baby."

"By killing Tige?" Her voice quavered.

"I'm taking him back to stand charged with murder, yes."

"Then take me along—me and my baby."

He shook his head. "No. I can't do that."

"You're taking Tige. He is part of me. You might as well take me."

He sank back in his chair. She sat on the raised brick apron before the hearth. He appeared ready to expend whatever time necessary to show her how wrong she was. He said, "I'd wish my own daughter to be like you, Nell."

"If I were your daughter, you wouldn't break my heart."

"I've got a daughter, Nell. No. Not Lydia's children—a daughter back home born to my late wife, Blanche. Her name is Sophie. She must be—eight or ten years old by now. . . . Her little eyes are crossed. She'll never be as lovely as you are. But I'd do for her what I would for you—what I know is going to be your best interests in the long run."

"Is it best to take Tige back to the States—to die?"

"He kilt a white man, child. He can't be allowed to escape punishment—less'n some other violent Nigra thinks he can kill a white man an' git away with it. Our whole society—back in the South—is built on establishing and maintainin' white supremacy. You know what that is?"

Her pretty mouth twisted. "White people are gods. Niggers are animals."

He almost smiled. "We keep law and we keep order by treatin' Nigras just, but firm. You wait and see what happens if that way of handlin' Nigras ever breaks down. You're going to see theft, and rape and murder so nobody is safe in his own bed. But as long as Nigras know they place, they don't rape white ladies. They do, they know they hang. Fast as they caught, they hang. They hang where other Nigras can see 'em hangin'—an' learn. They behaves, we takes care of them, we all live in peace. They kill—or rise in rebellion—they shot, hung or sold off to die workin' shackled in the cane fields. Nigras is animals. They got to be treated fair—but they got to be punished when they evil, fast an' hurtful. That's the only way we can be safe with them on lonely farms, on plantations where—with torches and pitchforks—they could destroy everything we hold dear."

"Tige doesn't need that lesson. Tige is not like that. Tige has learned."

He shook his head. "It's already too late for Tige. . . . I'm thinkin' about other Nigras now—and how we can control them."

"We're not in Alabama," she said. "We're deep in the Texies. . . . I am as guilty for my stepfather's death as Tige. Far guiltier . . . I would have killed him if I could have. But I couldn't. I was too weak, too afraid of him. Whatever Tige and I did—in Louisiana—we've paid for it. In agony. In running. In terror. But that could all be behind us—we could make new lives out here—"

"That's what I want you to do." He nodded and sat smiling at her, his eyes gentle.

"What?"

He nodded again. "I've give it thought, girl. You can start a new life. You must stay in the Texies. . . . I have to speak plain to you. The fact is, there ain't no place in the States—leastways not in the South among decent, Godfearing, churchgoing civilized people—for a white girl what's been violated by a black. That he raped you—an' you consented. That don't help. That makes it worse. But you *can* stay out here. You can start a whole new life out here. You—and your baby."

"Without Tige?"

He exhaled heavily and nodded. "I'm doing you a favor, girl. Can't you see that?"

"You're breaking my heart."

"I don't want to do that, girl—in the long run I don't think I am."

"If you take Tige from me you're destroying me."

"No. I'm making it possible for you to redeem a— a ugly, dirty mistake. A mistake you made as a child, too young to know better. That black out there forced hisself on you. You was too young to know better. Like you say, all that can be behind you. Out here, nobody points a finger at you. Nobody knows you. You and your baby will be better off here—among Texicans, half-breeds, Indians and Mexicans."

"I'm trash. And you see these people as dregs. You want to leave me with the garbage."

"Don't go low-ratin' yourself. I didn't say you was trash. Or think it. I don't believe that. I said they ain't no life for you—or your mustee child—back east. You can build whatever life you can—but out here. That's the best gift I can give you. I can't see nuthin' else."

"I don't want a new life. I want to be with Tige."

"We couldn't travel slow enough to accommodate you—a genteel white girl—an' a newborn baby—"

"I don't care. I'll take care of the baby. I won't complain. I'll be all right. As long as I am with Tige."

"It wouldn't help none, girl. You'd make that trip— if you survived it, if your baby survived it—only to see Tige go back to what he is—a black slave. A slave that's sure to die by hanging."

She shook her head, gazing about her, frustrated and helpless. The silence of the Texas night pressed in upon her as if the world around her were an empty void, without warmth or compassion.

Her eyes glittered wildly. When she jerked her head around her hair bobbled like a mane against her shoulders. She looked as if she'd wail out in her agony. Instead she only whispered it, "I can't stay here— alone."

He swung his arm, dismissing the matter. "I'm sorry.

You must. I've thought it out. That's the way it is. . . .
That's the way it's got to be."

When Ham closed the bedroom door and turned
around, Lydia stood naked before him. Her gold and
bronze body gleamed sensually in the saffron lamplight. Her rich black hair toppled like damasks about
her face and shoulders, accentuating her nudity. Her
liquid black eyes seemed to swirl with unknown cur-
rents, unplumbed depths and unshared secrets. It was
as if for the first time she allowed him to gaze into
the dark panes behind which she kept her hidden
desires, her innermost emotions. Her full breasts,
topped with dark ruby nipples, the shadowed planes
of her belly, the shadowy dark at her thighs, the sculptured elegance of her legs acted upon him as an overwhelming aphrodisiac. For the moment everything else
except her lush Latin beauty was swept from his consciousness. He looked at her and he wanted her, he
even *needed* her as he never had in the six years he
had used her body as a careless vessel. The faint musk
of her body aroused him. He forgot the hundreds of
times he'd possessed her over the years, using her,
shoving her away. Abruptly, it was as if he had never
had her before. She was new to him in her silken
nakedness, her seductive surrender. He knew it was
sorcery, some kind of spell. He was seeing her for the
first time as *she* wanted him to see her. He had truly
never seen her before like this. He was conscious of
sharp lancing pangs in his groin, the distended agony
of his swollen phallus.

"My God," he said.

She merely smiled, faintly, voluptuously. Looking
at her, the taunting succubus, he felt a raging desire to
overpower her, to master her, to beat her down to
submission with his mouth and his arms and his quiveringly rigid manhood. He limped to her, reaching for
the sensuous body dripping lamplight.

"Not so fast," she said. The soft Latin music of her voice added to her allure. "Don't you want me to help you undress?"

"In a moment," he said. He put his arms about her, sliding his hands to the satiny smoothness at the small of her back, the firm rising flesh of her hips. He closed his fingers possessively, drawing her up against his aching staff, kissing her. Her lips parted under his. He tasted the heady winelike sweetness of her heated mouth. Holding her, he slipped his probing fingers through the dainty mound of her femininity into the liquid wetness between her thighs. His breathing rattled and ached in his chest. "My God," he said again.

He felt her hands loosening the buttons of his shirt, expertly disengaging his belt buckle, freeing the fetters at his fly. His trousers slipped, crumpling about his boots. She peeled back his shirt and let it fall behind him. He tried again to pull her upon him, but she waltzed him easily to the bed, pushed him gently down upon it. He gazed down and laughed at his rigid phallus standing like a tower above the glabrous sea of his bare abdomen. Master. Monarch of all he surveyed.

Lydia worked the boot off his stiff right leg, pulled off the other boot, his stockings and his trousers. He tried to smile at her. "I don't want to wait anymore," he said. "I don't know if I can."

Her smile was that of a Mexican Mona Lisa. "You don't have to wait," whispered the musical, throaty voice, accented, heated, thrilling.

He pulled her down to him. She kissed his mouth and chin and throat lingeringly. His hands explored her, trembling with anxiety. She wriggled to the mattress beside him. When he would have rolled over upon her in the only position acceptable in his inhibited lexicon she spread her legs, locked her ankles about him. He protested from old habit, but she was astonishingly strong. She held him. She drew him closer inside the

222

vise of her legs. "I want you inside me," she said. "I want you deep, deep inside me."

Overcome by the fiery bubbling liquidity of her, he could not oppose her no matter what immodest, shameless thing she did. He found himself thrusting, driving himself to her, in an exquisitely tormenting rhythm. He stared down at her, even the pressures inside his skull making his eyes bulge. Her face was gone all out of focus. Her locked legs clasped him to her. Her arms bound him tightly, their bodies adhering. He rocked upon her, blinded by the pounding pressures in his temples, driven by the fearful urgency to fulfill his need, until he could endure it no longer.

He sobbed out and fell heavily upon her, his hips still bucking almost involuntarily. His mouth chewed in mindless suckling at her mouth. He panted for breath. He gasped for breath. He cried out in blissful agony . . . and he fell away from her.

He toppled facedown into his pillow, totally exhausted. Dimly, and as along a long corridor, he heard her musical voice caressing him: "You'll never find me—nowhere else—in anyone else—wherever you go, you must need me—as now. . . ."

He snored loudly.

Lydia fell away from him. After a long time she got up from the bed and stood staring at her reflection, yellowed and shadowy, in the wavy mirror. She slid her splayed hands down along the smoothness of her heated flesh. Her ebon eyes filled with tears. She had laid before him all she had to offer—herself, everything she was without reservation. And he had taken her, as he had a hundred times before, and plunged into stunned sleep. Old habits, brought from Falconhurst! Use a bed wench as a convenient vessel for relief and release and fall asleep, uncommitted, unobligated, uncaring. She turned and stared at Ham sprawled out across the mattress. How differently this little episode had ended from her dreams. She'd been so certain of her charms, so sure of herself. But in six years she had not cultivated his emotional dependence on her. She had become only another of his bed wenches. A brown one. Nothing more.

"Stay with me," she whispered, knowing he didn't hear, and that it wouldn't matter if he did. She had lost him.

She blew out the lamp and lay down on the bed. She stared upward through her welling tears into the smoky, lonely darkness of defeat. . . .

In the next days, Lydia moved silently about the ranchhouse.

She said little. She was too stunned by loss to cry out in protest. Her hurt over her rejection went too deep for tears. As she'd grown up she'd seen in other's eyes—even the anguished, veiled gazes of the priest that she was lovelier than other girls, set apart as diamonds are different from sapphires. It bought her nothing. She was a bed wench, used, discarded, rejected. She seldom smiled. She was inordinately gentle—even for her—with her children. When someone spoke to her, she appeared to respond with a start, as if deeply preoccupied with grief.

She watched Ham prepare to abandon the ranch as one watches preparations for some doomsday for which one is totally unprepared, and totally incapable of understanding. She knew he was going. She could not believe that he would go. He was leaving her, abandoning her, and she could not believe he was leaving her. He must not go. Yet nothing could keep him from going. He packed an old trunk with clothing, personal belongings. He was a man on an undertaking from which he could not be turned, dissuaded or delayed. He moved with a quiet, firm purpose. Everything he did was carried out for the final time, with an air of finality that left her shaken. He was leaving no loose ends; he was carefully and finally locking all gates behind him.

There came that somber day when there were no more last-minute preparations, no final chores, no reason to delay. He stacked his belongings just inside the front door in the parlor to expedite their storage in his carriage. He limped out across the sun-struck yard to say goodbye to the men in the bunkhouse. He ordered a Concord carriage hitched and made ready for travel. Everything was matter-of-fact, final, concluded.

Lydia searched for a trace of regret in his face, and found none. He was like an animal abandoning a fouled lair. She had the sickening feeling that he would never even look back, would soon forget.

She stood inside the kitchen door and watched him walk in his uneven gait toward the house for the very last time. His planter's hat was set squarely on his head. His broad shoulders and thick chest were held erect. There was that faintly arrogant tilt to his chin she'd remarked in him the first time she saw him—a look that declared he might not know who you were, but he knew who he was. *My mother was a Hammond, you know.*

Lydia pressed her palm against her aching throat. She hurt so badly she was afraid she could not speak. Yet when he came into the kitchen, she spoke, shocked at how calm she sounded when inside she was confused and terrorized and heartbroken. "And what about me, Hammond? What about our children?"

"You'll be all right." He glanced about the room, not really meeting her gaze, but certainly not reluctant to look at her. He simply didn't care. "They'll be all right with you. I'm not worried about that."

"You mean you don't give a damn."

"We've had what we could have, Lydia. Six years together out here. I've tried to be good to you."

"Why can't you take me—take us—with you?"

"You wouldn't be happy back there, Lydia—"

"Do you think I'll be happy here, with three children to raise, without you?"

He spread his hands. "You'll be better off. I know that. A Mexican. No matter how lovely you are—you are a Mexican. Your dark-skinned brood. . . . People don't mean to be cruel—back east. But they can be, hardly realizing it."

"Yes. I'm sure they can—I've known you for six years."

He winced. "I've given you all I ever said I would—"

"Have you?"

"I never said I'd marry you, Lydia."

"No. Not in words."

"I never meant to marry you. From the first day. . . . I don't believe you thought I would."

"But you're wrong. I did think you would. My mother thought you would. My priest thought so. If I came and lived with you, they said. If you got to know me." She laughed bitterly. "And most stupid of all, I thought so."

"You could have gone, anytime you wanted to."

"Could I? Would you have let me go? With another man? Or would you have killed him? And killed me? You—who walk away now without looking back."

"I'm sorry. But you are a Mexican. That does make some difference. Even here in Texas."

"You're wrong. I'm a Texican. I was born here. I belong here."

His voice hardened. "Then stay here. Be happy here."

"You owe me something, Hammond. Me. Our babies. . . . There isn't one law for you, and another for us . . . there should not be. You can't just walk out on us."

He made a sharp downward gesture. "Hell, Lydia, you must have known I would sometime. I never lied to you about that."

"No, I suppose I'm the only one who lied. And I lied to myself."

"You knew who I was—what you were. . . . Why did you become—my—my woman?"

Her head tilted. "Because you were rich and power-ful and I was very poor, Señor Maxwell . . . poor as Ramon and Maria are poor at sweet springs . . . hun-gry. Because I was willing to—to give you my life. Be-cause I thought maybe—in time—*con tiempo*—you might give me your love."

He poured himself a drink. "Well, I'm sorry about that. . . . Maybe I'll never feel about no other woman as I do about you. . . . But where I'm going, it wouldn't work out, Lydia. You might as well make up your mind to that." He reached into his inside jacket pocket and removed a folded deed. "I made this here deed out to you. The ranch. Lands. Stock. Equipment. Water rights. It's all yours. Yours and the children's. You run it even halfway decent, you'll get along. . . . I signed this deed over to you. Cook and Paley witnessed my signature. You take it in to the county seat and have it recorded. An' there's money hidden in the hollow bricks beside the fireplace—I left some of it for you. . . . I'm sorry. That's all I can do."

"If you loved me—"

"How could I, Lydia? My God. Try to understand. I'm who I am—"

"I know." Her mouth twisted. "Your mother was a Hammond, you know."

"—and you're what you are, and that's the way it is."

She took the deed, crushing it in her white-knuckled fist. "Yes." She nodded, tilting her head. "Yes. That's the way it is."

Nobody bothered to tell Tige what was going to happen to him. Nobody had to—the answers flared in the atmosphere, the entwined expectancy of a lynching, the forlorn gloom of a funeral. Nell clung to him, sobbing. She didn't discuss Ham's plans because she believed Ham had told him—vindictively explicit. Nell could think only to spare him as much and as long as possible. Lydia remained lovely and kind, but she was remote, as if bemused, bewildered. The cowhands came into the barn to visit him, but they were uncomfortable and ill at ease, puzzled and troubled to see him crouched there like a chained animal. Two of the newest hired hands drifted, not liking the look of chains, or a chained man. There was a heavy air about the ranch. Ham's decision to return Tige to the United States was a kind of legal murder. According to law, as well as the code of the slave states, Tige Frazee, chained in the barn, had been slain. He no longer existed as a free man, no longer a man at all, or even a human being. Once he crossed that Sabine River into the United States, he was a slave, a sub-human beast, an animal that could talk passably and think along simple lines, but born to die in bondage.

Tige fought at his chains until blood spewed from his torn hands and calves. He could not go back to slavery. He could not endure the auction block. He could never again be a slave. He would rather die, but he felt no guilt for the death of Foye Randolph.

Sprawled in exhaustion against the barn wall, denied even the least trace of human dignity, Tige almost prayed for it to end. He wished to God he had been born as meek and humble as the most cringing toady on the cruelest slave farm. He wished he were all black. Then he could live with it, with what his white masters said he was, a black beast of burden. He would never have tasted, even so briefly, the sweetness of freedom, the exalting pleasure of Nell's love. No never again.

He rolled his head back and forth. He couldn't return to that—to having his life and health and existence subject to the humors and caprices of white master, white mistress. No, by all his ancient gods. Never again. He felt pity and compassion for his black brothers, but he could never be one of them anymore.

He slept only finally and then in exhaustion, blood leaking from his torn arms and hands and legs.

Ham limped into the barn and stood over him, gazing down at him. Ham kicked him awake. "Hey, you, boy. You ready to go, boy?"

Tige sat up, burning with instant rage. His tone matched Ham's. "Go where, *sir?*" His voice mocked that title.

"I'm taking you back—to Alabama."

Tige gaze up at him, unblinking. "I'm ready to go," he said. "But you better know in advance—it's a long way across the Texies."

Ham's grin was cold. He shrugged his thick shoulders. "Oh, I'll git you there, all right. Don't you ever think I won't git you there."

II

THE JOURNEY HOME

XI

Hammond drove away from the ranch, taking Tige as his shackled prisoner, just after daybreak. No one on the place was sleeping in that noisy, crimson dawn; few had slept all night. There could be no doubt that the destinies of every human being were affected by Maxwell's departure. Nothing could possibly be the same. The ordinary security they'd all taken for granted as recently as a week back was shot to hell. Hammond called out the men and they loaded his best carriage— his trunk, guns, blankets, oilcloths, gear. Hammond Maxwell was a methodical, disciplined, careful man. He seemed to have overlooked nothing except the welfare of those he left in his wake, and about this he appeared totally indifferent. He checked all details carefully. The metal box containing a fortune in gold was bolted to the flooring under the front seat of the carriage. Its lock was large, cumbersome, practically impregnable. Shackles and chains had been secured to the sideboards and carriage underpinning. It would be a long hard journey, but Ham apparently was not troubled. He was supremely confident of his own abilities and strengths, and the desire to return to Falconhurst accelerated with each passing hour. Nothing would stop him.

As always, prudent and taking no chances, Ham ordered Cale Lambdin to stand guard with loaded shotgun while Paley and young Tyler led Tige in chains from the barn. Cale held his breath, perhaps the only person on the ranch glad to see Maxwell go, sweated with anticipation to have him gone.

Ham supervised shackling Tige on the front seat. A spancel was secured to Tige's scabbed and torn right ankle. This hobble was often used to fetter animals as well as slaves, to keep them from straying. Even if he broke his shackles, Tige could not run as long as he was spanceled. Chains from iron cuffs which linked the boy's arms were run through the spancel eye and locked to both the flooring and sideboards.

"Won't you need the boy to help you with the drivin', and tendin' the animal?" Paley asked.

Ham shook his head. "Won't need him."

"It's a fur piece to Alabama."

"Won't need him." Ham tilted his head at an obstinate set. "Come out here on my own. Don't need no nigger helpin' to git me back."

Paley shrugged. "Wish you luck, boss."

Ham nodded. He peered at Paley for a moment. "Hope you'll stay on here—for a while anyhow. Miz Lydia's goin' to need help, right at first."

Paley shrugged again, but said nothing. He made no commitment and Ham did not pursue the matter. After all, he was totally aware of the situation from Paley's viewpoint. A prideful man from the States like Paley might find it difficult—or damned well impossible— to work for a greaser woman . . . even Lydia. Well, it was Paley's decision. Ham made no effort to push him. He respected a man's pride and self-respect. He would not want to be pushed if he were in Paley's position.

"Well, take care of yourself, Paley," was all Ham said.

Tige's and Hammond's departure was marked and orchestrated by open lamentations and bitter silences. Nell pressed against the carriage and clung to Tige.

234

She held him in her arms and wept inconsolably. When Hammond slapped the reins and started the horse forward, Nell ran along beside the carriage weeping. The others watched, uncomfortable and saddened. The children were accustomed to their father's coming and going on horseback or in the carriage, but they too were aware instinctively that this departing was different. They sensed the tension crackling in the atmosphere, the quiet agony of their mother, who stood rigid and silent, watching. They clung to her dress, desolated but not crying, somehow afraid to cry.

When at last Hammond touched the whip to the horse and rode away from her, Nell sank to her knees in the sand, crying helplessly. Tige felt as if the speeding carriage had broken something precious—and tangible —between him and Nell. He twisted on the seat, looking back. His eyes brimmed with tears. Lydia, Estelle, the children and most of the hired hands had straggled slowly out to where Nell crouched on the ground. They watched her impotently, unable to comfort her because they had no comforting words. They could promise her nothing. Today was bleak; tomorrow promised pain. There were no reassurances, no hope for reprieve. She slumped in the strong morning sunlight, tiny and forlorn, and lost.

Tige remained half-turned on the seat staring back toward the ranchhouse until the roof of the house itself dissipated and disappeared in the blue-hazed distance. "No sense in you starin' back there," Ham told him.

"Go to hell."

Ham caught his breath raspingly. His voice was low, controlled, but quivering with suppressed rage. "You listen to me, nigger. I ain't never tolerated no nigger talkin' to me like that, an' by hell, I don't no way intend to start now."

"Don't you?"

"Damn your black hide. Don't you dare take that

235

tone. Why can't you be civil, polite, like a slave ought to be? Looks like, you claim to be so smart, you'd realize you git along with your betters by being civil. Hell, I don't no way understand a biggety, uppity-talkin' Nigra like you. I try to be fair—"

"Fair? Why you hypocritical son of a bitch. If you had one ounce of fairness in your body, I'd be ridin' free, heir to Falconhurst, recognized and accepted as your son—your firstborn son—"

"My son?" Ham's laugh was humorless, withering. "Jesus. The drop of a Nigra bed wench—"

"Your bed wench. Your son."

"That's the kind of crooked-headed, mixed-up thinking that has you actin' uppity. You ain't my son. No way. Even if I had *married* the black wench that bore you, you wouldn't be *my* son. Not before God. Not before the law. Miscegenation . . . you know what that means?"

Tige stared straight ahead and said nothing.

"Miscegenation. I'll jus' tell you what it means to clear up any fool ideas you got 'bout bein' my son. . . . That's intermarryin' between races. That's a criminal offense in Alabama. No such marriage could ever be legal."

"It means somethin' else, too."

Ham jerked his head around, eyes cold. "Does it, uppity-talkin' Nigra? Does it mean something else?"

"It means *interbreeding* between races, too. Jus' as criminal—before Alabama law."

"Don't talk so goddam smart, boy. Don't try to tell me the *law*. What the hell can an ignorant Nigra like you know about the *law?* I obey the law—"

"Shit. You double-dealing bastard, you. You obey all the laws that profit you. That don't no way inconvenience you—"

"I warned you once, boy, 'bout that smart-brass talk—"

"What can you do to me? Drag me behind the

carriage until I bleed to death? Do you think I give a damn whether I die in the Texies draggin' behind a carriage or live to hang in Louisiana? What can you do to me? Make me walk—chained? Hell, do you think I'm in a hurry to hang?"

Ham stared at him, face chilled. "You're a smart nigger, ain't you?"

"Why not, *Masta?* I'm *your* son."

They drove uncounted miles without speaking. The carriage rolled steadily forward hour after hour across the profligate waste of flatland. Up over gray ascent, across a flat-topped knoll and into a slight declivity, until after a while, it was as if all hillocks were the same, all shadowy vales identical. Ham let the horse plod the ill-defined trail at its own pace, down a gray slope, up a mesquite-fringed incline and down another. The wind blew across them, hot and grainy, stinging like winged ants. The sinister blaze of the sun attacked relentlessly, depleting men and animal. One looked ahead on the dim trail and found only more yellow ridges like humps on a washboard, their plateaus sun-splashed and the light seeming to spill over on all sides in widening rims of shadow. When Ham did speak again it was as if he continued their conversation without a break.

He laughed, a sound without mirth but choked with contempt. "So that's why you reconciled yourself—a born slave—good enough to marry the Murdoch girl, huh? You reckoned yourself *my son.* That put you right on eye level with the Randolphs and the Murdochs, eh? Good enough to marry the daughter, good enough to kill the father."

Tige shrugged.

Ham cursed. "It's that kind of limber-headed thinkin' that's causin' the trouble with you Nigras. That and that goddam Quaker abolitionist propaganda—"

"You forget, *Masta.* I can't read."

"Hell, boy. You blacks don't shit me. I know them abolitionist whites sneak around down here an' *read* them lyin' tracts to you—"

"I don't know anything about abolition. . . . I know only how I feel . . . inside. I'm no better than any other man—but, by God, I'm no lower—"

"You son of a bitch. You ain't a man, no way. You a animal. A slave. A beast of burden." Ham put his head back, raging with savage, angered laughter. "By God, I feel like I heard it all now! Like I in some kind of nightmare! That I'd ever sit and hear a black slave talk uppity like this! I ought to knock you in the head and throw you to the buzzards. Right here. Save the world a lot of trouble an' do you a favor."

"Be a waste of a nigger, Masta," Tige taunted him. "Don't want to hang a nigger less'n you get a profit, Masta. You want to hang me where I'll serve as a 'zample to other niggers. A warnin' never to lift their heads up—"

"Don't care you lift your head up." Ham made a savage downward-cutting gesture with his hand. "Hits jus' when you go deceivin' yo' own self—an' hurtin' other people when you do—that I objects. And objects violently. It's when you fo'gits you're a *Nigra*. When you get the insane notion in your burr head that you're a *human being*—"

"You're a human being, ain't you?"

"You goddam right I am. I purentee white—a human being—"

"Then I don't want to be one." Tige spat with the wind.

During the long unrelieved heat of the afternoon, Ham stopped infrequently. He found water for his horse in a meager creek. He permitted the animal an hour of graze while he stretched beneath a red oak and let Tige find what shade he could on the carriage seat. Tige dozed until his head fell back, or sank abruptly forward, waking him painfully.

238

They met no one on the trail that first day, came upon no dwellings, no signs of human habitation between the horizons. Ham rode, seemingly bemused, preoccupied. Tige discovered how alert his jailer was when Ham suddenly grabbed up the gun beside him on the boot of the wagon and shot a quail startled from a mesquite clump. Later, Ham killed three other quail. He made camp beside a scant and thirsty creek in the lavender-tinctured sunset. He cooked a meal, ate his fill, gave Tige the remainder of the food on the same tin plate from which he'd eaten.

Tige had thought Ham would take him from the carriage at night, but he was quickly disabused of this mistaken judgment. Ham spread branches, overlaid them with oilcloths, heavy quilts, blankets and a pillow. He stretched out on this cot beneath a cottonwood tree. Tige was left to shift for himself in the carriage boot. He managed to slide off the seat to the flooring. He curled, chilled, miserable and uncomfortable. He was bone-cold but damned if he'd ask Hammond for a blanket. He fell asleep at last in the darkest hour before dawn.

Ham poked him awake with the butt of his shotgun soon after daybreak. He fed him black coffee and hoecake. Tige awakened in such a fury of hatred for Ham that he drank off the strong black liquid and chewed the dry biscuit aware of no more taste than that of bitter straw in his mouth.

For exercise, Ham permitted Tige to run alongside the carriage for an hour or so morning and afternoon. Tige was allowed to relieve himself like an animal on the side of the trail. During the day Ham killed rabbits that hesitated in his path, or shot quail flushed from the chaparral. Tige felt a grudging admiration for his natural father. The son of a bitch was self-reliant, self-disciplined, self-sufficient and self-assured. And for each of these admirable qualities carried to a vice, Tige hated Ham with violence that roiled in his stomach and threatened to make him vomit.

On the third day they reached a crossroads settlement flung down carelessly around an open well in the eternal flatlands. A few bleak buildings, sun-dried and sand-whipped, some meagerly shaded by locusts, cottonwoods, or Texas oaks, a public watering trough, a general store with back rooms skimpily furnished for a night's lodging, a stable for horses—this was the nameless village.

A tall, thin-gutted man came out on his merchandise-piled stoop and squinted at Ham and Tige in the carriage. The man wore a derby, a striped shirt with arm garters, a splattered apron, twill pants and dusty boots. His nose was large and hooked and his lips tight and gray. His sun-baked skin was splotched, his sandy hair fading, a man of any age, no age at all. His pale-blue eyes widened at the sight of chains and shackles securing Tige.

"Your boy loco?" He came down one step into the stunning sunlight, gawking first at Tige and then at Hammond. One could not say which was stranger and more curious to him—the boy in chains, or the calm man who chained him. "Your boy—dangerous?"

"Ain't my boy," Ham said.

The man laughed indecisively. "Aw . . . you might deny your own name, friend. But you can't no way deny your own whelp. That's you son, all right. Plain as your face is plain. Why he's your spit an' image."

"Go on, Pa," Tige taunted Ham in exaggerated accent. "Tell him why I'm in chains."

Ham's face grayed out, his eyes glittered. "This here boy is a slave, mister. Not that it's none of your concern. He's a nigger. A mustee. Runaway nigger. He may favor me somewhat—but he's a black slave, born a slave, the worst kind of Nigra—a white one—an' I can tell you, he's on his way to hang."

"Well, I'm damned," the storekeeper said. "Don't

that beat all? . . . Reckon I can sit here on my stoop and see things nobody'd believe. . . . Now you, takin' your own son back to the States to hang . . . sounds almost like Abraham and Isaac."

Ham growled in his throat.

XXII

Vultures and jackals can smell approaching death; they crowd in and settle, ready to pounce while the carcass blood yet runs hot. It was like this with Ham's departure from Maxwell ranch. The odor of fatal illness emanated from the land itself and permeated the ranges in every direction, luring in the scavengers. In the middle of the second day after Ham drove away east from the ranch, four armed men rode thick-chested, glossy-maned, heavy-muscled range horses into the ranch yard. Dust and tension smoked in ahead of the fast-moving animals. The men rode directly to the front stoop of the house. Only one of them dismounted.

He was a big man, impressive. Though six feet tall in his range boots, he appeared to tower over others as a giant might, a massive monolith of congealed power and strength, from flat-crowned Stetson to trunk-like legs in tailored whipcord. His very presence overwhelmed strangers and inferiors—which comprised the bulk of the human race. His craglike features seemed to have been hewn by the slow, fierce cut of Texas sand blown on the wind. His blue eyes squinted habitually under ragged graying brows. His mammoth shoulders bulged and bunched with hawser-sized muscle cords, and his muscular chest resembled a shirted hogshead.

He stood, legs apart, just outside the line of overhang shadow as if toeing some disputed line. He removed his hat, his thick sandy gray hair curling and bobbling in the breezes. He called, "Miz Lydia, ma'am. You home, Miz Lydia? Could I talk with you, ma'am?"

His voice carried like the growl of the puma. Men came out onto the stoop of the bunkhouse and stood peering uneasily across the sun-basted yard, recognizing Elihu Kinlaw and his riders.

Lydia came out of the kitchen. Small brown faces like peonies formed a bouquet behind her. Lydia crossed the dog-trot, drying her hands on her bright apron. Even with her cheeks pink and moist, her dark hair framing her face in damp tendrils, there was classic beauty about her. Her beauty had never stirred Kinlaw's interest, nor did it impress him now. He admitted to a certain old-fashioned attitude, perhaps anachronistic in Texas in these modern days of the 1840s, but without apology he opposed mixed marriages—even or perhaps especially those between the Mexican Catholic and the Protestant American. He'd always been irreproachably polite toward Hammond Maxwell's woman—taking a Mexican woman as one's blanket squaw was somehow less offensive in his nostrils than marriage—but he never forgot her origin or her status.

"Good morning, Mr. Kinlaw." Lydia stood on the shadowed stoop and bobbed her head, briefly caroming a smile across Kinlaw's three silent riders.

"Mornin', Miz Lydia." Kinlaw nodded curtly. "Bright Texas mornin', ain't it?"

"If you're looking for Hammond," Lydia said, "you missed him. He rode east two days ago."

Kinlaw shook his head, marveling in astonished duplicity at this intelligence. Then he smiled and shrugged those massive shoulders slightly. "I had heard Maxwell had returned east. Do you expect him back . . . soon?"

"I don't know."

"I see. . . . Well, I'm a blunt, plain-spoken man, Miz Lydia. I reckon that's part of our Texas heritage that we speak straight from the shoulder, say what we mean, deal right off the top of the deck, eh?"

"I do not play too much cards myself, Señor."

He allowed a faint smile to tickle his mustache. "I think maybe you're playin' cards with me, right now."

"Sir?"

"It's all right. Long as we just keep the deck out on the table—all the cards in plain sight, eh? . . . Way I hear it, your—man—Maxwell is not coming back to Texas."

"I don't know."

"Oh? You expectin' him back?"

She spread her hands. "I am here. His three children are here."

He nodded, shrugged. "Word is that you have recorded a deed making you sole owner of this land and property."

"Word gets to you quickly."

"I find that appropriate. Only appropriate, ma'am. I opened this land to settlement, Miz Lydia. Come here as a boy. In a Conestoga, drawn by oxen. Overland. Slow, wearyin' and uncomfortable way to travel. 'Twas pleasanter to walk beside the wagon. Reckon I walked most of the way out here across Texas from the Sabine River."

"One has to admire your determination, Señor."

"My point is, ma'am, I care what happens out here. . . . This is my nearest neighborin' ranch. We're more'n fifteen miles from your ranchhouse and my land stretches a two-day ride in three directions. I've always fancied this range. Seems Ham Maxwell come in and picked up land and water rights I neglected—simply because I never thought it'd be taken—"

"You'd have to talk to him about that."

"Now wait a minute, Miz Lydia. I intend none of this in a hostile sense. What he done was just good business. Maxwell and me got along neighborly. I admit to a few disputes. We had our arguments and disagreements. Land boundaries, they are always troublesome, water, straying cattle. Nothin', though, that we never settled amicable. Most amicable."

She waited.

"Guess you've divined the reason why I've rode over here this mornin'? I let good range, water, forage slip away through negligence. That's water under the bridge. But I don't intend to be caught nappin' twice, eh? Once, shame on him. Twice, shame on me, eh? Well, first, let me inquire your plans—for this here ranch."

"I'm going to run it."

"A—lady? A Mexican woman? You expect to oversee this operation?"

"Yes."

His laugh was oddly warm, as if he were delighted and somewhat touched at the precious innocence of this idea. He swung his great head and glanced at his riders, who laughed briefly with him.

Kinlaw stopped laughing abruptly. His craggy face looked raw and cold as the bared mountain cliffs. "That ain't practical, Miz Lydia," he said. "And we both know it."

"This is my land. I have lived here six years. I have learned from my—from Hammond. I have men to work for me—"

"You do now," he said. "How long you expect they'll stay on here—working for a woman? A Mexican woman?"

"If they go, I shall hire new men."

"Maybe you will. Maybe you won't find it that easy to find men willing to take their orders from a—woman. Meantime, strays are lost, steers are stolen. Springs are clogged, streams muddied—the place slides into

246

disrepair. . . . It can happen fast, and it will—you don't have riders out all the time."

"I deeply appreciate your concern."

"I am concerned. I don't mean to sound callous. Sometimes the truth just ain't pleasant. There just ain't no way on God's green earth a woman like you can run this big ranch."

"Still, I must try."

"No. You don't. That's why I come ridin' over early. Neighborly. Still, with a business proposition. . . . I'm willing to buy you out—lock, stock and barrel—and do you a favor in the process."

"A favor?"

"Saving you from sure ruin, ma'am. Buy you out. Good fair price."

"Is not for sale, Señor."

"Well, now for God's sake, ma'am, wait a minute. Wait at least till you hear my offer. I pay you cash. In gold. Dollars you can spend in the States. Texas. Mexico. Twenty-five cents an acre on each and every acre recorded at the county seat. . . . Now you know well as I do, that's a fair offer. Some of this land is rock garden, some it won't even grow rocks, some is alkali crusts. Averaged out, twenty-five cents is a mighty reasonable offer."

"I can say this, Señor. If that day comes when I want to sell—when I must sell—I shall come first to you, Señor Kinlaw."

He shook his head, laughing without mirth. "That won't cut it, Miz Lydia. Let's look at it straight on. I'm making you an offer for house, lands, stock and equipment—as Ham Maxwell rode away and left it to you. Today. I ain't offering you a quarter an acre at some future distress sale."

She spread her hands. "It does not matter. I cannot sell. I shall not sell. I am going to raise my sons here—"

"Now you're talking nonsense. It's all right to have ideals, and big dreams, and look at the world the way it ought to be—but ain't. But you might as well look at the facts. Fact one is, no Texan is going to let you—a Mexican—"

"I was born here! It's far more my home than it is yours."

"You're still a greaser, ma'am. Face it. You—a Mexican holding this much property? This much prime property? Well, no sir. That just goes against everything we formed this here Republic of Texas for—to open land to white people."

"I am white!"

"Sure you are, ma'am. Don't mean to insult you. But, you know what I mean. I don't like to sound callous. But you're—well, latin blood. Spanish. Mexican white. Ain't really the same."

Lydia's eyes glittered. She tilted her head, her chin thrust defiantly. She was as beautiful as some creation by a savage master of the violently natural—but Kinlaw saw no beauty in her. He saw a sweaty Mexican girl—barely in her twenties—standing between him and land he meant to own. "I have no more say to you, Señor."

"Well, I got more to say to you, ma'am, and you best hear it now. Now. I'm a fair man and I don't want it charged later that we didn't lay it all on the line for you."

"You want to buy. I don't want to sell. We have nothing left to say."

"Not goin' to have you running this land—" Kinlaw began. He stopped, turning at the sound of wagon wheels creaking and squealing drily into the yard. He half-turned, his slitted eyes widening, then narrowing, his whiskered mouth pulling taut and gray. "Who are them goddam greasers?"

Lydia did not answer. She walked out into the yard to welcome Ramon, Maria, their new infant and Maria's parents. They came, a rickety wagon piled high with their dilapidated belongings, the cart drawn by the

248

rib-framed horse Ramon also used as saddle animal. Maria's silent father, hunched with mortal weariness more than with age, handled the reins. Maria held the baby on the seat beside her scrawny father. The mother sat on a small space at the tailgate. Ramon walked, in his painful boots, beside the cart.

Lydia winced. Ramon's family presented a sorry picture of poverty and desolation. Lydia had sent for them and she welcomed them now, directing them to the tack room at the barn, which was larger, cleaner and more open than their adobe hut at sweet springs. She felt a flaring of guilt and shame that she might wish Ramon's family to arrive at a more seasonable time. Their moving onto the ranch would only fuel Elihu Kinlaw's rages. Well, to hell with him. This was her ranch. Hers alone. She would invite upon it whomever she wished. She would run this place as her own conscience dictated. Still, the arrival of the deprived and ragged nesters would only harden Kinlaw against her, make him more determined than ever to run her off.

She stood bareheaded in the sun and watched the wagon rock and bump across the yard to the barn. She could see Ramon and Maria shrivel almost visibly under the contemptuous gazes of Kinlaw and his riders. Ramon was relieved to drive beyond the ranchhouse and to the tack room at the barn; it was a kind of escape. Lydia remained where she was, her back to Kinlaw, her shoulders set, until the wagon was almost to the barn pulling in under the shade of a locust tree.

"Greasers," Kinlaw said in a tone of disbelief. "Squatters." He strode across the sand to Lydia. "You mean to tell me you're takin' them greasers on this place?"

"It's my land."

"You ain't makin' it no refuge for greasers sneaking across the border. You ain't keepin' that squatter here."

Her voice was quiet, almost defiantly gentle. "They will stay. Ramon will work for me."

"Work? Doing what?"

"There's much he can do. . . all those chores done by the boy Hammond has taken east with him."

Kinlaw's own voice lowered into a chilled tone of reason. "Now, look here, Miz Lydia. A boy with grit in his craw doing ranch chores is one thing. But gettin' a lazy greaser off his butt to do anything except steal— is something else."

"You are insulting. These are my people you are talking about—"

"Your people? Relatives?" He stared at her, mouth agape.

"No. They are not related—"

"I thought not. Just the first of the greasers who'll come in here and foul this place. . . . No, Miz Lydia, I won't have it."

She peered up at him, chilled. "There is nothing you can say about what I do—on my own ranch."

"Well! That's where you're wrong, young woman. I warn you. I'll buy you out. Now. A fair price. Or I'll run you out. But, before God, no greaser's going to hold all this valuable range land."

She met his gaze. "Then you will have to run me off, Señor Kinlaw. But for now, I ask you to get off my land."

Their gazes struck like flint, held, the unyielding blue against the fiery brown. After a long time, he shrugged. He walked back to where his riders held his mount. One of them tossed him the reins.

His grin was akin to the grimace of a panther. "Why shore, ma'am. Long as we understand each other. . . . Sell out or get out. Either way, you ain't stayin' on this property."

Lydia stood alone in the ranchhouse parlor. She'd poured herself a long splash of whiskey into a tumbler. A drink. Against her loneliness, her helplessness, against the threat of useless tears. She brought the glass to her mouth, the acrid fumes from the corn whiskey making her gag slightly. Before she could drink she heard a sharp rapping on the screen door behind her.

She almost wished she could hide. She was depressed, she didn't want to see anyone. She took a quick drink, set the glass down and turned, dabbing at her moist lips with the backs of her fingers. "Oh, Paley," she said. "Thank you for coming."

He entered the room, frowning. "Why are you thankin' me, ma'am?"

She smiled and gestured. "I was feeling—so alone—so abandoned. Then I looked up and saw you . . . I was so grateful."

"Grateful?"

"You must have heard Mr. Kinlaw . . . his threats. I'm sure his voice and his threats carried as far as the bunkhouse."

"His voice carried as far as Dallas," Paley said. "But I didn't come about that. . . . I come up to ask you, ma'am . . . you permittin' that Mexican family to move into the tack room?"

"Ramon? Maria? Yes."

"Mr. Ham wouldn't no way approve—"

"Mr. Ham isn't here, is he?" Her voice quivered faintly, forlorn.

He winced. "I don't want to make you no trouble, Miz Lydia. It's your ranch. You do what you want—"

"Ramon *can* help us, Paley. He can do the same chores that Tige did. Work you and your men dislike so much—"

"That's your decision, ma'am." He shrugged.

She tried to smile. "But you don't approve?"

"It ain't up to me to say. It don't matter what I think, ma'am. . . . I just wanted to be sure you gave that—Mexican boy—permission to move in."

"Why?"

"Well, like I said. Mr. Ham wouldn't have had it—he'd of been dead set against it. Reckon I'm dead against it, too. So are some of the men at the bunk-house. . . . But none of that don't matter. Except it helped me to make up my mind. I come to give notice, Miz Lydia, an' ask for my time, ma'am. I'm drifting."

She caught his arm. "Oh, Paley, no! Please. I would be—in deep trouble—without you. Is it—do you want more money?"

"No ma'am. That wouldn't change my mind. Pay's fair. Mr. Ham was always most fair about pay and found. Food and found. I put away most of my pay. Don't even know for what. . . . No, ma'am, I just want to move on. Lots of reasons . . . but there ain't no call to go into them. You been most kind. I wish I could stay on, but I can't."

"Kinlaw threatened me, Paley. . . . I do need you —you must know that."

"No, ma'am. I heard his threats. I reckon he does mean to get this land—one way or another. I wouldn't be much help to you there."

"What do you mean?"

"I mean I'm no good for fighting—not a man like Kinlaw. That's the biggest reason why I'm travelin', ma'am. . . . I don't pride myself—walkin' out on you like this. But there is going to be trouble. I'm a cowhand —I ain't no way no gunfighter."

"Then there's no way I can get you to stay?"

"I'm sorry."

"You don't want to work for a woman—even if there wasn't this other trouble?"

He winced, nodded. "There's that fact—I don't think I could work for a woman. . . . It ain't right for a man."

"And—you *won't* work for a Mexican woman?"

He bit his lip, bobbed his head, eyes bleak. "That, too, I reckon."

XXIII

Cale Lambdin snuggled down under the coarse blanket on his bunk. He would have been content to go on lying there, but the long narrow communal room bustled with activity. There sure hell was no privacy. Cookie sweated over the big wood-burning stove at the far end of the room, frying pancakes and steaks. The aroma permeated the place, hot and pleasant. Cale kept his eyes tightly closed. He wasn't hungry. He'd lain stricken with painful erection most of the long night. When he was convinced every other man was asleep in the bunkhouse, he'd crept silently out to the barn and temporarily relieved his agonized satyriasis with his fist. He felt himself growing hard again. He stirred uncomfortably. He couldn't go on lying here and he sure hell couldn't walk around with a hard-on. He felt sick with anticipation and apprehension. Since the moment Ham Maxwell drove his carriage off the ranch, headed east, Cale had been unable to think of anything except Lydia. Lydia forsaken. Lydia naked and lovelier than sin itself. Lydia reaching for him willingly—more than willingly—anxiously! She was everywhere he turned, overseeing the ranch, running the house, walking across the yard, laughing at something on the dog-trot. Out of his sight, she erupted in sharpest images inside his mind. He was torn between need to conquer her and the sick wish to be accepted by her. She had tricked and humiliated him that day out on the prairie. But she hadn't reported him to Maxwell. Anyway, that was all behind him. Now his mind teamed with pictures in which she submissively redeemed every wrong, redressed every bitter injury. She'd pay for taunting him; she'd pay with her body, and she'd never stop paying.

He heard the other hands talking around him, desultorily, aimlessly, as they dressed, preparing for the day's work. He took no part in this activity, partly because he did not want to but more because he was unable to enter into any action or any conversation that didn't center around the upthrust fullness of Lydia Maxwell's breasts. His desire was rising like mercury in searing sunlight, and he ached, on fire inside. There was no room in him now for anything except the heated memory, the bittersweet anticipation, the obsessive need for Lydia.

"Hey, Cale, you lazy bastard," Cookie yelled from the far end of the room. "Stir your stumps. Breakfast is served hot. It's served once."

"Go to hell," Cale said. But he sat up and hung his legs to conceal the guilty upright towering there.

Paley paused at the foot of his bunk, eyeing him oddly. "You sick, Cale?"

"No." Cale shrugged. "I'm all right."

"You planning to stay on working here—for the woman?"

"Here?"

"Hell yes, here."

Slipping his arms into his work shirt, Cale stared up at his longtime saddle partner. "You mean—you're thinking of drifting?"

"Hell yes, ain't you?"

"I ain't give it no thought."

"Well, what in hell else you been thinking about?"

"I just ain't thought about leaving, that's all."

"I gave her my notice. Yesterday."

Cale pulled his trousers up over his legs, pulled on

his stockings and thrust his feet into his boots. He could not reconcile riding away from here now. It was like sticking around till Christmas and then riding away without eating the turkey. He hated the idea of staying behind when Paley rode away. In a lot of ways he'd be lost without Paley. If there were any brains between them, Paley had them all. It was easy to drift, leaving all the responsibilities to Paley. But leave Lydia now? After Ham Maxwell had just pulled stakes, leaving her without a man in her bed? He shivered. "You give her notice?"

"And asked for my time."

"The hell you did."

"Hell I didn't."

"You didn't say nothing to me."

"I figured you'd be with me. Like always, for Christ's sake. I reckoned you'd feel the same way about taking orders from a woman—a Mexican woman, too—the same as I did."

"You could of said something."

Paley spread his hands and stared toward heaven, concealed beyond the bunkhouse roofing. "For Christ's sake, Cale. Said what? Ham Maxwell's gone. His Mex woman owns the place now. She's already brought in some other greasers to live on the place. Be a little Matamoros in a few weeks. An' Kinlaw was around. He's going to make trouble. What else is there to think about? What was there to say? I figured you'd drift when I did."

Cale nodded, but said nothing. He was deeply troubled, his stomach queasy. He finished dressing with Paley standing there watching him. They walked down to the rough pine table in the kitchen end of the long barracks room. They sat on pine benches and ate in silence. Cale was especially aware of a couple of Paley's annoying habits—the way he slurped his coffee through his mustache as if it were a filter, and the way he dabbed at his mustache with the back of his hand after every gulp of liquid. As the finished off stacks of pancakes with a couple fried eggs and a steak, Cale wiped his own with the back of his hand. "I just wish you'd of said something, that's all."

Cale was disturbed over the fact that he could not loiter around here without revealing his secret to Paley. This would be deadly. Probably Paley already suspected that he'd had the stallion itch for Ham's woman for months. But Paley was one of those fortunate men who could take a woman when she was handy, forget her when she was not. He envied Paley that mind-calming trait, but he admitted he wouldn't want to be like that. He had never been casual about a woman that roused him since he was thirteen. Once one of them got inside his mind, it was like an infection; he was incapacitated, and stayed that way until he was bedridden.

Cale shuddered involuntarily in the heated room. When he needed it, he was sick with the need for it, and that's the way it was now. It was nothing he could make Paley understand, even if he were fool enough or brave enough to talk to him about it.

He exhaled heavily and let Paley believe he was drifting along with him, when really he hadn't made up his mind. But it was easier to let Paley believe he agreed with him all the way down the line.

He went out to the shower rigged under a rain barrel behind the barn. He undressed, soaped himself lavishly and let water spew down from the barrel until he felt cool and clean. Then he shaved. He did not confront his plans in his own mind. He carefully refrained from thinking at all. He was due to ride line out south today. He didn't tell himself he was not going to do it. But he dressed in fresh clothing and wished for some of that talcum powder and perfumed water they had in barber shops. By the time he was dressed again the bunkhouse was comparatively quiet. Most of the hands had ridden out.

"Where you going, all duded up?" Cookie wanted to know.

"Hell. Can't I take a bath? I felt dirty."

"In the middle of the week?"

He did feel better in a clean shirt, fresh underclothes, new stockings and soap-scrubbed trousers. He sweated slightly. He had not stopped to think how things would be here with Lydia as heir to the Maxwell ranch. Paley had put his fears in words. But the idea of working for a woman didn't outrage his pride as it did Paley's. It was something he could live with.

He felt a sweetly uncomfortable flaring in his loins. One thing was dead certain. Lydia was going to need a man to help her. Days and nights. He had no aversion to being that man—for a price.

He glanced critically at himself in the shadowy mirror nailed to the rough wall. He didn't look bad, not half bad. He was younger than Ham Maxwell by some years; hornier, that was for sure; built better; taller, thinner; toughened by work Ham hired others to do. It provided him a slight sense of security to know that Paley had pushed Lydia into a corner as far as needing help was concerned. She needed somebody to run this place for her. Now, he expected, Lydia would not turn him out, or scorn him. He wondered if she might just take him right into the house with her. He had heard of less reasonable arrangements. Perhaps she would see quickly and clearly how much it would be worth it to her to have him around.

His heart pounding raggedly, he paused on the bunkhouse stoop. Until now he had not really considered what it would mean to face Elihu Kinlaw and his hired toughs. If Lydia Maxwell was Kinlaw's enemy, every Maxwell hireling would automatically become a Kinlaw target for violence. And Paley would be gone. Damn. He was willing to do what he could for Lydia—for carnal payment—but he was no gunfighter. Mentally, as commander or executive, he was no match for Elihu Kinlaw. He admitted to a certain cowardice when it came to fighting of any kind. He had been in a couple of cathouse brawls, and he'd been hurt badly more than once. Some of these bastards, if they couldn't get you with their fists they came at you with knives. He had no stomach for fighting.

He sweated. He was no warrior, he was just what he was, and he admitted that: a gut-hungry man with an unreasoning hard-on. His was a thirst gone out of control. On the other hand, not even a famished man slaked his thirst at a poisoned pool. A man could become suddenly dead opposing Elihu Kinlaw. Still, in his present ravening condition, it made sense to make whatever deal he could with Lydia. He would have to take what he could get—and later, run when he had to. It wasn't a pretty thought, seeing himself in this true, unflattering and relentless light, but he was being honest. Life wasn't too goddam pretty when you stopped to think about it.

Lydia looked up when Cale Lambdin knocked on her kitchen door. She sighed and told him to come in. He glanced around at the others in the room and said he'd like to talk to her—privately. She sent the children into the parlor with Nell, told Estelle to take a breather in the old red-oak rocking chair on the breeze-cooled dog-trot, speaking to her quietly in rapid Spanish.

She gazed up at Cale bleakly when they were alone. "I suppose you want to give notice?"

He placed his hat on the table, arranged it carefully. "Paley did say he had asked for his time."

"And you want to leave with him?"

"We been partners—Paley and me—a long time."

"Yes. I understand."

He shifted uncomfortably. "Still. I hate to walk out.

Leave you in the lurch like this and all. . . . Your—man—gone . . . you're going to need somebody."

She looked up, puzzled, hopeful. "You mean—you might stay?"

He met her gaze, then let his eyes fall away. "That would be—up to you."

Her eyes widened. She read his meaning in his face. Her mouth twisted as if she'd tasted something tart. She shook her head, laughing at herself. "And I was fool enough . . . I hoped you were really offering to help."

He straightened. "Well . . . I am. Much as I can. . . . I know runnin' this big ranch—I could help with that. . . . I could give your orders to the men—"

"Take Paley's place?" she suggested.

He grinned. "No, ma'am. I had it more in mind—takin' Mr. Ham's place."

Blood suffused her cheeks. Her voice chilled, though its cutting edge remained sharp. "You come right to the point, don't you? I suppose next you'll be jerking your fly open again."

He flushed. "You were pretty rough on me that day out there. . . . Maybe I had it coming . . . but I'd dreamed about you for a long time. . . . Anyhow, Mr. Ham's gone now. You *will* need somebody."

Her eyes brimmed with tears of anger and self-hatred for her weakness. She stared up at him. Yes, she needed someone. Someone strong—to depend on, to lean on, to trust. She couldn't trust Cale Lambdin, nor depend on him, and if she leaned on him, he would see it as license to rape. She shook her head again, her black eyes glittering. "You may as well ride on out with Paley," she said.

"You better think about that," he said. "You need somebody to help you. And not just somebody—somebody that knows the ropes, knows this ranch and this grazing range. Now, I'm honest. Paley would be your best choice. But Paley won't stay—at no price. I will."

"That's a lot of points in your favor, isn't it?"

"I think so."

"What help do you think you'd be—against Kinlaw, or Kinlaw's men? If they drove cattle off, or spoiled springs, or ruined creeks—what help would you be?"

His face flushed red, his eyes showed raw pain. He shook his head. His voice was flat. "I don't know. I honest don't. . . . With a gun? Not much. . . . Maybe I couldn't no way stand up to Kinlaw. I don't know. . . . But if it came to that, we'd have to hire guns. I *could* help you do that."

"You sound—honest. But you don't sound like a great bargain."

He spread his hands. "Ain't no sense tryin' to fool either one of us, ma'am. You need me. I'm willin' to stay. I'll help you all I can."

"And your price?"

"I think you already know that, ma'am. . . . I been stallion-wild for you for years now. You've known that. It ain't let up none—the way I feel about you. No reason now—if I was to stay—I couldn't share your bed."

"No."

He gestured helplessly. "You really find me that—that repulsive?"

She shrugged. "You are a handsome boy, Cale . . . but you are not a man for me. You are not what I want."

"My God, Miz Lydia. Don't low-rate it till you try it."

She shook her head, gestured, dismissing him. "I told you. I don't want you to stay—not on those terms."

He hesitated, then came close to her. He looked ready to weep with the need that spurred him, the frustration she roused in him. "I couldn't want you so bad and you—not even know I'm alive."

"I know you're alive."

He touched her arms, his hands hot and trembling. "I know you do. You got to, or I couldn't want you so terrible. You do need me—maybe not as bad as I need you, because I ain't lived with nothing but my need for you. But you will want me. Give it a chance. Give me a chance, Lydia. God knows that's all I ask. I swear it. You will want me. I'll make you want me."

She drew a deep breath, shook her head in a chilled gesture of finality. She placed both hands flatly against his chest. "Listen to me, Cale. . . . Don't do this. Don't try to do this. One of us—will get hurt. . . . I am not some Mexican *puta* for you to crawl and ride away from."

His arms slipped around her. "My God, Miz Lydia, I never said you was."

"You don't even know what I'm talking about."

"I know I want you. I'm crazy for you. I know that."

He had slipped his hands to the small of her back. He pressed her softly padded femininity upon his rigidity. His breath quickened, painful in his throat. His entire body shook with the violent force of his need. "You can't live—with nobody—you got to have a man. You'll want me—"

"Let me go." Her voice was cold. "I am not a whore."

His voice quavered. "You don't have to be a whore to want it. You do want it. I can tell—"

"Whether I want it or not, I won't." She struggled in his arms. "Let me go."

"Kiss me. Just kiss me. You'll see—you'll see."

"Damn you! I don't want—to see."

He tried to capture her mouth with his. She twisted her head and his parted lips pressed against the squared line of her jaw. He held her tighter, forcing her to move her hips against him, totally convinced she had only to be roused to be as wild as he. He spoke breathlessly against her face. "Why?" He laughed. "Will you kill me if I don't let you go?"

Her voice was level, if slightly shaken. She inclined her head toward the screen door behind him. Going taut, he straightened and checked across his shoulder —this house had too recently belonged to Ham Maxwell for him to be at ease in it. His heart sank. The fat Estelle stood just inside the door holding a shotgun fixed on him. He heard Lydia's voice as above the pounding of a violent waterfall—the throb of blood in his own temples. "No," Lydia said. "I won't kill you. But Estelle will."

Cale dropped his hands to his sides, his shoulders sagging. Empty-bellied and more than faintly nauseated, he stepped back from her. For a moment Lydia wavered as if she'd lost support which kept her erect. Then she straightened. Her voice raked him. "I think you better get out now. As for staying on after Paley leaves, I don't think you should. There will be danger here, Mr. Lambdin. I don't really think you've given that danger any thought. . . . Now you can ride away with Paley—with a clear conscience. You offered to stay and protect me—but I would not pay your price. Someday, you'll thank your God."

Sweated, miserable, he spread his hands, watching her. "No matter . . . about this—between us. . . . You are going to need help. . . . Maybe I'll just hang around until you need—a man. . . . I know what I want—and I'll be here when you decide what you want."

Her mouth twisted. "You could get yourself killed."

He shrugged. "Even so . . . I reckon a man has to figure the cost of anything he does. He decides to pay the cost or let it go. I've decided to pay it— whatever it is."

"You are a fool because it will not buy you what you want." Her eyes glittered. "If you come near me like this again, I will kill you."

He grinned and shrugged again. "Or Estelle will, or Kinlaw might. There's a big price tag on you, lady . . . it don't sound promising."

She stared at him, still doubting his decision. "I never thought you'd—put yourself in such a position to take such chances, against such odds."

He exhaled. "You don't know me as well as you thought." He shook his head and grinned ruefully, looking suddenly younger and more vulnerable than ever. "Honest, I didn't know I'd do this, either. But—you'll meet the price."

"I told you. I won't let you near me."

"I heard you. But I'll wait. No matter how long it takes. One thing you got to know—night and day—is how bad I want you. You ain't going to forget that, either. . . . So I'll wait . . . I won't push you. I'll wait—till you come to me."

She laughed in spite of herself. "You can save yourself a great deal by riding out with Paley."

"No. I'll stay—even with Estelle's shotgun fixed on my belly. . . . I think I can wait as long as you can, Señorita."

Lydia awoke early the next morning despite a night of fitful sleeping, exhausting nightmares and empty hours of staring sleeplessly into the gloomy vault of the night. She was lonely. It was a wrenching experience, lying alone at night after six years of pressing against the male hardness of a man. She wanted Ham; she found her undisciplined thoughts following him east across the Texies; she saw him sharing her loneliness, her need, wanting her as she wanted him, turning back. Her eyes brimmed with bitter tears. She knew better. Thoughts like those were a kind of wishful insanity. The promise one made to oneself when the truth could not be endured, the lies that helped one make it through an eternal night. There was not even the trace of reality in her wishing; it was a softening agent to smooth the edges of a hard and troubled time.

She got up in the purpled dawn, the room shadowed, thinking with a kind of empty triumph that she had made it through one more lonely day. She saw her future stretching dark and lonely ahead of her like last night—all the nights to come. Only time would help her. Please God, time had to help her; she had no other ally.

She went quietly past the children's room, glancing in to find them sprawled in their varying positions on their bunks. The oldest sucked his thumb in his sleep, noisily.

She found Nell already in the kitchen, making coffee.

"Couldn't you sleep either?" Lydia put her arm about the girl's slender shoulders.

Nell turned a bleak face to her. "I'm not going to sleep. Ever. Not without Tige. . . . I need him. . . . It's more than that, Lydia—I'm not whole without him."

Lydia bit her lip. "For your own sake . . . you'll have to—to plan your life without him." Oh God, how easy it was to parcel out helpful advice to others.

"No. I'm going to follow him. Back east."

Lydia stared at the girl, speechless. It was not that she doubted the girl's intentions. Nell's sanity might be questioned, but not her purpose. Nell's gentle voice was firm.

"The only trouble with your plan," Lydia said, "is that you're not thinking clear."

"I don't want to think. Not at all. I'm not going to think. I'm going to do what I must. I have my wagon. My horse. I'll take the baby—and go."

Lydia drew the girl into her arms. "Oh, Nell, I wish there were some chance you could do it—"

"I've got to try."

"The baby would not survive such a trip."

"Maybe I won't make it. Maybe Tige will already be dead before we get there—if we get there at all. You think I haven't thought about all that?"

"But that won't stop you?"

"I'd rather die trying to get to Tige than to try to live without him. I can't sit here knowing that he'll die—alone—back there—without me."

"Nell . . . hundreds of miles . . . wild country—"

"I told you. I won't think about that. I am going."

Lydia sat down at the table. Nell poured coffee and they drank it without tasting. Nell stared through a window. Nell said, "If I could find Tige . . . if I could bring him back here . . . he could save your ranch for you, against that Kinlaw. . . . I know Tige could. He's strong—like his father. . . . The difference is, he's good inside."

Lydia sighed. "No sense both of us wasting time on dreams that can't be made real. . . . If you are going—we must *think*. We must think how we might make it possible for you to go—to make it all the way. . . . First, the horse. . . . Your horse is too old. But I can trade you a better horse. . . . We can give you money—a mattress for the bed of your wagon. . . . But no. There is no way a new infant could survive in an open wagon. . . . If you go, you must leave the baby here."

"Leave my baby?"

"You said you were coming back. You and Tige."

Nell's laugh was forlorn. "We know what kind of dream that is."

"But—if you did come back—your baby would be alive—here. . . . But it will die if you—try to take it with you. . . . Maria has milk—she is breast-feeding her baby . . . she could nurse yours."

Nell stared at her. She had made her decision to go, but for the first time she began to see how she might possibly accomplish it.

Lydia said, "At least you'd know your baby was

taken care of, fed—and safe." After a long pause, Lydia added, "And you—alone. . . . No . . . it is impossible. You could not make it alone."

"Still, I've got to try. No sense trying to stop me."

"If we don't stop you, then we must help you make it. Eh?" Lydia got up. She went through the kitchen door to the dog-trot. She called out to a man working near the barns, instructing him to send Paley to the house.

She returned to the kitchen, fried eggs and steaks as she waited, made fresh coffee. Nell was silent, slumped at the table. When Paley knocked on the door, Lydia told him to come in. She smiled at him. "Have you had breakfast, Paley?"

"Not yet, ma'am."

"Sit down. There at the table with Nell. Have eggs and steak with Nell and me."

He hesitated, then, "Thank you, ma'am." His smile was sheepish. "But I better warn you, I ain't gonna change my mind about staying here."

Lydia served him. "No. But you are leaving. I know that Nell means a great deal to you. I thought you might enjoy breakfast—with us. There are no strings attached. . . . You were most kind to Nell—when she had her baby."

Paley flushed. "I was scared to clabber . . . don't know what the young lady and me would of done without Mr. Ham."

"Still, you do care what happens to Nell."

"Yes, ma'am. . . . If I had a daughter. . . ." He laughed. "Well, I never will."

"Nell is going to drive her wagon—back to Alabama," Lydia said.

"Alone?" Paley's head jerked up. He reached out, covered Nell's gentle hand with his own callused paw. "Why, you couldn't do that, ma'am . . . no way at all."

266

Nell met his eyes. She tried to smile. Her voice shook. "I must get there before—anything happens to Tige."

He shook his head, his face set. "But not a young girl like you, alone in an open wagon. You just couldn't do that."

"She'll have to—unless she can find someone willing to drive her."

"Well, she'll just have to find somebody," Paley said. "And it's got to be somebody we can trust."

Lydia nodded. "Since you are leaving the ranch anyway, Paley, why don't you drive for her? I'm going to pay you your time. In gold. I'll give you—a second poke of gold, if you will drive Nell east to Benson, Alabama. . . . From there, you could take your horse—and your gold—and go where you liked. With a grub stake and knowing you did all you could to get Nell back to Tige—safe."

Paley tried to laugh. "Ought to have knowed. Steak and eggs ain't ever free."

"They're free," Lydia said. "It's just that Nell has no one but you—no one we could all trust."

He winced. "That's a tall order, you're asking me, ma'am. I'd have to think on it," Paley said.

Lydia nodded. "I know you will," she said. "Have another steak. Another cup of coffee. More eggs will be ready in a moment. You can always think a lot better—on a full stomach."

XXIV

They were just finishing a melancholy breakfast the next morning when they heard a rattle of wagon wheels and clop of hooves of horses in the yard. Lydia felt her heart leap. *Ham had come back. He had missed her and he had come back. Please, God, let it be him.* The children sprang from the table, glad for an excuse to escape the cheerless tensions which they could neither understand nor ignore. They stood, shouting and pointing, at the screen door. Estelle waddled over to them from the stove and gazed out through the screen. Her face paled slightly. She turned and told Lydia in Spanish that it was the two men who had come earlier looking for Tige. Nell dropped her fork and sat immobile, staring at her plate. Lydia got up tiredly from the table and crossed the room. She sent the children, protesting, back to Nell at the table. Lydia brushed at her apron and went out onto the dog-trot to greet the bounty hunters before they entered the house.

"Mornin' ma'am." The two men doffed their hats and squinted at her in the blaze of sunlight. She returned their greetings without warmth.

"Wantin' to see Mr Maxwell, and appreciate you tell him we out here an' await his convenience," Milford Thigpen said. The tall thin man removed his beaver top hat and slapped at his dusty clothing. He

269

swung down from the wagon and stepped just inside the rim of shade provided by the overhang.

"Señor Maxwell is not here." Lydia shook her head and turned as if to retreat into the kitchen.

"Well now, just a minute, ma'am," Thigpen said. She turned and faced him; he forced a smile. "This is a matter of some importance." He nodded emphatically. "Mayhap you could say when you expect Mr. Maxwell back? We are in a kind of a hurry. . . . Still, we got a rule—Mr. Bugas there an' me—we never move so fast we leave any stones unturned. You understand? We hurry where we can—but never no way at the expense of moving cautiously and covering ground thoroughly."

Lydia shrugged. "I don't know when Mr. Maxwell will be back. Not for . . . many days."

Thigpen turned his head; he and Bugas exchanged glances. Thigpen returned his gaze and exhausted smile to Lydia. "Then we'd like to talk to you, ma'am . . . and to your riders."

"About what?"

Thigpen explained their mission without mentioning the five-thousand-dollar bounty offered for capture and conviction of the fugitive mustee. His spiel sounded almost as if recited by rote. He had repeated these words so often they sounded flat and mechanical. "Maybe your riders can be of some help," he said.

"What do you think my riders might know?" Lydia asked.

Thigpen gave her a pained glance; he was tired, edgy. "If we knew that, ma'am, we wouldn't need to question them at all, would we?"

"I don't like my men disturbed," Lydia said.

Thigpen's face flushed slightly. It was with some exercise of self-discipline that he kept his voice moderated and respectful. His impatience underlined each word, despite his gray smile. "Ma'am, we do represent the law."

Lydia gave him her own bland, empty smile. "Then you will have a warrant of some kind?"

"My good Lord, ma'am." Thigpen spread his hands. "We just want to ask them some questions. This is just an investigation. We ain't tryin' to arrest or harry nobody."

Bugas's voice cut softly but decisively across Thigpen's. "Mr. Thigpen is a good man, ma'am. But he does get a mite impatient when he has to deal with— ladies—in a business way."

"Don't intend no offense at all, ma'am," Thigpen said.

"And all we wish to do is to check out some facts which we possess," Bugas continued in that syrupy tone. "In solving any crime, ma'am, or finding a missing person or stolen valuable, there's one rule that both Mr. Bugas and me has found to be most infallible. We take one fact, Mrs. Maxwell. One fact that can't be disputed or disproved. Then we look for other bits of information, or objects, to match that one indisputable fact. Something matches, we add it to our first fact and start to build case—always making any new information match up to what we know to be fact. You can see how that would work?"

Lydia shrugged, watching them. Bugas continued to smile. He said, "But, we find something that don't jibe with the fact we are working from, then we throw that information out and start over—"

"No matter how promising—or true—this new information seems," Thigpen said.

Lydia watched them and waited, unimpressed.

Bugas's smile grew mildly forced. But he nodded with feigned enthusiasm. "Mr. Thigpen's right." Bugas nodded his head several times. He mopped his sweated face with a damp handkerchief. "Now take the case of this here runaway mustee we seek. Fact one: He headed into the Texies. We found witnesses, undeniable proof that he headed into the Republic. So we

271

followed. We checked every town, every village, every house, every ranch. Had these people seen a man—driving an open wagon—with a girl along, we proceeded along that trail. Had they not seen him, we tried a new tack, a new trail."

"It ain't fast," Thigpen said. "But it is thorough."

"Working to solve any crime, or find a missing person, is seldom fast or easy," Bugas said. "It's a dull routine of asking questions of folks like you and your riders, of checking out every lead—following a trail or discarding it. Finding a new trail, or turning back on the old one—working always, you understand, with that one fact that can't no way be disputed."

"Which brought us here to your ranch in the first place," Thigpen said. "And which brings us back here now."

Bugas nodded. "You see, ma'am, the fact is, that mustee left the main trail, headed this way. Now we knew that. That was a fact can't be disputed. We had witnesses. We had proof. We followed signs which we recognized by now. . . . We trailed him here. . . . We went on down the road a two-day trip. We fanned out on side trails whenever we found he had not passed some given point."

"And we wind up back here," Thigpen said. He no longer made any effort to smile at all.

"I can tell you the man you seek is not here," Lydia said. There was chilled finality in her tone.

"Yes . . . all right. But you got riders. They spread out over great areas of this here range. Maybe they seen something they ain't mentioned to you because it didn't seem important to them at the time. You know? Now, we got no wish to inconvenience you," Bugas said. "But the answers to a few questions would be most helpful."

Lydia shrugged. "I suppose the sooner you ask your questions, the quicker you will be gone?"

"That's surely true, ma'am," Bugas said.

Thigpen glanced past Lydia toward the kitchen. "Maybe if we start with the folks in the house?"

"No." Lydia straightened as if to bar the way with her body. "There is only my servant. She speaks no English. She has not left the house. Also there is only— my husband's daughter-in-law. . . . She cannot help you. She has just had a baby recently and so has not left the place. I do not want her disturbed."

Thigpen checked over his shoulder with Bugas. The stout man shrugged and nodded. "All right, Mrs. Maxwell. We are glad to accept your word that they ain't seen nor heard nothing that might be helpful to us."

"They've seen no more than I have," Lydia said.

Thigpen mopped the sweatband of his beaver high hat. "Hope I ain't no way upset you, ma'am. . . . But we are dead serious—we are looking for a murderer. We can't always be as polite as we'd like."

"Sometimes we have to intrude where we have no wish to," Bugas said.

Lydia shrugged. She returned to the kitchen, where she found Nell, taut and gray-faced at the table. She had not moved. The children pressed against her, sat upon her lap. She appeared only barely aware of them.

"It's all right, Nell," Lydia told her. "They are not going to bother you."

Lydia remained inside the kitchen door. She watched the bounty hunters through the screen. Thigpen drove the carriage out toward the bunkhouse. Noticing the Mexican family in the tack room, Thigpen turned his horse there. Ramon, Maria and their parents came out into the shade of the locust tree and stared up at the strangers, squinting against the leaf-diffused sunlight. The questions were detailed, lengthy, the answers brief and far from satisfactory to the searchers. Lydia could almost *feel* the sweated frustration and annoyance which provoked the detectives. Thigpen finally gave up in disgust. He yanked hard on the lines and drove away to the bunkhouse.

273

Most of the cowhands were finishing breakfast or packing gear, preparing to leave for the day, when Thigpen and Bugas entered the bunkhouse. Thigpen introduced himself and his partner, smiling and shaking hands all around. "Like to chew the fat with you fellows for a spell," he said in his most affable manner.

Glad to find any reason to delay embarking on a long day in the saddle, the young men loitered, sitting on benches, the pine table, or leaning against the wall. Their gazes were neither friendly nor hostile. They were curious and they were in out of the sun, for which they were more than mildly thankful.

Thigpen talked unhurriedly and with great calm. In immoderate detail he outlined the crime which had been committed in Louisiana, the flight which followed, their own long trail across Texas, the sudden disappearance of tangible evidence here in the Brazos wild country.

"There's a lot of land where a man could lose himself," Paley said. "In Texas flat country, a man don't have to follow a trail."

"Especially a man on the run don't," Cale said. "Lots of places to hole in."

"But this man's got a pregnant woman with him. Just a young girl really," Thigpen said. "He can't let hisself get too far from some kind of medical help for his woman—even if it's just a midwife."

The young riders glanced at each other. Both Thigpen and Bugas, long trained to catch significant expressions in the eyes and faces of people they interrogated, perked up.

"You fellows seen such a man—and his pregnant woman? In an open wagon?" Bugas asked. He smiled encouragingly and leaned forward across the table.

A brief, fragile silence ensued. At last, Paley said, "What did Mrs. Maxwell tell you?"

"Said she ain't seen nothing," Thigpen admitted.

Paley shrugged. "Then we ain't seen nothing."

Neither Bugas nor Thigpen was discouraged. They were like salesmen who never truly begin their sales pitch until they induced a "no" from a client. Thigpen laughed. "Come on now, men. You're tryin' to hide something. Why? They did pass this way, didn't they?"

Paley shook his head. "They didn't pass here," he said.

"Now look, fellows." Thigpen reached into his inner jacket pocket and removed an aged and battered pocketbook with snap lock. "I got—fifty—yes, fifty dollars here for the fellow willing to give us any information at all."

The brittle silence tautened, the tensions growing strained in the room. Bugas laughed. "Come on now. A man needs money. Here's a month's extra pay for one of you fellows willing to help us."

One of the young riders said, "Put your money on the table, friend."

Thigpen looked up, smiling broadly. He laid Texas greenbacks on the table, smoothing them with the flat of his hand. He kept his fingers on the money and stared at the youth, grinning. "What you got for us, lad?"

The boy shrugged. "Hell, you're gonna find out sooner or later. I can use fifty dollars—even Texas money. Mr. Ham headed east—a few days back—with a boy in chains. Don't know—but he might be the one you're looking for—"

"That son of a bitch." Thigpen clapped his tall hat on his head. "Trying to beat us out of that re-ward."

Bugas, astonishingly light on his feet, was already striding toward the door. He spoke crisply across his shoulder. "Come on, Mil. Let's go after that sneaking bastard."

Thigpen tossed the money across the table at the

young informer and strode from the bunkhouse. Bugas was already scrambling into the carriage. Thigpen bounded into the vehicle, took up the reins and laid the whip across his horse. The open coach lurched, then raced out of the yard, headed east.

XXV

They drove east across the Texas flatlands, but the
land itself didn't change much. Ham traveled at a
steady but unhurried pace. The bare trail was rarely
traveled. Infrequently, they met oncoming covered
wagons, families, or men alone, traveling west. These
people paused only briefly, nervous, suspicious, exchanging bits of news or information and then heading
out. None appeared exultant in their discovery of new
land. They trudged across the open country, exhausted,
sweated, thirsty and, even with abundant game, usually empty-bellied. They had often been unable to
hack out a living for themselves in the east. They
had heard exciting and alluring stories about the rich
lands beyond the Texies, but the deeper they penetrated this broken prairieland, the lower their hopes
sank. There might be substance out here, sustenance
for a man and his family, but it was no Eden of milk
and honey. A man would slave out his guts for anything he got. They plodded forward because they could
not turn back. They could not even look backward,
except in regret, and there was little joy in looking
ahead.

Tige learned to hate it when they met travelers on
the road. All stared at him as if he were some two-
headed monster in a side-show. There was little in this
unvarying land to entertain a traveler. They gazed in

awe at the youth chained like a vicious animal in the smart-looking carriage. Tige seethed, watching them nudge each other, sniggering.

The gaping people crabbed along, staring over their shoulders at the strange sight for a long time after they passed. Ham appeared uninterested and unmoved by the stir Tige's chains created in every hamlet, at every encounter along the trail.

They crossed wider, deeper streams now, and rivers which had gouged steep ravines in the bare brown land. Someone had flung temporary timber beam-and-slab flat bridges, trussed to abutments at each end and without railings on either side. Huge beams were tied along the flat wood plankings, and these rough-sawn logs, sometimes a foot or so in diameter, were the only sidings. These roadway bridges were wide enough to accommodate one vehicle; the first to arrive crossed, the second waited. Usually men led the horse or team across the span, gripping the bridle sidecheck. Sometimes they threw crokersacks over the animals' eyes as blinders, especially as many of these bridges hung suspended forty or fifty feet above the white rocks and white-spuming, fast-running waters.

Ham stopped each night for camp an hour before sunset. As horizons grayed and skies burned tired orange and vermilion, he made a fire, started a pot of coffee, tended the horse and staked it out in the best available graze. Some nights they were forced to make dry camp, but the foresighted Hammond always packed the purest spring water he tasted—refilling his bottles whenever he found fresher clean water—for such emergencies. Greasewood was abundant and made starting and feeding fires easy. Ham never allowed any fire to burn past sundown. He wasn't interested in lighting some highwayman to his bivouac.

The rains started and the earth showed greenery—bluebells glittered in the gray clumps of forage grass.

When rains persisted through the night, Ham made his bed in the rear of the carriage. During a raging storm he condescended to toss Tige an oilcloth. Tige huddled under it, miserable and sleepless.

When he slept at last he dreamed about Nell and the life they'd promised each other they'd find together out across the Texies. He awoke in the morning aching and depressed. Ham lay asleep in the rear of the carriage. The rain had stopped and the sun boiled steam from the mud puddles. Tige threw off the oilcloth. He stared at Ham, thinking that if he could reach him, he could kill him. He could take the wagon and return to Nell. His mouth twisted in bitter frustration. Ham was too smart to be taken like that. He stayed out of Tige's reach; he carefully kept all firearms out of the boy's range.

Tige sat, sick and shivering with morning chill and the despair he'd come to recognize as part of his existence. Down below were long stretches of verdant hammock land, trees growing greener than he had seen for a long time. This did not stir Tige's hopes—this meant they were approaching Louisiana, coming back to that hated state where his life was held forfeit.

Tige tugged impotently at his shackles and turned away from the stand of green trees, the cool mists. He gazed back toward the brown, bare broken land where Nell was.

He glimpsed movement in the distance. At first he thought it was a bird rising up along the horizon, an eagle perhaps or a vulture. Then the distant figure appeared again, racing overland, speeding on that trail behind him. He watched it for a long time until it took vague shape as horse and carriage. After a while he became aware that Ham had opened his eyes and was watching him.

"What's the matter, boy?"

Tige shrugged. "Nothing very serious."

Ham sat up and followed the direction of Tige's gaze. Ham cursed. "You son of a bitch," he said.

"What's the matter, Pa?" Tige's voice taunted Ham. "Are you in trouble?"

"No. But you may be, you bastard."

"I was born to trouble, Masta. Remember?"

"Don't take that smart-ass tone of voice to me, boy. . . . Why didn't you wake me up when you first saw that carriage back there?"

"I didn't think about waking you up. I thought about killing you, but I didn't think about waking you up."

Ham threw back his covers and oilcloth. He slept in his boots because it was almost impossible for him to remove them without assistance. He was too clever to trust Tige near him. He leaped from the wagon and strode, limping, out to where he'd staked the horse.

As he worked, Ham frequently checked the dust bolls raised by the vehicle on the distant backtrail. He guided the horse between the carriage shafts, hitched it, ready to travel.

"Those men are after you, boy."

"How do you know? From that distance? Do you recognize them?"

"Don't have to. Know 'em. Seen 'em before. Know they after you. After your carcass. Your hide is worth five thousand in gold to them men."

Tige shrugged. "Seems a fair price."

"Ain't you got good sense? They mean to kill you. We got to get out of here."

"Does this mean we don't have coffee, Pa?"

"Damn you, boy. I can smash your face with this here whipstock. An' I'll purentee do it if you keep that tone of voice. I been expectin' them fellows since we set out. . . . I can tell you this. Them men catch up to us—they kill you first." Ham slapped the reins. The horse responded, pulling the carriage up the slight incline to the trail. Ham touched the animal with the whip. The sleek animal raced forward. The carriage rolled smoothly and at a swift pace along the pocked trail. "You best pray they don't catch us, boy."

Tige shrugged, the wind slashing at his face. "I told you, Pa. Dying in Texas is like dying in Louisiana as far as I can see."

"Well, you might want to die. I don't."

Tige thought about this for a moment. He grinned coldly. "You mean they are after you, too?"

"They're bounty hunters."

"No bounty on you, Masta," Tige taunted.

Ham shook his head. "They probably reckon I'm going back to Louisiana to beat them out of that five thousand reward."

"Are you?"

"Hell, boy. I got a hundred blacks—like you—at Falconhurst that I could sell at five thousand each."

Tige grinned. "You think you'll get a chance to explain that to them?"

"We ain't stoppin' to explain nuthin'."

Tige shook his head, laughing savagely. "You going to outrun them all the way to Falconhurst?"

"If I have to."

"My money says you won't make it," Tige said, watching the other carriage approach behind them.

"Where'd you git any money?"

After a while Tige said, "Have you considered—if you don't wreck this carriage and they start shooting—they might kill you first?"

"You hang on. They ain't in range yet."

Tige glanced at Ham, eyes cold and questioning. "I thought you were smart, Pa."

Ham laid on the whip. "What the hell does that mean?"

Tige continued to watch him, unflinching. "How long do you think your horse can keep up this speed?"

"As long as theirs can. Longer, maybe."

"No." Tige set himself against the sway and bounce of the carriage on the pot-holed roadway. "No.

You're not as smart as I thought, Pa. Their carriage is light—a hell of a lot lighter than yours. Carrying less than half the weight of this one. It's cut down to move fast. Racing wheels. You'll kill this horse running from them, but you won't get away."

Ham swore. He checked across his shoulder, struck with the whip again. "You so goddam smart. You got airy better idea?"

Gunfire snapped distantly behind them. The sound was like the crack of a twig in a high wind, yet it had its intended impact. They heard it in the lead wagon. Instinctively, Ham's horse moved faster. The carriage swayed from side to side on the rough trail. Hammond's knuckles grayed on the lines. He glanced over his shoulder again, his face taut, eyes like blue slits. "Ain't firin' tryin' to hit us. Not from that distance. Just tryin' to scare us," he said to no one in particular.

"Worked real good," Tige said.

"That was just their warnin' that they're after us."

"They're closing in fast." Tige checked over his shoulder and spoke in a conversational tone, his voice scattered in the wind.

Ham hurled him a malevolent gaze. "Whose side you on, anyway, you bastard?"

Tige laughed and shrugged. "Sorry, Pa. You've taught me to hate all whites—equal."

Ham's mouth twisted. "They'll kill you and they won't think twice about it."

"How much thinking you white people do don't really interest me all that much." Tige gripped the side rails and slid down in the seat as the carriage wheeled precariously on a curve in the trail, bouncing wildly.

Gunfire was closer now, more sharply defined.

"Got to stop 'em," Ham muttered between clenched teeth.

"Yeah." Tige nodded. "You got bad trouble, Pa, and that's a fact."

"Ain't just one of us going to die in this little melee, boy." Ham's voice was savage.

"Just so I live long enough to see you go first," Tige said. He savored that thought for a moment. "What more can I ask of a god that branded me a slave?"

"You stop that goddam sacrilegious talk! That's a hell of a way to mock the Deity at a time like this."

"Don't worry, Masta. God don't pay me no nevah mind." Tige crouched low as a gun cracked behind them. "Sometimes, I think if there *is* a God, He's a full-time white man's God."

"Certainly that's the way it is, boy. Only human being's got souls—" Ham began. The guns rattled closer behind them and he broke off in a breathless tension, brandishing his buggy whip.

"Wonder where God is, right now?" Tige inquired, taunting him.

"I see you puttin' as much barricade as you can between you and them guns."

"I'm a nigger, but that don't mean I'm too stupid to be scared, Pa."

Ham rode some silently taut moments, his face gray, his fists tight on the reins. At last, he spoke grimly, between his teeth. "I'm going to give you one chance to stay alive, boy."

"For how long?"

"Long as you're breathin', you're alive. Long as you got life, you got hope."

"That's a real movin' sermon, Pa. . . . You reckon to pass the collection plate now?" Tige crouched as low on the boot of the carriage as he could get. The gunfire sounded sharply defined now, and deadly.

"You listen to me," Ham yelled over the blast of wind, the rattle of the carriage and pound of hooves. "Them bounty hunters goin' kill you first thing—"

"You look like a fine target, sittin' up there. I think we come to a fine place in this road where it don't matter who is black or white, or who's going to die first."

Ham slashed the horse with the whip again. Gunfire crackled as if to mock his trying to escape.

Tige laughed. "If you let me handle the horse, you could at least fight back, Pa."

Ham glanced at him, face gray and cold. "I don't trust you. You wreck this here carriage, you stop us all."

"Figured all the angles, ain't you?"

Ham bent forward as far as he could. "I'm tryin' to stay alive, you son of a bitch."

"Too bad you ain't got a fine, strappin' seventeen-year-old son to help you."

Gunfire shattered any thought Ham might have put in words. He took up a gun and held it out to Tige. Tige stared first at the weapon and then at Ham, incredulous. "Take it," Ham told him. "You git up on your knees and fix that gun restin' over the seat back."

"I could turn it on you—"

Now Ham laughed at him. "With this horse gallopin' full-tilt, I don't think you will. You a nigger—but you smarter'n that. . . . We wreck now, I might be thrown clear—but you chained, your neck's broke sure."

Tige took the gun. He eased himself up to his knees and rested the barrel over the seat back, steadied it. "Comanche Indians shoot enemy horses first," he said.

Ham was staring ahead, studying the trail. "All right. You aim for the dead middle of that horse's head. . . . You don't fire till I tell you."

The bounty hunter's carriage was clearly gaining on them now. The light, steel-rimmed wheels seemed to skim across the hard-packed road. Tige stared back at the pursuers. The thin man in his tall hat whipped the horse; the fat man, kneeling in the boot, loaded, aimed and fired a rifle. The sound of gunfire was distorted, but fearfully loud on the wind. Tige admitted it may have been imagination, but he sensed the slap of the bullet beside him.

"Hold your fire," Ham yelled.

Suddenly all other sounds were obliterated as Hammond's carriage rattled out upon a narrow beam-and-slab flat bridge. The vehicle seemed to waver as the terrified horse, racing at full speed, instinctively slowed. Ham gripped the lines fiercely, urging the animal forward. Tige glanced out over the log-beam siding to the rocky rapids, the white flashing far below.

"Now," Ham said.

Tige held his breath. He fixed the gunsight on the other horse, which now raced out upon the bridge, plankings thundering. Tige was aware Ham had slowed their own animal. The pursuing carriage raced toward them. Tige saw the kneeling fat man prepare to fire again.

His mouth dry, Tige sighted along the gun barrel. He saw the bobbing head of the racing horse, its eyes wild, slaver blowing from its distended mouth. He pressed the trigger, watching fascinated.

It all happened with incredible, terrible slowness. It was as if that horse tripped on an invisible wire. The carriage tottered out of control, rocking on its thoroughbraces, swinging erratically from side to side on the narrow plankings. The fat man and his gun were thrown clear first. The gun went flying out over the side of the bridge and in some unreal flight, the fat man followed, flinging his arms and pedaling his legs madly as if fighting all the forces of gravity. The horse plunged off the left side of the bridge. As if his hope for safety depended upon his remaining with the carriage, the tall man gripped the lines. He was hurtled forward and fell, spinning over and over, still clutching the lines.

Ham's buggy rattled on along the bridge and rolled from it to the trail, and Tige felt the vehicle slowing. He gazed backward in horrified fascination. The men, carriage and horse were gone from the bridge as if they'd never existed at all. Ham's carriage slowed to its usual unhurried pace. Tige saw that Ham did not even look over his shoulder toward where the dead men had plunged from the bridge.

His rage gorging up in him, Tige gripped the rifle and turned it toward Ham.

He found Ham's pistol cocked in Ham's left hand and fixed on his belly. Ham's grin was cold. "I'll just take the rifle back now, boy. . . . Reckon we can stop up the road a piece and make coffee. . . . "

XXVI

The road climbed in a long slope upward from the riverbank and entered a thick stand of longleaf pine, post oaks and towering gums. Ham drove slowly, crossing the shaded corridor under a thick canopy of boughs. They followed the dim tunnel, sunlight brightly white at both ends. Tige rode slack-shouldered, numbed.

They drove past a few widely separated houses along the road, ugly, windbitten structures nestling against scabrous windbreaks. The road was more crowded with wagons, carts, men walking along the shoulders and plowed and planted fields damp and dark with rich earth on both sides. They could see the town ahead through faint mists rising from a river. The town was loud and busy with a fevered activity which was strange after months in the back country. It was like entering a different world. They crossed a short, narrow bridge and passed a sign which read: "Garretsville, Texas. Fastest Growing Town in Our Republic."

They came into the town on a narrow brick-paved main street with many damp gravel arteries running off from it. People on the boardwalks and lounging on porches gazed at them, curious and intent. They had never seen anything quite like them before. Dogs yapped at the vehicle wheels and children ran along beside the carriage, pointing at Tige and his shackles.

Ham pulled into the hitching area before the

Garretsville Hotel. This slab-sided false-front frame building was three stories tall, paint-blistered and wind-scratched. Most upstairs windows were open, curtains billowing like gray flags of surrender in the heat. Ham ignored the gawking curious who gaped at Tige, nudging each other and grinning nervously. Tige slumped in the seat and stared straight ahead.

Ham called out to a white-bearded sage on the hotel veranda. "How far to the Sabine River crossing?"

The old man spat tobacco and pointed east with arthritic fingers. "Depends on how foolish you push your horse, mister. But going at a reasonable pace it's no more than a day or two to the ferry crossing at the river."

Ham thanked the oldster. Ham said to Tige, "I'm going in and eat dinner. I'll bring you out a platter when I'm finished."

Tige shrugged. The children grew braver, ventured nearer now, wide-eyed, pale, holding their breath, ready for flight. Older youths and loitering men hesitated, paused, stopped and peered at Tige, shaking their heads, puzzled, fascinated. Several walked all the way around the vehicle and horse. One man kicked a wheel as if considering purchasing it as it stood, replete with manacled captive.

Finally, as Tige had dreaded, the questions began, the jeers, the taunts. Smaller boys threw rocks and sticks at him. Only the fact that Ham had hobbled the horse kept the animal from bolting. Tige remained silent on the seat.

The crowd grew larger, noisier, rougher. When Tige refused to answer the questions the older men fired at him, one of them found a cane pole and prodded him with it.

Tige became aware of two men on the shaded veranda. He noticed them for several reasons. Their rough buckskin pants and animal-hide jackets set them apart from the villagers. They stood apart, aloof from the

288

others. Their faces were weathered, bearded, their eyes as cold and empty as animal eyes. They wore guns strapped to their thighs in belt holsters, high-heeled boots and short Mexican spurs. They watched the rising excitement in the sun-blasted street but took no part in it. Their faces remained implacable. They neither smiled nor frowned. They merely watched and studied.

Tige would have selected the pair as the last two from whom he might reasonably expect aid. They did not move until several of the younger men, tired of poking at Tige with the cane pole, grabbed at his arms and tried to yank him out of the carriage to the street.

"Hold it, you loco bastards." The deep, rough voice of the taller man stunned and stopped the crowd in its tracks, cracking like a muleskinner's command across them.

The older men straightened, the younger men paused looking around, the children retreated. Several on-lookers, at the rim of the crowd, drifted.

The two strangers came down the plank steps from the veranda into the blazing sunlight. Both were taller, heavier than the townspeople around them. Armed, they looked dangerous, with violence tamped down barely under the surface. People backed away, and gradually but certainly the crowd broke up and dispersed.

The two men crossed the boardwalk. Tige said, "Thanks."

The younger man, red-bearded, pale-eyed, shrugged. "Hell, partner, we done rock-and-cell time. Both of us. We know about chains and cages."

Tige had the uneasy sense that while the rough-garbed strangers spoke to him, their eyes prodded and probed about the carriage, the supplies, the guns, half-concealed under oilcloths and far in the rear beyond Tige's reach, and most especially, the metal box bolted under the front seat.

"We just rode into town to look around," Redbeard said. "Maybe pick up a little grubstake somewhere."

"Yeah. And do a little fancy ridin' over at Miss Fanny Whitaker's," the older man said, leering.

When Tige's face remained blank at the mention of this lady's name, Redbeard laughed. "You ain't never heard of Miss Fanny Whitaker and her stable of fancy ladies?"

"No."

"You did come a long way."

"Yes. Out past Washington-on-the-Brazos."

"This fellow takin' you back to jail?"

"Yes. In the States."

"He some kind of bounty hunter?"

"No. He's a slave breeder—in the States."

The older man's chilled gaze brushed across the metal box again. "Figured him for a high-roller. What the Mexicans call a *caballero*, a *don*, a *patrone*."

Redbeard grinned emptily. "Must be he's pretty well fixed?"

Tige shrugged. "I don't know."

Redbeard nodded toward the bolted chest under the seat. "Carries his money screwed in tight. I'd say he's loaded with gelt, huh?"

Tige spread his hands. "It means nothing to me."

The darker man laughed. "That's 'cause you figure you can't git your hands on it."

"I guess so."

Redbeard said, "You goin' to let him take you back?"

"I don't know."

Both men laughed, though neither of them bothered to meet Tige's gaze. "I can see you don't mean to make the full trip," the older man said, nodding his approval.

Tige shrugged again. "I'll do what I can."

"My money's on you," Redbeard said.

"Yeah," the other said. "I been in chains. A man don't like it. It makes him wild."

290

The two men glanced once more at the bolted chest under the seat, then looked at each other. Their faces remained expressionless. The older man glanced briefly toward Tige. He said, "*Hasta luego, amigo.*"

"*Vaya con Dios,*" Tige said.

"Who's he?" the older man said, and laughed. He nodded again, in farewell.

The younger man tapped at the edge of his slouch-brimmed hat with the backs of his fingers in a salute of parting. The two men grinned emptily at Tige, then turned and walked lazily back up onto the shaded hotel veranda. They went to the far end of the porch and sank into rockers, slumping there inertly. They sat silently, unmoving, somehow bringing to Tige's mind the infinite waiting patience of vultures. . . .

Hammond walked into the crowded hotel dining room and bar. There were no women in the large chamber, though a huge painting of a nude woman dominated the bar. The men appeared well-to-do, businessmen mostly, with a sprinkling of farmers, ranchers, lumbermen.

A waiter bowed to Ham just inside the drapery-lined double-doorway of the dining room. "Is the señor alone?"

"Yes." Ham looked around. This wasn't the St. Louis Hotel in New Orleans, but it was the grandest-looking eatery he'd seen in six years at least. The tables appeared taken, men laughing, talking, loitering, none hurrying. Cigar smoke stalled in thick clouds between tables and high ceiling. "You got a dinner menu?"

"I'll bring it to you at the bar, sir," the waiter said. "Be just a few moments. I'll have you a table. A fine table. By the window. Very cool."

The waiter waited, his smile fixed unyieldingly on Ham's face. After a brief pause, Ham remembered the way to a New Orleans waiter's heart. He supposed waiters were alike under the skin, everywhere. He placed a gold dollar on the waiter's palm. The obsequious smile widened, intensified. Ham had bought a beautiful if transient friendship. "Be just a few minutes, Don Caballero. Just a few minutes."

Ham shrugged and limped over to the bar. A man had made a place for him at the railing. He appeared to be about Ham's age, but with graying hair, sunblistered face lobster red and marked with thick white brows above large, protuberant blue eyes. "Name's Shaw, suh. Samuel Austin Shaw. You a stranger in our fair city?"

"Yes. Just passing through. Name's Maxwell. May I buy you a drink?"

"What? And desecrate our noble reputation for Texas hospitality, suh? I should say not. And not again. . . . Bartender, the usual for me and—a—what is your pleasure, suh?"

"A hot toddy," Ham said.

Both Samuel Austin Shaw and the bartender eyed Ham oddly, but the drinks were prepared and delivered. Ham and Shaw discussed the weather, the crops, the sad state of Texas currency, over further libation.

"Texas may indeed be experiencin' growin' pains," Samuel A. Shaw said. "But this is not true of Garretsville. No, suh, you've ridden into the crown jewel of the Southwest. You have chosen for your reposoir, a veritable paradise where money flows freely, commerce moves swiftly and only time ambles calmly, recognizably in no haste to depart the confines of so elegant a watering place."

"You sell land or something?" Ham inquired.

Shaw laughed and shook his head. "No, suh, I do not. I am by profession and passion a banker, suh. But I have seen this town grow from a crossroads to what may yet be the greatest metropolis in our beloved Republic. But the growth of our town is not nearly so remarkable as the reason for its unprecedented mushrooming. I am shore you have seen many large

292

towns—and found the reasons for their burgeoning. Seaports. Trading centers. Riverports. Lumber towns. Gold-rush towns. Seats of governments. Railheads. Every town has its basis for growth. Ours is a great and lovely lady."

"A lady?" Ham stared, certain his acquaintance was setting him up for some kind of joke.

"A lady. Have you perhaps never heard the name of Miss Fanny Whitaker, suh?"

"No, sir. I can't say I ever have." Ham ordered refills for himself and his new friend. They drank together.

Shaw shook his head. "Well, sir. There would be no Garretsville—a bustling metropolis—today. I ask you to drink to the glory and long life of Miss Fanny Whitaker."

Every man at the bar stopped whatever he was doing and raised his glass in a toast to the lady. Someone insisted upon buying for everyone at the bar for a second toast to Miss Fanny Whitaker. Banker Shaw then ordered drinks for everybody and proposed an even more elaborate toast to the lady. Ham had five drinks before Shaw joined him at a table window to regale him with excellent food, wines, liquor and the story of Miss Fanny Whitaker and the phenomenal growth of Garretsville.

"Started out this here was a trail crossing, without even a given name," Shaw said. "Long before my time—and yet not too many years back, as time is recorded. It was to this lonely outpost that Miss Fanny Whitaker came. Many times she's told me the story of how she set up business in a vacant house near the river bridge. She says she ran her place hand to mouth, front and rear, till she could afford another girl to help her with her growing trade. It seems a traveler stopped here, rode on, mentioned Miss Fanny, and her fame spread. Travelers began to go out of their way to come to Garretsville—as it was named, for the minister of our first Baptist church. And there's a fine structure you must see before you leave town—after, of course, you visit and enjoy the delights of Miss Fanny Whitaker's mansion."

"A cathouse?" Ham said.

Shaw nodded. "In the vernacular, yes. But a cathouse with a difference. Pleasures you won't find among the thousand whores in New Orleans. Miss Fanny has at least fifty girls at present—some of them recent virgins, and others who can give such a rendering of virginity that it is preferable to the true article. Fresh young lovelies. But you'll see all that when we visit over there later—as my guest, of course."

"No. I am right interested hearing about Miss Fanny. But I'm not one that's really partial to white ladies. . . . It may sound strange to you, but my stomach turns at the sight of that white, dead-fish flesh. And, too, my pappy taught me to revere white ladies. . . . I gits downright impotent when I'm around a white lady—even a whore. I likes to think of our white ladies as up on a pedestal. I'm sorry."

"No apology required. None! You'd be surprised at how many men feel as you do. I put it down to the way they're raised. But you don't have to go over to Miss Fanny Whitaker's mansion to see her and her girls. Every afternoon—round five when the sun goes down enough so's it's cool—Miss Fanny takes a half-dozen of her lovelies out in her gold-painted carriage for a drive through town. It's a sight you'll never forget."

"Don't the good churchgoin' folks object to such carryin-on?"

Shaw laughed and shook his head. "Not here in Garretsville, Texas, suh, they don't. We all know what we owe Miss Fanny. Our debt to that great lady is real and can hardly be repaid. We stand and bow and tip our hats when Miss Fanny Whitaker rides past with her lovelies every day in her polished phaeton. . . . Church folks—if they mention Miss Fanny Whitaker at all, it's in their prayers. Miss Fanny has singlehanded made this town what it is.

"Cowpokes, politicians, travelers, trappers, farmers, ranchers—you name the man—he comes from as far out of his way as a hundred miles to visit Miss Fanny's mansion.

"It wasn't like that at first. Travelers come here with money to spend, and no place to spend it, except with Miss Fanny. Soon a cafe opened, then a saloon. A general store was next. Then somebody built a six-room hotel to accommodate the transients. A saddle-bag dentist settled down here after a night at Miss Fanny's. He opened an office, as did three lawyers and a saw-bones.

"I come along then, seeking my fortune. Well, sir, I seen what this here town could be. I opened a bank. It has done nothing but grow. Soon, our town became a scheduled stage stop. Farmers began bringing in their produce when they came to visit Miss Fanny's mansion. Deals were made in the hotel, at the saloon, or in Miss Fanny's parlor for all manner of things—for cattle, for land, for commerce. Trappers piled their furs at the stage depot. Lumbermills opened. A cattle pen. A mayor, sheriff and city council was elected."

"And you credit it all to Miss Fanny Whitaker?"

"Everything. As does every right-thinking man. We all pay homage to Miss Fanny Whitaker—and her ladies—every afternoon at five." Shaw nodded and clapped Ham on the shoulder. "You must stay for those festivities, even if you do not care to visit her establishment."

Ham shook his head. He mopped his mouth with his napkin and dropped it on the table. He agreed to one final hot toddy to be drunk in salute to Miss Fanny Whitaker, that civic-minded matron.

Tige glanced up, going taut, when Hammond

emerged from the hotel lobby with the stout, gray-haired, red-faced man in his wake. Ham was laughing and talking over his shoulder, and he stumbled slightly coming down the steps.

Tige felt his heart hammering. Ham's eyes were glazed, his face flushed, his movements uncoordinated. He was drunk!

"Goodbye, Mr. Shaw," Ham said. "It's been a real pleasure dining with you."

"Just hate to see you set out like this in the midst of the afternoon," Shaw said, clapping Ham on the shoulder. "You ought to wait around to see Miss Fanny's phaeton."

"Reckon we best git on down the road," Ham said. "Gettin' so close now, I can smell Louisiana—gettin' mighty anxious to set my feet under my own table."

Hammond and Shaw shook hands in the middle of the walk. Ham went unsteadily around the hitching rail, taking up the hobble and dropping it into the rear of the carriage. Tige saw that Redbeard and friend had not moved, but watched them with deadly eyes from the far end of the shadowed veranda.

"Maybe I won't make it. Maybe Tige will already be dead before we get there—if we get there at all. You think I haven't thought about all that?"

XXVII

When Hammond cracked the whip over the rump of the horse, moving his carriage along the street and out of the busy town, Tige sat taut and watched him narrowly. Ham seemed on the brink of a drunken stupor. He was keeping his wits under control only through incredible self-discipline. He sang as he clung to the reins—songs unknown and unrecognizable to Tige, delivered in a flat, off-key baritone which seemed to please the singer immensely. Ham would round off a song and laugh in immoderate delight. His hat blew off and fell to the rear flooring. Ham checked on it casually but did not reach for it. "Hell with it," he said and laughed fatuously.

The wind blew Ham's hair into his eyes. He loosened his shirt collar another button and complained of excessive heat—it was hot even for Texas. He belched loudly and apologized for forgetting to bring his captive either food or water. "Unf'givable of me," he said and laughed loudly. His breath was hot with the rancid smell of sweetened corn whiskey.

Tige sat, unable to relax. He kept his face averted, afraid Ham might sense the thoughts battering behind his eyes. This was that moment he had patiently watched for and fervently prayed for to all his gods.

His heart pounded. He had prayed to his gods and

now they had answered his prayers; they had handed him this one chance for freedom. Damn! They had delivered it on a golden platter. It was his responsibility to guarantee that he didn't throw it away or let it slip through his fingers.

His mind reeled with the awesome terror and anticipation. He kept telling himself there would come one perfect moment for striking at his captor. Tige delayed for what seemed like a long time, but was only a matter of minutes while his brain whirled with confusion, plans, fears. He was faced with a lifetime habit of regarding Hammond Maxwell as his superior, almost as an immortal, a tyrant and a deity so far removed above him that he had no weapons and no defenses against him. All Tige's life Hammond Maxwell had held supreme power, all weaponry, whips, guns, the auction block.

He sweated. He had to make his move—now. By all his gods, he had his chance now! It would never come again.

Suddenly, Ham jerked hard on the lines. The horse stopped. Tige was thrown forward but quickly righted himself. Ham held up his hand, warning Tige to silence. He stared at something in the roadway ahead.

At first, Tige thought it was a patch of shadow in the open trail. Then he saw it was a Virginia white-tailed deer. This country was infested with the animals. For some reason, the young buck had hesitated in the middle of the roadway, head tilted, sniffing, upwind from them.

"Deer meat for supper," Ham whispered.

Ham half-turned on the seat and reached over the backrest to lift a rifle.

Tige lunged toward him. At the last second, Ham sensed trouble, reacted, tried to straighten. He was too late. Tige caught him about the throat in an arm lock and yanked his head back, pressing his forearm, vise-like, against Ham's Adam's apple.

Ham struggled, trying to fight free. He managed to close his fingers on the rifle stock, and he brought it swinging upward like a battering ram.

"Drop it." Tige increased the pressure on Ham's larynx.

Ham gasped, trying to suck in air. He struggled a moment longer, wriggling like a gaffed fish, then he released the rifle. The gun struck the flooring. Tige released his grip only slightly.

Ham sucked in a breath, rasping, and fought again. He shoved his hand into his jacket pocket and brought out his pistol. Mercilessly, Tige closed his arm on Ham's throat. Sinews and muscles corded on the boy's bicep. Veins and tendons stood out as sharply on Ham's throat and neck. "Drop it," Tige said. "So help me God, I'll break your voice box. I'll break it."

Ham's face showed a violent red; his blue-lipped mouth parted, though he was unable to draw a breath into his throat; his eyes bulged in their sockets. His arms flailed a moment, before he let the gun slip from his fingers and fall beside the rifle on the boot flooring.

Still holding a fierce grip on Ham's throat, Tige knelt and got his hand on the pistol butt. He straightened, holding the gun. He turned it in his fist and pressed its mouth against Ham's temple. "The key to the shackles," he said between clenched teeth. "Give me the key."

Ham resisted less than five seconds. His body writhed, seeking oxygen. His face showed a blue cast beneath its blood red. Tige released his grip only enough to permit Ham a gasping suck of air. He tightened his arm again. Ham thrust his hand into his pocket and came up with the key.

Tige laid the gun on the seat beside him and took the key from Ham's trembling fingers. He unlocked the spancels at his ankles and loosened the shackles chained at his wrist. The chains fell away. Exultant, Tige wanted to cry out like an animal that's broken a snare. Instead, he spoke, very softly, his voice edged with regret, but coldly determined, "Looks like this is as far as you go, Masta."

As they'd fought, the untended horse had wandered off the trail down a slight defile. Here it stopped and grazed in dry grass clumps.

Tige pressed the gun against Ham's temple, his fingers tightening on the trigger.

He hesitated, trembling. Every instinct in him screamed at him to hurry, to get it over and get out of here. All the reasons for hating Masta Hammond Maxwell, slave breeder, swarmed in his mind. Against this justification for murder rose the thought that this man—heartless as he seemed, totally insensitive toward his own flesh and blood—was his father. The thought rolled through his mind, shatteringly. Maybe he didn't have to kill Hammond. Maybe he could tie him up, throw him out of the wagon, turn around and race west.

His heart sank, seeming to slip its moorings. He wished to all his gods that this alternative was open to him. This was what he wanted to do. But common reasoning told him better. Ham would run him down. He'd never afterward have a free moment unless Ham was dead. No matter where he would run, Ham would pursue him. He would always be waiting, taut—for the knock on the door, the footstep behind him in the dark.

"Damn you," he said aloud, agonized. Ham Maxwell was going to see his escape as the kind of wrong which had to be rectified, at all costs. He didn't want to kill Ham, but he couldn't let him live.

Suddenly, Tige went empty-bellied, sick. Instinctively, he realized they were no longer alone. There had been no sound on the roadway behind him, or his own blood pounding in his temples had deafened him to anything outside his own mind.

He jerked his head around and stared into the mocking face of Redbeard. The dark-haired older man circled the carriage, coming up close on the other side. "Better drop that gun, friend," Redbeard said.

Tige let the pistol slip from his fingers to the floor.

XXVIII

Ham straightened on the carriage seat when Tige released his armlock on his throat. He sat up, seeming suddenly and coldly sober. He said, gasping and wheezing, "Thank God you men come along. I am thankful to see you men."

The dark-haired man grinned flatly. "We're pleased to find you, too, *patrone*."

Redbeard laughed. Sensing wrong, Ham jerked his head around, staring at the younger man on the far side of the carriage. "What is this? What you fellows want?"

"Why don't you just let us ask the questions, *amigo?*" the dark-haired man said. He reined in close against the side of the carriage, nearer Ham.

"This—this nigger—" Ham jerked his head toward Tige. "This nigger was going to kill me." Ham shrugged his jacket up on his shoulders, trying to regain his dignity, watching the dark man warily.

The older man laughed. "Yeah. We seen what the boy was doing."

"He meant to kill me," Ham said.

"Well, an' Red and me appreciate the kid doin' the spadework for us, too." His voice hardened, chilled. "We'll take over now. Where's the key to the money chest, boy?"

Tige shook his head. "I haven't got it."

"Why in hell ain't you?" Redbeard said.

"You done a nice clean job, kid," the dark man complimented Tige. "An' Red an' me ain't standin' in your way. We goddam glad to see you go free. . . . Live and let live, that's Hawgans's way. Our business is with your elegant friend here. . . ."

Ham stared at the two highwaymen. "What is this?"

Red laughed. "Like the kid told you, *caballero*. This is as far as you go."

"What you men want from me?" Ham spoke coldly. He did not back down.

Hawgans shrugged. "Simple. We want the money in that chest, *amigo*."

"We git the money, nobody gits hurt," Red said.

Hawgans laughed. "Can you think of a fairer way to do business?"

"You go to hell," Ham said.

Hawgans grinned easily. "I wish you wouldn't take that attitude, *caballero*."

Moving with sidewinder speed and deception, Hawgans lunged forward in his saddle. He caught Ham by the coat collar and yanked him forward off the seat. Ham straightened and was flung out of the wagon to the ground. He struck hard on his belly and lay still, facedown, for a moment, his fingers digging into the earth.

Hawgans dismounted, taking his time. He stood over the prostrate Hammond, unemotional, methodical, deadly. "Now, I want that key, my fine cock. You want to give it to me friendly, or you want me to take it my way?"

Ham turned over slowly. "You go to hell," he said.

Hawgans calmly kicked Ham in the face, his boot smashing Ham's nose, splitting his mouth. Ham toppled back in the sand, blood spewing from his lips and nostrils.

Tige watched the big, dark Hawgans, empty-bellied. Behind Tige, Red laughed, a fluting sound. He swung down from the saddle and came around the rear of the

carriage. He stood beside Hawgans, staring dispassion-
ately at Ham writhing in bloody agony on the ground.
Red said, "You smart, friend, you give up the key. You
ain't smart, we take it."

"I—don't have the key." Ham spat blood. "Can't
open chest—till I get to Falconhurst."

"Well, that's going to be too goddam bad for you,
amigo." Hawgans's voice rasped. " 'Fore I'm through,
why, you goin' to wish to God you had that key—and
a dozen like it—in your pocket."

Red laughed, putting his head back. Hawgans
abruptly kicked Ham in the stomach with such force
that Ham vomited, doubling over on the ground, the
whiskey and food gushing through his throat, mouth
and nostrils. "Now, *amigo*. The key."

Ham managed to spit out vomitus. He stared up at
the two thugs and shook his head. Tige winced, admir-
ing Ham's bravery despite himself. Ham was proving
again he wasn't afraid of anything on God's earth.

Tige shook his head. Ham was brave, but was he
smart? Ham tried to roll away on the ground, and
Hawgans kicked him in the side again.

Ham moaned aloud, crouched doubled up with pain.
Hawgans's voice pursued him pitilessly. "I don't want
to have to kill you, but on the other hand, I can do
it—an' lose no sleep."

"Yeah," Red said.

Ham rolled over. He lay unmoving on his belly for
a moment. Suddenly, he set himself on his good leg
and sprang toward Hawgans's legs, arms outflung.

Hawgans kicked him in the face. Blood streamed
from the broken flesh of Ham's cheeks, nose and mouth.
Ham sprawled, face down. Hawgans cursed him.

"We goin' to have to teach you, *amigo*. You got to
learn to do what folks ast you. Tried warnin' you. You
won't let us be good friends. All right! You want it the
hard way. You like the taste of your own blood. I

don't give a thunderin' goddam. You want it the hard way, you git it the hard way."

Hawgans's boot cracked like a rifle shot against the side of Ham's head. Tige caught his breath, wincing as if he were being struck. Ham's head flopped awkwardly on his shoulders. Sick, Tige thought Hawgans must have broken Ham's neck. Ham lay still on the grassy earth, the sand stained red with his blood. His legs were stretched out like those of a rag doll carelessly thrown aside.

Ham's neck wasn't broken. He was barely conscious, but he tried again to lift himself. Those black boots flashed again and smashed into Ham's bloodied face. This time Ham sprawled flat and lay unmoving. "I think he's finally got the idea," Hawgans said.

"Yeah. Finally." Red nodded and laughed.

Hawgans jerked his head toward the prostrate figure on the ground. "Search the bastard, Red."

Red nodded. He knelt beside Ham's inert body and threw him over on his back as if he were a lifeless animal carcass. Red rummaged through Ham's pockets, taking everything of value he found until Hawgans swore at him, hurrying him.

"I'm *looking* for the goddam key," Red said, glancing up, squinting. "I can't find it."

"Find it." Hawgans's voice rasped.

Red's hands moved, searching. "Maybe he *ain't* got it."

"He's got it."

"We could shoot the box open."

"I want as little noise as possible. I want to move quick as we can. *¿Sabe?*" Hawgans drew his long-barreled pistol, held it negligently at his side. Red came up with a small ring of keys.

"Reckon this is it, Hawg?"

Hawgans nodded. "Good enough. Get back and I'll put a bullet in his face."

For one moment in eternity, Tige sat staring at the

three men beside the carriage. He felt incapable of moving, watching them, fascinated and horrified. Red crouched on the ground a few feet from Ham, holding the leather key ring. Ham lay unmoving, his face bloodied, unconscious. All he could think was, they didn't have to kill Ham . . . and if they killed Ham, would they leave him alive, a witness against them? All this boiled through Tige's mind while Hawgans raised the long-barreled gun and sighted along it at Ham's unconscious form sprawled on the sand.

Tige's hand, as if in reflex action, clutched up the pistol from the carriage boot. He heard himself cry out, "No! No, don't kill him!"

The next moments were dreamlike. Hawgans spun around. He saw the gun in Tige's fist and jerked his own gun up. Still in his nightmare, Tige drew his hand up, cocked the pistol and fired it at Hawgans, point-blank.

Hawgans's own gun cracked like an echo. He bent double in a terrible slow motion. He dropped the gun, fingers splayed and lifeless. He toppled slowly to his knees. His contorted face was already graying and blood stained the whole chest front of his shirt. He pitched forward.

Tige grabbed up the rifle, trying to fix it on Red, who remained, in that quick flash of time, still crouched beyond Ham, the key ring swinging oddly from his fingers. All Tige could think was that if Red drew, he could fire a pistol before Tige could hope to raise the heavy rifle.

But for that strangely unreal instant, Red seemed stunned, totally unaware of Tige, the rifle, or anything except the body of his dead partner. Staring at Hawgans's prostrate form, Red began to shake his head. His eyes widened, his face contorted in mindless grief. He screamed, almost like an agonized woman. He leaped up, backing away, still staring at his crony's body. He shook his head. Suddenly he heeled around and ran to his horse.

The animal shied and Red cried out again, grabbing the reins. He swung up into the saddle, jerked his mount's head around toward the trail. Then, like acid etching through his agony and terror, Red glimpsed Hawgans's horse. It must have crossed his mind that a horse could be used to pursue him, to run him down. Sobbing, he rode forward, grabbed the ground-tied lines and dragged Hawgans's horse after him up the incline and west along the roadway. He rode fast and he did not look back.

Holding the rifle fixed and ready to fire, Tige watched Red ride away. Something seemed to flood down through his body. It was over. It was ended and he was alive. Then he looked down at his arms and ankles. The chains were gone. He was freed. He could ride out of here and never be enslaved again. Somehow, he felt, an evil part of his life was over and ended. Forever finished. He was free.

XXIX

Tige hesitated, staring around in the crimsoned brilliance of the sunset. He really saw nothing; he was only aware of himself, deeply affected by this painful point in time. For the first moment in his life he was free. Free! A whole new life lay ahead—rewarding or fearful—he had already entered this strange and alien world of freed peoples. Once, while he was still a little boy called Tiger on the Falconhurst Plantation, he'd dreamed that Masta Hammond would pick him up in his arms, kiss him and love him—he who had never been kissed or caressed—call him "son" and declare him free. Well, that never happened. He had bought his freedom the hard way, one slow, agonized step at a time.

But he had made it. By all his gods, he had made it! The road back west lay open for him. Where would it take him? He had to move and move quickly—the first step on that long, unknown journey. He had to find sanctuary for Nell and their son. But where? At what cost? Whatever the cost, by God, he would pay it.

He shivered. He had never before felt so terribly alone. The very wild country around him appeared tautly silenced, as if everything hung suspended, waiting for something. What? The world itself waited, not even a jack-oak leaf quivered. Waiting? For what?

Loneliness shook him physically, almost like the chill

of an ague. Always, in his unhappiest slave days, he had been surrounded by people—the blacks and whites of Falconhurst and Hiddenbrook. He and Nell had been complete—even in their nightmarish flight they'd been together, close. Now he stood alone, between two worlds—the black world of slavery, and that bright new promised land of freedom.

He shivered, his body wracked with revulsion. He forced himself to face the truth. Ham had to die. It came down to that clear cold choice: Ham Maxwell's life or his own freedom. He had saved Ham's life when Hawgans threatened to kill him. But the fact was, Ham had to die. Here. Now. Alive, Ham was too dangerous, an implacable threat to Tige's survival.

He forced himself to move, to act. Tige tied Ham's wrists at the small of his back, secured his ankles, left him lying trussed like a poled hog in the sand.

Tige stared down at Ham's inert body. He looked around. He had to get out of here. If he returned to Garretsville driving Ham's carriage and without Ham, he'd rouse the people. They'd recognize him without fail. They weren't likely soon to forget that he had come to their town as Hammond Maxwell's *chained* captive. They'd never let him pass west.

Yes, unless he was smart, he'd run into deadly trouble at Garretsville. Then he found the only possible answer. He had to hide in the copse of red oaks until after nightfall. By ten or eleven tonight, he could start back west. When most of the town slept, he could make a run for it.

He experienced a sense of relief. He was thinking again, looking ahead, planning, finding trouble before it found him. He caught the heavy corpse of Hawgans by the boots and dragged it deeper into the under-brush. He kept plodding, working his way deeper into the thicket between low, thick-branched trees. He reached the rim of a ravine and rolled Hawgans's body over its brink. He stood, listening to the slide of rocks and pebbles and the thudding of Hawgans's thick carcass.

He stared toward the sky, willing the darkness to flood in and blacken the countryside. It was still brilliantly light! The eternal sunset looked as if it would delay forever. Long purple shadows laced the hammocks, and the first bats darted up screeching from the twisted, broken dry ravine. But the sun continued to flare like some savage fireball above the horizon, casting thin tapering streaks of silver over the crests of distant foothills.

Tige returned to the carriage. The horse grazed on the dry forage. Tige knelt beside Ham, who lay unmoving. Tige lifted him in his arms and placed him in the rear of the carriage. He could not say why he delayed that fearful moment which had to come—that price he had to pay to be free. He had to kill Ham, and yet, he told himself, it made more sense to conceal himself and the carriage first, and with all haste.

Grasping the sidecheck in his fist, Tige led the horse deeper into the undergrowth. When he could still see the trail through the trees—silvered in the infuriatingly lingering sunset—but had the carriage hidden from even the most curious passerby, Tige ground-tied, fed and watered the horse. He left the animal hitched between the shafts, ready to move out fast.

He heard Ham whimper and stir in the carriage. Tige walked back to the vehicle and stood beside the rear step. He placed his foot on it, staring at Ham's battered face, the broken lips, blood crusted around his eyes and nostrils.

Finally Ham was able to force his eyes open. He said, "Tiger? . . . Boy?"

"I'm here."

"Where . . . are they?"

"They're gone!" After a pause Tige said, "One is dead. I shot him. The other ran away."

His eyes closed again, Ham croaked, "Where's my money?"

"Don't worry about that," Tige said.

Ham thought about this for a long time. "You—risked your life."

Tige said nothing.

"You done it for me." After a long time he asked, "Why?"

Tige's laugh was self-reviling, bitter and puzzled. "Because I'm black inside. Because I ain't a white son of a bitch like you."

There was a long silence. At last Ham whispered, "You mean to keep me tied up like this—like some animal?"

Tige grinned in cold irony. "That's right. . . . You'll stay trussed up until I decide what to do with you."

Ham winced. "What . . . are you waiting for?"

Tige shrugged. "Dark. I can't go back through that town until late tonight."

"You mean to go back—west?"

"I'm going."

Ham's head rolled from side to side. "What about me?"

"What about you? I'm not going to let you stop me."

Ham's gaze struck against Tige's and held. He shook his head, looking broken in the weird red sunlight. "You—meanin' to kill me?"

"There ain't no other way to stop you."

"But why? . . . You saved my life."

"It beats hell out of me . . . but that's the way it is."

Ham stared at Tige for a long time, seeing Tige's determination to kill him, and the boy's inner conflicts. Suddenly, Ham wept openly, sobs bursting across his broken mouth. Tige said, "What the hell's the matter with you now? You that scared of dying?"

"Admits I'm scared of dying," Ham said, crying

aloud. "But . . . dying like this, that's what is so evil—kilt by my own son."

Tige laughed coldly. "So I'm your son now, am I?"

Ham cried a moment, tears running through the sand and blood crusted under his eyes. "God knows you *always* been my son. But it took this—this terrible *revelation*—from God Hisself—"

"What revelation is that—that you're about to die?"

"No." Ham wept uncontrollably. "The God-given revelation that you *are* my son. . . . That you put aside the hate in your heart for the wrongs I done you—the way I stood between you and your freedom— that you put all that worldly evil aside when you had to—"

"When I *had* to?"

"When God made you *see*. See the truth. That you is my son. I is your pappy. . . . So you couldn't let that man kill me. . . . And now God Jehovah Hisself has made *me* see. . . . You *are* my son. . . . Oh, I is wronged you, but if I live, then God's my witness, I got somehow to make up that evil to you—if I live."

"I wouldn't count on that."

"Please, my son—don't take that cruel tone to your pappy," Ham pleaded.

Tige's voice remained chilled. "I ain't changed. . . . I don't think you have."

"Son . . . oh, my son . . . if you could just know the revelation I is had," Ham said, his voice tremulous with emotion.

"Why you calling me *'son'?*" Tige said. "Why not *'boy'?* You spent my whole life denyin' I was your rightful son."

"A man changes, Son, when God rips the scales from his eyes," Ham said. He shook his head, crying. "I lived cruel—but I loved you—as my son—when you were a little tyke at Falconhurst. . . . But you was the son of a slave girl. By *law* you was a slave." He spread his hands, his face grave. "I had no choice. . . .

I had to deny you—if I was goin' on livin' among my kind of people."

Tige gazed at his father warily. "You sayin' now—out loud—that I'm your son?"

"Praise God, you are my *son!*" Ham nodded vehemently. "You are my own son what killed a bandit and drove another away—and saved my life. I thank sweet Jesus for what you done for me."

Tige sighed. "I couldn't let Hawgans kill you. But that don't make much sense. . . . Looks like I'm going to have to kill you after all." Tige shuddered. "Terrible as it was watchin' him, it would have been easier had I let them kill you."

"But that's it, Son! Don't you see? . . . You *couldn't* let them men kill me . . . any more than *you* can kill me—your own father—your own sweet flesh and blood."

Tige shook his head. "It's good to finally hear you call me your son—"

"You are my son—my own flesh and blood."

"That didn't keep you from chaining me up—tearing me away from Nell—taking me back to the States to hang. . . . I can't trust you. I don't trust you."

"Oh, sweet Jesus, listen to my own son profane my love for him! . . . Oh, I admits I was blind and stubborn—yes, and evil. . . . But ain't you never made a mistake, son? Done something you wished with all your heart you could undo? I been reborn, Son! I'm a reborn Christian, I am. I swear it at sweet Jesus's altar. . . . I seen that revelation when I opened my eyes and seen what you done—"

"You didn't see what I did—"

"Didn't have to!" Ham's voice shook with his emotion. "Before Gawd, I didn't have to *see* it! God seen it! And he made me see it in my heart! My heart purely knowed. . . . I was still alive, I was still breathing! . . . And all because God had put it in my dear son's heart to save my life—"

314

Tige shook his head. "Pa—"

"What is it, Son? What you want to ask of me—your own pappy?"

"I told you . . . maybe the biggest mistake I made was keeping Hawgans from killing you. . . . Maybe that's the mistake I already regret—with all my heart."

"Great God, Son! My son! My own son! What are you saying?"

Tige's voice was low. "There are things I go to do, Pa. . . . Things more important than you being suddenly *reborn* on this here road, suddenly deciding I *am* your son all of a flashing revelation. . . . I been your son for seventeen years. I lived all them years in hell. But I was your son. . . . Now I got one chance to be happy. One chance to be free. Free as you are. A chance to go back to Nell and my son. And right now, there ain't but one thing stands in my way. You, Pa."

Ham's eyes filled with sad, unreproving tears. His battered face contorted. "But ain't that what *I'm* sayin'? Ain't no need for no more violence . . . no need for hatred. No need for you to fear me—"

"I don't fear you, tied up—"

"Oh, Gawd, Son, don't break your father's heart in this sweet moment of revelation! I has seen the light. I is reborn. I tell you I has got a new vision of life—"

"Come awful fast, didn't it?"

"This here part may be sudden—my sayin' out loud what I wanted to say all your life, but that I never had the strength or the courage to say! To go against all I been taught. My whole way of life! Against my own people! But that sweet feelin' for you was always there in my heart—even when I seemed to hate you the most."

Tige hesitated, because Ham's words struck a responsive chord in his own mind. Ham's profession of love against reason had a fearful impact on him, because he had loved Hammond Maxwell. Tige shook his head, wavering despite every clangoring warning of his common sense. "I don't know. I don't know."

"Of course you don't, Son! You all tore up inside like I been. Like I was, but ain't no more! Glory God! When you a reborn Christian you see things in a whole new light! I see now that when my own dear sweet pappy died alone in Alabama—with me a thousand miles out west when he needed me most—I begun then to change. It was like dear sweet Jesus was gettin' inside me right then. . . . I'd wronged my own pappy and I knowed it—and something kept tellin' me I'd wronged you, too."

"Didn't keep you from bringing me back here in chains."

"That's it. Don't you see, Son? The devil still had his hands on my heart! Don't you see that? I *wanted* to be reborn—but I couldn't let go of my old evil ways—until this terrible violence when God came within a lick of lettin' me die . . . and my own sweet son saved my life. . . . Oh, the truth all came to me then like a blindin' flash of light, washin' my heart pure and clean."

"I'm going back across Texas," Tige said in a cold, flat tone.

"Ain't you heard a word I said? Of course you are going back, Son! Of course you are going free."

"And you ain't stopping me. With guns or words or tears. Dead or alive, you ain't stoppin' me—though alive, I know you be bound to try."

Ham wept afresh, struggling against his fetters. "That's where you *are* wrong, Son! Dead wrong! I grateful in my heart for what you done. I reborn! The devil done let go of me. . . . I belong to sweet Jesus now . . . and I *want* you to go free. I do want you to go free," Ham went on, crying and nodding, his nose running, helpless to blot it. "You don't have to kill me after all—don't have to have the blood of your own father on your hands."

"I don't want that, God knows."

"God knows, and I know, Son. I know how tore up with guilt I was when my pappy—your own sweet daid grandfather—died. I didn't *kill* him. But I was tore up with guilt because I knowed in my heart that if I'd of been there I might have saved him, might of helped him, spared him, made his passing easier. Oh, I was tored up with guilt! Think how you gone be when you put a bullet in me—in your own flesh-and-blood father. How you goin' to live with that, Son?"

Tige was silent for a long time. At last he said, "I don't know. . . . I don't want to kill you, but I am going back to Nell—"

"Of course you are! I want you to go back to her, Son! Trust me!"

"It ain't that easy, Pa. I hear what you say. But I also know what you done to me—all my life."

"You got to trust me! Not for me, but to save your own soul from torment. You can trust me. I reborn. A reborn Christian. You can trust me now. You don't have to kill me. . . . I worthless, but you don't need the stain of that violence on your conscience. . . . They don't have to be no more violence. We father and son now. I yell it out to God Jehovah Almighty up beyond them Pearly Gates. You are my son! You are my son an' I want you to go free. You spared my life . . . now, I set you free. Before God—and our debts are squared, Son—can't you see the glory in that?"

Tige shifted his shoulders inside the constriction of his shirt. He felt as if his own skin were too tight for him. He couldn't live with his doubts, but equally, he couldn't buy wholesale this sudden conversion. True, his father had been on the brink of death. They say that changes a man. He had stared hell in the face and he had been delivered. But his thirty-odd years of life had forged him into what he was, unyielding, unforgiving, unbending. Had he changed—even in the face

317

of death? Was it in him to change, no matter what he said?

"Listen to me, Son," Ham said urgently. "If I was free of these ropes, I'd take you in my arms to show you how deep I love you, that I have been reborn in Christ! Listen to me. . . . I'll make you see how it can be. . . . Drive me on east—"

"Oh, no—"

"Hear me out, Son. I beg you. It solves it for all of us. It ends the need for violence. It proves my love for you. . . . That's what we both really want, ain't it, Son?"

Tige shook his head, sweated. "I don't know," he muttered.

"Then drive me east to the Sabine River. Not one step further. They's a fine livery stable there at Aaron's Ferry where I bought a horse when I headed west. My own come up lame. I walked to the ferry on the Louisiana side and traded for a fresh animal when we crossed into Texas. . . . Take me that far. Then I open my gold chest . . . I divide it with you. One for me. Two for you—"

"Why would you do that?"

Ham's eyes welled with tears. "You my own son, ain't you? You feel I cheated you all the days of your life, don't you? Well, I through cheatin'. I through hurtin' my own dear son. . . . I need only enough to get me on home to Falconhurst where my pappy—your own sweet grandfather—lays daid. We got pots of gold eagles buried at Falconhurst. . . . I want you to have a full poke of gold to help you git started on your new free life with your Nell. An' I buys you a horse and a saddle. You rides free—back west—and I cross the ferry to the States, alone."

Tige was silent for a long time. He stared at the backs of his hands, the darkening sky, the silent countryside.

Ham shrugged as well as he could, trussed up on

the seat. "All right then, go. . . . Ride free now. . . .
Take my wagon. All my gold. Leave me here tied up
in the wilds of the Texies. Or daid. That's what you
mean to do. . . . Go on, kill me if you got to. . . . I
wants you to be free—even if it breaks my heart, the
way my own flesh-and-blood son is turned from me."

"Bein' your *son* is hellish new to me."

"An' to me! Don't you see? I want to *repay* you—
for the evil I done you, the wrongs, an' I in your debt
for savin' my life. . . . I'd be dead now but for you.
I thank God and I thank you for that. . . . Still, I
want you to be free more than anything else. It's all I
can do to repay you. . . . But—if you leave me here
—my face broken, afoot, in pain—I might as well be
dead. . . . Ain't more than a day's drive to the Sabine
River. There, we could part like *men*. Like father and
son. . . . There, I buys you a fresh horse and saddle,
gives you gold, blesses you, an' kisses your cheek . . .
an' we is through with violence forever. . . . One more
day to see your beaten father has a chance to stay
alive and get home to his own father's graveside—is
that too much to ask of a son what's already risked his
hide to save his father's life?"

Finally, Tige nodded. "All right. I'll take you to the
river. To Aaron's Ferry crossing. . . . But you'll go in
chains—the way I come this far."

Ham nodded, head lowered, body slumped. He
barely whispered, "Amen. So be it. . . ."

XXX

Darkness closed in around them while they talked.

They heard a wagon rattle past on the road and later a horseman, alone in the gathering dark. Animals moved through the underbrush and bats whistled along gloomy corridors in the broken land.

Tige was exhausted, but now that he had determined what to do, energy and optimism returned. He lifted Hammond in his arms, still trussed up, and moved him to the front seat. He placed the spancels and shackles on Ham's wrists and ankles, locked them. Ham kept saying in a sorrowful tone of melancholy, "You don't have to do this, son."

"I have to," was all Tige said.

Always, to Tige, the slave master Hammond Maxwell had been beyond understanding. And now, in this new conciliatory role, he was more puzzling than ever. Now that they were preparing to move east again, Ham was quieter, as relaxed as possible in shackles. He spoke less of the attack on his life and how, except for Tige's intervention, he would have been shot as he lay unconscious. He was able to put his close brush with death behind him. He rode silently, and in his mind looked ahead to the ferry crossing at the Sabine River and farther east—to Falconhurst.

"It all goin' to work out," he said once.

Tige didn't answer. He was pleased by Ham's silence.

He swung up into the seat, took up the lines and slapped them across the rump of the horse. The carriage rocked and bumped over the rough ground and up on the trail. Tige headed east. He thought he heard Ham exhale heavily, as if he'd been holding his breath. He could not be sure.

He watched the dim trail in the smoky-blue darkness and he exulted in his new freedom. No shackles! No spancels. No chains. He scrubbed involuntarily at his wrists. There was a sense of excitement and pleasure in finding his arms unbound. His mind raced to Nell and their life together in a world of free people. A place where they'd raise their son to be free. He wanted to rage out in his fierce exultance.

"What you plannin' to do?" Ham said after a long silence.

"I'm going to drive on to the river."

"All night?"

"All night."

"You ain't makin' no night camp?"

Tige shook his head. The chill night wind felt refreshing against his sweated face. He felt good, excited, hopeful—words unknown to him just a few hours ago. "I'm anxious to get started back west. . . . I want it over—and finished—between you and me. . . . I'm not tired. I can sleep when I get back to the ranch." He laughed. "Maybe I'll never sleep again."

"Might be dangerous, traveling all night on these roads."

Tige laughed. "I'm not afraid of anything."

Regret underlined Ham's voice. "I used to feel like that."

Tige put his head back, breathing deeply. "I reckon the fruit doesn't fall far from the tree."

He kept the horse moving at the same steady, unhurried pace Hammond had maintained across the Texies. The night deepened and the silences thickened, magnified by the stealthy forest sounds, briefly heard, quickly stilled. Huge gray clouds rode on the wind across the night sky. For a long time the stars shone bright as new coins, but then they were obscured. The wind rose and there was a smell of rain in the night.

After some twenty miles they found the sky lightening and breezes freshening. Dawn stole in through jagged pink fissures in the bank of clouds along the far horizon. Tige was hungry. He glanced at Ham, found him asleep, his battered face back, his mouth parted.

Tige drove off the trail near a shallow creek. He swung down from the wagon, stretching. He worked out his cramps and washed his face. The water tasted sweet and cold. He built a fire, using greasewood, pine knots and dried oak limbs walled between large slick creek rocks. He let potatoes roast in the hot coals. He found a bottle of cane syrup, flour and salt. He made pancakes. When the food was cooked, he filled a tin plate for Ham, a tin cup of black coffee. He carried the steaming victuals to Ham. Ham said, "I supposed to eat, tied up like this?"

Tige shrugged and set the food on the carriage seat beside him.

"I can't do it, Son," Ham said, voice plaintive.

"You'll learn—Pa."

Tige finally settled against the bole of a shortleaf pine. He poured cane syrup thickly over the water-flour-and-salt pancakes. He wolfed down potatoes, skins and all. Energy returned again The sense of being free swelled inside him. He cleared up the camp, washed dishes and pans in sand at the creek. The sun was just up, clearing the distant hills and growing hot, when they set out on the trail east again.

The reached sight of the Sabine River and Aaron's Ferry before ten that morning. The town seemed to hang suspended in a blue river-mist, a clutter of weathered buildings under giant elms and twisted-limbed live oaks on the very brink of the water. All life was centered around the ferry landing. The road led past the houses and buildings down a steep incline to the plank docks, where one of the ferry boats was tied up. The other was being winched across the wide channel on wet and dripping cables.

Tige stared at the swift flowing watercourse. The Sabine. It had never meant anything to him until this moment. Even crossing it with Nell there had not been the impact he felt now. Then it had been just one more river to cross in their headlong flight. They had run blindly, fugitives, across Louisiana. Once they'd forded the Sabine, they had relaxed slightly. They were out of the States.

But his emotions were different today. Now he saw the Sabine as the boundary between his old existence as a slave and his new life as a freed man.

He stared across the river toward the far bank. That was Louisiana over there. A slave state. Even the Republic of Texas permitted slaveholding, but didn't enslave or enforce slavery. A black could run into the Republic and, if he made it alive, live in freedom. Soon, he and Ham would part. Ham would cross that river and he, Tige, would finally be free.

Ham spoke in a sharp commanding tone, as if he held the reins and Tige might be in chains still. "Stop this wagon."

Tige continued to let the carriage roll forward. Ham stirred, writhing on the seat. "Please, Son, listen to me. You got to loose me from these here chains now."

Tige glanced at him. "I don't have to do anything, Pa."

Ham was silent another moment as they approached the outskirts of the river village. "You got my pistol, ain't you?"

"Yes. I've got all your guns and I mean to keep them."

Ham shrugged, nodding. "Keep them, Son. Load the pistol. Cock it. Do it. Fix it on me if you won't trust me. . . . But before we git into that town, I got to

324

open that chest. I got to have money—to buy you a horse and saddle, buy my own ferry ticket. And I mean to fill a poke of gold to carry in your saddlebag."

Tige gazed at him silently, wanting to trust his father, afraid to.

Ham's voice pressured him. "You jus' goin' to make trouble for me—an' for you—takin' me in town in chains." Ham nodded. "Hold that gun ready in your pocket, fixed on me. But stop the wagon and take off these chains."

Finally Tige assented. He pulled up on the lines, halting the horse in the middle of the roadway. He unlocked the spancels, removed chains and shackles. He held the gun in plain sight where Ham could see it, hammer cocked, ready to fire. "Go ahead," he said. "Open your chest."

"I need to git the key—from the carpetbag in the back."

"Bring it up here. Open it where I can watch you."

Ham nodded, complying silently. He removed a key from a leather case, unlocked the chest. The front wall let down. Gold coins spilled out. Ham drew a thick buckskin poke from his carpetbag and silently filled it, without counting. He tied off the mouth of the bag, held it out to Tige.

"Just lay it on the seat," Tige said, but his voice was gentler.

Ham looked sad, deeply hurt. "You bought my love and trust when you saved my life. . . . I wish they was some way I could buy your trust."

"I wish there were, Pa."

"Maybe someday—when you've had time to reflect. Maybe then, you'll recall me kindly," Ham said. He was slapping his jacket, brushing his trousers, straightening his soiled shirt and string tie. He recovered his hat, slapped it against his leg and set it straight upon his head. "Maybe someday, Son."

"Maybe. Someday." Tige slapped the reins and the

carriage rolled forward into the somnolent little river town. People looked up from their yards, pinked curtains at windows, watching them pass. Even at a ferry crossing between the States and the Republic, strangers created a stir. Tige was conscious of Ham's sitting straighter, preening slightly, recovering his lost dignity.

Tige grinned tautly. In this way at least, being reborn hadn't changed Ham Maxwell very much. He still wanted to be recognized as a person of status.

"Pull in yonder—at the livery stable," Ham said. I'll buy you a horse and saddle."

Tige glanced toward the half-dozen white men loitering under the cottonwood outside the wide double doors of the livery. He felt a faint sense of uneasiness. He shook his head. "I got gold. Why don't I buy the horse and saddle—after you're on the ferry?"

"You goin' wait and see me off?"

"I want to see you crossing that river." Tige sighed. "Then I'll worry about gettin' me a horse."

Ham sighed and nodded regretfully. "If that's the way you want it. . . . I just hopes they won't cheat you—you a young boy an' all."

"I hope they won't," Tige said. He could not say why, but the nearer they came to the river, the sicker he got. Panic moiled in his belly. He felt a terrible nausea, almost as if he had to vomit. There was the smell of hot tar, of burning pine logs, of long-dead fish. But none of this could account for his illness and fear. It had to be the very sight of that river—and the land beyond it—the slave states where he was wanted for murder, for miscegenation, for unlawful flight to avoid prosecution—for the crime of being black.

He looked around, sweated, feeling the eyes of the people fixed on him, the strange white, alien faces. For a moment the whole village spun about his head and he gripped the lines, knuckles graying.

The carriage rolled out of the shade of a huge old live oak and began the steep descent to the pier and the waiting ferry. Tige saw a dozen white men on the sun-splattered dock, watching them approach. Behind the carriage, the loiterers lazed on boxes or broken kitchen chairs outside the livery. They seemed to have suspended all dialogues, watching the sleek carriage in silence. Tige sweated, feeling suddenly boxed in.

He pulled up on the lines. He dropped the taut-packed poke of gold coins into his pocket. "No sense me going down there," he said. "Why don't I leave you here? I can see you across the river from the top of this embankment.".

Ham lunged at him suddenly, yelling from the depths of his lungs. "Help me! Help me! He's trying to rob me!"

Raging, Tige fought Ham off. Terror and hatred gave him incredible strength. He brought his knee up into Ham's crotch. Ham heaved audibly, buckling. Tige struck him backhand across the face, driving him back. As Ham wavered, his torn face bleeding again suddenly, almost unconscious, Tige shoved him. Ham toppled backward. He clutched wildly at the splash board, at the supports, for purchase. He missed, his fingers sliding past the supports, and he plunged outward to the road.

Not waiting to see what happened to Ham, Tige jerked the lines, turning the horse. The steep incline made a quick turn dangerous and impossible. The horse struggled in terrible slowness against the shafts, the restraining gear, the very tug of gravity itself. Tige kept straining on the lines, leaning against the tilt of the vehicle. The carriage teetered, wheels squealing, as it slowly made the turn, hanging a moment before it righted itself, headed upward.

Tige slapped the reins, cracked the buggy whip, and he prayed. . . . But it was no good, and he knew it had failed. He could not escape. By the time he got the carriage turned on the incline and righted, he was surrounded by cold-faced white men, armed with shotguns.

There was always threat of trouble along the boundary marker, and these men stayed ready.

Tige pulled up on the reins, dropped them and lifted his hands in surrender.

A half-dozen armed white men surrounded him, their guns menacing. But Tige saw only Ham in that crowd. Ham had leaped to his feet and grabbed a gun from somebody. He held it, fixed on Tige.

Tige stared down at him, meeting his gaze evenly. "You sneaking son of a bitch," Tige said.

Ham's face remained chilled. His voice had all its old remoteness and strength and implacable power. "I'm what I am, boy—I ain't changed. Never has, never will. . . . You made your mistake thinkin' that I might change."

XXXI

They crossed the Sabine River about noon that day. The village smithy had forged a metal choke which clamped about Tige's neck. This could be removed only with a chisel. It would not be taken off until Maxwell arrived at Falconhurst.

As the choke collar was forged to chains, Ham sat and talked with his supporters. They had become his born companions and drinking friends. Almost without exception, they were from the South. They'd crossed into the Republic for sundry reasons—when times got hard back home, when they needed a change of scenery, an altered climate. They'd come looking for work, excitement, change. But few had forgotten or put away their old ways. They were "good ole boys" who knew how to handle Negroes, keep them in their place. As townsmen at Aaron's Ferry, they were used to dealing with obstreperous or runaway blacks. They kept firearms, chains, whips and shackles handy for such emergencies. They agreed, over pots of ale, that they looked forward to disturbances over escaping slaves or lawbreakers as their only relief from boredom.

"Now your man," one of them said to Ham. "He wasn't much. Put up no fight a-tall. We've had them ornery bastards fight till we had to kill 'em."

Laughter burst anew as others recalled hair-raising incidents of violence and comedy in which they'd had to shoot or maim a black to subdue him. Finally, the metal collar was placed about Tige's neck and secured by a short chain to the rear floor of the carriage. The smithy laughed and yanked on the restraint so that Tige choked, flinging his arms in a way the onlookers found uproariously comic. "Well, this here nigger won't jump you no more, Mr. Maxwell. Or, if he do, he chokes to death."

Ham bought a final round of drinks all around, but merely sipped at his own mug of beer. He climbed up into the seat, slapped the reins and waved goodbye. The carriage rolled down the incline and was carefully set in place and wheel-chocked aboard the ferry. The townsmen gathered on the docks in the midday sun, drinking ale and yelling out to Ham as the flatboat was winched into the swift-flowing current.

Tige begun to tremble violently as the craft moved into the dock, Stateside. He bent forward as far as the choke collar and chain would permit. His stomach was twisted painfully with cramps. It seemed an eternity before the carriage was permitted to exit to the dock. As Ham slapped the reins, starting the vehicle up the incline from the river, Tige tasted the first hot spewing of stomach garbage. He groaned desperately and just managed to topple his head over the side of the seat before he vomited. The sweet-sick fluid gushed hotly up his throat and spewed from his mouth and nostrils. He gagged, his eyes burning, his nose choked with vomitus. He hung there, shaking visibly, and vomited until he was able only to lean outward weakly, grasping the sides of the carriage, heaving drily. . . .

Near dusk of that first day east of the Sabine, Ham said, voice vibrant with righteous fevor and suppressed hatred, "Well, you a purentee nigger again now, fo' sure." He seemed taut with the memory of the hours he'd spent shackled. By a nigger! By a slave!

Tige spoke for the first time since he'd been chained

at the ferry crossing. "When you turning me over to the law?"

"What?"

"Why don't you turn me in? The next town. That's what you brought me back here to Louisiana for, wasn't it?"

"Ain't none of your goddam business what I plans to do."

"We're in Louisiana, ain't we? This is the state where I killed a white man. Turn me over to the law—"

"Why you in such an all-fired hurry to git hung?"

"I want to get away from you. I want out of your sight. . . . I *smell* you. I don't want to smell you anymore."

"That's a fine way for a nigger to talk. I clean. I white. It's you niggers got the musk."

"I want you to turn me over to the law."

"Too goddam bad what you *want*. You a nigger—a purentee slave nigger now—and your *wants* don't amount to a hill o' beans."

"What about my trial? I should be tried here, not Alabama."

Ham raged with cold laughter. "Jesus Christ! Will you listen to this biggety nigger now? Trial? What trial? What ails you, boy? You gone soft in the head. That's it, you gone crazy. Black niggers ain't tried, you coon. A white man accuses a nigger of a crime—and that's his trial. His total trial. He accused and he hung. That's what's goin' to happen to you, nigger. Only you gone hang at Falconhurst—where my herd of blacks can see yo' punishment and learn from your crime. You'll hang where it suits me to hang you."

Tige stared at Ham, incredulous. "And who'll accuse me?"

Ham shrugged. "Don't worry about it, boy. You'll get accused. Clean and open where everybody can hear your crime. Then you'll hang. Where my herd can see you hang. I'll accuse you. An' by God, I'll hang you."

Tige did not speak again. They reached a settlement by nightfall. Ham engaged a room for the night. The tavern owner and a large black man took Tige from the carriage and bolted his chains to studs provided for slaves in an airless tack room. The black servant girl brought Tige's supper and placed it mutely on the floor near him. Later, as silently, the black man removed the untouched plate of food. At daybreak, the same slave placed corn pone and clabber in tin plates on the floor within Tige's reach and then returned and took them away before Tige was shackled once more in the carriage.

Ham gave Tige a sour glance. Ham looked refreshed after a good night of sleep on a corn-shuck mattress and rope springs. He'd washed his face and shaven. He looked healthy, robust, affluent. He'd eaten two heavy meals. He belched loudly as he turned the carriage east on the trail again. "Hear you didn't eat nuthin'. Not last night. Not this morning."

Tige seemed not to hear. Ham shrugged. "You cuttin' off your nose to spite your face, nigger. You don't eat, it don't hurt nobody but you."

The days passed silently, one much like the other. Ham found an inn or an ordinary each afternoon well before sunset. He stopped at these country taverns, had his captive secured in the barn or stables, ate, drank, swapped stories with locals or itinerants, and slept in tavern beds, satisfied with his accommodations and belching his pleasure at the food.

It was as if Tige existed in a fevered world of unreality. The forests, farms and fields they passed had no substance; they were unreal, all alike. He no longer dreamed of Nell or his son. It was as though their images had been expunged from his mind along with his hope of manhood, his last chance at freedom.

Somewhere—he had no idea where it was—he was served food in a stable lockup by a lovely black slave girl. She sank to her knees, watching him, her gentle smile and liquid black eyes compassionate. She begged him to eat when he did not touch his food. "Eat," she whispered, "to keep up your strength. You need strength to hate him." He shook his head; he no longer believed in anything, even hatred.

She offered to feed him, but he seemed scarcely to hear her. Her voice could not reach him in that empty abyss where he crouched, lost, inside his own mind. "I'd come out— to be with you," she offered, "after them white uglies has gone to sleep, but your masta has paid for me."

Tige's head tilted slightly. She nodded, her ebony eyes bleak. "He say to Mr. Teller, he say he need a bed wench. Say he don't rightly feel he back home yet until he's had hisself a bed wench. . . . Mr. Teller, he done rented me to your masta—for tonight."

Tige sagged back against the wall. How could he exist in a world which belonged to men who believed only in what they could take? He had believed in goodness and decency and justice, and now he believed in nothing. Slavery had not beaten the last hope from him; contact with a white man he had wanted to trust had done that, finally and totally.

At last, the girl took his untouched plate of food and retreated. It grew dark. Like the swells of incoming tide, the laughter and voices rose, rolling out from the barroom, washing over him, leaving him filthy and sullied, and Hammond's voice was the loudest.

Gradually, sometime in the hours around midnight, the laughter and the voices receded like an ebb tide. Ham's room was in the rear of the ordinary's second floor. Tige tried to close his ears, but he could hear Ham talking drunkenly to the bed wench for a long time. Then he could hear his grunting, the squeals of the bed ropes, followed by his belching and his vast expansive farting and, finally, silence. . . .

Tige managed to fall asleep at last and was wakened by Ham's boots kicking him just after dawn. The tavern owner and two Negro slaves transferred Tige from the stables to the carriage, securing the links of the shackles. "He go on, not eatin' like this," Ham said, "I soon be able to tote him by myself . . . in one hand."

The slaves grinned, rolling their eyes, and the tavern owner laughed as if he had not heard such rib-tickling native humor in a month of Sundays. Ham was a substantial, admired, jovial and genteel aristocrat. He was one of the gentry who knew how to comport himself affably among the unwashed so that they liked him and seldom resented him. Commercial and professional people toadied to him, bowed, smiled and laughed with him. Tige hated them all. But he hated no one more than he despised himself for having been duped by this self-assured master.

The first day east of the Mississippi was blustery and ended in a rainstorm. Ham drove into a huge plantation where he was warmly received and his captive accommodatingly chained in a cell for the night. The next morning the entire family came out onto the portico to wave goodbye and to entreat "Dear Mr. Hammond" to "come back soon, ya hear? Real soon . . . 'cause we going to be looking for you."

Midday brought them to a weathered tavern at a crossroads. Ham left Tige in the carriage while he ate a heavy meal of sliced fried ham, fried eggs and corn pone. He came out belching and massaging his stomach. They drove all afternoon through prosperous country dominated every five or ten miles by a plantation chateau, set like a showplace among laurels and oaks, remote from the trace. These magnificent mansions were fringed by slave quarters and trailed by decrepit

334

shacks of poor whites perched like alms seekers along the winding, verdant roadways.

"Beautiful country," Ham said. "Beginning to look like home. . . . Yes, sir, beginning to *feel* like home."

Tige was aware of Ham's increasing inner excitement as they entered familiar territory. They spent a night at an ordinary, though the owner admitted to Ham they were no more than ten miles from Benson, Alabama.

The next morning, Ham was too agitated and ebullient to eat breakfast. They set out just after dawn, dogs barking them away from the tavern on the Benson road. It was after noon when they rode through the haphazard grouping of stores, tavern, church and weathered dwellings in the town of Benson. But the place might have been a striking landmark, the way Ham reacted. He pointed out sights of interest, places erupting from his memory. "Only two miles now!" Ham said, exultant as they drove out of Benson. "I almost home—back home at Falconhurst!" His blue eyes filled with tears and he wept openly and unashamedly. "Gawd, boy . . . too bad you only a nigger, cain't noway feel the joyousness of comin' home like this."

Suddenly, Ham let out a yell and laid the whip across the rump of his laboring horse. Ham paid no attention to the flagging energies of the animal. He could see the black rooftop of Falconhurst through the trees.

"I home. Thanks to God, I home at last!" he cried. "Thanks be to God."

Ham's gaze touched at everything as they approached Falconhurst. Fields, trees, houses, creeks, cattle grazing in blue leas had him trembling in an orgy of nostalgia. He had fished this brook. His horse had thrown him in that meadow, broken his knee so it never set straight again. And yonder ahead, the lane leading up to the old Falconhurst manor house itself.

"Oh Gawd, boy," Ham wept. "I home! You know what that mean?"

Falconhurst was a far cry from the grand, tall-pillared colonial homes they had passed crossing Louisiana and Mississippi. There was nothing pretentious about the big, boxlike square structure which showed its additions like rough, ill-matched appendages. It was a back-country farmhouse and it had neither beauty nor dignity. But it was set far back from the trace, in magnificient landscaping kept trimmed, manicured and raked by slaves.

Laughing, his pleasure bubbling out of him, Ham touched his horse with his whip and the fagged animal broke into a brisk trot, perhaps sensing the end of his own hard journey. They rolled up the long, tree-bordered drive which led to the manor house. Ham's excitement preceded him. News of his arrival spread across the broad acres, swelling, first a cry, a yell and then the growing rush of joyous welcome from slaves, many of whom had never even seen the long-absent young master.

"We here! We home!" Hammond yelled as the carriage rolled between swarming children and slaves who came running from every direction.

Hammond's shouting rattled the great house itself. The front door was thrown open. A stout Negro amazon of a woman in red bandana and calico dress bounded out to meet them. Her loose slippers slapped rhythmically against her pink heels. Ham raged with pleasure. "Lucretia Borgia! Lucretia Borgia! I home! I home!"

"Oh, thanks be to God!" Lucretia Borgia wept. She ran to meet them—as a girl twenty years younger might run—a hamlike hand pressed over her copious, bouncing bosom. "Thanks be to God, after all these lonely years! My own Masta Ham done come back home to Falconhurst!"

XXXII

Falconhurst spun upward in a frenetic orgy of rapture at Hammond's return. Delirious excitement affected the least slave and turned the entire plantation into that kind of mindless celebration which must have marked heroic reentrances in ancient walled cities, where the release afforded through such festivals warded off insanity by unleashing insanity. The madness and delirium boiled and seethed out of control to a pitch of violent, temporary derangement. Slaves grabbed each other in their outspread arms, weeping and laughing hysterically in the same breath. They danced each other about. They ran past the manor house trying to catch even a glimpse of the restored liege. They sang, yelled, sobbed and put their heads back in a cacophony of unbridled delight. If some one of the slaves came into briefest contact, or were actually touched by the master's hand, or spoken to by him, that transported soul was hurtled into spasms of distracted undulations, quaking, wriggling and squalling.

No plans were formulated, no orders issued, no suggestions exchanged, and yet the celebration became a feast and the feast a revelry. No one authorized it, but Mem broke out gallon jugs of pure corn whiskey, some of it almost as old as he. The jugs were set up on temporary tables in the yard. Slaves came running with cups, gourds, bottles, any unblemished vessel. Children were permitted to pour cups of liquor for themselves. It wasn't a matter of permission; no one said they could or could not. In this frenzy of self-indulgence and permissiveness, no one noticed. Soon the tots were staggering, vomiting or crumpling up to sleep in the flower beds. No one noticed this, either.

No word was sent out from that place, and yet the news flared and flew across the countryside. Hammond Maxwell was home again at Falconhurst!

People came from miles around in every direction, classes mingling together happily who ordinarily did not exchange civilities. Poor whites from subsistence farms, most of whom had never passed the time of day with Hammond, joined the plantation gentry in a bright parade of carriages, carts and wagons on the driveway. Even the townspeople came out from Benson. Pearl Remick closed the local tavern for the day. He brought along a gallon of whiskey to add a fillip of pleasure to the festivities. But when he saw the jugs of Falconhurst liquor, he hid his own away under sacks and coats in the bed of his wagon.

Lucretia Borgia moved, heart and hub of all this frenzied activity. "More people a-comin'," she sang out, perspiring and watching the procession of well-wishers entering along the tree-shaded lane.

Mem had been sampling the whiskey since an hour before he decided to set it out for general consumption. He no longer cared who came or went. He sat rigidly on a cane-bottom straight chair and grinned vacuously at Lucretia Borgia whenever she passed within his orbit, but she was too busy and preoccupied to upbraid or punish him. He belched contentedly.

"All these good folks! Come to welcome Masta Hammond back home!" Lucretia Borgia wept. "It a plain outpouring of God's goodness."

Lucretia Borgia felt that her heart would burst with the joy and delight she felt in this moment. She wished she could gather it and hold it within her full

338

bosom forever. She was almost hysterical in her passionate agitation, her emotions gone out of control. She laughed and wept in the same moment. She ordered more and more food prepared, new tables set up, new silverwear broken out, new chairs produced from somewhere, as she propelled her bulk through every phase of activity.

"Heavenly father," she gasped aloud every few moments. "I just cain't believe this outpourin' of love. My own sweet Masta Hammond, come home to us all. Praise God, he come home to us."

The din and uproar swelled as people shouted ever louder to make themselves heard above the tonitruous clamor. Lucretia Borgia could not remember so much excitement and laughter and pleasure at the old house in her lifetime.

"A purely joyous occasion," she'd announce to anyone she happened to pass, black or white. "It a happy day. A happy day that has brung my own Masta Hammond back home to my heart!"

The black people grinned and mumbled, "Yes'm, Miz Lucretia Borgia, ma'am."

The white people—even the rigidly correct Gassaway family—were most tolerant and lenient toward Lucretia Borgia during this joyous event. She was black and, since she was, should not speak directly to white people without being spoken to—she was forward. But one saw her heart filled to bursting with happiness. She could, under these circumstances, be forgiven, her trespasses excused. . . .

Hammond awoke early the next morning. He overate, declaring he had tasted no food to equal Lucretia Borgia's cooking since he rode away from Falconhurst, eight years ago. Lucretia Borgia dissolved into tears, sobbing, at his praise. She stood silently behind his chair while he stoked away scrambled eggs, ham and popovers so light he swore he had to eat two to taste one. Lucretia Borgia's creamy chocolate face beamed. Her own sweet Masta Hammond was home! She jerked her head, ordering his coffee cup refilled before it was emptied, his plates removed, new ones set in their place—all accomplished under her command with a fluidity that could only amaze and delight him. "You gone sp'ile me shore, Lucretia Borgia," he said.

"Wants to," she wept. She dabbed at her eyes with her fresh apron. "Gwine spend the rest of my days sp'ilin' you, Masta Hammond."

He smiled and nodded. Many things had changed in the eight years of his exile. The house, the furnishings, the hand-woven carpets, the very family portraits, forbidding in heavy frames on the dark walls, all of it looked a little shabbier. The Seth Thomas clock—well recalled from his childhood!—ticked louder than he remembered, wheezing its age as well as the hour. But some things had not changed at all. Lucretia Borgia was the same. She was like a solid rock for him always to depend on. He uttered a silent prayer that he owned such a good and faithful Negress. Unless you knew she was a nigger—as he did!—you'd almost think she was human, finer than many humans. Well, it was just a quirk of nature, and the white blood in her veins that made her different, set her apart. It was easy to forget, though, that she was just a beast of burden like the rest of the blacks—but more like a house pet than a work animal, that was for sure!

His father's chair remained unaltered at the head of the table, but it was empty. This emptiness reminded him forcefully of the sadness which had set him on his return trek to Falconhurst. How he missed his father! He remembered, his throat tight, how each morning when he came down to breakfast in the old days, he had kissed his father. And he recalled with bittersweet agony the way his father had always clung to him for that extra moment, as though he loved him deeply and dreaded to part with him! He glanced at his father's old chair. Its worn cushion remained in place as if awaiting his arrival, waiting to make it more comfortable for the ailing man's painful joints. How he wished he could see his father one more time! How much he had to say to him that he had never said, that could never be said now! How he would want to reassure his father that he had indeed loved him devotedly, even though he had abandoned him in his advanced age and illness. It was so important that his father understand this, and forgive him. But now he could never say those words to his father.

Chilled, he walked up to the family cemetery alone in the early-morning sunlight. The whole plantation glowed with a saffron cast at this hour. He found the plot kept immaculate by slave labor. He sighed, pleased that Lucretia Borgia—black, and less than human as she was—had thought to keep the family burial ground cleaned, trimmed and repaired. Sometimes, he'd almost swear that Lucretia Borgia *was* different from other niggers—set apart from them, she was.

The sun glittered and gleamed upon the marble of his mother's headstone. The reflection of the sun lanced into his bleached blue eyes, blinding him for a moment and prickling tears from his lids.

Ham sighed and let the tears well in his eyes unashamedly. Like any other mature, red-blooded male, he had only contempt for grown men who gave in to their emotions and cried. "Weak sisters," he called such males. But, alone like this and deeply affected as he was with poignant memories, he felt he could excuse his own tears.

His heart swelled. Lucretia Borgia had not failed him. She had ordered a headstone for his father—an exact replica of the marble tablet marking his mother's resting place. Ham felt a rush of gratitude and deep satisfaction. The world was as it should be, after all. Yellowhammers and blue jays and mockingbirds chattered in pines and elms. Sounds of the farm coming to life swelled up from the barns, quarters and fields. This plantation was an oasis of beauty and quiet and dignity. These matching headstones gave the family plot the precise touch of somber elegance it needed. A man need not feel shamed, no matter who walked into his private burial grounds. He had provided the best for his parents in the very finest expression of that filiation which had always marked his devotion to his father.

He knelt beside the grave, extending his stiff leg awkwardly behind him. He pulled out a few slivers of wire grass and bunched little bold patches of periwinkles and four-o'clocks. Kneeling there, he tried to tell his father how sorry he was that he had not been present at the time of his passing. But his words sounded empty and inadequate. Still, he could not feel too grieved, or defeated. These marble headstones matched. The Maxwells were located and defined for the ages.

He stood up awkwardly, feeling relieved, released and expiated. He had provided the purest marble, the richest visible proof of his devotion. He had done all he could, and for this he could be proud, and it seemed to him that if only he could feel his father's gnarled hands on his, hear his father's voice, see the pride and love in those pain-flooded blue eyes, it would be vouchsafed to him that his father *did* understand. . . .

There were few opportunities for extended conversation between Ham, trying to make inspection tours, trying to work himself back into plantation routine, and Lucretia Borgia, attempting to direct the daily activities of the huge stud farm. She told Hammond often how pleased and relieved she was to have him back, how difficult and long the years had been without him.

She told him, tearfully, how his father had died. She made no effort to conceal her hatred for Cousin Charlie Woodford, whom she blamed for Ham's dear father's tragic and untimely death.

Masta Hammond held his daughter on his lap. Sophie had grown weedlike, he kept telling her. She was getting to be quite a young lady. But he could not choke out the lie that she was lovely. She was not. She was stringy, leggy like a new colt, and more crosseyed even than her uncle Charlie Woodford had ever been. He caressed Sophie and attended in horror and grief Lucretia Borgia's account of his father's violent passing.

Despite himself, Ham was offended that Lucretia Borgia should speak with such ill-concealed contempt and low regard for Mr. Charlie. After all, Charlie was white, and one didn't suffer accusations from blacks against other whites. It just wasn't fitting. Especially since Charlie was a distant blood relative and his own brother-in-law. Still, Charlie had, according to Lucretia Borgia—if a black's accusations could be credited!—hounded his ailing father, tried to steal his gold, and had caused Warren Maxwell's demise as surely as though Charlie had choked the life out of the helpless old man with his own dirty hands.

Hammond decided for the moment to pass up the reprimand he felt Lucretia ordinarily should have received.

"Don't know what on this earth we'd of done without that Brass Door."

"Brass door?" Ham said.

"Brass Door—he a mustee. His real name turned out to be Herman Hengst. He taken over Falconhurst after Mr. Charlie kilt your pa. Brass Door, he pretend he was white—purentee white—an' he in New Orleans now with a coffle of blacks, selling them off at auction for you. Don't know what we'd of done without that man."

Ham brushed this debt aside brusquely. Evidently, Herman Hengst, with Lucretia Borgia's assistance, had run this farm profitably. But he could not accept or condone the fact that a mustee had dared to pass himself off as a white man—even in the dire emergency of threat of losing Falconhurst without a white man to manage and oversee it. As faithful and efficient as Lucretia Borgia was, she was black. She would never have been permitted to remain as head of the estate. He could understand this; it was a clear part of the code he lived by. Only a white could control such a huge operation as this.

He scowled. Though Herman Hengst had saved Falconhurst for him, he could not approve such actions, such illegality and fraud. Still, he would not think about it now. He would deal with the upstart mustee when he saw him. Perhaps after he settled this business with Tiger, he'd go immediately to New Orleans and confront this Herman Hengst once and for all.

While his mind whirled with these thoughts, Lucretia Borgia continued to provide Hammond with a full report on farm operations. He admitted grudgingly that Falconhurst had never shown such a profit, even in the best years when he himself had been driving great herds of fancies to market in New Orleans and Natchez. Well, he wouldn't think about that now, either.

Lucretia Borgia answered all his questions quickly, expertly, completely. More often than she even realized she boasted on the new "Falconhurst Fancy" named Jingo Jim. She especially stressed and made certain that Hammond was unable to brush aside the fact that *she* had purchased Jingo Jim when he was only a muddy, sickly thirteen-year-old in an itinerant slave peddler's sorry coffle.

"This Jingo Jim, he more fancy and prime-quality than any buck we ever had here at Falconhurst—even Mede. Mede was a Mandingo. They pretty special. But Mede was quiet. This Jingo Jim, he even walk like a king."

"He a biggety nigger, that's what he is," Mem said. He had remained in the background, discreet and silent as long he could stand it. He could not restrain

344

himself any longer. "He no better than I was at twenty."

Lucretia Borgia's laugh was scathing. "Maybe not. But Jingo Jim, he jus' seventeen. By the time *he* twenty, he look like a god aside *you*."

Hammond waved aside all this bickering impatiently. He warned Mem to keep his nose out of conversations and affairs of others, and to speak not at all unless he was asked a direct question. "Maybe things been slack whilst I was away. But I home now, and don't you forget it. Maybe you need a tetch of the rawhide?" Hammond glared at the servant. "Needs to be reminded who the masta round here?"

"No, suh! Oh, no, suh! I don't need nary no whippin'. Mem your nigger, Masta. Mem a good nigger."

"Mem's a *no-good* nigger, tha's what he is. A triflin', whiskey-stealin' lazybones," Lucretia Borgia said. "You plumb needs the whip, all right."

"Now wait a minue," Ham said. "I appreciate all you done, Lucretia Borgia, whilst I was away, but I back home now. I can run things without you tellin' me what to do. I master here. I makes the decisions."

Lucretia Borgia smiled broadly, nodding. "An' I thank the good God that you back home, too. You has come home. I ain't no pridey nigger don't know *my* place. I pray every night fo' eight *long* years for my sweet Masta Hammond to come home, an' now you heah, you sho' am welcome to do all the bossin'."

Ham laughed and nodded. "Well, you just remember that Lucretia Borgia. I indebted to you. You a good nigger. But you still a nigger. Wouldn't want to have to put a touch of the lash to yo' fat buttocks, either. . . ."

Ham sank down on the old butt-sprung rocker in which his father had whiled away uncounted hours on this shadowed gallery. He stared up at the handsome young buck.

Jingo Jim was bared to the waist, his Osnaburg pants chopped off raggedly at the knees. He smiled uncertainly, nervous in the presence of his master, but prideful in the physical perfection of the figure he presented. He was without fault, unblemished. His master couldn't help but be proud of him, approving.

Ham smiled as the young buck shifted from one foot to the other. The continuing celebration ebbed and flowed around them. "You Jingo, eh, boy?"

"Yas suh."

"Lucretia Borgia, she been braggin' 'bout you. Say you somethin' special."

"Yas, suh. I guess I is."

"Now, just because you built well, and strong, Jingo, ain't no excuse to be biggety or uppety."

"No, suh."

"Jingo, eh? Kneel down here, boy. 'Tween my knees."

Troubled, Jingo knelt on the gallery plankings. Casually, Ham kneaded Jingo's ears and shoulder muscles, and ran practiced fingers over his cheeks, the nape of his neck and along his jaw line. Jingo felt good, being caressed like this, and he quivered slightly, gooseflesh rising on his arms.

Ham pulled back the lids of Jingo's eyes, parted his nostrils and stared upward into them. Then he pushed his fingers into the boy's mouth, massaging his gums, pressing on his molars. Jingo's mouth filled with saliva and he swallowed guiltily.

"Seem sound, seem pretty strong," Ham said. "I reckon Lucretia Borgia she ain't exaggerate too much."

Ham thumped Jingo's chest as he might check a watermelon for ripeness. He pinched his paps, stroked his pectorals and ran his fingers under Jingo's armpits and along his rib cage, over the small of his back. He pinched at the satisfactorily healing welts across his belly but said nothing about them. He told Jingo to stand up, but Jingo hesitated. He'd suffered a painful erection, which would have to be apparent to his master,

346

and he was fearful of the white man's reaction. He had never been caressed in just that way before, and he had responded whether he wished it or not.

Ham's voice lashed him. "What's the matter, boy? An' I tell you to stand up, you stand up. An' fast."

His face burning and anguished eyes averted, Jingo leaped to his feet.

Ham laughed. "Well, look how you hung! I see you built well down here, too. Like a young bull. And plenty of sap, I bet, too."

"Yas, suh. Plenty." Jingo exhaled, pleased he was guiltless of crime in his master's view. He shivered when Ham ran his hands up inside his pants legs, hefted his gonads and tested and checked his thigh muscles. Finally, Ham ran his hands along Jingo's calves and ankles, checked his arches and bent each of his toes back and forth. Jingo had to bite his lips to keep from crying out.

Ham smiled, nodding. "Yes, suh. Lucretia Borgia didn't no way exaggerate. You a purentee fancy prime animal, all right. A prime animal. Reckon you bring five, six thousand at the right sale in New Orleans."

Jingo's heart sank at the prospect of being sold away from this home. "You ain't sellin' Jingo, Masta! Please!"

Ham straightened, his face going flat and cold. "Listen to me, boy. You don't nevah talk to no white man, less'n he talk first to you. You don't ast no questions. Ain't none of yo' goddam business what I plans to do with you."

"No, suh." Jingo shook his head, eyes brimmed with tears. He drew a deep breath and tilted his head to conceal those tears.

Ham remained unaware of the boy's emotions. He said, "I proud of you, Jingo. You new to me. But I prideful."

"Yas suh."

"Look like a real good boy. Nice and black. I partial

to blacks. None of this white-skin nigger. I like a nigger good and black."

"Yas, suh. I a good boy, Masta. Strong . . . I makes a *fine* stud fo' you, Masta. Covers as many wenches a day as you tells me . . . yas, suh. . . . Good strong juice, too. Spurts out—hits the ceilin' sometime. . . . Them wenches purely loves havin' Jingo Jim pesterin' 'em. No trouble with them black wenches when they know Jingo Jim is goin' to pleasure 'em. Yas, suh."

Ham seemed not to have heard him. "Reckon you don't recollect a white-skinned nigger name of Tiger? A mustee boy raised up heah."

"Naw, suh . . . don't recalls the gen'mun."

"Ain't no gen'mun, Jingo. He a nigger—even if'n his skin be white, he a nigger, jus' like you."

"I declare."

"He used to belong here. Onc't. When he was naught but a little sucker."

"Yas, suh. That mus' be before I gits here, I reckon."

Ham shrugged. "Well, Tiger's home ag'in now. He a bad nigger. . . . Sometime a nigger goes bad, an' ain't no way you can save him. Tiger's like that. A bad nigger. But you a big boy, Jingo. A big, strong boy. You a lot bigger'n Tiger. Stronger. Blacker. You a better nigger. . . . Tiger likely gonna try to run away. It's your job to see he stay put. Tiger git away— I gonna take it out'n your hide. You understand me?"

"Yas suh."

"Wants you should put Tige in the slavejail. By hisself. Put a spancel on he leg and lock him in. You do what I tells you, Jingo, you and me gone git along fine as hen's teeth."

Lucretia Borgia's liquid black eyes blinked against the dimness of the slave cell after the bright sunlight. She closed the door behind her. "Brung you some grub, Tiger."

Tige did not move, nor did he appear to see her, though he gazed up into her face. His eyes were empty, distracted, as if they looked only inwardly at the confusion swarming in his mind. He seemed to have succumbed to intolerable outer oppressions, to have withdrawn and retreated within himself.

Lucretia Borgia knelt beside him, despite her bulk graceful and fluid of movement. He stirred slightly, his gray eyes brimming with tears. He remembered her. The years had stoked poundage to her girth, had expanded her breasts even to fuller proportions, but seemed not to have etched a single new line in the light, creamy chocolate of her gentle face.

Tige shivered. He desperately longed to reach out to her, to press his face upon that copious bosom, to weep out the agony and desolation that spread like cancer inside him. He did not move.

"You, Tiger? I remembers you well," she said. Her tone was gentle, her voice compassionate. "You little Tiger what used to run around this place as naked as a jaybird? Always underfoot? Followin' folks around—especially Masta Ham? Grinning and watchin' everything? I swear—in a hundred years I never forget you. You a plumb cute chile, you was."

"I'm Tiger," he said.

She touched his face lightly with the backs of her fingers. "O' course you are. And how pretty you growed! Spit and image of Masta Ham, you are."

He shuddered. "Don't say that."

She smiled, her voice soft. "Won't say nuthin' you don't crave to hear. . . . Jus' want you to eat some of my good grub. Bet you ain't had no food good as this since you left this here place."

"You were always a good cook, Lucretia Borgia, ma'am."

"Then eat some. Just a little taste. Just fo' me."

"I couldn't. . . . I'd throw it up."

"Try." She laughed and waved her stout arm. "You

349

got to throw up, you go 'head and puke all over. . . . We got niggers to clean it up. We got niggers growin' like weeds at Falconhurst. I send 'em in—an' they clean up, every time you vomits."

Tige smiled. "You ain't changed."

"I reckon folks don't really change, Tiger."

"No . . . I reckon not. They born evil, they stay evil."

Lucretia Borgia's ebony eyes clouded over. "Now don't talk like that. Hate—hit like a terrible p'isen, it gits inside you. It a sickness. It start out aimed outside at who you hate, what you hate. But no matter how deep you hate, the ones you hate ain't hurt none by it. But you is. Hate turns you to gall and wormwood and vinegar inside. It makes those pretty eyes narrow up and go mean. Puts deep lines around that sweet mouth. But worst of all is what it do to your stomach and your liver—all yo' insides—they shrivel up and go sour. Even yo' heart gits like a rotted apple, all withered an' brown an' sp'iled."

"Can't help hatin', Lucretia Borgia."

"Yes you can. Nobody can make you hate, but you. Yo' own self. You sho' don't have to love ever'body. I sho' don't. They's blacks and they's whites I purely despise—'cause of what they is. Or what they ain't, despite what they could be, would they let theyselves. But I don't pay them critters no nevah mind. They ain't goin' to p'isen me and make me sick inside, and sour, and turned to vinegar. No, suh, not Miz Lucretia Borgia."

"I wish I were like you, Lucretia Borgia. Not hate—no matter what he does to you."

She lifted her head, held her breath. "You mean my Masta Ham?"

"Who else you know was born snake-low and dug hisself deeper?"

"Oh, no, honeypot . . . not Masta Ham. He a good, kindly man inside."

"An inhuman bastard."

"Oh, no . . . oh lawsy now."

"He has no feelings for anyone. . . . Oh, he thinks he has. He's so rotten and empty inside, he truly believes the rest of the world is as cruel and vicious as he is."

Lucretia Borgia shook her head. "You think he evil 'cause he raises and sells niggers?"

"No. He raises and sells niggers because he's evil."

She laughed. "You jus' tryin' to mix me up, honeypot."

"No." He clutched her hand. "I'm trying to make you see. If he ever had any human feelings, he's lost them bein' so inhuman to us—to you."

"Not never to me. Not my Masta Ham. He sweet and kind to me."

"How can you be so blind? He treats you like an animal. Worse."

She shook her head, distraught and miserable. "Don't say these terrible things."

"Has he ever been decent to you—unless it profited him? Has he ever once thanked you for doin' things for him better than he could do himself?"

Deeply troubled, she shook her head again. "I don't know what you sayin'. I swear I don't. I love my Masta Ham. He been good to me."

"He sold your twins."

She nodded, chewing at her full underlip. His voice pursued her, relentless. "He sold you, Lucretia Borgia."

"Yes. He did sell me off to N' Orleans one time. But he only done what he think was right."

"Lucretia Borgia, how many crimes been committed by people who tell themselves they doin' what's right—for them—and never mind nobody else?"

"I don't know. I don't know."

"He'd kill you if he decided it was right—for him. Others have rights, but not in his mind. He thinks only of his rights. He don't care about you—about nobody."

"Oh, he do! He do! I know he do! When I runned away from N' Orleans an' come back here, he never sent me off ag'in. He could of, but he didn't. Never said nuthin'. He saw he was wrong to sell me away from Falconhurst. An' he ain't nevah done it ag'in. An' he nevah will."

"And he's never whipped you?"

"Only when it seemed right to him!" she cried.

"It seems right to him when you don't lick his feet an' whine around his legs like a lapdog. It seems right to whup you when you try to hold your head up—to live—like he lives."

She jumped up, trembling, confused, distracted. "He—think true in his heart we black an' we ain't got that right—"

"Do you think we got no right to live like—"

"I don't know. Eat yo' food. . . . Maybe we *ain't* got the right. I don't know. He the masta. He our masta. He know what best for us."

"Don't lie to yourself like this."

Her heavy shoulders sagged round. "Why not? Why ain't it better to lie a little to yo'self sometime when it makes livin' a mite easier—for all of us?"

III

A FAREWELL TO FALCONHURST

XXXIII

The joyous celebration marking the return of the master of Falconhurst died away and a pall-like tension replaced the exuberance. Most of the slaves saw Tige shackled in the slave-jail cell. Those who did not see him heard the word. He was a bad nigger, a dangerous nigger. All other plantation black malfeasants had been removed from the jail; none was permitted to come into contact with the bad nigger, for their own protection. Tige was to be hung. They did not know why he was to hang, nobody bothered to tell them that, but they did know his hanging was to serve as an example to them, one which they were never to forget, and something they had never even heard of in the long eight years their master had been absent. Things were changing at Falconhurst. The old ways passed. Trouble seemed to be rising from the very earth itself.

Ham yelled, summoning Lucretia Borgia out to the front gallery, where he sat—without really relaxing—on the deacon's bench. His stiff leg was stretched straight and awkward before him. "Want you should pick out three, four of the best boys we got. Nice-lookin', perlite. Boys that know their way home. We gives them road passes."

Lucretia Borgia's heart sank. Sending three or four boys abroad with road passes meant an event of great significance. It was unlikely to be anything pleasant;

the coming-home party was over. There was only one dreaded event which would be published across the countryside.

"Yas, suh. I got some good boys." The way Hammond jerked his head up, scowling, reminded Lucretia Borgia and she added, smiling, *"We* got us some good boys."

"That's better." Hammond nodded. "I have written to the people at Hiddenbrook Plantation. Tole 'em I cotched Tiger. Tole 'em I brought him here. Tole 'em what I planned to do with him. Tole 'em they invited to come and witness the hanging. But I got no idea how long it take a letter to git from Benson down into Louisiana where-at Hiddenbrook Plantation is. Don't know when they might git here, even after they has my letter. I'se decided to send word around to all the plantations. The Gassaways. Redfields. Hamptons. Duvals. Far as twenty, twenty-five miles away. You tell them boys they gits too far to make it home before nightfall, they should spend the night at that plantation. To say to the white folks I say it all right. I want the word to go all around the area. I decided to go ahead and hang Tiger—"

"Oh, no, Masta . . ."

Hammond flinched but continued as though Lucretia Borgia had not dared to interrupt. "I want it behind me. I want it over. We gone hang Tiger. Here at Falconhurst. Plantation folks invited to bring they families, an' as many of they slaves as they care to have witness the hanging. It a lesson niggers don't fast forget."

Lucretia did not speak. Her eyes brimmed with tears and she pressed her clenched fist over her heart. She merely nodded, agreeing to choose and prepare the young black messengers. She let her master know by the tone and the dejected stance of her body how unalterably opposed she was to his edict.

Ham seethed inwardly at Lucretia Borgia's wordless

defiance. Damn her! There was no doubting it, you couldn't be nice to a nigger—they took advantage of it every time! He tried to be kindly toward Lucretia Borgia, but rather than showing her appreciation, she argued and protested and defied him, even when she didn't open her rebellious mouth. She'd gone too long without a dose of the whip. He said, "Goddammit, Lucretia Borgia. I won't tolerate your insolence."

She turned at the door, her face a portrait of sweet innocence. "I goin', Masta. Gwine do just 'xactly what my sweet Masta say."

"Goddam you. You don't have to talk back to be insolent. I won't have it. This is over, I take care of you." He would have said more, but at that instant a carriage that looked vaguely familiar to him turned into the driveway from the main trace.

Both Ham and Lucretia Borgia stood and watched the carriage approach under the tree-lined drive. For the moment their conflict was set aside. Lucretia Borgia let the screen door close softly and she crossed the gallery, squinting. "Don't stand starin' an' gawkin' like a jackass," Ham said. But he stood beside her, shading his eyes to get a better view.

He saw a man handling the horse, a young woman beside him. A second horse was secured to the tailpost of the carriage and trotted smartly behind. Ham felt his pulse quicken. He recognized the driver as Paley, the foreman of his ranch. And—yes, in God's name, that was Nell Murdoch riding beside him. Involuntarily, his fists clenched at his sides, his jaw set so rigidly that a small muscle worked in it. He knew why they were here, and he was damned if he would endure one moment's opposition.

Hammond limped out into the driveway, and Lucretia Borgia moved as his shadow. She could sense her master's tension, though she didn't understand it. Whoever these guests were, they were less than welcomed; they did not rouse in the master of Falconhurst that vaunted southern hospitality. Far from it. He looked ready to strike out in suppressed fury.

The carriage rolled up close to them. Nell did not try to smile. Paley leaped from the carriage and ran around it. He helped the girl alight before he turned and faced Ham. He did not bother to smile. He said, "Howdy, Boss. So this is Falconhurst I heard so much about?"

"Yes," Ham said. "What are you doing here—in my carriage?"

Paley still did not smile. "Whether it's *your* carriage or not is a point you'll have to take up with Miz Lydia. She believes she got a legal paper giving her control of the ranch and all its property—"

"Not to be givin' away," Ham said, gesturing sharply.

"Like I say. You have to take that up with Miz Lydia. I don't work for her no more. I don't work for you no more."

"Then why you here?" Ham cleared his throat. "Did Miz Lydia send some word to me?"

For the first time, Paley almost smiled. He shrugged and said, "She didn't send no word I could repeat in front of ladies, Mr. Ham."

Ham's face burned red. He glanced at Nell. "I know why you come—to try to stop the due process of the law. Well, it won't do you no good. You can turn Paley against me so his hatred is plain in his face, but you ain't changin' me."

Nell's voice was gentle. "I came because I had to. I thought even you would understand that, Mr. Ham."

His chin tilted slightly. "Well, I don't. You figure something you can say that will stop me from hanging that mustee, you dead wrong, Missy."

"He's your son."

Ham's face twisted. He limped back and forth, disturbed and agitated, in the sun. He stopped and stared, squinting into Nell's pallid face. "Now, you want to

358

spare yourself, you can ride on out of here with Mr. Paley in *my* carriage. Go where you like. But nuthin' you can say is goin' to stop me from teachin' these black bastards a lesson they ain't soon forgettin'."

Nell's voice was low, barely audible. "I'm staying. As long as Tige is alive here, I'm staying." Her voice broke.

Ham shrugged, dismissing her. He glanced at Paley. "Well, Paley, you care to stay a few days? Goin' to have some excitement. You're welcome to stay as my guest."

Paley shook his head. "I wouldn't feel right, Mr. Ham, stayin' here, puttin' my feet under your table, the way I feel about things."

"About things?" Ham's voice attacked him. "What's wrong with you? You from Georgia, ain't you?"

"Yes."

"You know a nigger's got to be shown his place—"

"I don't know, Boss. I reckon maybe I been away too long. It don't seem to matter a damn to me any more. Instead of seein' a lot of blacks screamin' like banshees and wavin' knives, I see one poor kid, scared and running—and maybe blameless. I see each black as one black. Worth whatever *he's* worth. See no more danger in one black than in one white."

"Hell with talk like that. Reckon I be pleased to have you off my place."

For the first time, Paley smiled. "Reckoned you would, Boss." He extended his hand. "We worked good together—for a long time. An' I thank you for all that."

Ham hesitated a long beat, then he shook hands. He did not smile. "You done let this here little white baggage turn your head from clear thinkin', Paley. That's what you done."

"That's plumb likely, Boss. She a pretty little thing—and I ain't forgot the way you and me worked to save her. Makes me feel a little responsible."

"Makes you soft in your head. That's what it makes you." Ham swung his arm, his face cold. "Go on, get out of here."

"Just a minute, Mr. Ham." Paley's voice was cold and level, clipped. "I quit takin' orders from you some time ago. Whether I look at things the way you do—"

"The way any *white* man does—"

"—or not, don't have to make us go at each other's throat. I'm leavin'. Got to saddle my horse, and I'll ride right out. But we never had no real words before, no sense startin' now."

"I nevah knowed what you was inside before."

"Well, I can't say that about you. I knowed." Paley shrugged. He turned to Nell, put out his hand. But the girl ran, sobbing into his arms. He held her gently, awkwardly, patting her back. "It's all right, Missy. Don't you cry . . . They is a God . . . an' He'll help you, Missy . . . when none of us can't. I believe that —and I don't believe much."

"What will I do—without you—without Tige—without you?"

He drew a deep breath, held it. "I ain't got no answers, Missy. . . . But I figure to stay on at the tavern in Benson a few days. In case you need me, I be there. . . . Hell, I ain't in no hurry to git nowhere."

Lucretia Borgia sent the carriage and horse to the barn to be tended. She yelled for Mem, who carried Nell's small steamer trunk up the stairs to the bedroom in which Miz Blanche had died. She prepared the room, had the bed linens changed, though they were crisp and whitely fresh.

Nell told her about her meeting with Tige, the way they had fallen in love, their new baby. The baby looked much like Tige, she said. She missed it fearfully, but had left it out in the Texies because the trip would have been too rough for the infant. "You done right, honey," Lucretia Borgia whispered. "You done right.

360

. . . You come here . . . that was right, too. . . . 'Cause we love Tiger here—like you do. It break our heart what's gwine happen."

Lucretia Borgia walked slowly along the upper corridor and down the stairs. She felt ill. It was no exaggeration that her heart was broken. The pain in her chest must be heartbreak, no matter what learned medics might say.

She saw Masta Hammond striding back and forth in the dim living room, but she did not go near him. When his voice rocked the house, yelling for her, she sent Mem in to him. She prepared the hot toddy Masta Hammond ordered, but again she had Mem deliver it.

Walking zombielike, she went down to the quarters and chose four of the smartest boys to send as messengers. There was no sense in delaying this aspect of the execution. It would only infuriate Master Hammond and cement his determination to go through with the hanging.

She shivered. There could be no hanging, and yet how could she stop it? She spoke for a moment with Jingo Jim outside the jail cell, then went inside to Tige with the news that Nell had arrived and would visit him as soon as she could.

Tige was desolated rather than heartened or elated by the news. His eyes filled with tears, and he gripped Lucretia Borgia's arms fiercely. "Get her away, Lucretia Borgia. Please. Don't let her stay here. Don't let her see—what happens to me."

"She love you so, Tiger. She can't no way leave."

"She must not stay and see me hang."

"Nuthin' we can do, Tiger. Nuthin'. I done wracked my brains until I sick to my stomach. . . . Jus' try to find what happiness you can with Miss Nell. Long as you can. Let her know how pleased you is your baby is healthy and well. . . . Let her know how much you love her."

"Oh God, Lucretia Borgia . . . I can't think about

anything—but that man, the way I hate him. . . .
Listen to me, get me a knife. Just slip it to me. Then
when they take me out of here—to hang me—I'll use
it just once—on that bastard—my father."

"Oh no, chile. Don't git such thoughts in your head.
That ain't no way to solve it—"

"It'll stop him. He'll stop acting like God—"

"Lawsy, seems like you two jus' alike. He talkin'
about you got to hang—got to be an example to other
blacks. . . . An' you, you got to stop him—even if it
don't save you—so he stop actin' like God."

"I got to stop him, Lucretia Borgia. Help me. Help
me."

She drew him against her. "Is that what you want?
Just to stop Masta Hammond? Or is you just sick
inside so you can't think straight no more? So I gits you
a knife—a knife fo' you to use on my own Masta
Ham—and you kills him. Is you free? Is you free to go
with your Miss Nell and your new baby?"

"Can't ever have that."

"Can't if you kills Masta Ham, neither. They jus'
kills you—tears you apart—like wild animals they'd
tear you to pieces."

"I don't care," he sobbed. "I swear I don't, Lucretia Borgia. I done made my peace with God. . . . I
can't have Nell . . . I can't live free . . . I can't
know my baby . . . but by God, if I got to die, let
it *mean* something, Lucretia Borgia. . . . At least,
let me take that bastard with me. Let me stop him."

She held him for a long time until he quieted. But
inside she was in a more fearful turmoil than ever. She
got up and left the cell. She told Jingo Jim that when
a white lady came down to the cell, he was to clean it
out, and to put a chair in there for her to sit on. Jingo
tried to mess with her, but Lucretia Borgia shoved him
away, unable to respond, unable to think anything except that horror was coming back to Falconhurst.

She walked slowly across the yard in the sunlight.

She remembered in agony the hell into which all of Falconhurst had been plunged eight years ago. Ham's wife's baby murdered. Mede's child. Miz Blanche murdered. And Ham had boiled Mede in a vat and poured his flesh and bones and tallow over Miz Blanche's grave. And Ham had gone away across the Texies.

She went into the kitchen through the rear door. Her workers had the place almost spotless, but she found fault. They repeated their efforts, using more elbow grease, and when she was still not satisfied, she worked herself, thankful for anything that kept her hands occupied.

Somehow the day wore itself away, each second stretched out to its full tedium. Over and over in Lucretia Borgia's mind the thought spun, she had to stop Masta Ham—not only for the sake of Tige and his Nell, but for Masta Ham's own salvation. A man could not go on creating hell on earth without driving himself beyond sanity.

At dinner Nell and Ham sat across the table from each other, but they ate almost nothing, and spoke infrequently. Despite their tensions and silences, Lucretia Borgia sensed a mutual respect between them, even a feeling of love. Nell did not hate Masta Ham—she hated only the heinous thing he felt compelled to do.

After the silent meal was ended, the untouched plates returned to the kitchen, Nell excused herself. She said she was exhausted after the long trip, she would go up early to bed. Hammond nodded, seeming barely aware of what she said.

Lucretia Borgia knew that Nell went up the front stairway and down the rear stairwell, out the kitchen and across the yard to the cell where Tige was shackled. She supposed that Ham knew, too, though he said nothing. He had five hot toddies—unusual for him in a single evening—and went up to bed.

Lucretia Borgia remained in the kitchen long after the last scullery maid had slipped away to bed. Lucretia Borgia invented chores which required her deepest concentration, her closest attention. She polished silver, she scrubbed, changed drawer and shelf linings.

Midnight found the kitchen and pantry areas immaculate. She looked around, knowing she had to find something to occupy her mind and hands. She could not stand to go up to that bedroom and lie sleepless on that cot.

She remembered that Tige loved her beef stew. She smiled, recalling the way he had come to the kitchen door and begged for stew. The manor house was off limits for the slave children as well as most of the slaves, but Tiger had been unable to live within the boundaries of the law, even as a small boy. His sweet little face at the screen had melted her heart a hundred times. She had ladled up a large bowl of her beef stew, cut thick slabs of fresh bread and sat on the back steps with him while he ate it and told her how wonderful she was, the best and prettiest cook in the whole big world. She had tried to tell him he was just a little slave boy in a black corner of the world, and he couldn't possibly know about the best cooks. But he had smiled, his face smeared with stew and his fingers dripping with it. He had nodded his head, not to be denied. "They is some things you jus' purely knows for fact, Miz Lucretia Borgia, ma'am."

XXXIV

Nell crouched in the darkness. She pressed deeper into the stygian shadows when Miz Lucretia Borgia came into the small slave-jail cell. She watched the big mustee woman cross to where Tige was shackled to wall studs. A single tallow candle guttered and flared in the first gray slivers of dawn that sliced through the wall chinks into the rough room. Nell was thankful she was sitting even in half-concealment. She wished the crib in total darkness, because even the feebly guttering candle flame showed how wretched and beaten she and Tige were, how hopeless.

Nell watched Miz Lucretia kneel beside Tige where he lay on the straw-matted flooring. Gently, the amazonlike woman pushed his sweated hair back from his forehead. This simple act of kindness was more than Nell could bear. She choked back a sob.

"You all right, Tige?" Lucretia Borgia whispered.

"You bring me a knife?"

"You know I cain't do that, Tige honey."

"Then my accommodations are great," Tige said in the self-taunting voice Nell loved so deeply. How she loved him. The very sound of his voice excited her. She loved only Tige. She could never love anyone else; she was certain of this in that moment.

Nell did not move, but she shivered with an irresistible need to reach out and touch Tige. Her hands trembled to soothe the wild thick blond waves, to fondle his ears, trace her fingers along his chin, to caress the cordlike muscles and the dark coppery coins on his chest. He was so alive—his vigor and strength reached out to you. It was not only criminal to kill him in his eighteenth year; it was desecrating holy work, something permitted only to God Himself.

Tears brimmed her eyes and spilled along her cheeks. She sank against the wall, her body shaking with repressed sobs.

"Brought you a little beef stew," she heard Lucretia Borgia whisper to Tige. "Got to keep yo' strength up."

"Yeah." That voice had not learned to beg, even facing death. "Need strength—to hang."

"Dyin' ain't all that easy," Lucretia Borgia said. "Now you sits up and eats. This ain't no ordinary beef stew. I made this here beef stew my own self. Jus' fo' you. 'Members how partial you always was to beef stew when you was a little tike, runnin' round here with yo' backside hangin' out."

"Seldom got stew from *your* stove," Tige recalled. "Mostly, I got the greasy kind, full of fat and light on onions, potatoes or carrots. Felt like I'd died and gone plumb to heaven when I got stew from yo' kitchen, Miz Lucretia Borgia."

"This here stew right from my kitchen. Now you eat it."

Tige smiled tautly. "Kind of a little look at heaven ahead of time."

"You stop that flatterin' talk. You turn this here ole woman's head."

"You ain't old, Lucretia Borgia," Tige said, eating. "You ain't ever gonna get old."

"I gits old, all right," Lucretia Borgia said. "Things I see in this world makes me old. I see sadness. But worse'n the sadness is the meanness. People mean sometime—almost like they don't know nuthin' else.

366

. . . Was you here that time when Masta Ham slew pore old Mede?"

"I was here. . . . I was a little boy . . . but I recall."

"Masta Ham kilt that pore Mede. An' fo' what? 'Cause Mede been pesterin' Masta Ham's wife. An' she a no-good white trash what threatened to yell rape if'n pore Mede didn't mount her regular in her bedroom up there. . . . Masta Ham, he didn't no way want that wife of his'n. Po' unhappy little thing she was— needin' a man all the time—all the time—an' Masta Ham refusin' even to touch her. . . . But him not able to stand the idea of some other man a-givin' Miz Blanche what she had to have or lose her mind.

"Reckon Masta Ham loved few people in this world. His pa. He purely doted on his pa. An' I remember when he was throwed from that gelded horse an' broke his leg—how he cried for me. For ole black Lucretia Borgia what was as near a mammy as he ever had. Loved me, too, in his way. . . . An' he purely loved Mede. But that meanness got into him and he wouldn't listen to nobody. He kilt pore Mede—biled the meat right off Mede's bones. Just for a vengeance what kilt Mede all right, but what drove Masta Ham out of his mind, away from Falconhurst, all the way across the Texies."

Nell stopped crying. She stared in the flickering candlelight at the strength and beauty of Miz Lucretia Borgia's face. It was as if all the goodness God meant to exalt man was concentrated inside her, warming her black eyes, glowing in her unlined cheeks and softening the lines about her full mouth. Nell longed to stretch out her hand to Lucretia, to plead for her help. She was so strong! So good! Surely, if there were justice and human decency on this earth, Lucretia Borgia could find it. If Hammond Maxwell did love Lucretia Borgia as he might have loved his own mother, if he had ever loved her, wouldn't he listen to her now?

Nell shook her head. Why should she deceive herself, try to cling to hope when there was no hope left? Miz Lucretia Borgia looked like a monolith of strength. But what was she really? A Negress. Nothing else. As helpless as Tige. The only difference was that chains shackled Tige and kept him caged like an animal. That's what blacks were without exception to Hammond Maxwell. Animals with voices. Nothing more. He bought and sold them casually. Soon, as casually, he would destroy Tige.

"Oh God, Miz Lucretia Borgia!" Nell was startled to hear her own agonized voice burst out in the dawn silence. It was as if she spoke against her own will. "Oh God, Miz Lucretia Borgia! Help us!"

Tige looked up from his stew. His eyes were dark, even though his voice was kindly. "Don't drag Miz Lucretia Borgia into this, Nell. . . . I sorry I tried to. No sense gittin' her in it. No way she can help. She doin' all she can."

Nell's gaze moved from Tige to Miz Lucretia Borgia, and her heart lurched. Poor Lucretia Borgia. The dim flame illumined the tears welled in the big woman's ebony eyes and betrayed them, glittering.

Lucretia Borgia sat on the crokersacks piled at Tige's head. She extended her bulbous arms toward the girl crouched in the darkened corner. Sobbing, Nell flung herself against Miz Lucretia Borgia's bosom, clinging to her as a frightened child might—or as a bride, terrorized in the false dawn.

Lucretia Borgia stroked Nell's hair back from her forehead, patted her gently and, bending over, pressed her lips into the distraught girl's hair.

"My daddy bought Tige from this farm." The words spilled across Nell's lips in a rushing, involuntary way, as if she had no control over them. She needed to pour out their sad little story. Somebody had to hear how deeply they loved—she and Tige—before he died, and she lost him forever. Never to see him again. Never to hold him close. "I saw Tige the first day he came to Hiddenbrook. He was so pretty. I never even reckoned him black—"

"He Masta Ham's own flesh and blood," Lucretia Borgia said.

"He is white, Miz Lucretia Borgia. . . . The good Lord knows I hope you understand that I believe inside we're all alike—no different—black or white—we're what God made us."

Lucretia Borgia shuddered, her heavy body quivering so the girl felt her bulk shaken by the blasphemy. What Nell was saying, Lucretia Borgia had been hearing vehemently denied since her own birth, until finally she had come to deny it in her own heart. But Lucretia Borgia did not speak. She went on holding the sobbing girl, trying to comfort her. This was the least she could do. It was nothing. Less than nothing, but comfort in a joyless night was all she had to give, and she gave it with all her heart.

"You and I know black is skin deep. White is skin deep."

"Hit's good and evil that go deep to the bone," Miz Lucretia Borgia agreed. "That can go deep—don't matter the color of the skin. They's good and bad—black or white. Amen."

"But down here—today—the color of your skin makes all the difference in the way you can live—slave or free! A man like Tige. He's white—white as me. But a drop of black blood—that makes him a black slave. That means he can't ever be free."

Gently, Lucretia Borgia caressed the miserable girl. "You done a wrong thing, Miss Nell. You fell in love with a black man. That the way it *is*. We ain't talkin' about fair, Missy. We talkin' about *is*. We talkin' about life. Bout livin' amongst white folks—an' tryin' to stay alive."

"How can they be so cruel?"

"That's what you got to learn about white folks, Missy. They don't even know they cruel. They don't think about cruel."

"My stepfather was cruelest of all, Lucretia Borgia. He married my mother—to get Hiddenbrook Plantation. He didn't love her. I was only twelve, but I could tell. He didn't want my mother. I didn't know what he wanted then. My mother belonged to the finest family. We had slaves. I treated slaves—like slaves—till I saw Tige that day. It was like I was born new inside. Like I was singing inside with the way I felt. I thought at first he was the white overseer's son, but I didn't care *who* he was, or what he was. . . . I loved him then with all my heart—and I love him that much more right now."

Nell's ragged breathing shook her. Lucretia Borgia's arms tightened about her. "Well, Foye Randolph took over Hiddenbrook Plantation. My mother lived in terror. She moved through that big old house like a frightened shadow. When Foye bought Tige and brought him to Hiddenbrook, I was happy for the very first time since Foye Randolph married my mother. But that happiness didn't last very long. Foye was jealous of Tige—because of me! I was fourteen when Tige and I—first made love. I didn't know why Foye treated Tige so cruelly. Foye seemed to dote on me. He spoiled me, I was never punished. He was always kissing me, holding me on his lap, fondling me. I hated it. But I thought he was—my father—and I thought he was trying to be kind. . . . And I thought I could help Tige by being nice to Foye. . . .

"Then—after Tige and I fell in love—after we did it together that first time, I just flowered inside, you know?"

"I *know.*"

"All of a sudden I knew what life was about. What God meant it to be about. Tige and I—we had what

370

Adam and Eve must have had in Eden. . . . I couldn't stay away from him. I wanted him—loving me—all the time. . . .

"One night I thought Foye was away. . . . We went to my bed. I didn't even hear the corridor door open. But Tige did. He leaped up. Foye stood there with a lamp in one hand and a short, thick whip in the other.

"At first, Foye was cold with rage. His voice cut as he told me what a white slut I was to pleasure a nigger. I had never even thought of Tige as black, and by then, it wouldn't have mattered. I loved him so.

"Foye hit Tige with the whip. Then he called in two house servants, had Tige tied up and left tied up on my floor.

"Then he said—he said he was going to show Tige he could never have a white girl. He said that the only way to cleanse the filth of the nigger from me was to drive it—to fuck it out of me. He kept yelling that."

Nell covered her hands with her face. After a moment, words poured in another torrent from her lips.

"With Tige helpless and me watching Foye in terror, my stepfather came toward me. He whipped off his dressing gown. He wore nothing underneath. His body was covered with sweat. His face was strange, wilder than I'd ever seen it, deathly gray, as if he were ill. He had difficulty breathing. I could look at him—down there—and see how terribly aroused he was.

"I finally realized why he'd hated Tige so fiercely—because he coveted me so much. He wanted me not as a daughter, but as a teenage whore. He kept telling me he'd show me what being a whore really meant. As he crouched over me on my bed, I thought I was going to faint. Oh, Lucretia Borgia, can you understand how stupid and young and ignorant I was? I had not even suspected that Foye was driven insane

371

with jealousy—and was now obsessed with the need to *rape* the memory of Tige out of my body. . . .

"Foye grabbed my ankles and pulled me over to the side of the mattress. Then he forced my legs apart. Right in front of Tige, he forced me to do repulsive things. . . . I was weak and helpless with terror. He forced me—I had to do what he forced on me no matter how repugnant it was to me. . . .

"He lay with me and forced me to do things I'd never even imagined. I was afraid he'd kill me, choke me to death, tear me so I bled—down there. . . . I cried and pleaded and screamed. The more I wailed the more excited Foye became.

"The more I flailed my body to evade him, the wilder he was. Suddenly he came down upon me and thrust himself into me. . . . I fought and screamed. . . . And then it was as if it were not real anymore. It was a nightmare of violence. Foye was yanked back off of me. His face went away as if flying, contorted and blood-red. He was choking, gasping, fighting helplessly.

"Lying there, I saw that Tige had worked free of the ropes. He was bleeding where he had chewed and twisted himself free. He strangled Foye with the rope."

Nell shuddered and pressed closer to Lucretia Borgia, closing her eyes tightly as if trying to blot away the terrible memory. After a long beat, she went on, "Tige kept choking my stepfather even after we both knew Foye was dead. . . . All I could think was that we had to get away.

"Foye was evil, a vicious white man," Nell whispered. "He deserved to die. Tige thought he might kill me."

"Lots of white men you and me might count as better off dead," Miz Lucretia Borgia said. "Cain't kill 'em all jus' cause we know they skunk-mean. Tige broke the law when he killed that white man."

"I'd do it again," Tige said. His voice was dull and flat. "I'd do it a hundred times again."

"And I'd sing yo' praises loud, every time," Miz Lucretia Borgia said. "But it don't make it no easier. . . . A nigger kills a white man, it means a hangin'— no matter the reason. I sorry. . . ."

"I ain't askin' pity." Tige sat up. "I killed him. I meant to kill him. I told Nell not to burden it all on you. . . . Nothing you can do, Miz Lucretia Borgia. Nothing I ask you to do. Don't ask your pity neither."

Nell's voice rose, almost hysterically. "I do! Oh God, Miz Lucretia Borgia, I do. Feel sorry for us. Pity us. Oh God, help us, because we've got nobody else."

"Stop it, Nell." Tige's voice broke. "Ain't no sense makin' Miz Lucretia Borgia feel no worse. Ain't nuthin' she can do."

Nell clung to Lucretia Borgia as if to life itself. "You don't help us, Miz Lucretia Borgia, they'll hang Tige. They'll kill him. An' I'll never see him again."

Tige tried to smile. "We had a good time, Nell. We didn't have much time—but maybe there never is enough when you love somebody. What we had— it was good."

"Running all the time? Hiding? Scared in the dark?"

"Won't that be your life—even if you somehow got away from here?" Miz Lucretia Borgia said.

But the girl clutched at this, as if at a straw. "There's this lady, Miz Lucretia Borgia . . . she was Mr. Maxwell's wife . . . his woman, we found out. He walked off and left her to come back home here. She hates him as terrible as she once loved him. . . . She wants Tige and me back in the Texies, Miz Lydia does. She would welcome us back. She needs Tige to help her run that ranch. And we could live with her—white and free—in the Texies."

She began to cry helplessly. There was a haven, a sanctuary, if only she could get Tige safely there. The distance across the Texies no longer terrified her. Losing Tige terrified her. There was no other terror.

"Miz Lucretia. You love Tige. You care about him. I know you do. . . . You don't want Mr. Hammond to kill him. Tige's too young to die . . . too good. It ain't right . . . it just ain't right."

"I reckon life just ain't right. . . . It's just life and it just goes on."

"You can help Tige. Only you. . . . If Mr. Ham would listen to anyone on this earth, he would listen to you. You could help Tige live free—instead of hanging dead. . . . Help us, Miz Lucretia Borgia. Get us one more chance. Don't make me and my baby live out our life without Tige."

Lucretia Borgia held the girl close, rocking her in her arms as if Nell were a small child.

"It's all right, Miz Lucretia Borgia," Tige said. "I love you. I know you've done for us all you can."

"Can't you just tell Mr. Ham how it happened?" Nell pleaded. "He'll listen to you. Make him think, Lucretia Borgia. Make him stop and take time to *think* what he's doing."

"Time to think," Lucretia Borgia said. "Lawsy, how you gwine make a white man take time to think?"

She shook her head. With infinite gentleness, Lucretia Borgia drew away from Nell and stood up. Nell seemed to crumple, without hope, lying beside Tige on the straw-matted flooring. The big woman stood like a bulwark before them. She drew a deep breath. Masta Ham was good inside. In his way he did love her and he would listen to her when he would listen to nobody else. But Masta Ham was not in a listening mood—he was in a killing mood. No amount of begging or entreaties would force him to change his mind. He needed to think on what he was doing, but he was determined to hang this boy and there was no way to stop him, not even when they all knew Masta Ham would regret it to the longest day he lived. He would regret it, but he could not be stopped. . . .

She kissed Tige gently and pressed her cheek against Nell's. She said nothing more. There were no more words. There was only pain that was too deep for words. Her proud head bowed, Miz Lucretia Borgia walked out into the morning sunlight, her slippers slapping against her heels.

self off as a white man—even in the dire emergency
of threat of losing Falconhurst without a white man to

himself any longer. "He no better than I was somethin'!"
Lucretia Borgia's laugh was scornful. "Maybe not.
But limp Ham he don' contented, an' dey time he

XXXV

Hammond limped back and forth across the musty
parlor as if he were a sore-pawed animal in a cage.

He sat down in his father's old chair, but he could
remain there for only a few moments. He yelled for
Mem. When the servant finally arrived, Ham ordered
hot toddies. "And hot, damn your black hide. Hot,
you lazy lout. You hear me?"

"I hear you, Masta. It so good to have you back
home again, Masta honey."

Ham swung his arm savagely. "Shut your lying black
mouth and get my hot toddy."

"Yas, suh." Mem retreated from the room, shuffling
and bobbing his graying head up and down, stretching
his lips achingly wide in the falsest smile Ham had
ever beheld.

Waiting for his toddy, Ham plodded into the hall.
The house was quiet. Too quiet. The silence hung like
an oppressive miasma. He yelled for Lucretia Borgia.
A tense stillness spread in the kitchen as if everyone
in there held his breath.

After a long moment, Mem appeared in the doorway, eyes white-rimmed with fear. "Miz Lucretia
. . . she ain't heah jus' this second, Masta. She be
back mos' any moment, I sure."

"Get my toddy, damn you."

Mem's dark face disappeared from the doorway.

377

Ham scowled. There was much to do, many preparations to make. The house, yard, slaves, the scaffold, must be readied for the hanging. This would be no ordinary execution for which the clanging iron plantation bell would summon all the Falconhurst inhabitants as witnesses. Guests would be arriving, gentry folks in their best, some expecting to spend the night, all looking forward.

"Lucretia Borgia! Goddam you, Lucretia Borgia, where are you?" Ham's voice rattled dishes in dining room cabinets, echoed through the rooms, but then died ineffectually. Lucretia Borgia did not appear. Mem brought the toddy. Ham found it strong but not hot, and he cursed Mem, promising to blister him as soon as this hanging was off his mind.

Mem blubbered. Tears streaked down his cheeks. "Please, Masta. Don't hide ole Mem. Mem a good boy. Mem yo' own boy, Masta."

"The hell you are. I'd have skinned you years ago. Only reason you're here now is Pa liked you—"

"Yes, suh! Your paw purely doted on old Mem—"

"Pa was old, getting soft in the head. Damn you, I'm not. Now fix me another toddy. Sooner or later, you stupid ape, you got to get it right."

"Wants I should take this one away—?"

"And drink it your own self? Hell no. If I had any hope this side of heaven that your next toddy would be any more palatable than this one, I'd throw this one in your ugly ape face. But I know better. I won't git a decent toddy until Lucretia Borgia git back. Whereat you say she was?"

"Say she be right back." Mem looked ready to cry. Lucretia Borgia's helpers bustled in the kitchen, but the big woman was not there to supervise them. Mem did not know where she was but was too terrified to admit this.

"Get out. Get out. Get me another toddy. And it's

378

not hot, jus' right hot, mind you, I adds ten lashes to the hidin' I got in mind fo' you."

"Oh Gawd, Masta—"

"Shut up—and bring my drink. Move your lazy bones."

When he'd had two more of Mem's tepid toddies, issued all the orders he could remember or invent, Ham wandered about the house aimlessly. He ordered his breakfast when it looked as if Lucretia Borgia had forgotten him and none of the other servants would act without direct orders.

Seated alone in the old dining room, Hammond could not eat the food set before him. He refused to admit the anguish roiling around in his belly, but he admitted to himself that if he swallowed any of the food on his plate he would vomit. He did not acknowledge inner turmoil but said aloud that the slop prepared without Lucretia Borgia overseeing the kitchen was slop not fit for pigs. He did not eat. He kept seeing Nell Randolph's stricken face, kept seeing the mustee Tiger, as if looking at himself in a time-lapse mirror. Aye God, he wished these terrible decisions didn't redound to him, but they did.

He stared at his clenched fist. His father had taught him well. He carried out his responsibilities and obligations, no matter the price, or he was less than a man and he sank swamped under all the wrongs he left unmended. That mustee boy had killed a white man. There was no recourse but punishment by death—an example to other blacks. Tiger had to be destroyed but it was not easy. It did not sit well to kill the boy, but Hammond Maxwell lived by the code of his peers. The mustee boy would die.

Ham pushed the plate from him. Getting up, he limped out of the room, out of the house. He did not put on his slouch-brim hat or even his jacket. The morning chill closed in, damp and misty. He did not care. He plodded up the knoll to the family cemetery in the pine copse. He gazed briefly at his parents' matching headstones, at the graves of other white people who'd died at Falconhurst, at the slabs and stakes marking the resting place of the slaves beyond the snake fence.

For a long time Ham stared down at the still-raw yellow mound over his father's casket. His eyes brimmed with tears and he brushed them away with the backs of his fingers.

Painfully, Ham knelt beside the headstones Lucretia Borgia had ordered placed at the grave. The lettering was simple—his father's name, birth and death dates. This was all. Ham felt a rush of gratitude toward Lucretia Borgia. Instantly, his mood altered and he cursed her. Where was she, with so much to be done?

His badly healed leg stretched straight behind him, Ham placed all his weight on his good knee. He bowed his head and spoke softly, "Mornin', Papa. Come up to talk with you. Need your counsel, I do. Bad. Know you'd agree what I got to do—what I'm *going* to do—is best. But an' you was here, I could see your face, I'd know. You'd help me know I was right."

He pulled a wire-grass plug from his father's grave and crushed it in his hand. "Tiger is a good Falconhurst nigger . . . my own git, Pa. Out'n that Lilith gal. Remember her, Pa? She was nigh on as white as you or me. Octoroon, she was. Lots of fire in her. . . . Tiger like that. He a nigger what act like he white, better'n other folks. But I knows he's black—he jus' an animal, no matter he got human blood in him. . . .

"Do seem a sin to kill him. But I knowed when I brung him back here it would have to be done. And I gone do it. . . . It's jus' he do look the spit an' image of me—ten or twelve years back. An' he'd just whimper, or beg, it'd be easy, but he's pridey. Tryin' to die like a man—still won't admit he jus' a nigger—a killin' nigger. You know, Papa, once a nigger go bad, he bad forever. An' a mustee? Gawd knows, they the worst of all.

"So that's what I got to do, Papa. . . . It's a little

easier now, since I talked to you like this. Thankee, Papa . . . and—I love you."

Tears leaking down his cheeks, Hammond stood up. He felt cold. He shivered and massaged his chilled arms roughly with his hands, up and down. He limped back downhill. Entering the parlor, he yelled for Mem to build up the fire.

XXXVI

Mem shuffled into the parlor with unusual alacrity. Watching him, Ham scowled. Then he saw the reason for Mem's spryness. Lucretia Borgia entered the room at Mem's hurrying heels. Lucretia Borgia looked like an army with banners. Mem quaked with fear. Seeing her, Ham experienced a sense of relief and release. Some of this sickening responsibility would be lifted from his shoulders. He would share his anguish with Lucretia Borgia. He smacked his lips. She carried a tall glass of steaming hot toddy on a tray. It would be just right. He knew this as certainly as he knew his own name.

"Where you been, you black slut?" Ham said, taking the toddy from the tray. He drew a deep draught, feeling its warmth and sweetness eating through his inner chill.

"I heah, Masta," she said, without hint of apology or explanation. "These no-good trashy house niggers been neglectin' my Masta Ham, I takes the side of my hand to 'em."

"*You* been neglecting me, you black wench."

"No. Nevah . . . but I is been busy—"

"You been pleasurin' some randy buck out'n the barns, that's what you been doing."

Lucretia Borgia shrugged. "You know ole Lucretia Borgia, Masta. She a big black gal. She git itchy inside her skin an' she goes too long without'n a good pesterin'."

He did not smile. "We got too much to do."

She matched his tone. "Got to hang that pore Tige boy, Masta?"

"That's right. Got to get this house ready for guests. Got to slick them slaves up. You know every time people visit here, they finds five or six slaves they want to buy. Company comin' today. Quality white folks."

"To watch a nigger hang, Masta?"

"A murderin', runaway nigger. Yes. Ain't no use you trying to talk me out of what I intend to do."

"Please, Masta. Don't do this."

"Goddam your black hide. You mighty biggety, ain't you? Argufyin' with me. Think 'cause I trust you to run this heah place, it make you somethin' more'n a black wench—a uppety black slave wench."

She remained unmoved. "Ain't nevah thought that, Masta."

"I could whip them ideas out'n yore head. Don't you nevah fo'git that. I still master here. I'll cut the skin off your back."

She nodded, unflinching. "Yes, Masta. You done that to Lucretia Borgia. I recalls well. An' I shore you do. I was hung up like a sow to be slaughtered. Naked before all them niggers whilst they whipped me—"

He burst into tears. "Damn it. You acted bad. Papa had to whop you. Gawd almighty, Lucretia Borgia, that was back when I was fifteen—ain't you evah fo'give?"

"Nevah nothin' to fo'give, Masta Ham. You my masta, I yo' nigger. You wants to hang me up naked and whip me, that your right. Ain't nevah said that wasn't your right."

He wiped at his eyes. "Yes. An' don't you fo'git I has got that right. I wish someway I could make you remember that."

Lucretia Borgia sighed. "Only tryin' to make *you* remember, too, Masta Ham."

He prowled the room, limping, moving as if the walls crowded in on him. There was much he could have said, but when he turned and faced her again, he said no more about that evil memory. Instead, he said, "Stir your stumps. Bring me another toddy. An' you fix it. Don't let that no-good Mem near it."

"I wouldn't let that triflin' nigger wait on you, Masta. You *my* masta."

"Yes, goddammit," he yelled at her retreating back, "I am your master."

When she returned to the parlor with his toddy, Ham stood at an open window, staring into the yard where carpenters set up the scaffold. Their hammers and axes were the loudest sound in the morning. Ham turned, his ruddy face gray, and took the toddy.

"Why you tryin' to make me remember bad things like when we whupped you, Lucretia Borgia?"

She smiled and shrugged. "Jus' wantin' you to think on Falconhurst, Masta. The good. The bad."

"What else you believe I ever think on? Falconhurst. Clear across the Texies, I never forgot for a minute. I was pulled back here, because I belonged here."

She smiled again. "We'se had us some good times here at Falconhurst."

He nodded. "We raise the finest black fancies money can buy. Cain't buy no better slave than at Falconhurst."

"We raise good niggers, Masta. Fancy. Extra fancy. We careful who pester who. We got us a good nigger farm. . . . I recall once when you come home from Natchez, you brung me a red petticoat—like them Under-the-hill whoahs wore, you said. Made me try it on fo' you and yo' pappy. We all laughed. Big fat ole me in a whoah's red petticoat. Mostly, you been a kind, good man, Masta. 'Cause you a good man inside."

"Reckon you purely raised me after my mother died," Hammond declared fairly.

She nodded, remembering. "I done what I could, Masta. I done what I could. But we's had our bad times, too. Times when things so sad, wasn't even no tears for 'em."

He slashed his hand in a cutting gesture. "I don't want to talk about it."

"Think, Masta Ham!" she persisted. "Think how

"Ain't no way faultin' you, Masta, fo' what you done. to Mede."

His voice was dead. "I done to Mede what I had to do."

"Ain't no way faultin' you, Masta, fo' what you done. You a good man. You done what you see as right—"

"It was right! Damn you, it was right."

"It was right to kill Mede. He done pestered a white lady—"

"He raped my wife!"

She shrugged and let that pass, but through her mind flashed the memory of Miz Blanche's sending for Mede, day after day, and Mede going slow up those back stairs—afraid to go, afraid not to—as if he were on his way to the death chamber . . . as, of course, he had been. . . .

Her voice lacked spirit. "Then you shorely done the right thing, Masta. Mede rape a white woman, he had to die. You killed him. A white man couldn't do no less—"

"That's right." He nodded emphatically. "They's a code an' a white man lives by it, or he no man at all."

"Nevah questioned your righteousness, Masta. Nevah. Jus' askin' you to recall what it done to you— inside you—to kill Mede. . . . He was black, Mede was. A prize Mandingo. He worship you—you loved him. . . . You didn't kill him, Masta, not without dyin' some inside yo'self."

He shook his head, refusing to look at her. "You lie."

"You kilt Mede, but you destroyed yourself—all your dreams for a great race of Mandingo men like Mede—"

"Liar—"

"—you destroyed your own sweet life heah at Falconhurst. Your own dear pappy here, but you couldn't live here no more—because inside it was not your Falconhurst—it was the hell where you and Mede died together—"

"You're crazy . . . a crazy old black woman."

She appeared not to hear him. Her voice pursued him. "So you run away. Clear across the Texies. . . . An' you live there—try to make a life fo' yo'self— your roots torn out and pulled up from here. Your life here all fouled and ruined. And we missed you— all them long, lonely years. . . . You lived with yo' heart a-breakin' an' so did we."

"No." He limped across the room as if he were running from her, as if he could not escape her no matter where he went.

Ham was sweated down now. His shirt was damp with perspiration, discolored at the armpits. He could smell himself. He breathed raggedly and plodded about the room, touching glass, a table, the Bible, the back of his father's old chair. At last, he whispered, "Didn't say it was easy. Nevah said that. Didn't no way say it had to be easy. All I ever said, it had to be done, and I done it."

"Yes, Masta. And you paid a terrible price. . . . Now you goin' to pay that price ag'in?"

"To hang Tiger? Yes."

"Don't do it, Masta. Please."

"He murdered a white man. He got to die."

"But I not sayin' that. I not sayin' whether it right or wrong, I thinkin' only about you. About my own Masta Hammond what I raised up from a baby. . . .

I thinkin' 'bout what it will do to you—jus' when you come home again an' all."

Hammond's voice rose, thundering in the room. "You tellin' me what to do, wench?"

Lucretia Borgia extended her hand toward him, then let it fall to her side. "No, Masta. I nevah do that. I know my place. . . . You know Lucretia Borgia love you . . . no matter what you do. . . . I agrees with what you do—"

"Don't sound like it."

"I jus' beggin' you to take a little while. Time. Ain't no hurry. Time. Jus' a little time, Masta. Time to think about if first. What it do to you. What a fine young boy that Tige is."

"Don't matter how fine he is. He a killin' nigger. A runnin' nigger." He swept his arm outward. "He kilt a white man. He run. He got to hang—as a 'zample."

Her voice remained low, persistent. "Time. Time to think that Tige—he yo' own flesh and blood, Masta."

"I tole you. It makes no nevah mind. No matter whose blood he's got, or how white his skin. He still a nigger. A bad nigger."

"Maybe they some reason why he kilt that white man."

"What reason? Law don't allow *no* reason for any nigger to kill a white man."

She shook her head, as if trying to understand something too deep for her to comprehend. "Jus' hard to think we raised so good a boy heah—so good an' all here at Falconhurst—that he would kill—'thout no reason."

"I done tole you, wench. Ain't no reason a nigger can kill *any* white man."

"Still . . . Tiger. He one of the best boys Falconhurst ever raised—"

"He went bad."

"Cain't understan' that. He seem such a fine nigger

388

boy. He go on vendue in N' Orleans right today for four, five thousand dollars, I wager you."

He nodded. "At least that. He got no blemish. He extra-fancy."

"He so white he bring a extra price! Like burning all that money. Wasting that young boy."

"I nevah said I liked it, damn you. I nevah said I liked it. I said it what got to be done. Now, I won't heah no more argufyin' from you. . . . You got one job—less'n you wants to be spraddled bare-ass naked before them quality white folks and whipped till you bleed—a-fore the hangin'. . . . You want that? Then you stir yo'self. Bring me another toddy."

Her voice was low but it was not weak or timid. "Toddy's ain't gwine make you blind to what you doin'."

Ham swung around and faced her. His face grew red, his eyes murderous. He clenched his fists and advanced upon her. His voice rose and shook, hoarse. "Get me a fresh toddy, you black bitch."

Lucretia Borgia nodded, but in the same breath, said, "Ain't you had 'nuff, Masta?"

When he spoke, it was as if he forced control of himself, though his voice quivered with rage. "I decides when I had 'nuff, nigger."

She nodded and turned to leave the room, her great shoulders set. He raged after her, his voice lashing her along the hall, "I will hang Tiger. You hear me, you black meddlin' ole bitch? I will drink . . . I will drink. When I like. Much as I like. You hear me, goddam you?"

He found himself breathing raggedly through parted lips when Lucretia Borgia was gone and he was alone in the room. He paced slowly about. His flat palm stroked the huge old family Bible. He pressed his hand upon it fiercely, but did not open it. Then he hobbled over to his father's old chair. He drew his palm along the oil-stained doily pinned across the headrest. He wiped sweat from his face even as he shivered. Damn Lucretia Borgia! She could not be allowed to talk back to him like this. It was unthinkable! He had not really hated talking out his problem with her; he had used her as a sounding board. He had delineated the case against Tiger; he had put it all in words. He had set in his own mind what had to be done. Nothing would alter his course now. Still, he couldn't permit Lucretia Borgia to sass him like that. Damn her. Where was she now? All he asked was a hot toddy. Why did she take so long over such a simple task?

He prowled the room, trying to find that old lost warmth and familiarity which had always sustained him. He continued to sweat, chilled. Damn it, there was no reason to doubt, no sense in doubting. He was doing what was right, according to the code of this land. He was a southerner, he belonged to the Hammond family, the Maxwells. His was the best blood of the South. This position gave him prerogatives, privileges, but had its responsibilities as well. A man lived by that code. A southern gentleman must take any steps, no matter how heinous, to wipe out a stain on his honor or he had no honor left; he was no longer a gentleman. God knew, he had poisoned Blanche when he discovered her faithless. There had been no other way—he had had to defend his honor. In the same way, a southern slave owner had power of life and death over his slaves. He must not abuse that power but he must mete out justice—even death—fairly, or there was no justice. Slaves were animals to be protected and treated as animals with the power of speech, but, as they are protected, they must also be punished. And, dammit, Lucretia Borgia could prattle about a reason why Tiger killed Foye Randolph till the cows came home, but this was without consequence. A black could not testify against a white in a court of law. Nothing a slave said against a white man could be admitted as evidence. No. It was settled by a power greater than he. Hammond Maxwell was doing what he had to do; he was living by that code which had made the South a lovely, gracious place in which to live.

"Lucretia Borgia! Goddam you! Where's my toddy?"

"I comin', Masta."

"Rustle yo' fat ass, damn you. A man could die of thirst a-waitin' on you, you triflin' black woman."

Lucretia Borgia entered the parlor while fragments of his angry voice still echoed through the long corridor. The toddy steamed on the tray. She opened her mouth to speak. Knowing she was going to protest against his drinking another toddy, he gestured sharply, warning her to silence. Her face seemed somehow gray, muddy under its creamy chocolate surface. Her eyes held such shadows of sadness that he looked away from them, disturbed and angered. His hand trembling, he took up the glass and drained off the toddy defiantly.

He did not remove it from his lips until the last drop was gone. Then he slapped the glass back on the tray and glared at her, his gaze defying her to oppose him by word or gesture. She merely stood, unmoving.

"Now, damn you," he said. "I'm going out to check on the scaffolding for the hanging. Something got to be done right, I do it myself."

"Yes, Masta."

"An' I reckon you to git this here house ready for my guests."

"Yes, Masta."

"This mustee going to hang. Hang, you hear me?"

She nodded, and ethnic acceptance of agony pumping through her, her face tranquil.

He shook his head oddly, as if trying to clear it. She reached out to him, but he brushed her hand aside. He grabbed up his jacket and, carrying it over his shoulder, he took a long step toward the front door.

Something happened. It was as if he tripped over

an invisible wire. He fell straight forward. He did not even throw his arm up to cushion his fall. He landed heavily, the room trembling under the impact of his dead weight. He was unconscious by the time he struck the floor.

XXXVII

A shroudlike stillness settled over Falconhurst. From where Lucretia Borgia stood in the parlor of the old house, she could hear no movement. Either the world stood still or she'd gone abruptly and totally deaf.

Her mind spun. It seemed to Lucretia Borgia that she drifted into a strange, half-waking state where time lost its meaning and there was no reality. It was almost as though she stood apart from her own body watching her own movements, detached.

She stared at her master's inert body sprawled on the floor. She kept thinking she did not belong here. She should be safe and secure in her kitchen. But she was not. This room had suddenly become a hole beyond hell, and she was trapped in it with her unconscious master.

Her eyes brimmed with tears. She did not move for a long beat, but she spoke aloud as though Masta Hammond could hear her. "I sorry, Masta. I dreadful sorry."

The tears spilled along her cream-smooth cheeks. She felt anguished compassion for her master, but a part of her crying was for herself. Trouble was temporarily past for Masta Hammond—he was beyond the reach of pain or confusion or retribution, but she was not. She would never be again. Whatever her old life had been—good or ill—it was over and could never be the same anymore.

She exhaled and put this out of her mind. There was too much to do to waste time on self-pity. How long Hammond would sleep she did not know, could not guess. But this much she did know. Whatever she was to accomplish, she had to get it done before Masta Hammond awakened.

Ellen cried out behind her, and Lucretia Borgia spun around, as light on her feet as a butterfly, despite her bulk. "What you doin' in here, gal?" Miz Lucretia Borgia demanded. "Why ain't you in the kitchen?"

Ellen did not answer. She ran past Lucretia Borgia and knelt beside the prostrate man on the carpeting. Ellen stared at him, sobbing. "He daid! Oh my Gawd, Masta Ham is daid."

"He ain't daid," Miz Lucretia Borgia said. Inwardly, she prayed he was not dead.

Ellen's wails brought other workers and Mem, running from the rear of the house. "Oh Gawd," Mem said. Instinctively, he started backing away.

Without even looking around at Mem, Lucretia Borgia said, "You stand where you is, you triflin' nigger. Might need you to help me git Masta Ham upstairs to he bed."

Mem wailed. "I cain't touch no daid body."

"You touch what I tells you to touch," Lucretia Borgia said. Her anger roused her to action. She was thankful for this. She would stay busy, too busy to think about later, about consequences.

"What happenin' heah?" one of the undercooks said. "Why Masta on the floor?"

Lucretia Borgia swung her arm. "Ain't got no time to 'splain nuthin' to you now." Her agony and fear slipped deeper into her mind. "Want you people to git all the victuals up on my back porch. Got to git ready for the gatherin' of quality white folks. Masta

Ham invited quality white folks, an' soon they be comin'."

"Comin' fo' the hangin'," Mem said.

Lucretia Borgia spun around, her voice flaying him. "Ain't gwine be no hanging. We gwine have a party for quality white folks what's a-comin'. They expectin' a hangin'—got to give them a scrumptious party so's they don't be too disappointed not seeing a nigger danglin' at the end of a rope."

"Kinda hankered to see that myself," Mem said.

Now Miz Lucretia Borgia did slap him. Her hand caught him resoundingly at the side of his head and staggered him. Mem began to cry. "You got no call to do that."

"I clobber you when I feels like it. You lucky I ain't sold you down the river, nigger, since Masta Warren daid and Masta Ham away. You jump when I tells you jump. You gits half a dozen men and you bring fire-smoked hams, a crokersack of sweet potatoes, a bag of dried beans, a poke of coffee beans, three jugs of long-sweetenin' sorghum and a sack of flour. You puts it on my back porch. It ain't there time I come downstairs, I clobber you so you don't nevah fo'git it—if you recovah."

Mem nodded, retreating. "Yes'm, Miz Lucretia Borgia, ma'am."

Quietly, but with a cool authority none of the slaves would dare oppose, Lucretia Borgia sent all of them on errands, warning each that their very lives might depend on speed.

She kept Ellen with her. Lucretia Borgia knelt on the floor beside Hammond. Gently, she smoothed back his hair from his forehead. She glanced at the octoroon girl. "You gits yo' lazy hide up to Masta Ham's bedroom. You change his sheets and pillow cases. Put fresh covers on his bed. Have it ready when I gits him up there."

"How you gwine git him up them stairs and into his bed?"

Miz Lucretia Borgia glanced up, her face chilled. "I ain't wastin' yo' time askin' *you* fool questions, gal. Now git."

Ellen refused to be rushed, ordered. "You fo'git I used to be Masta Ham's bed wench afore he left Falconhurst. Even when he married to that Miz Blanche Woodford, he like me the best. You best be careful what you say to me."

"You do what I tell you, *when* I tell you, I don't have to say nuthin' to you, which is jus' the way I prefers it, yeller gal. Don't make me tell you again."

Sulking, Ellen walked out of the room, her shoulders back. Lucretia Borgia heard her mounting the stairs, defiance in the very way she walked.

Lucretia Borgia placed her arms under Hammond's shoulders and under his knees. Her face grew taut under the strain. She stood straight up, slowly, but without faltering. Master Hammond weighed nearly 175 pounds, but she cradled him against her as she had when he'd been a sleepy child—in a faraway, forgotten time.

Carrying her master gently in her arms, she went out of the parlor. She gazed up the narrow steep stairwell toward the cavernous gloom of the upper floor. She did not think about the distance or of the weight of the man in her arms. She carried him tenderly. Halfway up the stairs, she paused to get her breath. The unconscious man became deadweight. An irresistible pull dragged her backward, threatening to clutch her in its grasp and to fling her helplessly down the steps. She whispered softly, talking nonsense to Masta Ham to take her own mind off the distance and weight, as she had talked nonsense to him when he was a little boy to quiet his fears or sorrows. Remembering how easily she had carried him once—and with what love—made it easier. She had always loved him deeply, but never as she loved him in this ordeal through which they must pass together.

She drew fresh strength from some inner reserve. She came off the top step and walked along the corridor. Ellen came to the door of Masta Ham's bedroom and stood watching her helplessly. Ellen made no offer to help.

"That bed ready?" Lucretia Borgia said.

"It ready."

Lucretia Borgia shoved past Ellen, carrying Ham into his bedroom. His head and arms dangled loosely now like the limbs of a straw-stuffed rag doll.

"He gwine be all right?" Ellen said.

"You pray," Miz Lucretia Borgia told her. She laid Hammond down across his bed and leaned against the high mattress a moment, gasping for breath. "Gittin' old," she whispered. "Gittin' too damn old for all this."

"What you want me to do now?" Ellen said.

Lucretia Borgia exhaled heavily. She looked around at the mustee girl standing helplessly, then down at Ham's inert body. She breathed in deeply, hoisting her magnificent bosom under the inhalation, leaning against the bed for the last moment of rest she could foresee for herself.

Ham sprawled fully dressed across the mattress. He could not be left like this. His crooked right leg was twisted off the edge of the bed at an awkward angle. Lucretia Borgia lifted the leg tenderly and made him comfortable. "Ain't no niggers got no brains round this here house 'ceptin' me?" she implored, lifting her eyes and directing her question toward the ceiling. "I'll tell you what I want you to do, Ellen. First, you help me git him undressed. Then you tell that lazy Millie to bring a basin of tepid water and we bathes him and puts him under the sheets, so he can rest comfortable."

"I cain't undress Masta Ham," Ellen said, shaking her head. "We cain't see him nekkid."

"Seen him nekkid since the day he was born."

Lucretia looked as if she might smite the yellow girl. "An' you jus' braggin' how you sleep bare-ass with him.

"Never seed him nekkid."

"Well, you goin' to now. Git holt of that boot. An' be careful. He still git the misery in that game leg."

"He unconscious."

"Don't want him hurt, conscious or unconscious."

"Hope we doin' what right."

"We doin' what right." Lucretia Borgia lifted Ham's limp body and removed his shirt as Ellen pulled off his boots. Lucretia Borgia loosened his belt and unbuttoned the fly of his drill pants. Ellen backed away, but at a warning glance from Miz Lucretia Borgia, she returned, and working together, they pulled the trousers down over his legs. Miz Lucretia Borgia glanced at Masta Ham's flaccid manhood and smiled. "Hard to believe anything limp and ugly like that be worth a damn in hell to a woman, ain't it?"

Ellen was staring, her lips parted. She shook her head "I never saw it like that," she said.

"I jus' bet you didn't."

By now, Millie arrived with warm water in an earthenware basin, fresh washcloth and sweet-smelling cotton towel. Miz Lucretia Borgia gently bathed his face and arms. Ellen and Millie watched so avidly and enviously that she tossed the damp cloth to them. "Now, you two wash him—down far as possible. Then you wash him up far as possible. Then you wash possible. . . . I wants him nice and clean and comfortable."

Finally they had him in his nightshirt. Miz Lucretia Borgia lifted him and Ellen and Millie fixed the sheet over him. Miz Lucretia Borgia fluffed up the pillows then she smoothed his damp hair off his forehead and kissed his cheek lightly.

Suddenly, she heeled around, all business. "Come on," she said to the girls. "We got lots to do—and only God knows how little time we got left."

The girls looked at each other, nervously. They nodded, following her.

Miz Lucretia Borgia shuddered involuntarily going out of the room, along the upper hall and down the stairwell. She'd be all right, as soon as she was busy again. She had to keep her mind occupied, that was it. She sent Millie and Ellen to the kitchen, ordering them to wrap a dozen loaves of bread in paper and sacks. When they wanted to know why, she swung her big arm at them and they ran silently to obey.

She started toward the front door. Then, remembering something, she stopped as if poled and clutched her hand over her heart. She turned and ran into the parlor. The breath sighed out of her. The toddy glass and tray were where she'd left them. She sagged against a chair a moment, weak with relief.

She washed out the glass, rinsing it in scalding water and putting it away among dozens of others precisely like it. Then she glanced around the kitchen and walked out the rear door, letting it screech and slam shut behind her.

XXXVIII

Slave artisans from the Falconhurst carpentry shop worked desultorily at the scaffolding. The sound of hammers and axes echoed and reverberated incessantly across the yard, silencing even the yellowhammers in the elms. Children crowded around, watching silently. Older slaves avoided the area in a kind of superstitious fear. The blazing sun spread the malignant shadow of the platform like a stain out upon the red earth.

Lucretia Borgia bit back illness. She stood a moment in the blaze of sunlight, squinting up at the raw new lumber. She called, "Timothy."

The head carpenter nodded and touched his cap to her as he might to the most genteel white lady. "Yes'm, Miz Lucretia Borgia, ma'am."

Lucretia Borgia exhaled, feeling a deep inner satisfaction. No doubt about it, her authority had been established here at Falconhurst. Long ago, she'd been accorded the title of "Miz" among the slaves, a title never used toward any black, reserved only for white persons. To every Negro on the huge plantation, from the lowliest youngster to the aging carpenter-shop foreman, she was Miz Lucretia Borgia. She had earned that title of respect and she took full advantage of it. However, she had infrequently directly countermanded an order from Masta Hammond Maxwell. She meant to do that now; she meant to impress her power, to fight, if necessary for what she wanted. This moment, if it did nothing else, would prove how much real control she held on this farm.

She swung her arm deprecatingly toward the execution platform. "Can take that thing down," she told Timothy.

He stared at her, incredulous, long arms hanging loosely at his side, nails between his teeth. "Who say?"

The other workers stopped, sagging, slack-shouldered, to watch Timothy and Miz Lucretia Borgia. She kept her voice level, almost unconcerned, as if its fate were unimportant to her. "Want that thing tore down, Masta Ham do. Want that wood all chopped up—fo' my stove kindlin'."

The aging carpenter shook his head, involuntarily. "Chopped up? Chopped up? Them's good studs, good milled lumber—"

"Chopped up. Masta Ham say he don't want to see it. Don't want nuthin' left to remind him. Don't want you even talkin' to him 'bout it. Now git it tore down."

Timothy looked ill. He drew his sleeve across his sweated forehead. He opened his mouth twice to speak but words failed him. He wanted to protest, he felt he should check this order with Masta Ham himself, but looking at Miz Lucretia Borgia's face, he knew better than to put these thoughts in words, much less into action. He looked around impotently, ineffectually. He could not believe what he was hearing. He had no view as to the good or evil of the hanging itself. This was not in his jurisdiction. But to destroy all this work, chop up lumber! He stood there, shaking his head.

"You hear me, Timothy?" Miz Lucretia Borgia pressured him.

"Yes'm, Miz Lucretia Borgia, ma'am, I sho' nuff hear you. Don't believe it. But I hear you." He shook his head again, spat the nails from between his discolored teeth and reluctantly gave the order to dismantle the new scaffolding.

Miz Lucretia Borgia wasted no time to see that her orders were carried out. She turned and walked, taking long, imperious steps toward the barns. She did not even glance back to see if she were being obeyed. There was something about the arch of her back that said her command had better be followed . . . to the letter.

She came into the shadowed barn. The place was dark after the brilliance of sunlight and smelled of hay, old leather and something which Miz Lucretia Borgia always supposed was the smell of barn rats.

"Pollux," she called. "You, Pollux. Where-at you, Pollux?"

When Little Pollux, after a brief tense delay, came sheepishly from the hay, buttoning his fly, she ignored what he'd been doing. She said only, "Masta Ham say hitch two of his best carriage horses—fast ones—to Miz Nell Murdoch's wagon."

"Our best horses—pulling that carriage of her'n?" Little Pollux shook his head, revolted at the suggestion.

Miz Lucretia Borgia shrugged. "You have that carriage up to my back porch in twenty minutes, or you gwine feel my hand—and not the way you been usin' yours."

He nodded, pliant but miserable. He knew better than to argue with Miz Lucretia Borgia, but the finest Falconhurst horses hitched to the rig the Murdoch lady had arrived here in . . . it wasn't fitting. "Yes'm, Miz Lucretia Borgia, ma'am. It be there."

"It better." She gave him a look which would remain a strong image in his mind for the length of time it would require to hitch the horses and deliver the wagon. He would not dare try to substitute lesser animals.

Miz Lucretia Borgia heeled around and walked from the shadowed darkness out into the sunlight of the yard. She did not look back.

Jingo Jim lounged outside the slave-jail cell. He sat on a wicker-bottom kitchen chair with his long legs propped against a wall before him. From hooded eyes, Jingo Jim watched Miz Lucretia Borgia walk toward him. The bounce of full, taut, melonlike breasts, the swing of broad hips tormenting and exciting him in the same imagery. A big woman. A lot of woman. Too much woman for most men. Ordinary men beware. Just right for him. He felt his breeches growing tight at the crotch.

He let his chair fall forward and he stood up, lazily, with the grace of a panther going on the prowl. "Howdy, Miz Lucretia Borgia, ma'am."

"Mawnin', Jim." Despite the anxiety festering inside her, Lucretia Borgia found him comely, too. She sighed heavily. "They all right in there?"

He shrugged. "They like you left 'em."

He smiled, his gaze caressing her, fondling her, returning to caress again. "They gwine be like that till time fo' the hanging. . . . Masta say I gone git to hang Tiger. First nigger I ever hung." He nodded, considering the honor, the responsibility, the terror.

Miz Lucretia Borgia shared no part of his pride. She shook her head. "I seen hangings. They no picnic, boy—"

"No. Reckon not. Didn't think they was."

"—you git sick to your belly, just watchin', head swinging crazy, eyes and tongue poppin' out. Puke jus' spills out of your mouth, want it to or not."

He winced, swallowed back a mite of bile, but forced a grin. "That you. A woman. Ain't me. . . . You a good woman, you jus' weak-hearted."

She met his gaze. "You think I a good woman, do you?"

He nodded enthusiastically, now on firm ground. "You the livin' best, Miz Lucretia Borgia. . . . Lawsy, I ain't been able to git you out'n my mind fo' more'n ten minutes at a time—long enough to eat." He laughed.

Miz Lucretia Borgia smiled with him and cuffed him, none too gently. Miz Lucretia Borgia was the kind of woman who, even when she was flirting, did it with all her heart. "I been thinkin' kindly on that thing of yourn, too, Jingo . . . you some well-sct-up buck, all right."

"Ain't had no complaints."

"Bet you ain't. . . . Reckon you gettin' too busy for a old settin' hen like me."

He stopped smiling, bending forward suddenly, his face serious and his dark eyes troubled. "Ain't nevah gone git you out'n my mind, Miz Lucretia Borgia."

She patted his cheek. "That nice."

His gaze held hers, challengingly. "Then when I gwine git you on a bed—way God meant?"

"I tole you. When they time, I gits on a bed with you. Ain't no time. Not now. Too much to do. An' how you know what God meant? God might of meant it standin' up—"

"I don't think so."

She laughed, pleased with him, with his seriousness. "I let you know. You hung fine as frog hair. . . . I look forward to pleasurin' with you—but not now. Ain't no time."

He glanced meaningfully down at the rigid bulge at his fly, forcing her gaze to follow. "I got a bad need."

She let her eyes loiter for a moment at his waist. She smiled slightly. "I see you has. . . . Purentee sin to waste something like that, an' that's a fact."

"Lawd knows that's a fact."

She appeared to consider for some seconds. "I might walk over to the hay barn," she mused at last.

He looked ill. "I got to guard this nigger."

She shrugged. "All right . . . you don't want it."

He caught her arm, sweating visibly along the dark caplinc of his thick hair. "Didn't say that. I got to be careful, that's all. . . . This nigger gits away, it come out'n my skin, Masta done say."

"It's all right. I understand."

"Now don't take that tone! When a gal say 'I understand' in that tone, you can bet yo' life she don't understand nuthin' at all."

"You sound like you know quite a lot about gals."

"I know they funny critters. I know that. But I also know I want you . . . so bad I willing to risk my neck. Can't say I could want you much more than that."

"No. That sounds like a lot of want."

"That's what I got. A lot of want."

She nodded. "Then git on over there to the hay barn—an' you wait for me. You wait, even if it gits dark."

"Dark? How long you 'spects me to wait?"

"Till I git there. You got plenty in your favor. I wants its jus' as bad as you. I hurry. I be there—soon's ever I can—"

"But *dark!*"

"You scairt of the dark, nigger?"

He grinned. "Not an' you there with me in it."

She nodded. "I'll be there. Now git. Mayhap if'n it git dark, I'll bring us a lantern."

"That'll be nice." He laughed, fondling her breasts impulsively, unable to resist. "But I find you anyhow—even in the dark."

She stood beside the slave-jail cell door until Jingo Jim had walked past the barn. He glanced back once and she waved. She threw him a kiss. He caught himself at the crotch, meaningfully, and she smiled and nodded and waved again.

When he was gone out of sight, she opened the cell door and stepped inside. Tige lay on the floor with his head in Nell's lap. Nell's face was gray, set. She looked as if she'd abandoned all hope, as if she would never cry again. Never cry for anything. Never care for anything.

Lucretia Borgia wasted no words. She spoke in a

level, matter-of-fact tone, but with urgency. "Come on. You-all gittin' out of here."

"Oh, no. I can't leave him, Lucretia Borgia." Nell shook her head. "Not now."

"Ain't leavin' him." Miz Lucretia Borgia knelt and unlocked the shackles. She returned the key to her pocket before either Tige or Nell fully comprehended that he was free.

"He's free?" Nell whispered, shaking her head, unable to believe it.

"Ain't free till he get back in the Texies," Miz Lucretia Borgia said. "But he free as I can help him be."

Tige got up, the chains falling away. He rubbed at his ankle, stirring the circulation. Nell sobbed suddenly, full realization hitting her. "Oh, Miz Lucretia Borgia. How? How did you do it? How can we ever thank you?"

"No time to thank me. Less time to tell you how I done nuthin'. . . . We gwine walk out of here and up to my back porch. We walk slow and easy. We don't look happy. We jus' look like I takin' you up to the house—mayhap to see Masta Ham." She shivered suddenly. "No matter what happen, you walk slow and you walk right with me, you hear?"

They stepped out of the cell into the sunlight. Tige and Nell hesitated. They blinked, blinded by the stunning sunlight. Lucretia Borgia touched their arms. They walked slowly across the yard. Never had the big ugly old manor house with its sweeping roof and gables and bay windows seemed so far away. A distant cow lowed. Small dogs sniffed at Nell's heels, sagged away into the shade of a chinaberry tree. Chickens clucked in the heat. Beyond the barn, the scaffolding was being dismantled.

Tige stared at the platform as it was being destroyed. He shook his head, unable to credit it. But he said nothing.

Before they reached the back porch, Mem came shuffling toward them. Lucretia Borgia felt her heart sink. Masta Hammond was awake! Roughly, she caught Mem's arm, shaking him without even meaning to. "What is it?" she said. "What's wrong?"

"Nuthin' wrong, Miz Lucretia Borgia." Mem looked ready to cry. "I done what you tole me. I jus' wanted to know what you reckon me to do now."

Lucretia Borgia nodded. She released her fierce grip on his arms and patted his shoulder. "You load them smoked hams, sweet potatoes, dried beans, coffee, syrup, and flour in the rear bed of that carriage of Miz Nell's. An' mind you pile it careful—but you move them boys fast. Don't let 'em dilly-dally, 'cause we in a kindly hurry."

Mem stared at Lucretia Borgia, glanced at Tige and Miss Nell. Slowly full comprehension of what was happening struck him. He shuddered, looking gray, eyes white-rimmed. "Masta—he gwine kill you."

Lucretia Borgia tilted her head. "Masta cain't kill me till he wakes up. He wakes up 'fore that carriage is loaded and gone, you gwine miss all the fun of seein' Masta kill me—'cause I gwine kill *you*. Right on the spot."

Nell stood, clinging to Miz Lucretia Borgia's hand, as the last of the provisions were loaded.

"Git in the wagon," Miz Lucretia Borgia said to Nell. She looked at Tige and tried to smile. "I don't have to tell you to travel fast as you can. . . ." She spread her hands. "I done all I can. Cain't do no more . . . cain't stop Masta Hammond do he wake up and take it in his head to set out after you."

Tige nodded. His eyes brimmed with tears. He helped Nell up to the front seat of the carriage. Then he turned and caught Miz Lucretia Borgia in his arms. He embraced her fiercely. "No right," he whispered. "No right to put you in this awful danger—and then run off and leave you."

She smiled. "You git on to your baby. You make 'em happy. Know it was real costive—and you got to work real hard they be happy."

He kissed her. "They'll be happy. I vow, Lucretia Borgia. But you—"

"Nevah mind me. I bin here—seems almost as long as Falconhurst been here. . . . I be here—I go on bein' here." She clung to him for one more moment.

He turned away and climbed into the wagon beside Nell. All the folks in the yard stood unmoving. Dust smoked back over them as Tige drove out of the tree-lined Falconhurst drive and headed west on the main trace.

XXXIX

Lucretia Borgia stood unmoving in the sunlight until Tige's carriage turned on the trace and raced toward the Texies. She watched until the speeding vehicle was gone, until there were only clouds of dust smoking upward through the copse and finally the dust itself dissipated and blew away on the wind. She was conscious of her black folks around her in silent knots, the ordinary rural sounds of farm animals and fowls and of a tension in the very atmosphere unlike any she'd ever experienced before.

She sighed, looking around the familiar farmyard. She'd done what had to be done. It seemed to her that she had somehow secured the serenity and strength of Falconhurst by removing Tige from threat of Masta Hammond's hang rope. No matter what Masta Hammond was going to say, her first thought had been for him, for her beloved Masta Ham. She had seen him torn apart with turmoil and anguish before when driven to violence—violence which violated the inner goodness which she saw in him and goodness which he ignored in living according to a code imposed from outside himself. She knew that something of Hammond Maxwell had died when Mede was slain. And an evil miasma had settled over Falconhurst, and in the eight years since Mede's tragic murder, that leaden cloud had only finally lifted. For a long time when a slave child screamed in its sleep, everyone knew why—that child was reliving murder, as it had witnessed it, as it sometimes saw it still. . . .

She shivered involuntarily. She was thankful Tige and Nell had gotten away. She had done for them all she could—at what cost to herself remained to be seen. Still, she wouldn't have behaved differently. She would have to pay, but she had figured that cost, too. She wouldn't think about any of that now.

She drew the back of her hand across her eyes. It was not so easy to put it all from her mind. There were no magic words to make it all go away. No matter what she wished, it all remained: what she had done, and what retaliation she could expect from Masta Hammond. She had wanted to help the two young people and equally she had hated defying Masta Ham, and more than that she had feared putting her own life in forfeit. In the end, she had chosen to help Tige, not because she loved the young mustee and his young wife but because she loved this great plantation. She had been its surrogate mistress. She had kept it solvent and functioning—yes, and according to Herman Hengst's figures, profitable!—almost singlehandedly for eight long years. This place was her home, her own land, her roots were sunk in this red soil. And most of all, she loved Masta Ham and wanted to protect him from himself—from the evil which sometimes possessed and threatened to destroy him. Because she did love Masta Ham, she regretted what she had done to oppose and thwart him, but it had been necessary, vital and urgent. No matter what it cost her, she had done only what she had to do.

Despite herself, her thoughts whipped backward to that moment of panic and sorrow and compassion which had warred inside her earlier this morning when she fixed that hot toddy for her beloved Masta Ham. She'd sent the least child from her kitchen, complaining they were always underfoot, though they knew as well as she did that she loved them there.

Alone in that pantry, she had splashed sweetening and corn whiskey into the toddy glass—in most generous portions. Then, her heart slugging so hard it ached against her rib cage, she reached out and took down the bottle of laudanum given her by Dr. Redfield. "It'll knock a sufferin' patient out, and he'll rest till the pain lets up." Doc Redfield had been talking about the wounded slave, but to Lucretia Borgia, pain of the heart and soul and spirit could be as intolerable as any physical anguish. The evil moiled in Masta Ham, the stubborn set of his mind to do violence, the conflicts making him wild—all these seemed as much human ills as a broken leg to Lucretia Borgia. All she could think was, if only she could calm Masta Ham down, quiet him, force him to think with that sweet side of him which she believed to be a major part of his nature, then the violence would end. . . .

"Wonder what Masta Ham gwine say?" Mem said. Despite a deep secret delight that the biggety Lucretia Borgia was going to have her wings clipped, he was frightened. His voice shook and his shoulders slumped rounder than ever in his aged rust-black frock coat.

Lucretia Borgia's gaze impaled him. "Say? Masta Ham say? 'Bout what, nigga?"

Mem winced under her withering glance and retreated slightly within his shell like a disturbed turtle, but he stood his ground. " 'Bout you, that's who. You. Lettin' that mustee nigger go free. That nigger what Masta Ham planned most fondly on hangin'—hangin' wif quality white folks a-comin' from miles around to watch. What he gwine say 'bout that, Lucretia Borgia?"

"That's for me to worry about," she told him.

"I'd be doin' me up some fancy worryin' was I you," he mumbled. "Sick with worry."

She tilted her head, her red bandana catching sunlight like a furled banner. "Yes. Well, you ain't me.

413

You ain't nevah gwine be me. You jus' a triflin' nigga, 'fraid to think for hisself. Triflin' niggers and white trash. Ain't nuthin' lower on God's earth." But Lucretia Borgia's mockery lacked its old fire and spirit. She was worried.

Suddenly Lucretia Borgia shuddered, visibly frightened. A cold chill wracked her body in the intense heat. What she had done was right. There was not the least question in her mind about this. There had been no other alternative. But how was Masta Ham going to view her insubordination, her defiance, her betrayal? Right had very little weight in that real world where Masta Ham ruled and where Miz Lucretia Borgia passed the days of her life. No matter her inestimable value to this farm, her grasp on power or life was tenuous at best. Whims, vagaries, transient indispositions and cruel learned prejudices of white people were the staples of her existence. She lived or died at the casual pleasure of some white person. Right was a meaningless word in her world.

"Masta Ham, he gwine take the hide off your back," Mem said, nodding sagely. He dared not smile.

"I done what was right." Her voice rang, stubborn.

"We see 'bout that, when Masta Ham wakes up."

"You ain't gwine frighten me, nigger. I learned— things may not evah be as good as you hope, but they seldom bad as you fear, either."

Now Mem did permit himself the trace of a taunting smile. "Things don't have to be near as bad as I think they gwine be—and you still in a passel of woe."

She ignored Mem. She waved her arm, dispersing the silent, troubled black people grouped around her. They walked away, mumbling to each other as if afraid to speak aloud in this fearful day.

For some moments, Lucretia Borgia went on standing in the bare, hot sand of the yard. There was much to do and yet she lacked the will to pick up the strands of her life again. It was as if she wanted to delay this moment before the onslaught of the storm. She had to face facts. Masta Ham was a wilfull, stubborn, unyielding man. Though in the deepest wells of his heart and mind he might abhor the senseless murder of an innocent eighteen-year-old boy, once he had set his course, he could not be swayed, deterred or altered. Worse, she had betrayed him openly before his peers—the plantation quality folks invited by him to see a Negro hung as an example to other blacks. There was no way she could discover a glimmer of hope that Masta Hammond could ever forgive this mortification.

She glanced about helplessly. The familiar old plantation seemed to float in a gray mist of strange terrors. Everything was superficially the same—the maples, the chinaberry, the tall pines, the wide-reaching live oaks, the road into Benson, the patches of clouds in the faded sky, the animals at graze, the rows of slave shanties, the work barns, the ugly old manor house—everything the same, and somehow this was most disturbing of all. Everything was unchanged and yet nothing was the same at all.

Nothing would ever be the same again. She could delay the moment when she faced Masta Hammond, but she could not escape it.

Lucretia Borgia wiped her dankly moist hands on the checked front of her apron. She should be able to find some security. She'd devoted her adult life to this place and to its owners. She'd been reviled here, scourged and honored. Blacks called her Miz Lucretia Borgia, ma'am, and feared her more than they feared the Maxwells in the big house or God in His heaven. But she had never been secure—she'd been sold off like any other common slave. Sooner or later every slave was sold off at Falconhurst. There was no profit in aged and useless blacks, and Falconhurst dealt in profits. She'd been sent to New Orleans years ago, and she'd run away from that city, and she'd come back here, walking, like a stray cat. Warren and Hammond Maxwell had welcomed her warmly then. That hiatus in her service to them had been enough—more than enough, old Warren Maxwell used to tell her!—to convince them that Lucretia Borgia *was* Falconhurst, as Falconhurst was Lucretia Borgia.

"It my *home*," she whispered to no one in particular.

She heard a commotion upstairs; she felt the rushing of sick fear through her body. Masta Ham might be waking. Or, worse, since she'd doubled Doc Redfield's prescribed dosage of laudanum in Masta Hammond's toddy, Masta Ham might be writhing in death throes.

She shrugged her calico dress up on her broad shoulders. Whatever it was going on up there, she had to go up, she had to face anything that was ahead for her. She wouldn't run away.

"I ain't gwine run," she thought. "But I don't have to pretend I ain't too scairt to think straight—and jus' when I needs most to think clear."

She walked toward the house as if toward the gallows. She was going to face it, but God knew, this could be anything—death, mutilation, the whips, anything Masta Ham's mind concocted in its rage and turmoil. She drew her breath and held it. It would not be the whips. This she silently vowed.

The need to ensure she died before she was ever stripped naked and publicly whipped and humiliated, roused her. Spurred by the necessity to shield herself against that intolerable injury, she climbed the plank steps at the rear of the old house and entered the kitchen, letting the screen door slam shut behind her.

Ellen, Millie, Mem and the dozen other kitchen helpers sat around the big pine table, helpless and rudderless without her to direct and prod them. This morning, in her anxiety, she ignored them. Even when they questioned her directly, she appeared not to hear them. She went to the cutlery drawer and selected the sharpest carving knife. Its stone-honed blade glit-

416

tered as she lifted it. She dropped it into the full pocket sewn into her apron.

Ellen came across the room to her. "What we goin' tell Masta Ham, Miz Lucretia Borgia? What we goin' say to Masta Ham when he wakes up?"

Lucretia Borgia sighed heavily. "We gwine say to him what we got to say."

Ellen waved her hand impatiently; she had no time for riddles. "What we got to say?"

Lucretia Borgia sighed and met Ellen's gaze evenly. Her voice was very low, but not defeated. "What we got to say to save our skins, that's what." She licked at her lips and watched Ellen narrowly. "Like, you recall that Masta Ham wasn't total unconscious when you come in the parlor and found him on the floor?"

Stunned, Ellen frowned, her face going blank. "What?"

Hardly knowing where she was going, acting from an ancient instinct for self-preservation, Lucretia Borgia persisted. "You remember . . . Masta Ham tole me—tole me what to do . . . when he tole me to send Miss Nell and Tige away. . . . Recall? You must recall. . . . He was afraid he goin' to die . . . say he no way wanted to die with that hangin' on his conscience."

"I don't remember him saying that." Ellen's eyes wavered under Lucretia Borgia's, going bleak. She retreated, shaking her head.

Lucretia Borgia's mouth twisted. "Maybe you recall sneakin' into that mustee Herman Hengst's bedroom at night when you thought I was asleep. You recall that, don't you? Slippin' in there like a cat in heat—night after night—when you knowed Masta Ham vowed you to be his'n—an' his'n only—touched by nobody else. Reckon you done fo'got all that, too."

Ellen's tea-rose cheeks went pallid. "But I—was so lonely, Lucretia Borgia . . . all those years . . . surely, you understand."

Lucretia Borgia shrugged. "Sho'. I understand. I understand how pretty that German mustee was, too. I seen how he was hung. Sho', I know all about needin' and bein' lonely. . . . Sho', I understand. . . . All you got to do is pray that Masta Ham—he understand."

Ellen seemed to crumble inside, though she did not move at all. "Oh God, Lucretia Borgia," she whispered, "would you do that—would you tell Masta Ham— about that?" She caught her arm in icy fingers. "You know how jealous Masta Ham be—he likely kill me you tell him that."

Lucretia Borgia shrugged. "Seems like you ought to be able to recall the way Masta Ham talked—rambling—before he passed out. I was bending close over him and mayhap I heard him better than you, but I swear you was standing beside me and heard it all, most all, anyhow. You had to—the part about callin' off the hangin', an' sending Tige and Miss Nell away. . . ."

Ellen looked ill, as if she might vomit, but at last, she nodded.

XL

Lucretia Borgia dared breathe more easily. She was not safe yet, not out of the woods, but she felt better because she was taking some action, even if it proved futile. She was still alive, she was still trying, and where there was life Miz Lucretia Borgia never stopped hoping. She had a great and abiding faith in her gods—and in herself. Now that Ellen had agreed to support her—because she had left her no alternative!—she felt as if she'd found slippery footing in a raging stream. She hadn't made it across, but she was still on her feet. Some of her old vitality flowing through her again, she sent the loitering slaves into a flurry of activity. "Got to git to bakin'. Cookin'. Quality folks coming. Cain't none of you stand round here with yo' fingers in your bottoms. Now move!"

She took a long thirsty swallow of water from a gourd dipper. Her mouth felt parched. She gripped the gourd handle tightly, because she didn't like to see her hand tremble.

She glanced around her at the hurrying kitchen helpers, hearing no sound except the rutching of bare feet on the scrubbed pine flooring. She would face Masta Ham as bravely as possible. He might punish her—he might kill her. Well, she would pluck that chicken when she caught it. Only if he attempted to have her publicly whipped would she take violent exception.

419

She would die first. Her hand tightened on the knife in her apron pocket.

She was brought abruptly from depths of her reverie by something tugging at her skirt. She trembled involuntarily and had to bite down on her underlip to keep from crying out. She stared down at the dark-skinned urchin who gazed back up at her from ebony eyes the size of gold eagles.

"What you want, boy?" she said. "Ain't got no bread puddin' for the likes of you this here time of the day."

"Don't crave no bread puddin', thank-ee, Miz Lucretia Borgia, ma'am," the child said. His own wistful eyes branded him liar, and, even troubled as she was, Lucretia Borgia jerked her head toward Nellie, signaling her to spoon up a dish of bread pudding for the boy.

"What you want then?" she said.

"It's Jingo Jim, Miz Lucretia Borgia, ma'am."

Something stirred inside her, the urge to laughter and the sudden fierce heat of passion—that ultimate escape from any of life's woes. She remembered sending Jingo Jim to await her in the hay barn. She bit back her smile. "What 'bout Jingo Jim?"

"Please, ma'am, he say he dyin' of waitin', Miz Lucretia Borgia, ma'am. . . . He say to tell you you don't come soon won't be nuthin' left for you when you do git there."

She laughed. "You tell Jingo Jim I say to hang on to what he got."

The boy looked frightened. "Please, ma'am, he say you might say that—to hang on to what he got. He say that the trouble now, Miz Lucretia Borgia, ma'am, he say he done hang on so long—he nigh 'bout wrung its neck."

She scrubbed her hand through his tightly kinky hair affectionately—as she loved the sender, so she found delight in the messenger. There were few secrets on this farm, even from the least child. Tragedy. Murder.

420

Averted murder. Whatever happened for good or ill, life went on at Falconhurst, and Falconhurst was first above all a Negro stud farm. The children grew up from infancy seeing life in its natural course. "You eat yo' puddin'," she told the child. "I reckon I best git along to see 'bout pore ole Jingo Jim."

She walked across the bare, sun-struck yard, feeling the juices stir inside her, stewing out the fears. Her step was springy. She knew her hips bounced youthfully and her melonlike bosom bobbled against the restraining fabric of her calico dress for the world to see, nipples bold. Maybe she wasn't so old, after all. Perhaps life wasn't ugly and fearful and threatening. She walked faster, smiling.

She was most gratifyingly aware of the heated gazes fixed on her, the knowing smiles, the undeceived glances, the envious eyes. She straightened her shoulders, flaunting her breasts even farther forward.

As she came around the side of the hay barn, she stopped, feeling as if her heart had stopped. "Mem!" She cursed him. "What in hell are you doin' here?"

"Cryin'," he said truthfully. "Beggin' you, Miz Lucretia Borgia . . . don't do this . . . you make me laughin' stock 'fore all these folks."

"You makes your own self a laughin' stock, sneakin' around, spyin' on me. Followin' me. Now you git back to that house, or I swear I git you sold away frum here. I swear it."

He stood, slack-shouldered, crying helplessly for a moment, and then he turned and slunk away.

She brushed away the thought of Mem as of no more importance than a pesky deerfly. She patted at her dress, straightened her turban and dampened her lips with the tip of her tongue. She felt as excited as a sixteen-year-old. More. Few sixteen-year-olds knew what she knew.

She pushed open the door of the hay barn and halted just inside, blinking and bat-blind in the cavernous darkness after the blaze of sunlight. Finally, she discovered Jingo Jim. He sprawled on a pad of loose hay; he looked sweated, depleted.

"Well, if'n it ain't Miz Lucretia Borgia. . . . You sho' took yo' time a-gittin' here."

"Been busy. Still busy," Lucretia Borgia said. "I here now. . . . Don't waste my time frettin' 'bout things you can't change."

"Thought you wasn't comin' a-tall," he complained.

"Told you I'd be here. Now come here. I in a hurry."

"Damn. You always in a hurry." But Jingo Jim stood up, lazily, as pretty as a black man could be, Miz Lucretia Borgia thought, pleased and aroused. Strong-thewed he was, his shoulders as wide as a barn door, his belly as flat as a hound dog's, his dark, muscular body unblemished. "You always in some fuckin' hurry, Lucretia Borgia."

She laughed and kissed him. "That why I here, Jingo Jim. I in a *fuckin'* hurry."

He laughed. His hands closed on her overfull breasts and fondled them lovingly, but roughly, greedily. "Been thinkin' 'bout your tits somethin' fierce. Ever since that last time—remember?"

"I 'member last time we done it here, we done it dog-fashion," she said. "We got to do it that way again." She closed her hand on the bulge at his crotch.

"Why? Dammit. Why?"

"You actin' mighty biggety—like you own me, boy. . . . You don't. An' I tell you why we got to do it like that—or don't do it a-tall—"

"Oh, we do it!"

"—'cause we got trouble at the big house. I ought not be here. 'Cause if Masta Ham cotch us pleasurin' right now, he'd likely kill us both. . . . An' mostly 'cause you big and hard and pretty—and I wants it terrible bad."

His voice sounded forlorn. "When I gone git you nekkid in a bed?"

"When I ready." She kissed him passionately while she loosened the buttons on his Osnaburg cut-offs. His breath quickening, he dipped into the loose bodice of her frock and spilled her high-standing breasts free. Her nipples stood rigid. He fell upon them, suckling and nuzzling hungrily. She laid her head back for a long moment and enjoyed the ecstasy that flooded through her. This might well be her last pleasuring on this earth. She savored every flaring delight of it.

She let him fondle and suckle at her breasts for a long time. With one hand she hoisted her skirts above her hips. She found the knife an obstacle and removed it. "Good God," he whispered and took the glittering utensil from her. He tossed it behind him into the hay. She was too weak with desire to protest. Expertly, she knotted her skirt at her waist, baring her hips, thighs and shapely legs to him.

"Gawd, you lovely," he said. He panted helplessly, grinning. "You what my dreams are about, Lucretia Borgia—all my wet dreams."

"That do seem a waste," she agreed, smiling sleepily. She released his quiveringly rigid staff from his fly and turned her back to him. She bent forward, her smooth breasts hanging like mammoth clusters of dark grapes, her hips gleaming creamily in the musty darkness.

She braced herself against the loft ladder. Her rounded legs, set apart, braced her body like immovable pillars. For long moments they held fiery tableau, enraptured. He drove himself into her as if he meant to destroy her. He thrust upward on the balls of his feet, his toes digging into the hard-packed earth. He sweated, the muscles in his calves, tendons in his ankles and along the backs of his legs aching in exquisite agony.

"Harder," she gasped. "Deeper." She whispered it

in ecstatic command until he hated her. Great globules of sweat dripped from his face to her upthrust hips. He chewed at his mouth, forcing himself to wait until he heard her helpless moaning which would signal her orgasm. If he let go first he was afraid he would fall and he'd never satisfy her—he'd never see her again, and God knew he couldn't stand that. She was a lot of woman, but she was what he wanted. His mouth bled and sweat drizzled along his hairline, into his eyes, down his cheeks and over his neck. A man was a man if he overwhelmed her—and he meant to drive her to her knees. He grasped her breasts, squeezing her nipples, and worked himself pistonlike, growing giddy and dizzy and wild with pleasure and pain.

Gasping for breath, he sucked in a lungful of air and thrust fiercely. She moaned. She moaned again, her moans growing in intensity to a helpless, keening wail of delight and total surrender.

Jingo Jim laughed, his own blood and sweat tasting hot and salty in his mouth. He closed his hands brutally over her breasts and made one final lunging drive. The very life seemed to erupt from him into her. He bucked convulsively, helplessly. Then, his legs too weak to support him, he crumpled to the ground and sagged against a mound of hay. "Gawd," he whispered into the dried grass, "my Gawd, Lucretia Borgia, that was almighty satisfyin'. . . ."

She bent down and kissed him affectionately. She was tired, too, exhausted. She longed to sprawl beside him in the hay, but she knew better. "You pretty good today," she said in her half-taunting tone. "Better'n usual, even. . . . One of these heah nights, I gwine send fo' you . . . we have all night together . . . nekkid in a bed."

He nodded and smiled, too depleted to speak. He felt wrung out, trembling with physical weakness.

"Got to go now, Jingo Jim." She gazed down at him, her smile warm and her dark eyes liquid with approval.

He nodded again but did not move.

Pulling bits of hay from her apron and bandana, Lucretia Borgia shook out her skirts and patted out the wrinkles. She stepped out of the barn door and let it close behind her. She sagged a moment against it, closing her eyes against the pitiless lances of sunlight. She rested there as much to inform the curious who might be watching as to regain her strength. Let them niggers see her. She was some woman. Enough for any two men. Too much for one man. An army with banners. The only way to die. She smiled, thinking about Jingo Jim lying helplessly in that barn on the ground, and her full lips twisted into a pleasant-tasting smile. . . .

XLI

Lucretia Borgia glimpsed Hammond Maxwell as he stepped from the shadowed gallery and strode down the front steps of the plantation house. All warmth and remembered ecstasy dissolved into bile and fear that roiled in her stomach. She watched him plod in violent haste, limping toward her. Fright shook her and she glanced around wildly, looking for a place to run. Her heart sank, battering erratically. Her legs trembled, almost too weak to support her, but she did not retreat. Instead, she shifted her dress up on her shoulders, slapped at her apron and walked faster. She met him in the crosshatching shade of a chinaberry tree. The rest of the world hung suspended in tense silence around them.

Hammond's face was deathly pale, his pallid cheeks rigid, his faded blue eyes cold. He still looked confused, disoriented, but rage spurred him. "Damn you, Lucretia Borgia, what in hell's going on here?" he said.

She did not answer at once, and, watching her, Ham winced. He had been prepared to pound her into some kind of submission, to beat the truth from her with his fists, if necessary. Something was terribly wrong—the nausea in his stomach, the spinning in his head, the cottony taste of his mouth. But she was a distinguished-looking woman, despite her color, despite status as servant for life. Her gaze was level with his,

427

humble but unflinching. His fists clenched. Damn her! He wanted answers. He would have them from her.

"Now, ain't you a purty sight?" he heard himself demanding. "This here place can go straight to hell, long as you a-gittin' pestered by some young buck." This was nothing he had meant to say. There was so much that had to be explained, so much he meant to hear from her, but he was still fighting butterflies in his belly, the wheeling dizziness in his brain. He didn't know where to begin.

He'd waked up a long time ago; how long, he had no idea. He lay in bed wondering how in hell he got there, unable to make sense of the fragmented scenes that flashed across his mind, all out of focus. He was aware of fresh sheets, cool morning breezes through opened windows and a warm sense of his floating in an insubstantial world.

It was a long time before he could reconstruct any part of what had happened to him, and none of this was clear, nothing had a time frame. Why was he in bed? Why was he drifting in warm mists? Why did his body seem weightless? Where in hell was everybody?

He heard commotion in the yard. He wanted to get up from the bed and investigate from his window, but he could not force his body to move. He could only lie there, helpless prey to unreasoning fear. He'd had a stroke, a heart attack, he had fainted? What in hell had happened? What about the hanging?

He stirred on the bed. He'd invited people from nearby plantations to view a hanging. He couldn't lie here a slug-a-bed. Neighbors must be arriving by now.

But still he did not move. A hanging? Another violent death? God almighty, hadn't there been death and violence enough at Falconhurst? It was almost as if destruction and pain were the heritage of this plantation. He didn't want to hang Tiger. Justice played no role in his decision. If Tiger had killed a white man—

and Tiger admitted this!—then Tiger had to die. That his execution should not be a waste, his hanging had to be a public punishment as example to other blacks. This was his responsibility, and he didn't shirk this.

He closed his eyes tightly. It was the actual lynching which sickened and revolted him. If only they could hang the mustee, hang him quickly and cleanly and have it done with. If only it ended when the boy died, there would be no problem. But violence never ended with its ebb, never allowed any surcease—God knew he'd learned that from Mede's death. No, it never ended. Once the actual hanging was accomplished, it became an evil image to return and torment him, to rob his sleep, to poison his mind, to shape his nightmares. He had been through all this after he'd slain Mede. God knew, he'd been younger then, a boy. But he'd seen too much now; he had neither the heart nor the stomach for it.

Lying there, he pressed his arm over his face as if warding off physical attack. He had started this fearful atrocity—this public hanging. There was no retreat. And then, his mind clearing, he remembered Lucretia Borgia's arguing with him against the execution. Gradually, he recalled his drinking, his wrangling with Lucretia Borgia, so that even his drinking another hot toddy became an act of defiance, Damn her argufying soul! He couldn't abide a black with a smart mouth. Lucretia Borgia had risen too high. It was time she was slapped down and slapped down hard.

Suddenly, his eyes filled with tears. He must be weak, ill, unmanned to cry like a woman, to admit inner weakness. But despite his best efforts to blot out the images, he saw Lucretia Borgia holding him when he broke his leg. How tender and loving she'd been! He'd gone away from here and left her with his invalid father to care for. She'd run this place, even made a profit. Damn it. That didn't change the color of her skin, gave her no right to get uppity and telling him what to do. This he would not tolerate.

He forced himself to get out of bed. He drank great drafts of water from the earthenware pitcher. He scrubbed his face with cold water. He yelled for Mem and sat on the edge of the bed while the Negro forced his boots on his awkwardly unbending leg. He dressed. He had no heart to punish Lucretia Borgia. He remembered the last thing she'd cautioned him, he was drinking too much. She was thinking about his best interests, even then.

A man had to make decisions within himself; he had to do what he himself saw as right. He had to face what society demanded of him—living by the code, earning the respect of his peers—against what he wanted inside himself. The hell of it was, no man acquired the real wisdom to know what to do—at least not in time to save himself from hell. Reason and compassion came only slowly, almost thrust upon him. He learned to accept what life dealt him, and react in a way that made it possible to live in peace with himself. Maybe this was the only real wisdom. But had he ever found inner peace?

He walked out of the room, deeply troubled. Maybe what happened to any man—for good or ill—is most often beyond his control. He can determine only his own responses. If there is a plan in this existence, it was too complex, too deep and too mysterious for him to grasp. And finally a man accepts that he is only a grain of sand buffeted in overwhelming cosmic winds. He cannot shape existence, he can only live inside himself in a way that permits him to remain sane and self-respecting. If a man can meet his own eyes mornings in a mirror, he was doing all he could hope.

Now, he stared at Lucretia Borgia in the blazing morning sun. He swung his arm. "Who told you to tear down the gallows scaffolding?"

Her voice was bland. "Why, you did, Masta."

"I did? When?"

"Lawdy, Masta." She looked ready to weep. "Don't you recall? You drank that toddy I begged and begged you not to—"

"Never mind that," said Ham shakily.

Lucretia Borgia felt encouraged but tried not to show it. She bit her lip, nodded. "Yas suh. . . . then you fell down on the floor—"

"I remember that."

"You lay there, Masta. I was sick, scairt. And you was fearful you was dyin' . . . you begged us to send Nell and Tige away—stop the hanging. Oh, Masta, don't you 'member telling Lucretia Borgia?" She let herself wail and a flood of tears came very easily.

"Why, Ellen was there, Masta. Don't you recall? Ellen and me bending over you, frightened you was dying . . . oh, Masta Ham, it was terrible. Thank God you is all right." She grabbed his hand, kissing it wetly.

He jerked his hand away. "Ellen was there—with you?"

Lucretia Borgia's face contorted with concern for her beloved master. "Oh, Masta, don't you recall?"

"Damm it, I don't recall."

She lowered her head, her voice faltering. "You wants me to call Ellen? You can question her."

"No." He made a sharp downward gesture and then quickly pressed both hands against the shattering pain in his temples. "No . . . one lyin' nigger is too many for me." He stared toward the trace. "So they gone. You sent that murderin' mustee free—"

"I done what you tole me, Masta—"

"Stop that. Goddammit. I tole you. I don't believe you—"

"You wants me to call Ellen, Masta?"

He glared at her. "Reckon I could get the slave patrollers and run them down."

"Yas suh."

He licked his tongue across his feathery lips, almost overcome with thirst. "Jesus. What we goin' to do? All them folks comin'. They expect a hangin'. . . . Goddammit. I ought to hang you."

"All right, Masta."

"Damn you. I don't credit this look of innocence, all these tears and carryin' on. I know you behind this—I know you lyin' to me. . . . Damn you. You are behind this. Don't know how yet, but when I do find out, I whup you like you never been whupped."

Lucretia Borgia's voice was flat, dead, but determined. "No, Masta."

His head jerked up. At first he wasn't sure he'd heard her—not even Lucretia Borgia would dare speak in such brazen defiance. "What? Goddam you, you black slut. What did you say to me? What?"

He stepped forward, hulking over her menacingly. She turned to clabber inside, but she remained standing tall, her head tilted, that red bandana catching the sun. She shook her head firmly. "No, Masta. Nevah gwine whip Lucretia Borgia again on this earth. Nobody. Whupped her once . . . hung her by her heels. Nekkid. 'Fore the whole plantation of niggers. But no more."

"Damn your hide. How dare you talk back to me like that."

"Don't mean no disrespect, Masta. . . . But I nevah be whupped again—"

"We'll see about that, you black bitch." He shook his head, trying to bring her into focus. He felt weak, woozy, so dizzy the earth and sky changed places and Lucretia Borgia spun wildly about his head.

He thrust his hand out, grabbed her arm. His fingers closed with fearful pressure. He stepped toward her, glaring down at her, but the spinning, wheeling figure before him remained unaltered in one way, her face remained stubbornly set against him. "Damn you. I will flog you . . . you nevah go against me again . . .

432

you nevah raise your black voice to me again . . . by God, when them folks arrive, they gone see a whuppin' they nevah fo'git."

She shook her head. His hand tightened. Her silent defiance enraged him more. "Kin have you whupped when I say," he raged.

She simply watched him, her eyes bleak but dry and unyielding.

"Kin!" he yelled at her. "Kin! And by God, I will. . . ." He spun her from him. She twisted, lost her balance and sprawled on the ground just beyond the fringe of shadow.

"No, Masta." She stared up at him and she whispered it, but there was steel in her voice, and he heard her. He looked around wildly. Damn her! He was certain the whole plantation heard her insolence and defiance.

"Hell take you," he said, his voice shaking with rage, his face fiery, veins throbbing in his temples. "You don't think I master here? I show you who master here if I plain has to whop you to death. . . . I show you—I master of Falconhurst."

She did not move. She remained sprawled on the ground, her gaze fixed on his. He stared at her, raging, helpless, infuriated. He turned on his heel and strode away, limping, both hands pressed against the sides of his head.

XLII

Lucretia Borgia lay on the ground after Hammond crossed the yard, entered the old house, the door slamming shut behind him. She felt as if she were destroyed. She had no wish to move. The entire population of this farm had witnessed the final break between her and her beloved Masta Ham. Plenty of them would exult in her fall from grace. Old Lucy. Mem. How many others? Ellen? Millie? Most had felt the back of her hand, the singe of her scorn, and resentment festered, tamped down inside them. It would spurt forth now, like champagne from a bottle.

She no longer cared. No matter that she belonged here, that this place was her home, that she had kept it all together. It was over. She would not be hung up like a slaughtered beef for the cut of the whip, for the sportive, aphrodisiacal delight of white people—humiliated, tortured, tormented, whipped. No.

Listlessly, she pushed herself upward. She stood erect and brushed sand and litter from her dress and apron. She straightened her red bandana. Emptily, she glimpsed Jingo Jim in the gawking group at the big barn, Little Pollux, Omar and the others. Jingo Jim looked ill. He stared at her, sick, helpless. Clearly, he wanted to aid her, but he was afraid of retribution from the master. They all were. Those who were not elated to see how low Lucretia Borgia had fallen were too frightened to come near her. She didn't blame them. Let them live as protected lives as possible. It no longer mattered.

She heard footsteps near her, and a truncated shadow bobbed along beside hers, stopped. She felt a hand, gentle and timid, on her arm, apprehensive yet supportive. She turned, and tears sprang unwanted into her eyes.

Mem tried to smile. "You all right, Lucretia Borgia?"

She managed to smile. "I'm all right."

"Walk with you to the house," he said.

She nodded again. She walked beside Mem across that interminable distance to the big house. Mem held open the kitchen door, and she entered the room which had been her domain for so many years. She sat down at the pinewood table. Mem brought her a cup of steaming black coffee. She smiled and nodded, thanking him silently, but she did not touch it.

She was unsure how long she sat there, aware only that she determined in her own mind what she would do now. Everything was clearly mapped out for her. She gathered enough strength to order the workers from the kitchen, all of them, even Mem.

Alone, she traversed the silent room to the pantry. She entered and took down the bottle of laudanum Doc Redfield had given her. There remained only a few drams in the bottom of the glass. She turned it up and drank it slowly, taking the last slow drop on her tongue. "Don't need much," she reminded herself. "Enough to make easier what I do—not enough to stop me."

She went back to the kitchen table and sat down. She waited with great patience for the euphoric haze which she hoped would numb her mind to pain and reality. She loved life too fiercely to relinquish it easily.

Although the laudanum did not obliterate her agony, nor fully deaden her will to live, to survive, to overcome, it did ease her mind so that Lucretia Borgia sank into a lethargic, drowsy state of sleepiness. In this soporific half-world, it did not really matter whether she lived or not. And since she had made up her mind to die, she could calmly accept her decision and quietly carry it out. It was almost as though all this were happening to someone else and she stood safe and secure in her familiar kitchen, watching without even a very great interest.

She touched at the pocket of her apron, seeking her knife. Something was amiss and her sluggish mind spun, trying to find the wrong. She knew she had placed that knife in her pocket. That knife, honed to razor sharpness and kept ready against this terrible day; it was missing. She remembered dropping it into her apron pocket in that agonized presentiment of tragedy.

She scrubbed her fingers at her forehead. She got up and crossed the room to the cutlery drawer, her slipper heels clapping. She opened the drawer and stared at the knives laid out in their holders. Her knife was not there. Finally, memory wormed its way through the velvety haze clouding her mind. Jingo Jim. He had thrown her knife carelessly behind them— in the hay barn.

She nodded, pleased at this memory. The hay barn was well removed from the mainstream of ordinary farm activity. This time of the day it would be restful, silent and heated with pleasant memories for her. A nice place to die.

Sighing, she closed the drawer and turned. She stood some moments, letting her gaze fondle the furnishings of this familiar room. The awful realization that she was seeing this place for the last time penetrated into the deep dimness of her mind and shook her visibly. It took several minutes to drive away the agony of grief and loss.

She walked slowly across the room to the screen door. She heard a movement in the shadowed kitchen behind her, but she did not care. She did not turn around. It had nothing to do with her anymore.

"Lucretia Borgia." It was Mem's voice.

She turned in exaggerated slowness and braced herself against the doorjamb. "Let me alone, Mem," she said.

"Where you goin'?"

"It don't matter. . . . Ain't no way none of your business, Mem."

"Don't go, Lucretia Borgia. Please."

She saw his dark face was contorted with grief. The pain of jealousy. She realized he believed she was on her way to pleasure young Jingo Jim. Poor Mem. She had treated him badly. She tried to smile. "It's all right, Mem."

He shook his head. "No. Ain't all right." He drew a deep, ragged breath. "You mine, Lucretia Borgia. Old Master Warren say."

Her smile widened, gentle and kindly. How many years ago had old Masta Warren told Mem that Lucretia Borgia was his to cover? Twenty years? Twenty-five? Only poor Mem remembered the incident at all. But she no longer wished to hurt him. She nodded. "All right, Mem. I yours. At last, I yours. . . . Don't you fret about it no more."

She went out the door and made her slow, painful way across the yard. People passed her; they spoke to her, but she did not acknowledge them. She was aware of them only as shadows. Their voices barely penetrated the warm place inside her where she huddled, protected from them all.

She did not glance back, but she knew Mem stood at that kitchen door, watching her. She was vaguely aware of Omar, Lucy, Jingo Jim—a jumble of faces without reality against a tapestry of painful sunlight.

She paused outside the hay barn. The sun glittered oddly on the elm leaves, shining like the brilliant facets of diamonds. She stepped inside the cavernous room, leaned against the door, the world shut forever away from her. She was no longer conscious of misery or fear, she was simply very tired, drowsy, sleepy. How nice to sleep. . . .

She found a wooden bar and dropped it into the iron holders, securing the door. Even in her sluggish

438

state, she might cry out in pain. Someone might hear her cries. They might get to her. All that mattered was that they not get to her in time.

Pleased with her cunning, she padded slowly to the pile of hay into which Jingo Jim had tossed her knife. She found it easily. The steel blade winked maliciously up at her from the ground. She sank to her knees in the hay and took up the knife. She studied it dreamily, the needle-sharp point, the fine-honed blade. As she'd determined, she extended her left arm. She was thankful for the laudanum. How easy it made it all. The pain belonged to someone else. The blood spurting from her wrist was not real blood, though it spattered across the front of her dress.

She heard movement, but decided it was the scratching of rats in the hay. Her left hand was smeared and sticky and hot with her blood, but she was conscious of no pain. She transferred the knife to her blood-covered hand and extended her right arm.

Sleep . . . soon now it would be over and she would sleep. . . .

Vaguely, she saw Mem lunge at her from the shadows. She tried to fight him, but he wrenched the knife from her fist and threw it with such force that it bit into a wall stud and quivered there.

She fought him, blood spilling on both of them. "Damn you," she raged. "Spyin' on me. Always spyin' on me. Followin' me. Damn you. . . ."

Mem didn't bother to answer her. For one long beat he stared, wide-eyed, at the blood pouring from her wrist, then he yelled, screaming for help at the top of his voice. Still yelling, he leaped across the ground to the barred door. He hurled the bar aside and threw open the door.

Lucretia Borgia sank back into the hay and watched him languidly. He was crying, sobbing, but this in no way impaired his efficiency. He moved in haste she'd never witnessed in him before. He scratched up dirt and hay in his fist and clamped it over her bleeding wrist. He ripped her apron, bound the poultice in place. He was tying a second strip of cloth tightly about her bicep when the room filled with people.

Lucretia Borgia lay back, watching disinterestedly. She saw Jingo Jim crouching near her, his beautiful young eyes distracted. She wanted to console him, but it took too much energy. She was too tired.

From some dim and shadowy vale, she watched Hammond Maxwell thrust his way through the knot of blacks huddled around her. He stared at her, shaking his head, eyes agonized. "Lucretia Borgia," he whispered. "Jesus Christ, Lucretia Borgia, what have you done?"

She smiled, gently, but made no effort to speak.

After that long moment of grief which immobilized him, Maxwell took charge. He spoke rapidly, sending Little Pollux to Benson for the doctor. "You bring that son of a bitch," Hammond said. "Want him. The doctor. Don't want no vet. You tell that doctor I say." And then to make doubly sure, he dispatched Omar to fetch Doc Redfield from Six Mile Road.

Maxwell jerked his head toward Jingo Jim. "Lift her up," he ordered. "Careful." His voice had lost all its harshness. Its sound of gentle concern caressed Lucretia Borgia, washing over her warmly.

She became aware of Jingo Jim's strong arms lifting her. He swung her up easily, though God knew she weighed more than he did. She vaguely saw the dark faces, concerned and grief-stricken, the folks falling back to make room as Jingo Jim carried her across the yard toward the big house. Maxwell limped along beside them, his face as gray as ashes.

She felt flashes of pain, dizzying, threatening to make her cry out. She bit her lip and sank into a deeper warmer darkness where the only reality was the gentle strength of Jingo Jim's arms, the soft concern in Maxwell's voice as he directed Jingo Jim into the house through the front door, up the stairs to Miss Blanche's own bedroom, to her bed. Dimly, Lucretia Borgia felt it was not fitting, but she was too tired to protest.

She remembered little more than this for a long time.

440

How long she slept she did not know. She returned to consciousness to find her wrist professionally bandaged, which meant the doctor had come and gone. When finally she opened her eyes, she found Maxwell sitting in an old rocking chair beside the bed.

Hammond smiled at her. "You gone be all right Lucretia Borgia. Doctor say."

"No, Masta. Ain't. . . . Cain't stand the whip. No more . . . cain't be whipped no more. . . . I loves you, Masta Ham. Better'n life, I do. An' I do anything for you . . . but I die before I be whupped again."

He nodded. "We both come a long way, Lucretia Borgia. . . . Maybe we both a heap smarter. . . . I vow to you—you never be whipped. You got to learn not to argufy . . . but no . . . you never be whipped. No. . . . I'm a-goin' to make it up to you, Lucretia Borgia."

"You already have, Masta Ham, suh."

He smiled. "Still . . . I got to know you fo'give me."

"I fo'give you, Masta. 'Cause I loves you. 'Cause I know how good you is—deep inside."

"I hope so . . . I don't know. . . . Here we are, with all them folks arrivin' downstairs. . . . Expectin' a hanging, they are. No hanging. . . . Willing to watch a good whuppin', they are. No whuppin'. . . . What we do to entertain them, Lucretia Borgia?"

She sighed. "How 'bout a nigger fight? Bare-fisted. All them white menfolks dote on seein' nigger fightin'. . . . Most of them ladies never seed two nekkid black bucks a-fightin'. . . . They gits theyselves a mighty big frenzy out'n that. . . . Likely, they don't nevah stop talkin' 'bout it."

At last, he nodded. "Might do it. . . . Always favored nigger fightin' myself. Ain't seen such a fight as Mede used to put on for nigh on to eight years. . . . But—we got any bucks what could put on a fight?"

Miz Lucretia Borgia nodded. "There's Omar—he's part Mandingo. Part Hausa. He could fight Jingo Jim."

Ham thought that over, nodded at last. "They might put on a respectable fight."

She smiled faintly. "I could guarantee it—kinda promise the winner a little—extra-fancy re-ward."

He laughed. "Lucretia Borgia, you a hellion."

"Nevah said I was a good woman, Masta."

He shook his head, laughing. "I love you anyway, you black vixen."

"Reckon no law say a woman got to be good to be loved, eh, Masta?"

He shook his head, agreeing. Later, he would rant against this moment of weakness, regret his granting total amnesty as the vascillating unworthy of the master of a plantation. He would mutter against his own weakness, against Lucretia Borgia's duplicity, which he did not understand, but suspected, even now. But, for this moment, he was at peace. For the moment he was satisfied to go along, carried like a leaf in floodtide.

He stood up beside the bed and stared down at her, still puzzled, deeply troubled, but relieved and gratified that she was all right. But Lucretia Borgia knew. For this moment at least, she had won, she had made him delay, she had made him think, brought out the goodness deep inside him. Maybe it would change. But this present moment was all she had, all anybody had. There was no guarantee that Nell and Tige would cross the Texies alive or find sanctuary on that far ranch with Lydia. But they would try. As she would try to make Falconhurst as good a place as it could be in this imperfect world. Try. That was all anyone could do, against whatever odds.

She yawned tiredly. Her mouth stretched wide, muscles and flesh aching. Luxuriating on the deep and comfortable mattress, she found a strand of hay caught in her hair. She chewed it idly, watching the shadows the sun tossed across the ceiling.

Epilogue

A GLIMPSE WEST

XLIII

The sun blazed down, erasing every shadow from the ranchyard, steaming in the sand and sucking the last drop of moisture from the grass and bedraggled trees. A blast of tension rose to strike the three people who drove the carriage into the silent yard. They had left this place a busy, active cattle ranch. They returned to find it silent, withdrawn, a sense of terror pervading the very atmosphere. Paley pulled up on the reins just outside the overhang before the ranchhouse. "Hellish feeling," he said to Tige and Nell. "Feel like somebody's got a gun fixed on me."

He was right. At the remote bunkhouse, cowhands emerged to the stoop, armed, cautious, wary and watchful. Those men who remained as employees no longer ventured out on the far ranges, into the lonely draws, along dim trails or upon the open plains where death stalked, from ambush.

Tige swung down from the carriage. He called, "Miz Lydia? You here? Anybody home?"

The parlor door was thrust open and Lydia came through. She paused under the overhang, staring, incredulous. A breeze rustled her dark hair, bouncing a tendril against her pale, drawn cheeks. She carried a gun, but when she recognized Tige, Nell and Paley, she set the weapon against the adobe wall. She cried out in welcome and ran from the shaded overhang to greet them. Nell leaped down from the carriage boot and they met, crying and laughing and clinging to each other.

Then Lydia looked at Tige, not believing her own eyes. Clearly, she'd never expected to see him again on this earth. "Is it you?" she whispered. "Is it really you?"

"I've come back to work for you," he said. "If you want me."

Lydia stared at him and burst into tears. After a moment the parlor door edged open and the children appeared, timidly. They recognized Nell and ran screaming to her. She knelt and gathered them into her arms. Behind them came Estelle, carrying Nell's baby. Tige took the infant from her. The baby grinned up at him, eager and alert. Tige just shook his head, unable to credit the simple wonder of life itself. Nell pressed close, touching the baby's hands. "Oh, thank God," she whispered. "Thank God."

"God," Tige agreed, "and a lady named Miz Lucretia Borgia."

Paley swung down from the carriage. He came to Lydia, took her small hand in his. "Things look pretty rough, Miz Lydia. . . . Reckon Kinlaw's been making a mite of trouble for you?"

She tried to smile, failed. "Driving off our cattle. Shooting at our men from ambush—on our own range. . . . Most of our men have left." She shook her head. "I can't blame them."

"How about Cale?" Paley glanced around. "Where is Cale?"

Lydia bit her lip. "He's—been shot," she said. "Fighting Kinlaw for me. He's been—so brave. . . ."

"I'd never have believed it," Paley said, grinning.

"Nor I," Lydia answered seriously. "Would you like to see him?"

"Always longed to see me a brave man," Paley said.

Lydia led them through the parlor, past the children's

bedroom and past the guest room. Stunned, they found Cale propped up in Hammond Maxwell's own bed. Cale was swathed in bandages and he looked pale, but happy and content. Paley burst out laughing. "The one place I never expected to see you," he told Cale.

Cale grinned sheepishly. "Yeah . . . Miz Lydia finally let me in Mr. Ham's bed—but I had to get shot up to make it."

"He's a good man," Lydia said, her voice vibrant with pride of discovery. "We would have been lost—but for Cale."

Cale winced. "I done what I could. But we ain't out of the woods yet. . . . We need help—an' we can't get it."

"Maybe you got some now, partner," Paley said. "Don't know if I can stand working for you after all them years of thinkin' for you—but Tige and me are here to help you—if you want us."

"Want you?" Cale grinned. He sat forward, looking ready to get up and join them on the disputed range. "I want you, ole son! I know Miz Lydia wants you. She said I was *brave*. She didn't make no boast about how good I am at *thinking*."

"Then I'll take the job," Paley said in his laconic way.

Lydia wept, clinging to Paley's arm. "God is good," she said. She made a small sign of the cross. "And true. . . . He has sent you all—to save us. . . ." She laughed through her tears. "With you, Mr. Paley, to *think* for us—and Tige—and Cale—there's nothing we can't do."

Cale nodded. "Texas is big. Plumb big. We'll be big, too—big as all Texas."

"Can't hardly get no bigger than that," Paley said.

Tige said, "I'll bring our things in."

Lydia nodded. "Yes. Do that."

Paley nodded. "An' I might just as well put my horse in the corral and get my old bunk set up."

"Please," she said. She added, "And your old job—foreman—if you want it."

He nodded. "I think I can help you, ma'am," he said simply. "Me. And Tige. Kinlaw won't have the belly for fighting us—his taste runs more to widows and—" he glanced meaningfully and tauntingly at Cale—"orphans."

Cale sighed heavily as the others left the room. Lydia remained close beside his bed. "Thank God, they're back," he said.

"Yes." She nodded. "Thank God."

He grinned. "Now I can concentrate full time on my really important job."

"Important?" She frowned, puzzled.

He smiled broadly and winked at her. "You," he said.

She gazed at him, wonderstruck, awed, still unable to believe that this man was the arrogant boy she once repulsed. She reached out her hand and Cale took it, grinning. "Bigger'n Texas," he said. Lydia didn't ask him what he meant. But she blushed, her face radiant.